A LITTLE BUZZED

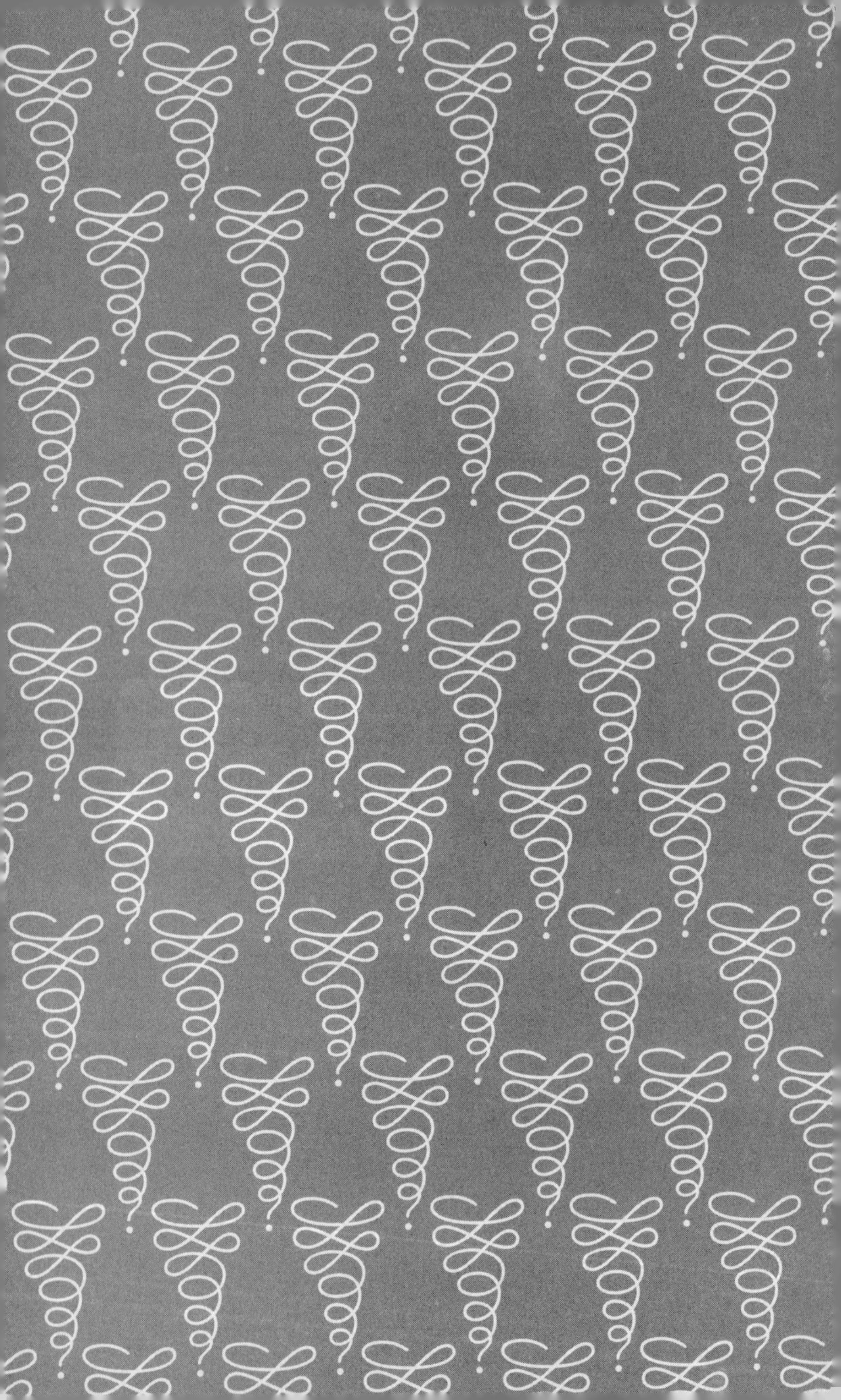

ALYS MURRAY

A LITTLE *BUZZED*

BERKLEY ROMANCE
NEW YORK

BERKLEY ROMANCE
Published by Berkley
An imprint of Penguin Random House LLC
1745 Broadway, New York, NY 10019
penguinrandomhouse.com

Copyright © 2026 by Alys Murray
Penguin Random House values and supports copyright. Copyright fuels creativity, encourages diverse voices, promotes free speech, and creates a vibrant culture. Thank you for buying an authorized edition of this book and for complying with copyright laws by not reproducing, scanning, or distributing any part of it in any form without permission. You are supporting writers and allowing Penguin Random House to continue to publish books for every reader. Please note that no part of this book may be used or reproduced in any manner for the purpose of training artificial intelligence technologies or systems.

BERKLEY and the BERKLEY & B colophon are registered trademarks of Penguin Random House LLC.

Library of Congress Cataloging-in-Publication Data

Names: Murray, Alys author
Title: A little buzzed / Alys Murray.
Description: First edition. | New York: Berkley Romance, 2026.
Identifiers: LCCN 2025016660 (print) | LCCN 2025016661 (ebook) |
ISBN 9780593819715 trade paperback | ISBN 9780593819722 ebook
Subjects: LCGFT: Fiction | Romance fiction | Novels
Classification: LCC PS3613.U7567 L58 2026 (print) |
LCC PS3613.U7567 (ebook) | DDC 813/.6—dc23/eng/20250626
LC record available at https://lccn.loc.gov/2025016660
LC ebook record available at https://lccn.loc.gov/2025016661

First Edition: February 2026

Printed in the United States of America
1st Printing

The authorized representative in the EU for product safety and compliance is Penguin Random House Ireland, Morrison Chambers, 32 Nassau Street, Dublin D02 YH68, Ireland, https://eu-contact.penguin.ie.

This book is dedicated to the lady in a Vegas sex shop who let me go into the porno theater for free to "check it out" because she wasn't "sure it was my scene."

You were right, Vegas sex shop lady. About the porno theater and about the Womanizer you encouraged me to buy that day.

Thank you for your service. Without you, this book probably wouldn't exist.

Sex is emotion in motion.

—Mae West

(Probably not. Like, she probably didn't say it.

But Google says she said it, so that's good enough for me.)

A LITTLE BUZZED

1

Start Off with a Bang

Hudson Bailey was as useless as my vibrator.

I'm sure that was just the sexual frustration talking. However, as I lay back against the headrest of my Cleveland Airport Ramada bed, that was all I could think.

Take the new guy to the sex toy convention, they said.

It'll be fun, they said.

"They" were Clara Mason. As my boss at BuzzCorp, a rising star in the sex toy industry, Clara was thoughtful, ambitious, open-minded, hardworking, understanding, insightful, and sharp-elbowed.

On the Hudson Bailey issue, she was also very, very wrong.

It hadn't been fun at all. Hudson was new to BuzzCorp. A contractor, he was brought in on a short-term deal to create the software for our latest, greatest, and completely top-secret sex toy—The Fantasy. According to Clara, he was at the top of his field when it came to, I don't know, numbers or The Matrix or binary or whatever it was he did on his laptop all day.

The problem was that he didn't know anything about the industry. When I explained to Clara that he was unsuitable for the job on every level but the most basic, she treated me to a ten-minute lecture on his résumé, which apparently included rescuing a failing music streaming app and keeping a multinational stock trading platform from collapsing. In her estimation, we were *lucky* to have him and his technical expertise. Not only that, but his inexperience was a benefit. His fresh eyes were just the thing we needed to take this potentially industry-shaking toy to the next level.

I should have called bullshit then. I should have pressed Clara to find someone, *anyone* else. But I had confidence in Clara. When she hired me two years ago, I was only BuzzCorp's second employee. We'd built this company, and dozens of sex toy designs, together. Maybe Hudson Bailey wouldn't be *that* bad.

But oh . . . it was bad. It really was.

During his first two weeks at BuzzCorp, he and I hadn't had much reason to talk. Until now, our work had been fairly siloed. I led the engineering team on the design and functionality of the toy itself, while he designed the app and software that would control that toy. Eventually, our work would marry up, but this trip was the first time I'd really hung out with him.

The proximity was torture. I was my job, and I liked to keep things as uncomplicated and unmessy as possible, which meant keeping everyone at a polite and professional arm's length.

But Hudson?

If I was the negative end of a magnet, he was the positive. If I was a drive gear, he was an idler gear. If I was peanut butter, you better believe that man was sweet and sloppy jelly.

Inseparable.

This convention turned into the tag-along show, starring me, the engineer who got shit done, and Hudson, the handsome sideshow who clearly didn't know what the fuck he was doing. He did a good dance of pretending to belong, but the signs were there. Like, for example, when we walked up to a booth and he asked one of the most famous porn actresses in the world about the technical specs of the product she was promoting because he didn't recognize her. Or when he very loudly whispered, "That couldn't possibly fit," during a demonstration of a fairly midrange butt plug.

I'm sure that my mask of professionalism had slipped this weekend. That he'd seen my frustration. As hard as I tried to hide it behind bland pleasantries and focus on the task at hand, I couldn't keep my annoyance totally at bay. And now, my time dragging his admittedly appealing dead weight around was interfering with my nightly solo session.

It wasn't even that there was anything wrong with Hudson. He wasn't rude or creepy or anything like that. On the contrary, he was . . . thoughtful. Eager to learn. Curious. Attentive, even. And despite his frustrating inexperience, he had his moments. Like when we'd gotten on our flight to come here and he'd lifted my carry-on into the overhead bin for me. Or when he'd slyly managed to shift the attention of various old creeps trying to chat me up during the convention mixers. Or when he'd bring me complimentary cookies any time they put out a fresh batch in the event hall.

Or this evening, when I'd been giving my final speech to a crowd of fellow engineers, and during the review of our client feedback—pretty explicit feedback, lots of orgasm talk—I looked down to see him staring up at me like I was a Playboy Bunny pinned up on his wall . . . and he was sporting the semi beneath his jeans to match.

Fuck, there it was. The thought I'd tried not to bring up again. The real reason I couldn't make myself cum tonight. The sight of him, semi-erect, as he watched me lecture about sex.

I shifted uncomfortably in bed. The sheets, which had felt so luxurious when we'd checked in, scratched at my hardened nipples and my exposed thighs, reminding me of the orgasm that had evaded me.

"Hmph."

Trying to push him out of my mind, I crossed my arms and refocused. I was not going to waste another second thinking of him.

Besides, I wasn't going to be able to go to sleep this horny. Something had to be done.

Taking long, slow breaths, I fell back upon one of my calming thought patterns.

Problem.

Proposed Solution.

Test.

Result.

That was just how my brain worked. No matter what I did or what problem I faced, I filtered it through the scientific method.

Problem: Need to cum, can't stop thinking about Hudson Bailey.

Proposed Solution: Find some way to stop thinking of him while also orgasming.

With that in mind, I set about step three—testing. But just how to go about that?

Given how tormented and sweaty and near-orgasm I'd gotten over the last hour, I probably needed a shower. So I started there.

Leaping out of bed, I dug through the various freebie bags I'd been given over the course of the convention. *Butt plugs, nipple clamps, paddles, Womanizer . . .*

"Ah, there you are," I muttered.

From the bag I retrieved two new items from one of our biggest competitors: One was a knockoff of a Hitachi Magic Wand, which would have been forgettable on its own, but unlike the Hitachi, it could be used around water, and the other was a thick dildo called The Spreader, which featured a suction cup bottom, perfect for solo play.

My entire body awakened as I put my toy cleaners to work in

the bathroom sink. There was nothing like it, that anticipation of knowing an orgasm was just on the horizon, and I bit my bottom lip to try to keep my excited breath from echoing off the marble bathroom walls.

But then, as I dried off The Spreader, my hands stilled as a memory caught up with me.

Hudson, handing this to me at the welcome party, after he'd won it in a door draw. He'd winced awkwardly when he'd opened the package and offered it to me with almost painful sheepishness.

"You know, in case you need it for market research, or whatever."

Instantly, that memory twisted into a fantasy. Hudson, feathering the thick dildo down my skin . . . Hudson, doing some market research on me.

I dropped the dildo to the edge of the vanity.

Fuck no. This was against the entire ethos of this experiment. Thinking about Hudson was the problem I needed to fix. I could not solve that problem by masturbating to the thought of my coworker. This was a bad idea. Time to abort. I needed to get in bed, take a melatonin, and forget about—

As I went to grab the melatonin from my makeup bag, my arm accidentally brushed my nipple.

"Fuck."

My body almost contracted at the contact. I gripped the vanity counter to keep upright. Oh God. I was even more pent-up than I thought.

The experiment was back on.

I clenched my thighs a little tighter. All thoughts but making myself cum—now and very hard—flew out the window.

In the bathroom mirror, I was pretty unremarkable. Curvy body. Shoulder-length black bob. Brown eyes. But my nipples were pebbled, ready to be played with, my cheeks were flushed, and my pink lips were parted as I panted through them.

Another intrusive thought.

What if Hudson thought of me this way? Was that why he'd gotten hard during my talk today? Was he picturing me pliant and fuckable?

Swallowing hard, I stared my reflection down. "No matter what you do," I muttered, "do not think of him while you masturbate."

You're a scientist, dammit. Don't let him ruin this experiment of yours.

My hand moved down to my breasts so I could thumb my hard nipple.

The relief was instant, but so was the craving for more.

I threw the shower to its highest temperature and teased my flesh as I waited for steam to fill the room. The dildo adhered comfortably to the shower wall, and despite the wetness growing between my legs, I generously applied lube.

When I stepped beneath the hot spray of the shower, it tickled my frayed nerve endings.

The Hitachi Magic Wand was widely considered to be an instant orgasm in toy form. The most powerful masturbator on the market. But even I was surprised when I turned it on and teased its head down my body, starting between the valley of my breasts and heading down . . . down . . . down . . .

"Oh!"

The first vibrations between my legs caught me by surprise. It was intense on my skin, but on my pussy, I felt ready to burst immediately. No good. I wanted this orgasm to be worth the hour of foreplay I'd accidentally endured.

I withdrew and turned my attention to the dildo, which stood at attention on the shower wall.

Positioning myself in front of it, I presented my ass and slowly—*oh my God, that's so fucking big*—sank my pussy back onto it.

"Yes," I hissed, relishing the sensation.

I let myself linger, not rocking the cock inside me or returning the vibrator to my clit. Its girth completed me, pressing against every button in my depths.

I wonder if Hudson is this big.

The thought came out of nowhere. My eyes snapped open.

No. No, this could not be happening. I could not be having a sexual awakening to my coworker.

Returning one hand to my nipples, I focused on that pleasure instead. But with every touch and every tease, I imagined his hands exploring me.

Slowly, I rode my dildo. Surely *that* would keep him out of my mind.

I whimpered as my clit throbbed, begging for contact, begging to deepen the fantastic tingles already stirring in me from penetration alone.

You could teach him so much about sex. Can you imagine if he saw you like this, fucking yourself to the thought of him?

Fuck, fuck. This wasn't working. No matter the parameters of my experiment, my thoughts kept circling straight back to him.

No amount of fucking myself was going to get Hudson out of my head.

Arching back against my dildo in earnest now, I lowered the wand to my clit.

"Ah!"

I shuddered around the cock. The vibrations were so strong, so good, so highly directed. It wouldn't be long until I came.

But he kept popping up in my head. His groans intermingling with mine. His hand toying with my clit as he thrust deep inside me. Him breathing praise as he delighted in every inch of me.

With each errant thought, I raised the vibrations a little bit, giving me enough blinding pleasure to erase him—at least for a second or two.

But then, as I ran out of breath, I also ran out of vibration speeds. My moans wouldn't stop. I couldn't hold it back . . .

Screw it. I wanted to cum, and I wanted the orgasm to be delicious.

I embraced the fantasy, picturing Hudson's hands firmly on my hips, rocking me back onto his big, thick cock as the vibrations on my toy reached a fever pitch. I climbed higher and higher. My own moans echoed off the marble walls.

This was it. I was going to cum. I was going to cum for him . . .

Before I could stop myself, I screamed—

"Hudson!"

My orgasm shattered over me, and my entire body racked around the cock buried in my cunt. Riding the waves, I clung to it until my trembling stilled and my heart slowed to a normal pace.

The effort exhausted me. I slumped back, more satisfied than I could remember being in a long, *long* time.

"Holy shit," I muttered, turning off the shower and letting the cold air of the bathroom bring me back to reality.

Mentally, I wrapped up the loose ends on my experiment.

Problem: Need to cum, have to sleep, can't stop thinking about Hudson Bailey.

Proposed Solution: Find some way to stop thinking of him while also orgasming.

Test: Fucked myself silly with the biggest of big guns . . . and still kept thinking of him. It made everything way hotter, in fact.

Result: Absolute failure. Seeing him tomorrow is going to be very, very awkward.

2

Morning Glory Hole

Science has proven that sexual climax is great for pain relief, improved sleep, and mood boosting. In evolutionary terms, this is supposed to incentivize reproduction. If sex lifts you up, soothes your worries, or kicks period cramps to the curb, then you're probably going to keep doing it, aren't you?

As an engineer in the field of sex science, I'd read the literature. I'd even conducted thorough follow-up studies on myself, and the data checked out. Orgasms always made me feel better.

"And what does 'glory hole' mean in this context?"

Unfortunately, the next morning, with every word that he uttered, Hudson made all those delectable happy-horny chemicals disappear.

Together, we sat at a small table at the OFest convention's farewell breakfast, surrounded by vulvar croissants and bacon strips and sausage balls artfully arranged like penises. I hadn't wanted to cut him in on this morning's bagelside engineering chat. But Hudson was as charming as he was persistent, as persistent as he was handsome, and as handsome as he was inept, which meant that he'd weaseled his way into my meeting with

Ichiro Ose *and* took every opportunity to make a fool of himself in front of our biggest buyer.

To his credit, Ichiro laughed at the glory hole gaffe. His eyes, though, flickered from Hudson to me, a small gesture that told me everything I needed to know.

Hudson was making a very, very bad impression.

Great. Fantastic. The guy had fucked me in my dreams last night, and now here he was, fucking me over professionally . . . while making my stomach flip with that oblivious, perfect grin of his. This meeting was the entire reason Clara had sent me to this regional OFest during the height of crunch time on The Fantasy. Success was vital here. It also seemed less and less likely with every word Hudson ventured.

"Scout," Ichiro said, picking playfully at his plate of lukewarm scrambled eggs. "What a charming gentleman you've added to your team. Where'd you steal him from? LoveHoney?"

"LoveHoney? Me?" Hudson answered before I could. "No, my last job was at GulfZGH."

A beat as Ichiro chewed his eggs *way* too many times. "The oil rig manufacturer?"

"Yep, I helped develop an early-warning app to alert the crews when to evacuate in the event of an oncoming natural disaster."

Nothing could hide the note of pride in Hudson's voice. It may have sounded unbelievably sexy, but I wanted to grab him by the shoulders and shake him. Didn't he know how this came across, him bragging about his total inexperience in our field? It made BuzzCorp look like complete amateurs, giving the reins of such an important project to a knob-headed novice.

"Well," Ichiro persisted, keeping a friendly, jovial air one only developed after a career in sales. "At least that means you're very familiar with lubricants, hm?"

Hudson just blinked. After a beat, he was forced to explain the joke.

"Petroleum is used to make some forms of intimate lubricants, son. Just a little industry humor."

Realization dawned and Hudson laughed. I forced myself to join, trying to focus on Ichiro and not Hudson's prominent dimple.

"Well, I'm happy to say that this job is *much* more fun than oil rig work." His eyes flickered in my direction. "And my colleagues are *much* prettier."

My stomach twisted as I thought back to last night. He thought I was pretty?

No. No, he was just playing Ichiro. And, God help me, it was working. Ichiro's slightly condescending chuckle broke into shards of real laughter.

As Hudson artfully turned the conversation from sexy fossil fuels to the banana nut muffins Ichiro had been eyeing at the center of our generic hotel breakfast table, I quietly reassessed him. Maybe . . . ugh. Maybe Clara did have a point in sending him here with me. The entire purpose of attending OFest Midwest at such a critical time in our development of The Fantasy was to assure Mr. Ose, who would undoubtedly tell the rest of the buyers in the industry, that our ambitious, ground-breaking—and *top-secret*—new toy design was worth their time and attention. With pre-orders from a company like Ichiro's, not to mention those who followed his movements closely, we could convince our investors to infuse us with some sorely needed cash. It was our job here not to give lectures or eat our weight in cookies (though I'd done both on this trip), but to prove to this giant of the sex toy retailers that the tech we were building was solid—even if we couldn't actually *show* it to him yet.

Hudson may not have been able to tell a wand from a rabbit, but he *did* have people skills. People skills I sorely lacked. Oh, I could hold a conversation about specs and drafting all day, but lighthearted banter about muffins and the big game last night?

Not a chance. It wasn't that I didn't like people or *want* to fit in at a cocktail party. I just spent so much time working that my people skills were as rusty as a Dremel saw after a rainstorm.

Their masculine chatter continued. A flicker of hope caught light in my chest. Yes, this had to be why Clara put him and me together: so I could talk toys, and he could talk with the boys. The perfect combination of business and pleasure. He would soften Mr. Ose up with chitchat, and then I would convince him to buy countless Fantasy units with my technical prowess. Why hadn't I seen it before? Of *course* this was Clara's plan.

"So, Mr. Ose," I interjected, ready to be useful. "We really wanted to talk to you about The Fantasy today."

The old man's face fell slightly. A twinge of disappointment hit me as I realized I'd made a mistake. Once again, reading the room wrong. That was the thing about me—you could always count on Scout Porter to bungle a social interaction. "Ah. Well. I should start by saying that I've read the brief you sent over last night, and after this talk with you and Hudson, I'm excited by the new direction the company's going in."

I furrowed my brow. "New direction?"

"Well, for starters, you've hired a man. It's about time."

"I actually have two men on my engineering team," I pointed out, as gently as I could.

"Yeah," Hudson added, "when I was first brought on, I was told that the company was almost forty percent women."

"But it's not really your *brand*, is it? Scout, you and Clara are the faces of BuzzCorp. Your entire identity is women. Women-owned. Women-designed. Women-first. Women, women, women. Hudson, with all respect, you may be completely inept when it comes to the world of sex toys, but at least you're bringing a new facet to the company. I hope you will be, anyway."

I always felt that I was two people. The calm, professional, remote, and reserved person I allowed everyone else to see, and then the slightly neurotic, highly emotional, tightly wound person I was on the inside.

I kept them separated for so many reasons. Public Scout was like argon—a totally nonreactive element. Very difficult to do harm to anyone with her. But private Scout? She was like fluorine—unpredictable and highly reactive.

In science, you have to quarantine elements like fluorine. If you don't, they're liable to run havoc through your lab. And through your life.

That was why I had such a hard time connecting with people outside of work. If I tried to get close to people, they might see the real me, and well . . . I couldn't let inner Scout ruin everything for outer Scout.

But oh . . . did I want to unleash a can of Fluorine Scout all over Ichiro's picturesque breakfast plate.

"And what, exactly, are you hoping he brings to the company?" I asked, voice strained.

"Men. I *hope* he brings men to your sales demo, anyway. I can't keep the lights on just selling your products to girls."

"You won't be worried when you finally see The Fantasy in person," Hudson said. "That toy is going to fly off the digital shelves, and people are going to become totally brand-loyal to BuzzCorp."

I didn't believe in knights in shining armor. But if I'd been brave enough to give him a look just then, I might have had to shield my eyes from Hudson's glistening chain mail and sword.

Because if he hadn't interjected, I might have lost my composure. Working at BuzzCorp hadn't been my first choice of profession, but bringing people pleasure, giving them control over their own sexual autonomy—those things mattered to me. I hated to see them written off as "girls' stuff" that needed a "man's perspective," especially by someone who clearly believed that he was helping me in some way, delivering folksy, paternalistic, tough-love truths.

With his brief interjection, Hudson saved me from myself. Which annoyed me *and* turned me on.

Ridiculous, confusing man. I couldn't *wait* until I got the hell back to my office in Dallas, where I barely had the time or energy to see him, think about him, or masturbate to the thought of him.

"Yeah," I agreed. "Exactly what he said."

"I hope he's right, then, Miss Porter." Ichiro gave a little shrug. "Or else that will be you out of yet *another* high-profile job, won't it? At least this time, nothing blew up."

The air evacuated my lungs. Even as a joke, throwing my biggest professional disappointment back in my face turned my stomach.

Though clearly confused, Hudson once again stepped in to pick up the conversational slack.

"I guess that means you're not committing to buy any Fantasy units today, then?"

"No. I won't. I understand that keeping the toy top-secret is your prerogative as an up-and-coming industry player, but I can't just take your word that this *thing* of yours will work." Ichiro turned his attention to me. "And considering the inexperience of this guy you've put in charge as your software engineer, as much as I may believe in your and Clara's vision, I don't have much faith that he has the skills to make this project a success . . . It would be unwise to commit to ordering any volume of this product at this time. You understand, don't you?"

Ichiro stood up. Hudson mirrored him. I briefly wondered if I could fake amnesia when having to report back on this meeting to Clara.

"Of course," Hudson said, shaking his hand. "We look forward to sharing more about The Fantasy when we can."

"If there's nothing else, I've got to get going."

"Have a safe flight, then."

Ichiro clucked his tongue. "Will do. This trip has given me much to consider. Your offerings, not to mention this new player entering the space who I met with yesterday . . ."

I snapped to attention. A new toy manufacturer was a big deal. I hadn't heard anything about it, not even rumors.

"There's a new competitor out there? No one new presented at the festival," I said.

"I'm sure they'll be at the national New York convention in November. The new owner's rollout strategy is a bit unorthodox. He wants to sneak-attack his competitors." Ichiro's cheek lifted playfully. "But *ssssshhhh*. You didn't hear it from me."

"Why'd you mention it to us, then?" I asked.

My relationship with Ichiro had always been complicated. He was friendly and polite. I sensed good in him. But his greater demons of capitalistic excess hung on to him like a parasite. One minute, he was friendly and insightful. The next, he was assessing your work at a sexual health company like an internet weirdo ranking women on their "feline hunter eyes" and "forehead ratio."

But when he looked at me, I didn't see any of that second Ichiro. The bottom-line devotee was gone, and in his place was a man who'd been around the block a time or two and needed a place to park his advice.

That worried me *more* than if he'd been a total asshole.

"Because I like you, Scout. You're a weird fish, but you're smart and good at your job. And I like Clara and your new friend here, too. I *want* to see you succeed. But with this fresh blood coming in . . . you should be very, very worried."

3

Fly the Sexy Skies

I felt bad for Hudson.

Not as bad as I felt for myself, but still.

I felt bad.

Before this convention, I knew Hudson as a golden boy. Always smiling, always happy, always leaving a trail of laughter behind him wherever he went. There wasn't a stranger he couldn't befriend or a room he couldn't work. I'd never seen a guy glow before, but even from the distance I kept between us, he did just that.

But once Mr. Ose left, Hudson and I made our way to the Cleveland airport for our flight. Somewhere along the way, he surprised me.

He wilted.

It was like someone had pulled his spark plug. All his intangible energy vanished. He didn't even try to talk to me—shocking, considering he'd barely let a minute pass between us without repeated attempts at collegial bonding.

At the beginning of the trip, I'd been thrown off balance by his questions, his jokes, his persistent chatter. Now that it was gone, I . . . I missed it.

Problem: The happiest guy in the world looks absolutely miserable.

Proposed Solution: ????

When I was stressed or upset, I turned to work, revising plans or rerunning calculations or cleaning my soldering irons. Hudson didn't seem the type. He seemed like the *talk about your feelings* type—not my strong suit.

So as we walked through the Cleveland airport in search of our gate, I compromised. Not feelings. Not work. But a secret third thing.

"Do you . . . want a Cinnabon?"

Great work, Scout. Were those dynamite conversational skills what they taught you in human interaction school?

"You don't have to do that. You don't have to cheer me up. You clearly had a game plan with Mr. Ose, then I showed up and said all the wrong things. I'm sorry."

"It's fine."

"No, it's not. I'm sorry. I'll explain everything to Clara. It was my fault Mr. Ose didn't convert."

Part of me wanted to agree. But I couldn't. No, going full-frontal with the news that he'd never worked on a sex toy hadn't been great optics. But in retrospect, Clara's insistence on top secrecy about The Fantasy's designs made selling this thing nearly impossible. Not even her best two nerds could sell it.

"I . . . I wasn't exactly stellar out there either," I admitted. "I don't *people* well."

"You're doing fine with me."

As we threaded our way through the hectic airport crowd, I shot him a skeptical look.

He took it in good humor. "Man, I really *haven't* won you over, have I?"

"Don't take it personally."

"Hard not to. I've just always worked to be the type of guy

that people like. It's my whole thing. My superpower. And here you are . . . human kryptonite."

Oh, so *this* was why I didn't like him. Not because he was too sexy. Not because he knew nothing about specifically coding sex toys. And not because he contributed to the mess of a deal with Mr. Ose.

It's because he was too *nice*. Most people who met me got my "Oh, she's intense and doesn't want to talk about anything but work and her lunch order" thing within seconds. He was persistent. Even when he was calling me *human kryptonite* (which, rude but true), it didn't feel like an insult. It felt like a self-own—like he was disappointed in *himself* that he couldn't find a way to reach me.

I had a hard time dealing with him not because I wanted to push him away, but because he made me want to keep him close. Or, you know, closer than I let other people get, anyway.

"I like to keep things professional," I said lightly.

"Right. About that . . . I know it couldn't have been easy, having me chained to your side all week."

"What? No, it wasn't a problem at all—"

His turn to flatten his gaze. "Scout, you had to explain to me what Ben Wa balls are. Jesus, what did you do to Clara to deserve such a cosmically bad punishment?"

I bit the inside of my cheek to keep from smiling. He was funny, too. Maybe it was hypocritical, coming from an engineer, but I hadn't expected that from the computer nerd.

Not today, anyway. For some reason, I couldn't hold back a joke of my own:

"I accidentally ate one of those twenty-dollar cookies Clara saves for her cheat day. I'm surprised she didn't try to send me to the Hague."

He laughed, and I felt it all the way down to my toes.

When was the last time I'd made someone besides Clara

laugh? In the office, I led my team with a detached, hyperprofessional air. I kept everyone at a distance besides my boss, and I only kept her close because once upon a time, she'd met me at my worst and decided to hire me anyway.

It felt nice to make him laugh.

I shook off the feeling. Must have just been my brain's final, lingering sex chemicals in the last flashes of their half-lives.

"Actually, I think she sent you here to help me make the sale. You were great with Mr. Ose."

"You think so?"

"Yeah, like I said, like you've *noticed*, I need a guide dog for human interactions. You were a very good service animal."

There I went again with another joke. Maybe Hudson was just being nice, but he laughed again.

"Maybe, except for the part where I told him the one thing he didn't want to hear. And I don't think Clara sent me to guide-dog you. Clearly she loves your work. I think she sent me along so I could learn more about the industry. I mean, why would she send me to close with Mr. Ose? I've never even used a sex toy before."

I nearly tripped into the girls' volleyball team shuffling ahead of us. "Wait, so not only have you never *worked on* a sex toy before, you've never *used* a sex toy before either?"

"Nope."

There was going to be an entire true crime docuseries about what I would do to Clara when I saw her at the office tomorrow.

"Actually," he said, a note of optimism creeping back into his tone, "I wanted to talk to you about that."

Don't like the sound of that. Not one bit.

"I'm not really familiar with this stuff. This sex toy stuff," he continued. "Not the way you are."

My jaw dropped. His eyes widened.

"That came out wrong! I mean *professionally*! You're the expert.

I know nothing. I never even held a dildo until my first interview with Clara. I'm out of my depth and clearly this is too important for me to be so unlearned. So I was thinking . . . what if you taught me?"

"What, like sex ed? Sex Toy Ed?"

"I'm a blank slate. Everything I know about sex toys is through cultural osmosis, and if we want to make The Fantasy the greatest one that's ever been built, I need more information."

A half-dozen horny vignettes crossed my mind. Oh, the things I could teach Hudson Bailey about sex toys . . . about making a woman scream . . .

Dammit. If I kept this up, I'd be joining the Mile High Club—party of one—in the Airbus bathroom.

He was right, of course, that he needed instruction, and I was probably the best one to give it to him. It would be simple enough. We could go through the BuzzCorp catalog of products, I could explain their uses to him, and show him the focus group reporting on how and why those toys were invaluable to our users.

Easy as (cream) pie.

But teaching Hudson about *anything* would necessitate us spending more time together. Teaching him about *sex toys* would necessitate *me* spending more time trying not to think about the sexy man at my side burying himself between my legs.

And given how important The Fantasy was to my future and my career, I just couldn't risk the distraction. Couldn't risk *him*.

"Why don't you just watch porn?" I asked.

"Ah, porn. Depicting healthy and equitable sexual relationships since the beginning of time."

Good point, but I had to hold my ground.

When we arrived at our gate, preflight boarding was in effect. The two of us settled into remote seats at the edge of the carpeted space. I purposefully put my backpack between us—to avoid any accidental touches that might lead to more horny fuel for sessions like last night's—and settled in to get some work done on my tablet.

But I should have known it wouldn't be that simple.

"What did he mean back there?" Hudson asked, after a pause. "Ichiro, when he mentioned your old job blowing up or whatever. What did that mean?"

Cool. Straight to the heavy stuff.

I guess I should have been grateful he wasn't asking for more sex toy training.

I'd done a lot of work on myself to be able to talk about my pre-BuzzCorp existence. I had to. Anyone who googled me would see everything and ask me about it no matter how I felt.

"Remember the GalacticSolutions disaster?" I asked.

"Sure."

"That was my project."

"Oh."

Such a small sound for a major humiliation. In my first job, I'd worked on propulsion for a rocket company, and well . . . it hadn't gone according to plan.

At least he didn't sound judgmental. That was more than people usually gave me.

"Yeah, *oh*. A multibillion-dollar rocket *literally* blew up in my face."

"That couldn't have been your fault."

Not entirely, no. But still.

"It happened on my watch and under my command, which is all that matters. And it happened because I wasn't focused on my work. There were other . . ." My throat tightened the way it did every time I got to this part. When I had to skirt the details and lie by omission. ". . . *things* going on behind the scenes at GalacticSolutions that took my attention away from the project. If I hadn't been so stupid, if I hadn't let myself get distracted, then the Ilium might not have been a disaster and I might be sipping cocktails on Mars right now."

"Yeah, but then we wouldn't be sharing this beautiful moment together. And how tragic that would be."

He was the all-time Make Scout Porter Laugh scoreboard leader without even trying.

I reappraised Hudson, daring to properly inspect him for the first time since my mental trip to poundtown last night. He had brown hair and eyes to match. His thick, dark glasses gave him an air of dignified mystery. The vibe was very *clean-cut NASA scientist from the 1960s by way of a soulful indie-guitar player.* I'd already known those things about him, but today I noticed other things, too. The big hands. The impossibly long legs. The sleeves of his button-up, which he kept rolled to his elbows. The soft, gentle way he spoke to me.

"C'mon," he tried again. "I'm not a distraction. Teaching me about the sex toys is part of your work. Help me out. Please?"

For a moment, I allowed myself to entertain the possibility of opening myself up to him. Just a little bit. Just for the good of our project.

No. Focus. Discipline. Control. That was how I kept myself on track and my career from going up in flames.

I would never have another GalacticSolutions disaster ever again. I wouldn't allow it.

"The Fantasy *has* to be my priority right now, not teaching you the finer points of penis sleeve extender usage and maintenance."

"But—"

"I agree that you need to learn, but it doesn't have to be from me. I'm sorry, Hudson. It's not personal, but my answer's no."

Could he hear how sincere that apology was? How I wished that things were different? That *I* was different?

He must have, because his eyes softened.

"I wish my last girlfriend had broken up with me as eloquently as that."

The tops of my ears burned at the way he lumped *me* and *girlfriend* in the same sentence.

"But I think I can change your mind," he added.

"You can try, but don't say I didn't warn you."

"Forewarned is forearmed, they say."

Please don't talk about forearms. I can't stop looking at yours.

He seemed so confident. Not in an arrogant *I'll get you because I'm a badass and no one can resist my charms* way. That would have been easier. However, it was an *I've seen the future, and I know this works out great for both of us* way.

"I wouldn't count on it. But don't worry. It's for the best. You'll look back on this and thank me someday."

He screwed up his face in confusion, opening his mouth to utter another devastatingly earnest response, no doubt. But before he could, a harsh ping filled the air. The gate agent made an announcement.

The direct flight to Dallas was boarding.

Grateful for the diversion, I joined the snaking line of passengers, leaving Hudson and his extra-leg-room ticket to lounge behind me.

By the time I made it up to the door, though, the stone-faced airline host informed me:

"Ma'am, we're going to need to check that bag to your final destination."

"I'm so sorry, but I can't. The laptop in it can't go in the hold. It has all my company's proprietary design information on it."

Mr. Gate Agent didn't even look up from his computer. "If you don't surrender the bag willingly, we'll have no other choice but to assume there's a nefarious reason and then confiscate and destroy the bag."

I shifted uncomfortably. Making scenes wasn't my thing.

"If I could just explain. I'd be happy to check the bag and carry the laptop on its own—"

"There's no room in the overhead bins to store your personal items—laptops included. I *just* said that. Are you going to hold up *everyone*?"

Fluorine Scout threatened to make an appearance, a chemical reaction rising in me, unbidden.

"But—"

Then a voice cut over the din of airport chaos, approaching until it reached just over my shoulder.

"Sorry! So sorry! Thank you, love."

Love?

I snapped around to find Hudson approaching me, confident and chipper as ever.

Oh no. Not just approaching me. Coming in for a cheek kiss.

Which I completely botched by turning my head at exactly the wrong second.

There wasn't enough time to avert. By the time I realized what was happening, Hudson's lips were already brushing against mine.

It was the softest of touches. Feather-light. Nothing more than a brush. Still, my knees went weak.

He kissed me. Hudson *kissed me*. By accident, but . . .

I'd just been kissed.

And worse?

I wanted more.

If he noticed my osculatory distress, he didn't let it show.

"Sorry," Hudson said, laying the charm on thick as I reeled, lips still buzzing with the taste of him. "She was just holding my bag. Here's that sweatshirt you left at the airport lounge, baby. My girl, always forgetting things. Everything okay here?"

I slipped the sweatshirt on, trying to play the dutiful girlfriend—

though not entirely sure why. My brain was still too scrambled from the lip-lock.

Mr. Check-In raised one eyebrow. "That's *your* bag, sir?"

"Yeah, and I have extra leg room, so I think I have a dedicated overhead bin, right?"

"Of course, sir."

"Great. Let's board. Shall we, dear?"

It took me a too-long beat to realize he was talking to me. *I* was his dear. At least for the moment. And he had swooped in, playing the boyfriend, to save my bag from the hell that is the luggage hold.

With two quick, resigned zaps of his ticketing gun, Mr. Check-In welcomed us aboard. Hudson reached for my bag . . .

At the exact same moment that *I* stepped forward to get it.

We collided, our tangled feet kicking the bag forward . . .

A familiar sound rattled from the beaten old fabric. My heart stopped.

The ticket agent's face tightened as he inspected it. "I'm sorry, is your bag . . . vibrating?"

Yep. It sure was.

The same vibrator I'd used on myself last night, buried in the depths of my backpack, was currently going so hard that its momentum was literally scooting the bag across the carpeted floor. I choked. "No, no, it's not—"

But Hudson reached for the bag with a casual air. Like everyone in the terminal wasn't currently watching us because they suspected we were carrying either a bomb or a vibrator. Mr. Check-In's expression flared, clearly delighted at the possibility of catching us in a bag-related lie.

"I'll ask again: That's *your* bag, sir? Remember, lying to an airport official is a crime, and *both* of you could be in trouble—"

Flatly, Hudson fished out the vibrator and held it aloft for inspection without a hint of shame.

"Between you and me, the BuzzCorp products are better, but this junk will get the job done when I'm traveling."

Mr. Check-In blanched. What do you say to a man pulling out a vibrator and brandishing it for an entire airport to see?

"Just take the batteries out before you board."

I must have entered a fugue state, because the next thing I knew, Hudson and I were walking down the jet bridge, side-by-side. It took everything in my power not to think about how soft his sweatshirt felt against my skin or how great it smelled.

Hudson, though, couldn't have seemed less bothered. He whistled.

Whistled.

Like nothing had happened.

"You *kissed me*," I finally managed.

The whistle fizzled out. "I'm so sorry, that wasn't supposed to—"

"And you kept me from maybe going to terrorism jail over a vibrator."

"I think terrorism jail is just called jail."

"And . . ." I wanted to be outraged, to put some distance between us. If I was angry at him, I didn't have to face reality: that I was starting to like him. "Shit. That was really nice of you."

"Try not to sound so disappointed," he teased.

I wasn't disappointed. I was confused. I'd just rejected his tacit offer of friendship, his request for help, *and* been a total ice queen to him all week, and he'd repaid me by . . . keeping me from humiliating myself in front of the entire Cleveland airport.

My better judgment told me to take the win. But as the open plane door approached and Hudson's shoulders brushed mine, I made a snap decision.

Dammit. Here goes nothing. I fiddled with the sleeves of the sweatshirt he'd lent me.

"Okay, so I guess I owe you one."

The brightness of his smile could have rivaled any supernova. "You mean—"

"Yeah, I'll help you. I'll teach you everything you need to know about the industry. But this is one hundred percent professional. I'm just doing this to make sure The Fantasy is a success."

"Deal." He put his hand out for me to shake. I took it, trying not to mentally compare how I'd imagined his hands last night to how they actually felt now, brushing against my palm. "And I owe you one. Whatever you want, it's yours."

Careful what you wish for. I may want you.

4

Clocking In at the Orgasm Mines

Monday mornings were for the fuck reports. I know what you're thinking. *Scout, I've worked in an office before. I know that people come in on Mondays and give way too many details about their personal lives, but really. Fuck reports? No need to be quite so unprofessional.*

Sure. I'd give you that. If my office were a normal office and I was just talking about my small engineering team chattering away about who they got lucky with this weekend, I'd be in total agreement with you that "fuck reports" was inappropriate.

However . . .

"Morning, Scout! Have you gotten through those fuck reports?"

"Not yet. There are a lot of them today, aren't there?"

"Huge storm front pushed through the Pacific Northwest this weekend. Guess people took the rain as God's way of saying *Go fuck yourself*."

The thing is, a sex toy company *isn't* a normal office, and *appropriate* is very relative when you're looking at pocket pussies all day.

To be clear, *fuck report* was not my terminology. And in my line of work, it didn't refer to my colleagues and their sex lives. Instead, it referred to the metric tons of data currently cluttering my laptop screen.

At BuzzCorp, we prided ourselves on being user-first. Testing was conducted at every phase of new toy development. Our talented QA team would be sent a product, use the toy for a certain number of days, and then write detailed summaries of how those toys functioned in solo use and (if applicable) with a partner or partners. Being the head of engineering, I could have delegated the work of poring over the fuck reports to someone else, but I never did. When it came to work, I was a control freak.

And when it came to sex, it was nice to know someone was having it, even if it wasn't me.

Our testers ranged from a grocery clerk at the center of a polycule to a housewife trying to reinvigorate her sex life to a single mother hooking up between work and her daughter's soccer practice. Rich or poor, fat or thin, sexually adventurous or meek, beautiful or ugly, young or old, nondisabled or disabled, men or women or otherwise . . . it didn't matter.

People were having sex. Great sex, with the help of the toys I was engineering.

Reading about them was my Monday workload. Just another day at the office.

The BuzzCorp offices took up one floor of a "reimagined" workspace in downtown Dallas. What had once been the cold, *Office Space*-y confines of a multinational bank was now an open-concept, glass-walled, potted-plant oasis built with collaboration (and splashy, stylish magazine spreads, probably) in mind.

Most of the time, I worked in the safe and secure confines of my lab, a private glass box of sterile space that made me look like I'd been sentenced to a thousand years in movie supervillain jail. It was as uninspiring and unsexy as a room could be, but I loved it. The seclusion gave me space to think and kept me from getting too mixed up in my coworkers' lives.

But on Mondays, the fuck reports called, and I was forced to answer them in the communal space in the office's open-concept center, which was comprised of a kitchen, call booths, a community garden, and group workspaces—the typical trappings of a too-hip-for-its-own-good, late-stage-capitalism office.

And not even the fuck reports could take my mind off Hudson. I'd been checking the door all morning, waiting for him to pop his unreasonably attractive head into the office. I needed to go back on my offer. As I flipped through fuck reports, his sweatshirt (which I'd forgotten I'd been wearing until I collapsed on my couch last night) sat in a little bag near my feet. Every time I brushed against it, I imagined how that conversation would go.

Hudson, I regret to inform you that I will be unable to teach you about sex due to a prior commitment. I have to get a Brazilian wax. I haven't shaved down there in a while, so by the time the waxing tech gets finished, your contract will probably be up anyway.

Or—

Hudson, here's my password for this women-owned porn site I visit regularly. They'll teach you more than I ever could.

Or—

Hudson, I'd love to teach you about sex toys, but then I might stupidly give in to my urge to ride you like a mechanical bull. You understand. It's for the best I keep my distance.

"Scout? Are you in one of your scientific fugue states again?"

I looked up at my small engineering team. There was Jared Blotcher, the loudmouthed wiring specialist who'd asked the question. Addie Cao, a fresh-faced recent grad whose parents still believed she worked in microchip development at an electric car company. And Terrence Ramirez, our fabrication expert, who I would have been able to describe in more detail if he ever talked about himself.

"No, I'm fine," I replied to Jared. "Just a little jet-lagged. Addie, how are things going with the marketing department?"

Addie, as the most junior of the team, was our technical liaison with the advertising folks and helped prepare all the packaging, branding, and marketing materials for The Fantasy. She scrunched her pert nose.

"I'm not totally sold on their concept, but we're looking at alternatives."

Jared wouldn't let it go, though. "Jet-lagged? There's only a one-hour time difference."

Addie cocked her head, turning on him. "Hey, didn't *you* miss almost an entire day of work the Monday after Daylight Savings?"

Thank God for Addie. I should have her nominated for sainthood.

"We're not talking about me here. We're talking about our extremely exhausted-looking boss."

Oof. Spoke too soon.

"You've been pretty quiet this morning, boss," he continued. "Going to regale us with all the shenanigans you got up to in Cleavage-land?"

He waggled his eyebrows.

Gag.

"She's going to refer you to HR," Terrence muttered, not looking up from his work.

"*Sorry* that I'm trying to ask my *friend* how her trip went. I didn't realize being *nice* was a *fireable offense*."

"Cleveland was fine," I said. There weren't many things I disliked about working at BuzzCorp, but Jared was certainly at the top of that very short list. If Hudson had a talent for making me want to at least peek past my strong in-office barriers, Jared reminded me why I kept them steel-nailed shut. "Now, if you'll all look at the fuck report from Mary Brighton—"

"Did you and Hudson get along all right?"

I made a mental note to cancel Addie's application for sainthood. She blinked at me with her wide eyes, completely oblivious that she'd just asked the *worst possible* question.

"Mm-hmm," I hummed. "Fine."

"You don't look like it went fine. Those bags under your eyes tell me it was *exhausting*. I guess you didn't get *any* sleep with Hudson Bailey around, did you?"

Terrence narrowed his gaze at Jared. "Man, why are you gonna say that to your boss?"

"I'm worried about her," Jared said, adopting an oh-so-innocent act. "Scout was out in a big bad city all by herself with some strange weirdo Clara scraped off the street somewhere."

Addie rolled her eyes. "Oh please. You're just fishing for more information."

"I think he's shady. Nobody can be that nice."

"Yes, they can," I said, the words out before I could stop them. If there had been a scientific experiment in man's capacity for kindness, Hudson would have thrown off the whole data spread.

Jared leaned in. "And she speaks! Finally! Details, please."

"There's nothing to tell. We went to the conference. I showed him the ropes—"

He cut me off. "I *bet* you did."

My blood ran hot. Jared always had a bro-y tenor to him, like he'd applied for a job at a sex toy company as a way to pick up chicks, and while I probably should have reported him to HR like Terrence suggested, I knew doing so would just rock the boat. And rocking the boat was the last thing I wanted to do. Not when the stakes were so high with The Fantasy and it required all of my focus—and my entire team.

"And we didn't land an order from Mr. Ose," I continued. "So, if we're all done picking apart my personal affairs, could we please get back to work and try to salvage this project before we're all filing for unemployment?"

Addie and Terrence both recoiled. Jared just blinked. I didn't blame them for their surprise. Snapping and harsh talk was not my managerial style. I preferred the aloof approach. Less complicated and messy. Less chance to get close to people and take my eyes off my goals.

Today's goals?

Recover after the psychic damage of that Mr. Ose meeting.

Retract my agreement to teach off-books sex toy lessons.

Stop thinking about fucking Hudson Bailey.

And stop thinking about *fucking* Hudson Bailey.

"Great," I said, once I believed their silence. "Now, no more distractions."

Famous last words. Because from behind me, the elevator dinged, and a familiar—too familiar—voice rang out over my shoulder.

"Morning, all! Scout, have you seen my sweatshirt?"

5

Seven Minutes in Kevin

I understood the scientific law around time. Time travel was never proven possible even in theory because of the reality that time cannot stop, go backward, or be tailored to our will.

The theoretical physicists could be wrong, though. Maybe it only worked if time bent *against* our will. Because as soon as Hudson's voice reached my ears, the world moved through a pane of molasses, allowing me to see Terrence's horror, Addie's confusion, and Jared's smug, shit-eating grin.

God, they all thought we slept together this weekend.

It was happening. My worst nightmare come true. Not only had everything gone wrong outside the office, but now *in the office*, I was going to be the center of gossip, my reputation was going to be damaged, our productivity was going to go down the drain, and I didn't even have a night of passionate, mind-blowing, world-changing sex to show for it. It was like GalacticSolutions all over again.

Human musculature is made up of roughly six hundred individual components. Every single one of the six hundred muscles in my body coiled in a cringe.

Snapping around in my chair, I found Hudson standing in

front of the elevators, his handsome face wrinkled in apprehensive confusion.

"Is everything all right?" he asked.

"Oh, I think everything's *better* than all right," Jared intoned.

BuzzCorp was small, and Jared worked fast; if I didn't nip this in the bud, everyone from Mario in Accounting to Aimee in Janitorial would be chattering about my sexcapades before lunchtime.

"No, Hudson. I don't have your sweatshirt. I think you left it on the plane."

Hint, hint. Yes, I had his stupid sweatshirt, but I'd wanted to return it in private.

"I don't think so. Didn't you have it last?"

"Nope."

Every eye in this room was on me, and I wanted to disintegrate. The discomfort was all-encompassing. *Please just shut up about your stupid, soft, amazing-smelling sweatshirt.*

"Oh. It's just I thought I—"

"Maybe you should call the airline. They might have it in lost and found. Now, are you using the conference room this morning? Your team should be getting in any minute."

I could not be hinting any harder if this was fucking charades. But Hudson persisted.

"I really could have sworn you had it last. I don't mean to be a pest, but—"

"Why would she have your sweatshirt?"

Hudson turned his attention to Jared, who slurped loudly and deliberately from a near-empty iced coffee.

"I gave it to her."

Slllrrrrrpppp. "Sounds cozy."

Addie threw her hand over her mouth to cover up laughter. Terrence, clearly smarter than the rest of us combined, closed his laptop and walked away from this whole pathetic scene.

I shot up to my feet, too.

"All right, well. Great meeting, everyone. I want to crunch some more numbers on these fuck reports before we talk any further about next steps. Let's circle back to this after lunch."

Collecting my things, I went for my office, only to be stopped by Jared, who got the last word.

"*You* need some time to crunch the numbers? You're the most prepared woman I've ever met. What gives? Someone keep you distracted this weekend?"

I didn't dignify that with a response.

Mostly because I couldn't bring myself to lie.

A moment later, I was in my office, highly aware that my audience could still watch me through the glass walls. I bottled my bubbling emotions deep down and tried to go back to work. Back to what I was good at.

That was all I wanted, after all. To get back to my simple, unaffected self. To once again walk the straight and narrow, with no complications or detours.

But then, probably because there's no God and if there *is* a God he clearly enjoys my suffering, there was a knock on the door.

"Scout? Can I come in?"

Hudson had only visited my office once, when Clara first introduced us. But there he was. In front of my transparent door. Being observed carefully by Jared and Addie.

I dropped my tablet on my desk but kept my backpack shouldered. There was no way I'd be having this conversation with him in the corporate fishbowl. We'd need privacy.

"Can you walk and talk?"

"Uh, yeah. Sure."

He fell into silent step beside me as I left the main, shared floor of BuzzCorp and toward friendlier locales. There were only four places with any privacy here: Clara's office, the bathroom, the freebies room, and Kevin.

Kevin, named for Kevin Costner, whose movies always made *Clara* cry, was the remote maintenance closet where she sent me whenever *I* needed to cry.

A tiny closet lined with bougie, cruelty-free cleaning products and fair-trade mops and brooms—only the best for my boss—it was much smaller than I'd ever noticed before. A fact I only realized when I led Hudson inside and locked the door behind us.

Trying to ignore the looming largeness of him, I reached into my backpack and withdrew the object of today's frustration.

"Here. Here's your stupid sweatshirt. Now take it and get out."

I want to cry in peace, thank you.

Hudson only followed the first half of my instructions. I should have had him written up for insubordination in the workplace. "You dragged me in here to give me this?"

"I couldn't return it in front of everyone."

"Why not?"

"Because they're going to think we had sex! Jared already *does* think that!"

With those two little sentences, it was like the air evacuated the closet. In the stillness that followed, I was hyperaware of Hudson's proximity, particularly his face, which fell, drawing new lines I'd never seen in his perfect features.

His long fingers curled around the sweatshirt, holding it to himself like armor—or a security blanket.

"I get the sense that I messed up back there."

"You could say that," I snapped. Then I course-corrected so he wouldn't think me a total asshole. None of this was his fault. It was mine. I didn't need to take it out on him. "Thank you very much for lending it to me. You were really helpful yesterday; I mean it."

"I sense a *but* coming on."

"But after sleeping on it, I don't think I can help you with the sex toy lessons. If it gets around the office that we're spending a lot of time together, the gossip is going to spiral, and we can't afford any—"

"Distractions, I got it. But we can fix this. Get them off your back and give us the space for our tutoring sessions. I spent most of last night *doing my own research*." The tips of his ears went pink. "I gotta say . . . I was overwhelmed. I need you. What if I cleared things up for everyone?"

"What, go out there and make a company-wide announcement that we didn't sleep together? I'm sure *that* wouldn't make them suspicious."

His glasses slipped down his nose. He nudged them back up. "Why does it bother you? Would it really be so bad if we had?"

There were a million ways that I could have answered that, all of them too revealing. I could have said no, because having sex with him probably would have been amazing—too good for me. I could have said yes, because if we'd had sex and I told the entire office we had a one-night stand, then I'd be humiliated for being *just* a one-night stand. Or that if we'd had sex and we were still having sex, then that meant I'd gone off the deep end and dove headfirst into a relationship, which I'd never allow myself to do again, especially not during crunch time at work.

Or I could have said, *Hudson, my last relationship destroyed my entire life, so I keep myself in a little emotional box where I can stop myself from hurting anyone else—or me. So if you and I have sex, that means that everything has gone very, very wrong. You understand. I just don't do fucking and relationships. I can't afford the chaos.*

"I just need to keep firm professional boundaries."

His face fell slightly. "Well. No one deserves to be made to feel bad at work. If they're bothering you, you should report them to HR. Or make Clara remind them about their hostile work environment training."

Yeah, you'd think that would be the solution, wouldn't you?

"I can't do that."

"Why not?"

I hate conflict. I hate attention. The only guaranteed way to go unscathed is to hide from anyone who could possibly hurt you.

I stared down at my hands. "It's just easier to be invisible. No one can touch you when you're invisible."

"That's why you don't want to teach me about sex toys. Because then you won't be invisible."

"Yeah."

There was a shift in the body in front of me, and suddenly we were so close the fibers of our sweaters brushed. I looked up, and there he was. Gazing down at me like I wasn't the problem I knew myself to be. He smiled again. A real one this time. "Well, you've already failed there. You've never been invisible to me."

My lips parted, and the air between us crackled. I thought about our kiss yesterday, accidental and fleeting as it was, and wanted nothing more than to close the gap again. To test if his lips were as warm and soft and welcoming as they had been the first time.

I'm sure I would have said something as meaningful and as profound as what he'd just said to me, but before I could—

Knock, knock, knock!

"Scout?"

I practically threw myself against the far wall of the closet, staring at the closed door with wide *oh shit* eyes.

Clara. Somehow, Clara had found me in here. Dammit, couldn't a girl spurn her office crush in peace?

"Just think about it," Hudson blustered to say in a whisper. "You can't go invisible again, and I'm sticking around the office until the end of my contract. You might as well help me out with our work."

Clara knocked again.

"Uh, yeah?" I replied through the still-closed door.

"Could I please see you in my office?"

"Sure. I'll be right there."

I heard her heels click on the floor for a few paces.

Click. Click. Click. Click . . .

Phew. I'd gotten away with it. She had no idea that I'd been in here with Hudson. Home free.

Click. Her heels stopped on the floor. My luck ran out.

"Oh," she continued, cheerful as ever. "And please tell Hudson that he should go back to work, too."

6

Between a Cock and a Hard Place

"I don't know what you've been hearing around the office, but I have not slept with Hudson Bailey."

That probably wasn't the best entrance I could have made into my boss's office. But hey. I was frazzled and horny and anxious and convinced that one night of fantasizing about a coworker was going to wreck everything, so give me a break.

Clara looked up casually from her computer screen, completely unfazed.

"Hello, Scout," she droned drolly in her posh Emma Thompson accent. "Can I get you anything? Alkaline water? Kombucha? Maybe some condoms to take home with you?"

"I said I'm *not* sleeping with him!"

"No, I imagine not, but it is very funny to see you so worked up. It's very unlike you. I couldn't resist."

The corners of her lips crinkled as she smiled, removed her brightly colored spectacles, and let them dangle loosely from the chain around her neck. Clara Mason was an empress of industry. Pushing sixty-five, she'd founded BuzzCorp just seven years ago and taken it from a one-person start-up to one of the leading operators in the sex toy space. A #girlboss queen of the highest order, she had a tall, willowy figure and white-blond hair that looked positively angelic on magazine covers *and* under our office's harsh halogen lighting.

She was powerful. She was beautiful. She was constantly closing some business deal or closing the bedroom door on her latest conquest. She was *everything.*

She was also correct. I never acted like this—at least not on the surface.

"So you haven't heard that we had sex this weekend at the conference?"

"No, is that what the rumor mill is saying?"

"Yes, and it's not true."

"I wouldn't blame you if you had, you know. He's leaving when his contract is up in a month and a half or so, which means it would be a fairly unmessy affair. And he's got . . . something, hasn't he?"

Something was the understatement of the century. How hadn't I noticed it before? For weeks, we'd been working in the same building, in the same company, attending the same meetings and drinking from the same damn water filter. But one rogue erection during a conference talk and suddenly I saw him as if it was the first time, with all his softness and infuriating kindness and stupidly kissable lips.

What was it, anyway, that something? *Something* special? *Something* sexy? *Something* more than both of those things put together?

Fluorine Scout wanted to run experiment after experiment on him. Argon Scout, the Public Scout, on the other hand, wanted to go back to the old way things were, without him.

No. Hudson Bailey and I could not be a thing—not even a totally platonic thing.

"I wouldn't know. I've been too busy trying to get this prototype finished. Remember? The one that we were blue-skying before you told the entire world it would be out and ready by next Christmas?"

She waved her hand at me, like the details of her "move fast and break things" ethos hadn't turned this office from *easygoing days at the sex toy office* to *nightmarish crunch to meet this insane deadline.*

"Do you ever think about anything but work?"

"You pay me too much to think about anything else. Besides, I think about work twenty-four-seven and it's *still* not enough."

She clicked her tongue. "Ah. You're still hung up on the Mr. Ose deal."

"You're not?"

The events of the last thirty-six-odd hours had given me *much* to stress over. Clara's disappointment over our Mr. Ose meeting was at the top of that list. But she couldn't look less worried.

"I knew it was a big ask, pushing him to order all those units without ever seeing a prototype."

"Then why'd you ask me to take the meeting? With a guy who *has never even used a sex toy*, no less."

Clara smirked. My stomach dropped.

"You *knew* about that?"

"He mentioned it in his interview. I didn't think it was relevant. Anyone good at their job should be able to port their skills from one vertical to the other, and he's proven himself quite adept at doing so, having worked in so many industries as a contractor. Besides, I thought he could learn on the job."

For a moment, I considered not telling her about his little request. But it was *Clara*. I told her everything. We were in this business together. She'd picked me up when I was at my lowest, after the GalacticSolutions explosion, and I owed her my unfailing loyalty. "Speaking of learning on the job . . . He wants me to give him sex toy lessons." Clara's eyes lit up, and I knew I'd said the wrong thing. "*Lessons*, Clara. Not demonstrations."

She pouted. "And you're going to, right?"

"I said I would, but I'm going to blow him off. It's too much. I can't afford any distractions right now."

"It wouldn't be a distraction," she countered. "Him knowing about the industry is important to our success with The Fantasy."

"Then *you* teach him!"

A longing sigh. "That's a young woman's game."

"We're not going to sleep together."

She pursed her lips. "A pity. But even so, I think you should do it. Especially since the dynamic is . . . changing . . . around here."

Her usually breezy manner shifted. It set me on edge.

"Oh God." I groaned. "Are you about to make my day better or worse?"

"I suppose that entirely depends on your point of view, but I imagine it's worse."

That was another thing about Clara. She didn't have time to bullshit—or the inclination. We were alike in that way.

"I wanted you to hear it from me. Or, at least, I didn't want you to find out from the internet."

"What's that?"

"Lloyd Exeter bought Please-U Inc."

When she'd said she was going to make my day worse, I didn't think it was actually possible. My best guesses were like *Our silicone supplier went bust* or *Add some new, ridiculous feature to The Fantasy prototype.*

I'd never, not in a million years, thought the name Lloyd Exeter would get thrown around like a punch straight to my jaw.

The strength in my knees took a vacation. I dropped into the nearest chair.

"Oh," I said, for lack of anything intelligent to say. Gears in my head turned until they clicked. "That must have been who Mr. Ose was talking about."

"I've been hearing rumors for a few months now, but Lloyd made the official statement publicly this morning."

Please-U Inc. was one of our biggest competitors in the space. Unlike LoveHoney, which seemed to be a very "basics" brand, and unlike Bellessa, which was explicitly for women, and unlike us, who embraced the fact that sex was and should be pleasurable and exciting for everyone, Please-U Inc. had an industry-wide reputation as the man's sex toy company—and not in a fun Pride Month way. In that toxically alpha male, bro-y, pickup artist, *making love is for pussies, I only fuck* way.

In short, a very fitting portfolio acquisition for my former boyfriend.

No, not boyfriend.

He was. . . .

Well, Lloyd Exeter and I had . . .

To me, Lloyd was . . .

A mistake.

Yeah. Please-U Inc. and my worst mistake would be a match made in hell. Or whatever was below that.

"Can I ask you a question?"

"Of course," Clara replied.

"How in the world could you even imagine that news would make my day better?"

"Look at it this way: He's entering *your* world now. This isn't like working at GalacticSolutions, when you were under his thumb. This is a chance to best him. To show him that you're on top, and he can't touch you—not ever again. Literally or metaphorically."

The hairs on the back of my neck stood on end. "You don't think this is about me, do you? Like, you don't think he bought a sex toy company because of me?"

"What? No." She paused and visibly reconsidered. "Well, even if it is, you know that I'm in your corner. I won't let Lloyd Exeter do anything to harm you."

"You're just saying that because you know you won't be able to get The Fantasy out without me," I grumbled, only half joking.

"And because my days would be *so* boring without your quick little remarks."

We both laughed, but I had to force the sound out. My chest was still tight.

"Are you okay?" she asked after a moment.

Was I okay? I mean, I'd always known that Lloyd Exeter didn't disappear from the earth when he disappeared from my side. It wasn't being reminded of him that bothered me.

It was that he was *here*. In my space. The very space I had to run to because he'd made sure no one else would have me.

I couldn't even claim this little slice of the universe as my own anymore. Now I had to share it with *him*.

So no. I wasn't okay. But I had to be.

After all, I was not going to let Lloyd Exeter ruin my fucking career. Again.

My voice cracked when I answered, "Yeah."

So much for strength and resolve.

Carefully, Clara placed a hand on my shoulder. Her eyes were so full of empathy; they swam with the understanding we shared. So many memories of what Lloyd had done to me, of the person he'd turned me into.

"You know what I like to do at times like this?" she asked.

"No."

Her lips curled. "Drink."

7

Cock-tails and French 69s

Clara loved team building.

"Drinks on me, everyone!"

She did it in many, many ways—resort getaways in the Dominican Republic and Hilton Head, afternoon sundae bars, excursions to bowling or rage rooms—but this was her favorite: putting her credit card down at a bar and inviting the entire company (yes, all thirty of us plus custodial and security) for "sips and snacks" on her.

The last thing I needed was a drink. I'd had an emotional roller coaster of a weekend topped off with a second, weirder roller coaster this morning, so it would have been safer all around if I had clocked out, gone home, and tried to catch up on some work. *Alone.*

However, unappealing as the thought of drinking or socializing was, I dutifully took an Uber with Clara to Josie's, her favorite spot in town. Drinking might have been a distraction from work—yikes—but at least it would also be a distraction from thoughts of Lloyd and Hudson.

With its low lighting, slightly warped wall-mounted TV

screens, and bottomless chips and salsa, Josie's was a run-of-the-mill Tex-Mex joint with a solid tequila library. Usually, a fun spot. But, of course, my most annoying coworker couldn't leave me in peace.

"Whoa, look who it is! Boss lady's in the house!"

"Hi, Jared."

At the bar, waiting for my second watermelon margarita, I didn't even turn to acknowledge him—just caught him in the already hazy corners of my vision. He sidled up beside me anyway. After our encounter this morning, I had gone out of my way to make sure our paths didn't cross again, but he never missed out on free drinks or free food. Our meeting here was inevitable.

I glanced toward the hallway where Clara had disappeared ten minutes ago with some well-dressed silver fox she'd found drinking alone at a corner table. Damn her. Getting some *and* abandoning me.

"Good to finally see you at one of these little office hangs. Tell the truth: You just came because your boyfriend's coming."

I offered one of those halfhearted smiles women do when they want men to leave them alone. "Don't have a boyfriend, Jared."

"You know what I mean!"

The waitress brought my watermelon margarita; Jared ordered a tequila shot for each of us.

Normally, I wasn't a *let's shoot tequila* girl. Given the extenuating circumstances, however, I downed mine the second it was put in front of me.

"Unless you're saving yourself," Jared mused. "For me, right? You're saving yourself for me? Just waiting for the right boozy opportunity to strike? C'mon, Scout. You don't need any liquid courage where I'm concerned. I'm a sure thing."

The worst thing about Jared—an achievement considering his docket of faults—was that he genuinely didn't see anything wrong with what he'd said. He was *always* "just joking."

I mumbled about needing the restroom, then disappeared for some peace and quiet. However, no sooner had I set myself up in front of the bathroom mirror than Addie appeared behind me.

"Jared's such bullshit, huh?" she asked, shooting me a sympathetic look.

"He's harmless," I said, repeating the same thing I told myself every time we spoke.

"I know, but still. I'm sorry he talks to you like that. You should tell him to go fuck himself."

Oh, to be twenty-one again and think the world was that simple.

"I would, but I'm afraid he'd think that was an invitation."

Addie nodded, smacking her lips as she applied a new coat of bright purple lip gloss. Not for the first time, I felt a sharp stab of regret. I'd never been cool and hip, not even when I *was* twenty-one. Purple lip gloss and cute miniskirts and telling asshole men to fuck off had never been in my skill set.

What kind of person would I be if I'd grown up normal like Addie, not a number-crunching savant who didn't understand the first thing about the real world beyond her calculator and slide rule?

Satisfied with her lip gloss, she turned to me again. "Can I say just, like, one thing, though?"

"Sure."

Her words slurred slightly, but there was a fondness to them I couldn't deny. "And to preface: I don't mean it in a weirdo-Jared way, but in a drunk-girlfriends-in-a-bathroom way. It's just that I've, like, noticed that you're not super, you know, like, outgoing or whatever. You keep to yourself. I don't think I've ever seen you go out to one of these things unless Clara forces you. And do you ever date or anything?"

"Not really. I like my job. I put most of my energy into work," I said.

"A job isn't a life, girl. And I think you're crazy hot. And smart. And accomplished and stuff. You should be, like, out there having all the sex, living it up all around town, partying with your girls. It might take a little of the pressure off at work if you did, you know, more nights like this. I mean, come on. You and me—we work in a boys' club. There aren't a ton of female mechanical engineers out there. We've gotta stick together, mama."

She gave a little shoulder shimmy that I assumed was meant to be a dance. I rolled my eyes.

"Did Clara put you up to this pep talk?"

Her face contorted and I realized I'd said the wrong thing. *Shit.* "Whatever. I was trying to be a friend. Sorry. Forget I said anything."

Yet another example of why I didn't talk to people outside the office. I couldn't get through a simple bathroom pep talk without hurting someone.

As she stalked through the swinging door, I realized that she wasn't talking generally. She had said all of that because she wanted to be my friend. That was why she'd been hurt. She thought I just didn't want to be friends with *her.*

Steeling myself, I left the bathroom to find her and apologize.

However, the televisions in the bar were on an evening news channel. A poppy *Entertainment Tonight*–style show. When I glanced up at the flickering screens, a bottomless pit opened in the center of my stomach. I staggered to a stop. All thoughts of Addie and apologies flew from my mind.

The news story was, apparently, about Lloyd Exeter and a recent appearance on *The Joe Rogan Experience.*

I grabbed two tequila shots from a random table and downed them—one right after the other. Then a third for good measure.

Built like a homecoming king, Lloyd had sharp-featured, all-American good looks. Once upon a time, the sight of him filled me with butterflies. Now, alligators. Or some other scary animal with sharp teeth and predator energy.

Jared noticed me lingering at the back of the bar and waved me over to the empty seat between him and Terrence. "Hey, Scout! You used to work for him, right? Talk about a blast from your past."

A blast from the past always sounded like a nice thing in theory, but in this case, *blast* meant "fiery explosion" rather than "good time." However, with the attention of all our coworkers squarely on me, when he waved again, I had no choice but to join them.

The television volume increased, and Lloyd's laugh filled the bar's speakers. Again, the laws of thermodynamics were clear on the practice of time travel. I knew that. But as I watched, it was like I'd been transported through the years to my old self—the one who'd fallen head over heels for him . . . and ruined her life because of it.

"So you're getting into the sex toy game. What's the story there?"

"You're gonna laugh."

"No, man. I think it's cool."

"Well, there was this chick I used to fuck . . ."

Out of the corner of my eye, I noticed Clara get up from a cozy corner booth and rush back behind the bar, but I paid her no mind.

My world narrowed around the TV screen. There was nothing but Lloyd Exeter.

"Beginning of all great stories."

"Right? And so, we used to work together at GalacticSolutions, building the Ilium. Remember that shit show? Long story short—she was the reason that the Ilium went kaboom, *so we don't work out, she gets fired, ends up working at some sex toy company. And I sorta, you know, I don't keep tabs on her or anything, it wasn't that serious, but she comes across my feed every so often. One day, I see this video of her, up on stage, at some orgasm industry conference. At first, I ignore it, but she keeps doing these conferences and she keeps popping up. And she keeps going on and on about* pleasure."

"Which I'm guessing you didn't think was her area of expertise."

"Uh, no. Definitely not. What this girl knows about pleasure could have fit in her very, very tight holes, you know? So, anyway, I thought if someone with so little skill could make a bag doing sex stuff, then I could do it, too—only, you know, I'd be good at it."

The clip ended and transitioned back to the *ET* clone commenting on it. Too late to save me, Clara finally managed to requisition the bar remote and turn the radio to Spanish-language pop hits.

The perfect soundtrack to my utter humiliation.

There wasn't any denying that the woman in that story was me. I was, after all, the only person who'd worked for Lloyd Exeter *and* at a sex toy company. We all knew it.

But no one had known we'd been together. That was the new information.

"Holy shit," Addie breathed.

"You can say that again," Terrence said.

They had the decency to sound sympathetic. Maybe even a little sorry for me. Jared on the other hand . . .

"You had *sex* with *Lloyd Exeter*?"

That was when the emotions hit, smashing through my shock. He'd lied about me. Lloyd Exeter had gone on the most popular podcast in the world and *lied* about me. Everything else that happened between us back then, I could handle. I'd made mistakes, I'd been a fool, mea culpa and all that.

But for him to tell the world I'd slept with him?

No, that we'd *fucked*?

"No," I said, my voice almost a whimper. "I didn't have sex with Lloyd Exeter."

"But he just said—"

"I didn't!"

He scoffed. "You can't just go on Joe Rogan's show and say anything, Scout."

"Yes, you can. It's sort of his whole thing," I countered. Heat was building in my blood. A cacophonic, whining, high-pitched din filled my brain, like the sound someone would play to trigger a sleeper agent. Fluorine Scout begged to come to the surface, go reactive, and leave this entire place in ash.

"She doesn't want to tell you," Addie interjected. "Leave her alone."

"There's nothing to tell," I snapped.

"Oh *please*. Who has more reason to lie? You or him? I want to hear all the horny details. He had to be good, right—"

My anger had made me irrational, thoughtless. But he was so careless and Lloyd was so cruel and Joe Fucking Rogan should be consigned to the Hague and I felt so small and helpless and tipsy and—

Fluorine can't be contained forever.

The words were out of me before I could stop them.

"I didn't have sex with Lloyd Exeter, Jared, because I haven't had sex with *anyone*."

Jared's eyes lit up. It might as well have been Christmas. "What was that?"

This isn't happening. It can't be happening. Shut it down. Shut it down.

Instantly, I was shy and retiring Scout again. Public Scout. I tried to claw back the girl I had been two minutes ago, before I'd let my anger get the better of me.

"Nothing. I misspoke. I'm flustered. I—"

But Jared saw right through it. They all did. I clocked understanding as it dawned on each and every face in that bar. And not just my team, either, but every BuzzCorp employee close enough to eavesdrop.

"No way," he crowed. "You're a *virgin*?"

Well, yes. In the technical sense. But in that moment, I felt well and truly fucked.

8

Beat Around My Bush

It was like a scene in a movie—all conversation, clinking of ice in glasses, all clattering of silverware ceased immediately. Everyone stared. Record-scratch moment.

When we were together, Lloyd hadn't known I was a virgin. That was good, because at least he hadn't told Rogan about that. For a moment, I'd had a scrap of dignity.

But I had to go and screw it up by blurting it out in front of everyone.

So there I was, surrounded by my employees and coworkers, not to mention the poor, unsuspecting bar staff, having just admitted that I, the sex toy engineer heralded by my boss as the future of the industry, had never actually had sex before.

"I have to go."

"Scout—"

That was Clara, approaching me, but I couldn't answer her. Not now. I knew she would be sweet and sympathetic, and I just knew that if I looked at her, I'd start crying.

I couldn't be a crier *and* a virgin in front of my colleagues. One of those was bad enough. Both of them? Beyond humiliating.

As I collected my things, I tried to dredge my thoughts from my devastated alcoholic fugue state and put them in order. *Okay. Everyone knows you're a virgin. Lloyd Exeter is spreading lies about you online. And you're probably never going to be the same after this. But there's a silver lining, I guess. At least Hudson didn't hear all of this.*

Except . . . he did.

When I turned around to leave, I discovered that he'd been sitting there, down the bar from me, for at least a few minutes. He still had his backpack slung over one shoulder, like he'd come in but froze when the fireworks started.

Fuck this.

Dropping his gaze, I stormed out of the bar, too drunk and too anxious to care about the mess I left behind me.

My steps out onto the darkening Dallas streets were shaky. It was hard to see the street signs through the haze of tears threatening to spill over onto my cheeks; the tequila brain didn't help either. But I let muscle memory guide me home.

I only got a couple of blocks before a voice rang out behind me, just like it did the day before when he cornered me for that accidental kiss.

"Scout! Scout, wait!"

Hudson materialized beside me, his cologne haunting my nose like the last, lingering magnesium carbonate from erased classroom chalk. I hated how that smell immediately made a few of the knots in my shoulders relax. How it reminded me of the soft, comforting embrace of the sweatshirt he'd lent me.

"I don't need you to try and make me feel better," I said, desperate to dispel the feeling.

"Ah, the bar's not really my scene anyway. I figured I could use the walk."

I shrugged. "Suit yourself."

We walked in silence. It was . . . surprisingly nice, to have his presence there. Nonjudgmental. Noncurious. Just there for me.

"Well," he said eventually, breaking the silence. "Look at it this way. At least no one thinks we're sleeping together anymore. Or if they do, then they're not talking about it anymore."

I couldn't help it. I laughed. Big mistake, though, because a few tears leaked out as I did.

"Do you want to talk?" he asked gently.

"So you *did* come out here to try and make me feel better."

"I've sort of noticed that you keep people at arm's length. Except for Clara, but you can't exactly talk about your virginity with your boss."

"What, so you thought I'd talk about it with a total stranger instead?"

"We're not *total* strangers. Remember, you kissed me yesterday." I opened my mouth to retort, but he cut me off. "And anyway, I thought, hey, if I was in her shoes, I'd want someone to talk to. Sorry if it was the wrong call. I just didn't want you to be alone. Especially when you're drunk and it's dark out."

"I'm not drunk," I said before *immediately* stumbling over my feet.

"You're right. Sober as a judge. Here." He offered his arm. I eyed it for a beat. "C'mon. We can't have our best engineer twisting her ankle. Let me walk you home?"

"Fine. But no feelings talk. And I'm *not* taking your arm."

Tossing my chin with defiant I'm-a-bad-bitch-who-don't-need-a-man energy, I went back to walking . . . and tripped over my feet yet again.

Damn feet. Who kept putting them there? And why wouldn't the sidewalk just stay put?

He offered me his arm again, a twinkle of humor in his eyes. This time, I took it, placing my hand in the crook of his elbow.

His surprisingly muscular crook.

"You can talk about your feelings, too," he said, once we got under way. "If you want. I mean, what's the risk? My contract with BuzzCorp is up in six weeks. You'll never see me again after that. I'm like . . . a self-destructing tape. You put all your feelings and thoughts into me, and then in six weeks . . . bam. Gone."

Maybe I was drunk, but this struck me as sound logic. I hadn't thought of it from that perspective. My two big worries about people? Them distracting me from my work and them bailing once they realize what an unsocialized loser I am.

Problem: I'm so, *so* isolated from other people. A weirdo, a freak who can't get through a normal conversation without humiliating herself.

Proposed Solution: Make a friend who won't judge you. And whose opinion doesn't matter anyway, because in six weeks, he'll be gone.

"I don't even know where to start," I muttered, taking my first tentative steps onto the friendship ledge.

"Are you . . . interested in sex?" Hudson asked.

From anyone else, it might have sounded like a creepy come-on, but from him, it was a genuine question. Asexuality was valid as hell, but unfortunately, I was afflicted with the curse of sexual desire. Every time I so much as smelled Hudson's cologne, I was reminded of that.

And now, with our bodies pressed against each other and the swirl of alcohol in my brain, I felt that sexual desire more potently than I could remember in a long, long time.

"Yes, I'm interested. The timing just never worked out. I mean, I was a child prodigy. I graduated high school at thirteen. I was out of college by my seventeenth birthday. I had my master's by the time I was twenty. Dual PhDs after that. My parents worked hard to get me through the best schools, to help me make the most of myself. So I was always studying. Always trying to make them proud. I didn't have time for anything but work. And even if I had the time, who would I have had sex with? Studies show that most first-time sexual encounters are engaged in during the college years. Well, how do you lose it when you're a fifteen-year-old in a class of nerds in their midtwenties?"

I was rambling, but he didn't seem to care. I continued.

"Then, after that, there was Lloyd. We didn't sleep together, but we had a thing and it ended badly."

"And he's why you blame yourself for the explosion."

He didn't phrase that like a question, so I didn't answer it. In truth, I didn't blame Lloyd. I blamed myself. But that was an emotional equation to balance another day, so I merely replied:

"I never wanted to let what happened at GalacticSolutions happen again. I didn't want anything to mess with my concentration. So sex just . . . I just haven't done it yet. I guess I've been waiting."

"For what?"

With a small tug on his arm, I indicated that we should stop. He lingered with me outside my little apartment building, looking like he belonged there. Like, if this was a scene in a movie, he'd guide me up the steps and into my apartment for some PG-13-rated, romantically scored escapades.

What *was* I waiting for? I turned the question over in my head.

When *would* be the right time?

Who *would* be the right guy?

Why *not* Hudson?

Slipping out of his grip, I gave a little shrug.

I don't know. I don't know what I'm waiting for.

It was the only answer I had for him. And the only answer I had for me.

"There you have it. That's what happened—mostly. So what's the diagnosis?" I asked. "Exactly how pathetic am I?"

"Nothing pathetic about you. You can have sex. Or you don't

have sex, who cares? I just . . ." He toyed idly with a piece of broken glass on the ground, then used his boot to guide it into the gutter, where it couldn't hurt anyone. "I wonder if you're letting this Lloyd-GalacticSolutions thing stand in the way of you being happy. Not just about sex, but everything. I know you like your work, but are you so wrapped up in it because you want to be, or because you're hiding behind it?"

I blinked. Hudson visibly paled, then nervously fiddled with his spectacles.

"Sorry, I overstepped. I didn't mean to—"

"No, no," I replied, soft but firm. The words were almost whispered. It was surprisingly difficult to articulate full sentences when sloshed on tequila and seen straight through by the most handsome man in the world. The truth was . . . he was right. I'd just never let myself understand it that way. "You're . . . surprisingly insightful, Hudson Bailey."

He chuckled. "What a pair we make, huh? The sex toy engineer who's never had sex and the sex toy app designer who's never used a sex toy."

"Clara always says that she's not in the sex toy business. She's in the people business. Getting the correct people together and letting them work their magic. I guess she had to horribly fail sometime."

His dimple appeared as his grin widened. "Fail? I don't know, Scout. I think we're a win so far."

It was so romantic. The stirrings of good to come, if only I would let myself have it.

If only I hadn't ruined it by immediately throwing up all that tequila right on his shoes.

9

Dildon't You Want Me, Baby?

Hudson was really nice about the vomit thing. Did he turn a little green? Yes. Did he politely excuse himself to (I assume) clean himself up and do the *Men in Black* memory wipe thing on himself so as to forget my existence and the unfortunate relaxation of my pyloric sphincter and subsequent emesis? Also yes.

But he did it all without ever once making me feel bad about the incident or his likely now ruined shoes.

After a thorough shower and a Coca-Cola mixed with two salt tablets (the most scientifically sound hangover pre-cure), I tucked myself into bed and tried to sleep, but my mind kept circling around the conversations I'd had in the last thirty-six-odd hours. Mr. Ose had basically called me weird and unsocialized. Addie said I needed to get some girls and go on some dates. And Hudson said I was holding myself back.

Two data points were interesting but not significant. Three data points were the beginning of a trend. Four or more data points were irrefutable.

If I was going to take Mr. Ose, Addie, and Hudson seriously, then I needed more data.

"I was wondering when you'd phone me," Clara said, answering my call on the second ring.

A hum of activity crackled behind her, and I pictured her in all her Goop-elegant glory, still slurping back jalapeño margs at Josie's.

"Sorry. Am I interrupting?"

"Not at all. We're just wrapping up here. I'm walking to my car." The sound dulled as she did just that. Then, easy as breathing, she informed me, "You'll be happy to know that Jared has quit."

"He *what*?"

"No one else thought his little spectacle with you was funny. He kept trying to get everyone in on the joke, to back him up as it were, but when no one would take the bait—in fact, Addie and Terrence gave him a pretty firm talking-to—he said that this was the last straw and he could no longer tolerate being saddled with such humorless, cancel-culture woke-ists."

Guilt and shameful relief mixed inside me like noxious chemicals in a test tube.

"I didn't mean for him to quit" was all I could manage.

"I'm sure you didn't, though I can't say I'm sad to see him go. He was my one true hiring mistake. I thought he might bring some balance to the team. It appears I was wrong. He caused discord wherever he went. I should have fired him ages ago, but I wanted to give him a chance. Ah, well. I suppose you can't win them all."

When she sighed, I was reminded of Hudson's sweet parting words. *I think we're a win so far.*

Thank God Clara got it right way more than she got it wrong. If there were more Hudsons out there to be found, and she hired them instead of Jareds, we'd be in good shape as a company.

"Anyway, what can I do for you at this late hour, Scout?"

"I wanted to pick your brain."

"By all means, I love to be kept from the warm embrace of slumber to have my cerebrum probed."

If she hadn't been teasing me, I might have pointed out that telencephalon would be more precise. But considering it *was* late and I *was* asking her for a favor, I bit my tongue on that particular point.

"It's come to my attention that some people are under the impression that I don't get out enough," I said, summarizing the opinions of Mr. Ose, Addie, and Hudson. "That I'm too closed off and should try to, you know, connect or whatever. Is that true? Do you see me that way?"

"Of course."

"Of *course*?" I screeched.

"I told you as much this morning. Remember? When I said you should have sex with Hudson."

She hadn't *exactly* told me to have sex with him, just that it wouldn't be the end of the world if I did. I brushed away the thought—I couldn't get distracted with my *God, I want to fuck Hudson Bailey* fixation right now.

"But . . . you don't think . . . I mean, The Fantasy is the most important thing we've ever done. If I take my eye off the ball, if I waste my time with people, then I might lead us into another GalacticSolutions situation—"

"*That's* why you haven't had sex yet? Because of what happened with Lloyd?"

"I wouldn't say that, exactly."

Mostly because I didn't want to admit it.

"Scout, you can't punish yourself forever."

"I'm not punishing myself—"

"You're afraid to fight, Scout. Afraid to get what you want. Afraid that maybe you don't deserve it. But you do. You should.

And, as your friend and not your boss, I'd like to see you try. All this stuff about being distracted from work? That's just a rubbish excuse."

"On the other hand, if word gets out that your lead engineer is a virgin, it could be a total disaster, Clara. You should have seen Mr. Ose's face when Hudson told him he was new to the industry. We'll be a laughingstock. I can't handle it if I bring down the company."

My own labored breathing echoed back to me through my cell's receiver.

"Listen, as the woman who will likely lose everything if The Fantasy fails, I want you to know that you have my full and unconditional support. Have sex, don't have sex. It doesn't matter. I don't care what anyone else thinks about you. Your work speaks for itself, and you're an invaluable member of this team. You've never let me down before. I don't anticipate you starting now."

That night, I slept fitfully. I'd never conceived of my inability to make friends or date as fear. I'd always seen it as quite practical. A symptom of my dedication to my career.

But Clara's diagnosis about me running away from intimacy made sense. And I couldn't help but wonder . . .

What would my existence be like if I wasn't afraid all the time?

THE BUZZCORP OFFICE was a friendlier place without Jared. I didn't have to worry about fending off sexist jokes or having anyone pry into my personal affairs, and while no one went out of their way to talk to me about the night before or its revelations, I felt their support. There were more waves, more "good mornings," more sympathetic glances that seemed to say *Don't worry about it; it's not a big deal.*

But it *was* a big deal. Last night changed everything. At least for me.

In my office, I chomped on salt-and-vinegar chips, ostensibly trying to brainstorm new pistoning techniques for The Fantasy but distracted by yesterday's revelations. I had permission now to start over again. To exist outside of work. But how? Where to start?

Well . . .

A salt-and-vinegar chip froze halfway to my mouth, coating my keyboard in crumbs.

I could lose my virginity. That was a place to start.

I wasn't going to let Lloyd Exeter control me anymore. He might have destroyed my life once, but I wasn't going to let him keep doing it. I wasn't going to keep sabotaging my own happiness because of him.

That little bit of determination turned my whole day around. As I fiddled with my tools, adjusting pieces on the first-gen prototype we'd been building for months now, my mind raced.

First thought? Ask Hudson. Just walk up and say *Hey, I'd like to fuck, would you also be interested in that?* Best-case scenario: hot losing-my-virginity-in-my-office story. Worst case: sexual harassment lawsuit.

Yeah, that was out. It was too Fluorine Scout. Too messy. Every time my mind drifted to him as a potential partner, I immediately came up with dozens of reasons why I absolutely should not.

So I holed away until everyone left the office that night. When I was sure I was alone, I fired up my laptop and did a quick google.

How to find a one-night stand

That was cleaner than fucking my office crush, anyway. Simple. Easy to walk away from. A one-night stand to remove my cloak of virginhood, then back to normal life.

However, the results that popped up required way more effort than I cared to give. I mean, really. Go to a bar? Hook up with some rando at a club? Nope. I amended my search.

Non-creepy hookup apps

No, that wasn't any good. I deleted and tried again.

How to find a non-creepy, handsome, funny, gentle, caring guy to lose your virginity to in a no-strings, safe, pleasurable, exciting, satisfying one-night stand

Color me shocked. That extremely specific search didn't generate a single useful answer.

I scrolled anyway. Someone had to have some idea of how I could rid myself of this meddlesome virginity.

Wasn't there anyone in the entire world who would just dick me down?

"Hey, boss."

Shit!

I jumped out of my chair, scrambling. As if conjured by my earlier, horny thoughts about him taking my V-card right here, Hudson stood in the doorway, looking every bit as sexy as he did in my completely impossible fantasies.

"Hudson! What are you—what are you still doing here?"

Everyone else had gone home ages ago, content to leave me with the late-night toil. It was unfair how good he looked after fourteen hours in the office—and how a little uncertain furrow in his brow only accentuated his natural appeal. "Is now not a good time? I'm sorry, I can come back . . ."

He trailed off as his eyes drifted over my shoulder. To my computer screen. Which displayed a hot-nude-male-torso-laden landing page for a discreet hookup website.

My stomach dropped.

"It's not what it looks like."

"And what it looks like is none of my business," Hudson said with a reassuring and knowing expression that instantly set me at ease.

"Right," I said quickly. But then a weird pang struck me. Yeah, my sex life wasn't Hudson's business. Another tally in the *never gonna happen* column. Bummer. "Right. How are your shoes after last night? I'm sorry about that, really."

"They're washable. Gotta love these innovations in sneaker technology, huh?"

I breathed a laugh, but I'm sure it wasn't convincing. To have Hudson barge in on my digital sex safari—especially when he was the one I really wanted—was too much. It reminded me of that night in Cleveland, when I fantasized to the thought of him well into the early hours of the morning, only to have him come to my dildo rescue the next day.

"I can go, if you want," he offered. "I was just getting ready to head out, but I saw your light on, and I just thought—I wanted to check on you. See if you're all right after last night."

"Yeah. I'm all right," I lied, lying like a lying liar would. *Just act natural.* "Why d'you ask?"

"Because last night was a lot. And it's slightly concerning that after all that, you're looking at an anonymous hookup site while your 3-D printer crafts a new dildo."

10

Midnight in the Sex App of Good and Evil

Heat flooded my face as I glanced over at the machinery in the corner of the room. I'd totally forgotten it was on—or that it was building a mock-up of the latest addition to our Monster Masturbators oversized dildos collection.

"That's not for me!" I insisted.

"The dildo or the hookup app?"

"The dildo!"

"Hey! I'm not here to judge."

"The dildo isn't for me," I reiterated. "But if you're not careful it's going to be for you."

He chuckled. "Don't threaten me with a good time."

"I thought you didn't know anything about sex toys."

"I don't" came his snappy retort. "But I think I've made it clear that I'm eager to learn."

I couldn't help it. I chuckled. But the chuckle quickly shifted into nervous resolve. I didn't *have* to tell him this. I probably shouldn't have. However, Hudson had a way of making me feel comfortable. Safe. Against all odds and logic, I trusted him.

"After due consideration, I decided that your advice last night was sound. I should change my outlook a little bit."

To my surprise, Hudson pursed his lips. Thoughtful. "You shouldn't try to lose your virginity just because I said so. Or because Lloyd Exeter was an asshole on a podcast."

"'Asshole on a podcast' is redundant," I mumbled. "But that's not why I'm doing this. I'm just . . . tired of living on the margins."

He leaned over my shoulder to inspect the screen. "How's the search going, then? Any promising prospects?"

Yes, you.

But alas, I wasn't looking to Hudson for this. I was looking at dating apps. So even if there had been promising prospects, they didn't matter when the one guy I wanted—but couldn't let myself have—was so close I could feel his breath on my neck.

"I'll just say this. If you could call a meeting of all the world's men and teach them how to take a picture *without* holding up a fish or a red Solo cup, that would be great."

"I'll get right on that. And how about this: I'm a consultant. Would it be helpful if I . . . consulted on this? First hit is always free."

What the hell did *that* mean? When I heard *hit,* my mind always went straight to sex. But surely he didn't mean it that way.

"Or is it too weird?" Hudson asked after a beat of my silence, stepping back from my chair. "Me helping you find a guy to hook up with? I think my services would come in handy, but I'd hate to be a Jared about it."

He could never be a Jared about anything, and his services could come in handy in many *other* ways, I was sure. I focused back on the screen, scrolling down so he could scan the site.

"You have more experience picking sexual partners," I reasoned. "And better luck, I imagine. I'd be grateful for the help."

Another one of those sharp, longing pangs struck me. In another universe, maybe Hudson would help me. Maybe he'd cut the crap with this online hookup stuff, boost me onto my desk, and ravish me right here. Fulfill my naughty fantasies. Give me a cherry-popping I'd never forget.

A silly dream. If he'd been interested in having sex with me, he would have said so. Not offered to help me find someone *else* to get the job done.

"It's scarier than I thought it would be," I added. "Trying to put myself out there."

"Firsts usually are. First time dating, first time having sex, first time making a friend. Go easy on yourself."

I'd never been easy on myself, not for one second.

"And when it comes to men," he continued, "you should be choosy."

"I'll keep that in mind while messaging . . ." I pointed at a random profile on the screen. "Brendan."

Hudson made a face.

"He's got a quote from that toxic masculinity influencer guy in his bio. The one who got arrested for human trafficking last year." I opened my mouth to retort, but he cut me off. "Even if your ethos is *don't be choosy*, I think *not a potential human trafficker* is the absolute minimum bar your guys should clear. What about that one?"

Jonathan. Straight teeth. Huge muscles. He'd do. He wasn't Hudson, with the barest wisps of smile lines at his temples and hands made for grabbing the sheets. But whatever. "Sure, yeah. I'll message him."

"C'mon, Scout. The first person you have sex with doesn't need to be your soul mate or anything, but don't just passively accept some dude because he'll answer your DM. Do you *want* him?"

I reconsidered the countless pixels making up Jonathan's profile picture. "He looks like he'd want me to get out of bed at six on Saturday morning for a jog."

"Not into the gym-bro stuff. Good to know. What about that guy?"

"That haircut makes him look sinister."

He pointed to another.

"C'mon. Cowboy boots?"

Another.

"He didn't even make his bed before taking the mirror selfie."

Another.

"Not my type."

Hudson barked a laugh. "And what *is* your type, Scout?"

Oh no. I shouldn't have brought up the *type* thing. I idly picked at a stray thread dangling from the cuff of my cardigan sleeve. Anything to avoid telling him the truth. That I didn't want any of these guys because they weren't him. "I haven't really thought about it."

"Don't overanalyze it. It's that *zing*. What guy makes you zing?"

I don't know how to answer that without totally giving myself away, dude. And I can't give myself away. Not to you.

He tried again. "Or maybe this: When you've imagined what sex would be like—real sex, good sex, the sex you've wished for—what's that guy like?"

Say something. Say anything. Just don't say He's exactly like you.

"Um. Tall."

"Pity for the short kings out there, but at least it's a start."

Hand back on my mouse, I scrolled down the seemingly endless pages of dating profiles, mostly for something to do. But the longer I looked, the longer the partialism of it all—shirtless torsos, crinkle-eyed stares, buzz-cut heads—spiraled me into something like a trance. Before I knew it, I was doing that nervous talking thing of mine. The one where I said entirely the wrong thing.

The truth.

"And gentle. And thoughtful. And maybe like he wouldn't necessarily beat me in a fight—you know, a little softer or lankier or whatever. None of those big burly types. Curly hair. Long fingers, nice hands. And he'd smell good—really good. He'd be able to talk to me about stuff that wasn't sex. Science or math or philosophy or the last museum he went to. But he can't be too serious. He needs to be able to have fun, too. A nice laugh. A good smile. Looks good in a pair of jeans. Bookish. Nerdy. Kind eyes—I don't care about the color. I like glasses. And . . ."

I trailed off, the weight of one particular set of kind, bespectacled eyes bringing me back to reality. Closing the tab on my screen, I stood up from my chair and leaned against my desk to face him.

"And I want him to care about me. When I do have sex for the first time, I don't want anonymous. I probably should. It'd be safer. Less risky. Easier to wham-bam, thank you, ma'am. But I want to be with someone who actually likes me. I don't need forever. Just a one-night stand. But still. I want to feel safe. To know that it'll be good."

For a few moments, all we heard was the whir of the 3-D printer as it went about its work.

"Quite the Mr. Right," Hudson mused.

"Don't make fun. I'm fully aware that it's ridiculous."

"I wasn't going to. I was going to say . . ."

As he trailed off, something strange happened. Something absolutely baffling. Hudson raised one perfect hand, ghosted the tips of his fingers up my knee, and lightly, almost incidentally, traced the hem of my skirt.

My entire body erupted in goose bumps. I licked my lips involuntarily.

Was he . . . was he touching me *on purpose*?

"Say what?"

Hudson glanced up at me from under his eyelashes. If I didn't know better, I would have sworn he looked . . . hungry. "Your dream man sounds a lot like me."

11

A Sindecent Proposal

I'm not sure how I managed to concentrate with his fingers dancing across my knee.

But somehow, a snap plan occurred to me.

Problem: Need to lose my virginity.

Proposed Solution: Find someone to have safe, emotionally unattached sex with.

Test: Have sex with Hudson.

Result: Some potentially amazing virginity-losing shenanigans?

"I have an idea," I said, breathless.

"Yeah?"

"Would you . . . How would you feel about a trade?"

His fingers paused on my knee. "I'm listening."

"If you still want those sex toy lessons, then I'll give them to you. And in exchange, we should have sex."

The air between us pulled—a bridge jumper's cable about to snap and break our necks or rebound and send us soaring.

Hudson let out a long breath. His expression turned wolfish. "I think that's a fair trade."

"It only makes sense," I said, trying to tamp down my swell of sentiment with good old-fashioned practical, scientific thinking. "I'll get to know what sex is like, which can only improve the quality of The Fantasy. And you'll know more about sex toys, which will achieve the same result."

"You don't need an excuse to do what you want, Scout," he said, leaning closer. "You can just have it. You can just have *me*. If that's what you want."

"I do."

"Good," he said. Once again, those fingers did their dance across the skin of my thigh, awakening deep, primal lust in me. "Because I want you. You're my type, too."

"That's so hard to believe," I muttered.

Hudson's gaze went flat, as if it was the height of stupidity not to think I was eminently bangable. "Haven't I made it obvious?"

Obvious? I tried to think back over the last few weeks we'd known each other, examining them in a different light. Yeah, he'd held doors open for me. Gotten me cookies at the conference. Listened to me. Stood up for me at the airport. Accidentally kissed me.

And yes, sure, he'd gotten an erection during my talk at the sex toy convention. But that wasn't . . .

He wasn't . . .

My surprise made him shake his head.

"You clearly don't know what you look like bent over a drafting table."

He'd been ogling me in the office? He'd been lusting after me from afar like Mr. Kinkz-william Darcy?

"And," he continued, "that kiss at the airport might not have been on purpose, but ever since, I've had a *very* hard time thinking about anything else."

Wow. Maybe the Lloyd thing messed me up more than I originally thought. Had I really gotten so bad at realizing when someone was into me?

Or had I just been hiding from it?

Well. No more.

"Prove it," I challenged.

"Gladly."

In a single bound, he captured my cheeks with his big hands, and breathed in my surprised gasp as our lips touched.

Whoa. He wasn't kidding. He does want me.

It had been so long since someone had touched me even remotely like that. Thank God my body acted on instinct.

Again, evolutionary programming at work.

Heart racing, I gripped at his rib cage with one hand and clutched the soft spot where his neck met his shoulder with the other, pulling him closer to me, deepening the kiss almost as soon as it began.

And I knew this was a bad idea, and that letting myself go after controlling myself so tightly for so long was a recipe for trouble and that I needed to shove him away and end this and never think about it again, but . . .

Clara was right. I'd been keeping myself from getting what I wanted. I was tired of it.

He tasted like spearmint and sex. I wanted more. This was what I'd been missing for the last few years. Maybe what I'd been missing forever. Kissing Lloyd Exeter was never like this.

When his tongue traced my bottom lip, I parted for him, wanting as much of this man as he would give.

Then my legs spread involuntarily, beckoning him closer. He pressed himself fully against me. My hips rolled, making contact with the hard evidence of his arousal.

"We have to stop," I breathed.

Without hesitation, Hudson retreated. Before I had time to blink, he was off me—a full step away, hands at his sides. "Of course. I'm sorry. I didn't—"

"I want to set some ground rules first."

Not ground rules. Experiment parameters.

If I was going to have sex with Hudson, then the only way to keep myself safe was rules. Last time, I'd rushed headfirst into my whatever-it-was-but-definitely-not-an-affair with Lloyd Exeter. This time would be different. This time, I'd make sure a workplace fling didn't affect me so deeply.

Making myself happy—but with guardrails.

The dimple returned to Hudson's cheek. "Right. Okay. Yeah. Whatever you want."

Whatever I wanted. What a strange concept. I couldn't remember the last time I'd let myself have *whatever* I wanted.

The power was intoxicating. Here it was. Everything I'd wished for. A solution to my virginity predicament and an offer to get off with one of the hottest guys I'd ever seen. All mine for the taking.

How *did* I want it?

"I want a one-night stand," I said, formulating on the fly. "No strings. Just take the virginity, thank you, have a nice day. Then we can focus on the sex toy lessons—absolutely no practical demonstrations. Can you do that?"

"Why? Don't you like me?"

His tone was playful, but I was too single-minded to joke back.

"I get that I'm trying to expand my horizons or whatever, but I really can't let this interfere with work. Besides, you're leaving in six weeks."

"We're both pretty professional. We could keep the no-strings and keep having sex for six weeks."

"My last coworker relationship didn't end so well for me. I'm not interested in letting history repeat itself."

He tipped his head. "Fair enough."

"Have you been tested lately?"

Suddenly, he was the one who couldn't meet my gaze. That

worried me until he explained, "I've been in a dry patch. Dry country mile? Dry multistate highway? It's been about a year and a half, but yeah. I test regularly anyway. They've all come back negative."

"And I have the coil, if you want to go bare. Or we can use condoms."

Hands drifted to my waist and pulled me in closer. Once again, I couldn't ignore the press of his erection. It was as obvious as that little smirk he wore. "*Condoms.* Multiple. Isn't she so confident about where this will go?"

"I'm only getting you for one night. I might as well make the most of it."

"I'll do my best to keep up. What about you? Condoms or without?"

My answer was irrational, but instinctive. "Without, please."

His eyes flickered down to my mouth. I pressed one hand to his shoulder, holding him at cautious bay.

Get what you want. You deserve it.

"And I want to orgasm. Believe me, I love using my toys, but I want to know what it's like to be made to orgasm by *you.*"

The words came out in a self-conscious rush. Hudson pressed a kiss to the apple of my cheek.

"Don't worry. That won't be a problem. I may not have a ton of experience in the toy department, but believe me: I am very, *very* eager to please. And to learn."

12

Delayed Gratification

Now who's the confident one?

As he continued his trail of soft kisses, I considered everything I knew about Hudson. It wasn't much, but he had such an easy, likable way about him. I never imagined that the same attributes that endeared him to everyone from uptight engineers to airline staff would extend to sex.

But I couldn't argue with results. He was so, *so* sexy.

"You're surprisingly smooth, you know that?"

He placed a kiss on my jaw. "I'll try not to take that personally."

"It's just that at work, you're so . . ." Friendly? Straightforward? Uncomplicated? I couldn't find a word that seemed to fit him right.

Another kiss. This one at the sensitive base of my throat. "It takes a lot of effort to function normally when all you want to do is crawl under your coworker's desk, spread her legs, and worship her until she screams so loud the walls shake."

Pinch me, I must be dreaming.

No—*fuck me*, I must be dreaming.

"So . . . you agree?" I asked hesitantly. This moment felt soap-bubble delicate. I didn't want it to pop. "We're going to do this?"

"One night. Relaxed. No pressure. No strings. Blazingly hot orgasms. Come to work the next day like nothing happened and get off-the-books sex toy lessons in our spare time," Hudson confirmed. He tucked a strand of hair behind my ear. I shivered. "Anything else?"

"No, I think that about covers it."

"Then, yeah. I agree."

And neither of us wasted any time sealing that agreement with a kiss.

No, not just a kiss.

We sealed it with foreplay.

Our lips met in a furious collision, and as they explored new territory, our hands did the same. I wandered the great plane of his chest, feeling every inch of him like I'd wanted to do since the day we met. He held fast to my hips, yanking me closer than I thought possible. All that separated him from my virginity was a few measly layers of fabric.

My hips unconsciously rolled against him, hungry for the friction against my center. Moaning into my mouth, he rewarded me with just that, pressing even tighter.

Not satisfied, I knocked the contents of my desk onto the floor and lay back, flush against its surface. It was torture to pull away from Hudson's attentive mouth for even a second, but it was all worth it when I gripped him by the collar and pulled him down on top of me.

Oh.

There he was, the spectacular all of him, pinning me to my desk. In my needy haze, I didn't have much capacity for critical thought. Not enough to dissect my form or worry that we were going to break the desk or wonder if I should slow down and savor the sex . . .

Just enough to relish Hudson's breath on my chest as he unbuttoned my shirt, and just enough to think:

This is it. I'm going to lose it. I'm going to lose it to Hudson—

A painfully loud mechanical shriek cut through the euphoria. Hudson broke away, looking up at what I could only assume was the 3-D printer finishing its work on the prototype phallus I'd been crafting all evening.

Nope. Not dealing with that right now. I had sex on the brain and for once, I wasn't going to let my job get in the way of that.

I went for Hudson's belt buckle.

"Scout."

The machine beeped again. I dragged my lips down his bare chest, toward the erection I struggled to free from its tailored khaki prison.

"Just ignore the printer," I said. "It can wait."

"It's not about that." He reached down and took my hands in his. I'd been a half second away from taking the length of him in my mouth, but it was the simplicity of that gesture that made me the wettest I'd been all evening. "I'm not fucking you in the office."

"Why not?" I asked.

"Besides the obvious HR implications? Your first time should be more than a quickie on a desk."

I rolled my eyes. "Why does it matter where it happens? I knew I'd never be one of those rose-petals-and-candlelight girls."

He flinched, like it was the most ridiculous thing he'd ever heard. "And what makes you think that?"

What *didn't* make me think that? I was a north-of-plus-size engineer with mousy black hair and no social skills. I'd never been one for romance, and I'd assumed that no one was going to be sweeping me off my feet for grand, romantic sexual escapades. That no one was going to make my first time special, no one was going to make *me* feel special. Although now that I thought about it, was that all a symptom of my relationship with Lloyd?

"I don't know. That's just how I've always felt."

"Want to unpack that at all?"

"Not really. This is just sex, Hudson. It's not a relationship."

"It's not *not* a relationship either. It's more of a—"

"If you say *situationship*, I'll find someone else to fuck."

After all the time we'd spent together in the office as colleagues, I'd never really noticed his laugh. I'd noticed that he laughed *often*, but not how it sounded. Clear and sure, like he wanted me to know exactly how much I delighted him. "Look, I don't have sex with people I don't give a shit about. I want to get between your legs *and* get to know you."

I squirmed. Could I even handle that? Or would the sex and closeness be too much for me? He caught my discomfort.

"Okay, okay," he conceded. "I'll let you lead on the friendship thing."

He pressed a kiss to my temple, soft and tender, and tugged me back to my feet.

"Now, about the sex part. How about tomorrow?" he propositioned. "We can have our first sex toy lesson, and then you can take me back to your place. Make sure you're totally comfortable."

There it was. That zing he talked about. *Zing!*

He cares about you. God, how fucking sexy was that?

Dizzy, I leaned back against the desk for support . . . and admired my handiwork. With his hair all askew, his shirt half-buttoned, his glasses slightly crooked on his handsome nose, and a slight dark spot punctuating the outline of cock hidden by his dark-wash jeans, he screamed sexual frustration.

And I'd been the one to make him that way. I'd been the one to get him hard and wet and a half second away from turning my office into a porn shoot.

I could have kicked my feet and squealed for how thrilling that felt.

"Yeah. That sounds great. Better than losing it on a desk, anyway."

"Exactly. Besides . . ." he said, gesturing over to the 3-D printer, where the painfully long and thick dildo I'd been printing now proudly stood. "It's hard for a man to perform when he's competing against that."

The sound of my laugh bounced gleefully off my office walls.

There were, it seemed, some criteria I'd forgotten on my perfect-man list.

He has to be great at making me laugh.

Then another thought struck.

Oh, and making me cum, but I guess we'll see about that tomorrow, won't we?

13

The Entrance Inter-You

The next morning, a question shattered me awake and I bolted upright in bed.

It's a Wednesday. Do people even have sex on a Wednesday?

A remarkably stupid question. Of course people had sex on Wednesdays. Wednesday was not a particularly unhorny day, and even if it was, there were probably some deranged sex freaks who would do it anyway. Statistically speaking, Wednesday sex was a mathematical certainty.

But that was how the day was for me. Whether I was building a rocket ship or a vibrating butt plug, I would never enter a high-status task without doing the research, asking probing (*haha*) questions, or having all the facts. My questions stacked up.

Should I wear lingerie? Or is that too try-hard? Do I even own virginity-loss-worthy lingerie? Should I google where the nearest lingerie store is? What if he's not into lingerie? What if he is into lingerie, but he wants to be the one wearing it? I'm not judging, I just need to know what to do in that case. Like, would he bring his own lingerie or am I expected to provide it? What size does he even wear? And where would I even get men's lingerie at this time of day on a Wednesday?

It was . . . a lot. Too much for a transaction that should have been simple. Meet boy. Like boy. Fuck boy. Never think of him again.

That last point was imperative. Hudson may have been comfortable with casual sex for the next five weeks, three workdays of his contract, and while I agreed with, well, everyone that I could stand to loosen up, loosening up didn't mean letting go completely. One night of freedom would be fine. Manageable, then right back to work. Blow off some steam. Prove to myself that I wasn't unfuckable and I wasn't incapable of human contact.

Five weeks, three workdays, though? The same five weeks, three workdays during which I needed to finish the prototype of the next generation of sex toy?

Impossible.

No matter how much I might want it. Our work was too important, and my Fluorine Scout propensity for letting my personal affairs interfere with my professional ones too strong.

So there I was, worrying over my impending virginity loss when Clara popped her head into the kitchen, where I'd been mindlessly searching for caffeine reinforcements.

"Scout?"

"Hm?"

"There's a young woman in your office. I've hired her to replace Jared."

Jesus, Clara. Again?

"That was fast," I said, when what I really wanted to say was *And you didn't even consult me on hiring someone for my own damn team?*

She did this all the time. I loved Clara like she was family, and she'd done more for me than my actual family, but for all the ranting and raving she did about me taking the back seat on decision-making, she sure did love to requisition the wheel at work.

Clara nodded and clucked her tongue. "She's really been put through the wringer. Her medtech start-up folded when her now ex-boyfriend embezzled the company's entire savings. She's brilliant, though. Aside from giving over her books to such a wanker, obviously."

"Is BuzzCorp just a rehab for wayward women in STEM now?"

"Someone's got to look out for you ladies. Might as well be me."

Five minutes later, I had an employment dossier, a huge tumbler of Diet Dr Pepper, and a Miss Leelah St. James at my desk.

Leelah was tall, stacked like a tennis player, and clearly terrified.

"Hi there," I offered by way of greeting.

"Hi," she replied, voice shaky. "It's nice to meet you."

"You, too. So. I'm sure Clara warned you that this was going to be a very rigorous entrance interview."

"She made me sharpen my pencils just in case."

Once again, I glanced over Leelah's résumé and Clara's notes. There were all the important things there—she was a Rhodes Scholar and UT Austin graduate, had founded a company before she turned twenty-one, was a few years older than me, had been featured in *Forbes* . . .

Her medtech company had made a name for itself by creating portable devices that could be taken anywhere—war zones, natural disaster areas. An EEG that weighed less than the average Stephen King novel was her signature invention.

Shit, I thought, *what the hell is this girl doing at BuzzCorp?*

A small voice in the back of my head, one that sounded like Hudson's, replied: *What the hell are* you *doing at BuzzCorp?*

I shook the thought free, though. I liked working at BuzzCorp, and not just because I'd been blacklisted everywhere else. Not because it was my last resort after the GalacticSolutions disaster. I found my work fulfilling. And not just because the dildos I took home to test after work were long and generously girthed.

Again, the little voice came back. *But maybe work and dildos shouldn't be the only fulfilling things in your life. Maybe it's a good thing that Jared's gone. Maybe you could open yourself up a little bit more. After all, you're about to have sex for the first time. Maybe finding friends is next.*

I scanned the rest of her intake forms. She ran dance classes on Saturdays in the park and spent a not-inconsiderable amount of her former fortune buying up original Britney Spears tour costumes. And her nails were painted like little Monet lilies.

She seemed fun. This office needed fun.

So did I.

But . . .

Problem: I don't have any friends.

Proposed Solution: Find some.

Test: Try befriending the new girl. She seems fun.

Could I do that? Surely one friend wouldn't distract me *too* badly from work. Besides, she would be a *work* friend. And work friends get shit done.

Look at me, engaging in some personal growth. I guess that's just what crisis does to a person—makes them do crazy things like make friends and have sex.

"Usually, I'd put you through some tests, but . . . I'm going to be honest with you, Leelah. You're overqualified and the culture's not good here right now. And I just need to know that I have someone in my corner. Can you be that person?"

"What do you mean?"

I told her the truth about the Jared Blotcher/Lloyd Exeter situation. What the hell did I have to lose? She'd find out within a few days of working here anyway. Besides, she knew what it was like to be screwed over by an ex-boyfriend. Might as well start this friendship with a little trauma bonding.

"How awful," she muttered when my tale concluded. "That guy's a dick."

"That's insulting to dicks. At least dicks are useful."

"Some of the time. I mean, they're clearly very replaceable." She gestured to the dildo I'd crafted last night. Damn. I really needed to put that thing away. "But I guess you're right. Sometimes you can't beat the real thing."

"Being a virgin and all, I wouldn't know, but I'll take your word for it."

Just like that, Leelah became an entirely different person. A light sparked inside her, and the tension withdrew from her body. If Clara was cool and I was neurotic and Addie was spunky, Leelah was excitable. Perky. "God, this makes me feel so much better. I was terrified to come in here. You know, you're terrifying? Everyone says so."

"Do they?"

"Yeah. Clara said not to be surprised if you don't even look at me."

How weird—I knew that about myself, that I wasn't effusive or anything. But I'd never thought people were *afraid* of me. "Let's just say I'm turning over a new leaf. Or trying to, anyway. Maybe the sky won't fall if I come out of my shell a little bit."

"Why? I mean, why come out of your shell now?"

Because the hot guy in the office got a boner while looking at me once and then everything went to shit. "A lot of reasons. But . . . when I started here, I probably looked a lot like you did a few minutes ago. Clara welcomed me. She made me feel like I was more than what happened to me. She was—and is—my friend. I think it'd be nice to have more friends in the office."

Leelah nodded, practically bouncing in her seat now. "I can't remember the last time I had a friend. People always say that I come on too strong, that I should just keep my head down, but I don't think that's any way to live. I mean, what's even the point?"

If I'd developed a friend in the lab, I couldn't have created a friend more unlike me. She was enthusiastic, beaming, and more interested in socializing than crunching numbers or working with tech.

In short, she was perfect. If I was going to try and make friends, I might as well go for broke, right? She could teach me a thing or two about peopling.

"This is just so exciting, Scout. I can't wait—should we do lunch today?"

Lunch. A friend was asking me to lunch. "We have a prototypes meeting over lunch today, but maybe tomorrow?"

"Awesome. You've told me so much about yourself, but I've got to get you caught up on all *my* lore!"

"Sounds great. Go ahead and look at these specs. They'll help you get ready for the meeting this afternoon."

I passed some papers her way. She took them and deflated. I guess it must have finally dawned on her where she was working—not just a friendly place with a newly friendly boss, but a place that built sex toys instead of the medical tech she'd been developing for years.

I knew that look. I still saw it sometimes when I looked at myself in the mirror.

"The pacemakers I was creating at my firm were going to change the entire way we treat sick people. My portable EEGs were going to save lives," she muttered.

I shrugged. "So you're going from helping the medically fucked-over to letting the helpless get fucked. How exciting for you."

A little of her old grin returned. "You know, I think I'm going to like working here. Thanks for everything."

"It's nice to meet you, Leelah. Glad to have you on the team."

And I was. I really was.

Not just because she seemed fun. A little intense, but very fun. It was also because, for the last twenty minutes, I'd barely thought about giving Hudson my virginity at all.

Then, of course, the man had to ruin the streak by walking past my office's glass wall. He didn't look in my direction, but as he walked, I leaned back in my chair and let my eyes oh-so-subtly follow him as he went.

Everything else in my world, like dildo prototypes and new friendships and questions about sex, disappeared. All I could think about was his ass in those jeans.

God, he had a good one.

I couldn't wait to see it for myself tonight.

14

Hot for Teacher

During standard business hours, I'd purposefully avoided talking to Hudson. Mostly because I wasn't sure I could keep a straight face around him. The last thing I needed was anyone in the office noticing the waves of lust rolling off me.

But once the office was clear, there was no avoiding him. Like magnetized machine parts, we collided not ten seconds after the last person swiped their key card to leave.

"Hi there," he said, hovering in the hallway between my office and his desk.

"Hey," I replied a little awkwardly. "I'm sorry, I don't know how to do this."

"Do what?"

"Talk to you like normal when, in the back of my mind, I know we're going to have sex later. Like, is this what dating is like? Do you really hold a regular conversation, all while thinking about how to get them in bed?"

Forcing myself to do anything else besides stare at him (and think about how his jeans and cuffed-sleeve sweater would look on my bedroom floor), I led us both to the conference room.

"Pretty much. Or, if you're unlucky and you have a sexy

coworker, you have to do all of that while explaining complex computing modalities to her." When I startled, he scoffed. "What, you're saying you *really* never thought of me that way?"

Yes, of course I have. And you don't even want to know how graphic my fantasies have been.

But there was a difference between fantasizing about sex and sex lingering just beyond your fingertips. On those other occasions, he'd been an impossibility. Now he was almost mine.

"If it'll help," he said, "just focus on the lesson part of tonight's activities. We can cross the sex bridge when we get to it."

"Hudson, we're literally going to be talking about sex toys for the next hour. I don't think I can avoid thinking about interpersonal copulation."

"And I'm going to have a hard time not being turned on by you saying things as sexy as *interpersonal copulation*, so at least we'll both be suffering equally." As if anyone could be turned on by *those* words. He held open the conference room door and gestured me inside. "Just try, Miss Porter. I'll be a good student, I promise."

We'd agreed on sex toy lessons followed by swift virginity loss, and to keep things professional, we'd decided to host the former in the office. As my colleagues had trickled out this evening, I'd drawn the curtains over the conference room and set up a veritable smorgasbord of BuzzCorp's finest sex toys for his inspection and perusal. Above us, the projector hummed, casting the entire room in anticipatory blue light.

"So . . ." I said, spreading out my arms, presenting the silicone-and-plastic-laden table for his inspection. "Welcome to *Dr.* Porter's School for Continuing Sex Toy Education."

"Wow," he marveled, staring at the toys.

He gulped. Visibly gulped. I rolled my eyes. It was the only thing keeping me from getting on tiptoe and kissing his Adam's apple. How could a gulp be sexy?

"Don't act so shocked. You know where you work."

"Yeah, but this is the first time I've let myself imagine using them on you."

A hand traced around my waist, almost as if he was going to spin me into him for a kiss. I wriggled out of it, trying to heed his advice. *Don't think about sex. Focus on the lessons. Be his teacher, not his fuckbuddy.*

"You're being a very bad student, Mr. Bailey."

"Sorry," he said, trying to stifle a laugh. He took a seat at the conference table. "I'll behave, Dr. Porter."

I hope you don't.

What an unfortunate turn of events. He'd told me to be his teacher, and I didn't even realize how much that would turn me on. We were back at square one—desperately horny and trying not to think about sex.

Putting some much-needed distance between us, I took the seat across from him.

"Now, before we start, I have a few questions for you."

Anyone else might have missed him wincing. It was a micro-expression, barely perceptible. But I noticed. I also noticed the way he tried to cover it by leaning back and feigning a casual air. "Shoot."

I should have let it go. However, I'd never known when to keep my mouth shut. To make matters worse, Hudson seemed to *like* that I never said the right thing, which only encouraged me to do it more. At least in his presence. "Why does that make you uncomfortable? Me asking you questions?"

"I like to focus on other people. I'm not very interesting."

He said those two thoughts as though they were nested subjects, when in reality, they didn't fit together at all. The first sentence was an oddity. The second sentence was an attempt to stave off unwanted follow-ups.

Why didn't he want me to know about him?

No one in this world is uninteresting. That, I believed to be a scientific fact. And if anyone *could* be uninteresting, it wasn't him.

Hudson Bailey was the Large Hadron Collider of people. Infinitely complex, staggeringly beautiful, and incomprehensible.

I wanted to take him apart, piece by piece, and understand how he ticked. What were the gears that made up his thoughtful mind? What sort of engine powered his caring heart? What was the exact function that made up the curve of his lips?

"You're plenty interesting to me," I replied.

"You're a scientist. Everything interests you. It's in the job description."

"Not *everything*. I may be a polymath, but my interests pretty much extend to chemistry, physics, engineering, and bagels. And you. You're interesting, Hudson."

"Not as interesting as you." Then he turned his attention to the table between us. "And not as interesting as these toys. What the *hell* does this thing do?"

He picked up a wand and waved it in my direction. At one end, it had a hard, black plastic handle; at the other end was a silicone sucker that might have looked like a cross between a tulip and a fish if I hadn't given the standard toy a redesign to keep it from looking so silly.

A blowjob simulator.

Oh right. There were, like, twenty sex toys on the table between us.

However . . . I still had questions for him.

"You're not getting out of this. We'll start off easy. What do you want for dinner?"

He shrugged.

"I'm good with whatever."

"I want Thai."

"Sounds great."

I frowned and ran a second test.

"Actually, pizza."

He never lost that winning smile, not for a second. "Fantastic."

"What do *you* want?"

"Anything you like."

"Hudson, I'm not having sex with someone who can't tell me what he wants. That's not fair to you."

"I want to make you happy. That's it. Now, are you going to teach me or what? That *is* our deal, after all."

A slight edge tinged the air. Desperation. He *really* didn't want me to know anything about him.

I let it go. If I pushed him, I might lose him, and I couldn't lose him tonight. Not when I was so close.

"Sure. Back to the sex toy lessons. But to get a baseline . . . you told me you don't have any experience with all this stuff. Tell me about that."

It was a teacherly instruction, not a question. Carefully crafted so he had no choice but to respond.

"I was in a long-term relationship. I met a girl the first day of college, fell head over heels, and then we entered a very vanilla relationship. I've never been particularly adventurous. I mean, I have fantasies just like the next guy, but she wasn't super open to them. I wanted to please my partner, whatever she wanted, and what she wanted was to touch herself while we had sex. Oral wasn't her thing. She didn't really like me touching her. And since she never brought them up, I never saw the point of trying out sex toys."

"Never saw the point?" I asked, my voice pitching up in surprise.

"Not really, no. We had good sex. We both got off regularly together. When that relationship ended, I had a few hookups, but believe it or not, none of them carried vibrators around in their purses, so I never had the chance to try it with anyone else."

My first reaction? I *carry sex toys in my purse; I'm not an animal.*

My second reaction? *Oh right. That's not normal. You're the weird one in this scenario.*

My third . . .

"Why'd you break up?"

"We were in business together and we had a big fight about the company. Fundamental differences of opinion regarding our direction. One day, she just . . . decided she didn't like me enough anymore to keep me around. Not in the office and not by her side."

A million more questions entered my mind. The first thought to bubble to the surface, though, was:

"Her loss."

"Back to the topic at hand," he said, carefully avoiding any follow-ups. "Toys always seemed to be for women to use on their own. I'm not a big porn guy, but the stuff I did watch never had women use them. It just didn't seem to be for me."

A stitch of anger made its way to the center of my chest. It reminded me of high school, that agitated pain that occurred when you'd eaten your weight at Taco Tuesday right before the Presidential Physical Fitness Test.

"Oh, Hudson. We've got so much work to do."

"Sorry to disappoint."

"*You're* not disappointing. The education on this issue is . . ." I said. I had a habit of pacing when I was frustrated, and now was no different. Rising from my chair, I marched back and forth along the elegant carpet. "The fact that you, a sexually active man, don't understand the importance of this technology is sad. Mr. Ose was right, BuzzCorp *is* proudly women-led, but is that our fault, or is it the fault of society for teaching men that they don't need to concern themselves with female pleasure?"

To his credit, Hudson let the rant continue.

"Orgasms are good for us. They improve our mental and

physical health, just like exercise—and more than that, they're just plain fun. People should be using every tool at their disposal to have more of them, and at BuzzCorp, that's what we do. We create things that give everyone, regardless of gender or identity or sex organs or relationship status, agency and autonomy over their own bodies and sex lives. Making our partners feel good, making *ourselves* feel good, should be a fundamental right. Toys like ours ensure that people reserve that right and enjoy it without shame or hesitation."

"You're proud of the work you do here" came his surprised reply.

"Yes," I said. "I know I'm not building rockets anymore, but when you hear stories from people—our focus groups are *very* vocal. I hear stories about women having their first orgasms at forty with our toys. Couples who have rescued themselves from dead bed. People who discover their sexualities, who allow themselves to explore their autonomy after leaving religious sects . . . all of it means that when I go to work every day, I'm making a difference to someone out there."

Oh God. It was too sappy. Too impassioned. I needed to get off this topic before I weirded him out with my intensity.

"And tonight," I said, turning my attention back to him. My mind conjured up fantasies of what lay before us. "I think I'm going to make a difference in yours."

"Oh yeah?"

"Mm-hmm. Your future girlfriends are *so* going to thank me."

A shadow flickered across his face. I couldn't quite read it, because he recovered too quickly.

"So, talk me through this display."

Yes, yes. The lessons.

"I actually have a PowerPoint."

"Of course you do, you beautiful nerd."

Trying to hide my blush, I reached for the stylus and called the projector up. An image popped onto the giant screen running along the western wall of the room. It quickly displayed my title page. In big, bold letters, it read:

WELCOME TO THE REST
OF YOUR FUCKING LIFE,
HUDSON BAILEY.

"Essentially, sex toys fall into roughly six categories. Vibrators, dildos, partnered toys, penis toys, anal toys, and BDSM materials." With each introduction, I clicked to a new slide and pointed to the corresponding toys on the table. "I'm sure with your time here so far, you've gotten a rough idea of those groupings, but seeing as you claim ignorance on all of these in practice, how familiar are you with them in the abstract? What's your baseline?"

He scanned the toys, then glanced up at me from beneath hooded eyelids.

Oh God. He was going to turn this horny, wasn't he? Gone was the sterile teaching environment I'd tried to harbor. We were in full-on foreplay now.

"Vibrators vibrate on your clit."

Your. Not *the user's* or *the person's* clit. *Your.*

An image flashed through my mind. Hudson's cock buried deep inside me while he held a vibrator against my clit, forcing me to orgasm.

I cleared my throat. "And can be used internally for the G-spot, yes."

Rising from his seat, he took a firm grip on a moderately sized dildo. How had he known that was my favorite model? As he lifted it, another thought occurred: him working it inside me while mouthing my pussy.

Fuck, I was already getting wet.

Correction: I'd already slicked through three sets of underwear today, just anticipating this night with him. Now I was well on my way to walking home without them, as I'd run through my emergency pairs.

"And this fills you up."

"We're not talking about me here," I whispered, trying to maintain my composure.

Tilting his head in a *fair enough* gesture, he continued his slow stride around the table toward me and gestured to the toys he'd been eyeing earlier.

"These I'm not familiar with."

"They're for penises," I said, my hand shaking as I clicked through my PowerPoint. As a last-ditch effort to keep from melting on the spot, I turned my back on him and kept my eyes on the screen. "This is a masturbator. This one's a blowjob simulator. This one's a cock ring. Fleshlights, pumps, and vibrators. And these?"

We reached a new set of slides. *Click, click, click . . .*

"Anal toys, I'm guessing." *Click.* That slide popped up on screen and Hudson watched intensely, eyebrows lifted behind his glasses. "And is that—"

"A strap-on, yes," I replied. Was it getting hot in here, or was my brain's imagined scenes of Hudson bent over a table, taking a long length of a strap-on deep inside him just making me blush? "They can be used anally or vaginally, depending on your partner's parts."

One of the best things about Hudson was he never let dead air hang in a conversation. When other people let my words linger in silence, I always got that twitchy sense that I'd screwed up somehow. Ruined the social interaction. Hudson never did that to me, never made me feel weird or out of place for anything that came out of my unsocialized mouth.

Now, though, as he shifted his eyes from the projector showing a variety of strap-ons down to The Lover, our top-of-the-line harness-and-dildo combination, he didn't say anything.

In my line of work, particularly when it came to focus group research and fuck reports, I'd noticed that more men than I ever could have imagined were into the idea of penetration or ass play. However, the stigma kept most of them from sharing that fact with even their most intimate of partners.

One of the most important parts of my job at BuzzCorp was breaking down *all* stigmas around sexual health. Not just for women or people with vaginas, as Mr. Ose had suggested in our sales meeting, but for *everyone*.

"Is this . . ." I asked, hoping I sounded as supportive as I felt, ". . . an area that interests you? The other day I mentioned it, and you said *Don't threaten me with a good time*, if I recall correctly."

A muscle in his jaw twitched. "I've never really thought about it before. Not seriously. That was just a joke."

"Think about it," I said with a small, encouraging nod. "I've heard they're really enjoyable. Our testers think so, anyway."

He nodded once, then moved farther down the table to the next set of equipment. I clicked through my PowerPoint to match. BuzzCorp didn't do much by way of BDSM materials, but we had a few nipple clamps for him to peruse.

It seemed, for a moment, that the sexual tension had left us. That we could return to emotional and verbal distance.

That moment passed, though, when Hudson reached the final set of toys. The ones closest to me. Not wanting to back away and admit the effect he was having on me, I held my ground, which only resulted in his hovering proximity, his body not touching mine but keeping me lodged between the table and his warm presence.

"These are all remote-controlled partner toys. They have actual remotes, whereas what you're building is an app-based remote. They all have the same penetrative, vibrating, and/or thrusting capabilities, though, as our self-operated toys."

As if I wasn't speaking at all, he reached around me to pick up a remote-controlled panty vibrator—a pair of underwear with a tiny vibe sewn in so one could discreetly pleasure their partner in public with the help of its corresponding pocket-sized remote. Then he reached out with his other arm, walling me in as he nonchalantly inspected the toy with both hands.

His entire body melded to my back and ass. No matter how I tried to keep myself from being affected—these were our *work lessons*, after all, not our personal, out-of-office fling—my entire body reacted at being trapped by him.

"Now that you know the basics," I squeaked, "what I want to teach you is not only what the toys *do*, but how they *feel*. That's the important thing. If you're going to build an app to help people with pleasure, you need to understand what sensations actually *are* pleasurable."

He dropped the panties. His arms moved down to my thighs, then up until they gripped my hips, pulling me back even harder against him. "You could show me."

"We agreed no practical demonstrations," I retorted, even as my head tilted back onto his shoulder, exposing my neck.

Hot lips pressed against the hollow of my throat. "Agreements can be renegotiated, can't they? After all, I'm going to be taking you home tonight and ravishing you all night long."

His hands moved from my hips, dragging up my waist and toward my breasts.

He cupped them, pointedly refusing to move toward my aching nipples.

"Speaking of . . ." I croaked.

"Yes?" he prompted, clearly enjoying my barely concealed desire.

"How much longer do we have to wait before ripping each other's clothes off?"

Pulling away, he turned me so we could face each other. "What happened to pizza or Thai food?"

"I'm not hungry anymore. You?"

"I'm hungry, but don't bother ordering." My entire body tingled as he inspected me from head to toe. "I'm looking at an eight-course meal right now."

15

Begin the Sex Scene

Somehow we managed to make it home without having sex in the office, the car, or the elevator up to my place. I'm not sure how, but it happened.

"It's very weird to have you in my house."

Not my finest welcome. I wouldn't be getting that embroidered on a welcome mat any time soon. But when I locked the door behind me, turned, and found Hudson towering over my kitchen counter, casually surveying my home like it was a guide to understanding me, it's all I could think.

When I'd been fired from GalacticSolutions, I'd given my parents the bulk of my severance package. However, I'd saved some to buy this apartment. I called it my Hush Money House, which wasn't a great way to look at one's home, but hey—at least I was honest about it. The apartment was simple and elegant and at least twenty years behind current trends, but it also had high ceilings and big windows and a kicking AC unit that beat the Texas summers back.

I didn't spend much time here, though, preferring to eat out and devote most of my waking hours to my desk, so now, seeing it through Hudson's eyes, I realized the messy bookshelves stacked high with academic texts and the takeout menus tacked up on the fridge made the place look a little sad. Slightly devoid of personality.

"Why should it be weird?" he asked. "It's just sex, right?"

"Right. Yeah. Just sex," I said, trying to convince myself more than anything. "Not a big deal."

His gaze burned everywhere it touched. My cheeks, my neck, the swell of my breasts peeking out from my sweater.

With slight pressure on my wrist—the only place our bodies currently touched—he navigated me back until I was pressed against the kitchen island. Nowhere to run. Just me, this handsome man, and the ghost of sex yet to come between us.

"Right. Yeah. This is casual. We're just two people . . . who happen to be attracted to each other . . . and we're going to have sex and . . . and . . ."

He released my wrist and let his fingers drift lazily to my waist, where he found an exposed patch of skin between my skirt and my sweater's hemline.

"Do you want to keep going, or would you like me to find a better use for your mouth?" he asked.

"You can try, but I'll just keep thinking like this even if I'm not saying it out loud."

"Then I'll need to distract your big, beautiful brain, too."

"Good luck."

Every inch of my body was almost painfully aware of his. He still only touched that one part of my body, that flesh at my waist, but the distance drove me crazy.

Why didn't he just bend me over and fuck me already?

"I love a challenge, remember?" he said. "It's why I like you so much."

"I hope there are other reasons you like me," I said, my hips unconsciously shifting forward into his touch.

"There are. Many reasons. And I'm sure I'll discover even more reasons to like you tonight."

Without taking his eyes away from mine, he let his hand drift down my back. He stepped forward. He cupped my ass, gripping it tight and pulling me against him—testing, judging how I felt in his hold.

I must have passed muster, because his cock stirred.

Which, of course, made a rush of arousal flood between my legs.

"You'd better not like me too much, though," I reminded him. "We have a deal. Sex tonight, and then we go back to the way things were."

"There's one thing I think you should know about sex, Scout."

"Yeah?"

He pulled me even closer somehow. My breasts were now flush against his chest. Our clothes were the only thing keeping my virginity intact at this point.

"We can never go back to the way things were. Once I see you like this, I'll never be able to unsee you like this. I'll never forget the way you feel, never forget how you moan for me . . . and it'll be the same for you."

I scoffed, sounding braver than I felt. "I'm a rational, responsible, clearheaded adult. I'm going to be able to blow off one night of passion."

"You don't sound so sure."

I kissed him instead of answering.

Why would I waste time talking about my feelings when I had a perfectly good cock standing at attention between my thighs?

This was why he was here, after all. For sex. That was it. Not talking, not heart-to-hearts, not getting-to-know-yous. Just fucking.

He must not have minded the distraction too much. As I kissed him in earnest, he answered back, throwing himself into every touch and every breathless gesture.

Picking me up, he hoisted me onto the kitchen island, spreading my legs and positioning himself between them. As we kissed, I angled my hips into his again, desperate for any friction. The heat that had been building up since the conference, that Hudson itch I'd not been able to fully scratch with any of my best dildos, all spurred me forward. I was greedy for him, ready for him.

And I knew that I was rushing, but I couldn't help it. My hands went straight from his cheeks to his shoulders, down the expanse of his chest, tracing every line and committing it to memory. But then I went for his belt, and suddenly, it was déjà vu all over again.

He backed away from me, stopping our seemingly unstoppable descent into sex.

"Wait! Cosmos!"

"Okay," I managed through panting breaths, responding instantly to the safe word we'd agreed to on the ride over.

"I almost forgot."

Untangling himself from me, he stumbled backward and dug his hands into his pockets. Even stumbly and awkward, he was unbelievably fucking sexy. My pussy throbbed. I'd never been this close to having sex with someone before. The waiting was unbearable.

A moment later, he found what he'd been looking for. He offered it to me.

It was a glass jar about the size of my hand. Inside, there were rose petals, some glitter, a tea light candle, and a few of those tiny fireworks that you set off by throwing them on the ground. A small tag hung from the neck of the jar. It read, in Hudson's blocky, mathematician's script:

Break in case of emergency virginity loss.

"You said you weren't the girl who got roses and candles and all that," he said, shrugging. "I just think you're wrong."

My chest was suddenly very tight. This felt too nice, too personal. I didn't need him to lie to me, didn't need him to pretend that I was some great prize. This was just sex. Transactional sex. I didn't need or want to feel special.

I couldn't want that. I didn't need to get addicted to the feeling.

I set aside the jar. Then I looped my fingers through his belt and pulled him back between my legs.

"I'm a sure thing, Hudson," I reminded him. "You don't need to butter me up to get me to have sex with you."

"And you didn't have to do a damn thing to get me to have sex with you, Scout. You just had to be you. You just had to ask." He took my face in his hands. One thumb brushed down my lips. I shivered. "Why has a woman as beautiful, as brilliant, as funny and sexy as you never been taken before?"

Because nothing had ever led me to believe that was possible.

"A long time ago, I posited a theory that I was not capable of trusting myself with big decisions. Like whether to have sex. And who to have sex with. And time and time again, my experiments have proven this hypothesis correct."

"Why did you finally choose me, then?"

"Because the cosmos is impossibly vast. We might as well be two specks of dust when compared against it. Then somehow, an understanding, handsome man with strong hands and a laugh like Christmas morning found me. And against all odds, he wanted me. You are the right man at the right time. And I'm trying to become a Scout who can welcome a gift like that. Who isn't afraid of it. Even just for one night."

"And what's been holding you back?"

"A million things, really. Like my second hypothesis, for example."

"Which is?"

"That I'm not sexy."

I was, after all, a twenty-six-year-old virgin who spent her days behind a desk. I wasn't fielding offers from eligible gentlemen in line at the bagel shop, nor was my last relationship particularly affirming. I worried, deep down, that this experiment of mine with Hudson would fail, and it would be all my fault. Just by virtue of who I was.

Hudson got that look in his eye again. That *I'm going to fuck you* look. The emptiness between my legs felt unbearable now.

"A good scientist should always be open to the possibility of being proven wrong," he reminded me. Then his hand traveled up my thigh. Beneath my skirt. And right to my parted legs, where his fingers toyed with the lining of my wet thong. "Are you open, Scout?"

16

Shall We Shag Now, or Shag Later?

If he just said the word, or moved his fingers a little more boldly, I'd be filled by him without hesitation.

"Yeah," I breathed. "I'm open."

But he withdrew his hand.

"Come on. I'm not going to fuck you on your kitchen island."

"That just displays a supreme lack of imagination," I huffed.

"Don't worry. It'll be worth the wait. I'll make sure of that."

"You'd better."

Bratty? Yeah, sure. I sounded it. But you have to understand—I was seconds away from breaking a twenty-six-years-long no-sex streak. The impatience coiled in my body, begging to finally be relieved.

Hudson helped me down from the counter, and I almost convulsed when our bodies brushed against each other again. How was I going to survive the walk to my bedroom? I might cum just from the friction of my thighs rubbing.

Hudson's hand on my hip didn't help matters. It just made me think about the better, more useful places he could put it. "How are you feeling?"

"Like I want to throw you to the floor and use you," I grumbled. "I'm tired of waiting."

"Not that I hate the sound of that, but I have plans for you. I want you to enjoy this."

"I'm pretty sure I'd enjoy riding your cock."

He pressed a kiss to the top of my head; his laughter ruffled my hair. "Then we'll put that on the docket for round two, shall we?"

Once in my bedroom, he stood at the foot of the bed, which loomed behind him like a promise. When I was close enough for him to touch, he tilted my chin up, so we were eye-to-eye.

"Do you trust me, Scout?"

"Yeah. I do."

I probably shouldn't. I barely know you. But you're nice and you're here and against my better judgment, I want you more than I want air right now.

And I've run the mental experiments.

Problem: I'm still a virgin.

Proposed Solution: Lose it.

Test: Have sex with Hudson and don't develop any sort of attachment to him.

Result: No more virginity, back to normal, and back to ignoring Hudson completely.

He leaned down, our lips so close they almost brushed when he spoke again.

"Do you want me to take the lead?"

"Please."

I leaned in to close the gap. He evaded, brushing his lips against my ear instead.

"One more question."

"Yeah?"

"Have you ever had your pussy eaten before?"

I shuddered. My thighs tightened.

"No."

"Would you like to?"

I smirked. Even with horny brain, I couldn't resist a quip: "That's two questions."

He growled, but there was an eye roll in it. Like he was caught between *Let me eat your pussy* and *You're incorrigible, woman.* He dove in for another kiss, this time slower. Almost reverent. Our kissing to this point had been fiery, more of a necessity than a luxury. A consequence of wanting each other so badly.

He threaded his hands through my hair, dragging his fingertips along my scalp, exploring my mouth with his tongue. I breathed into the kiss, deepening it.

Then his attention drifted.

Down my neck.

Past my collar.

To the first button of my sweater.

Pop.

It gave way easily, exposing more of my flesh. Its second and third cousin soon met it, and I gasped. The AC wasn't so cold today, but being so suddenly exposed sent a shock wave through my entire system that instantly hardened my nipples.

With one more nudge, Hudson had my sweater on the floor. And there I was, standing in front of him in nothing but a lace bra and my skirt.

He stared for a moment.

He was speechless.

I'd made someone speechless.

During orgasm, oxytocin and dopamine are released into the body in staggering quantities. And I'd had some orgasms that defied all scientific logic and known study.

But making Hudson speechless? I might as well have been shooting feel-good hormones out of my fingertips. It overloaded my senses.

Eventually, he managed to say: "Pretty nice lingerie for a virgin."

"Wearing lingerie to masturbate is unbelievably hot," I informed him, resisting the urge to cover my chest. I wouldn't hide. I wanted him to see me. I wanted him to want me. "This is one of my favorite sets."

He cupped my ribs, his thumb trailing the underside of my breasts, which were clad in soft, Cinderella-blue lace. "I can see why. I predict you'll look even sexier without it, though."

With the slightest of gestures, he tipped me back on the bed. Legs spread and dangling over the side, I was seated when he descended to the floor and kneeled.

He looked good down there, ready to eat my pussy. With his glasses peeking over my mound, I don't know if it was possible to conjure a sexier image.

Slowly, he palmed my thighs, dragging his hands up my body until he reached the straps of my bra. One at a time, he slid them off my shoulders. The fabric shifted slightly, and the tops of my hard nipples peeked out from the lip of the lace.

"Please," I breathed. "Please touch me for real. I need more. I think I'm going to go crazy."

Not fazed in the least, Hudson traveled to the central clasp between my breasts, carefully avoiding my nipples. Totally in control. Unmoved by my squirmy misery. "How does it feel? To be wanted this badly?"

"I think I'm the one doing the wanting right now," I panted. I had half a mind to reach between my legs and make myself cum—screw him and his games. I resisted, though. He would make me feel so good if I waited.

Hudson chuckled and slowly toyed with the gold clasp until it gave way. With every word, he worked the bra off my shoulders. "Oh no. This is what it feels like to be desired, Scout. To have someone so obsessed with you, with your body, that they keep their own pleasure at bay so they can enjoy every inch of you."

The bra fell. He took in the sight of my breasts. "I'm *relishing* you, my dear."

My throat dried. I said nothing, just enjoyed having a man in the palm of my hand, wanting me this badly. That hooded look in his eye, that desperate twitch in his jeans. It was so satisfying I might have been able to cum from that alone.

Famous last words. Because then he took my bare breasts in his grip and I moaned.

Fuck. It felt so good to be touched by someone else. No, to be touched by Hudson.

My moan must have awakened the monster in him. His control slipped. He descended to my left nipple as he kept a tight, massaging grip on my right. When he was satisfied by my soft pants, he switched, making my nipples harder than I'd ever believed possible.

"I want more," I whined.

"I was wondering when you'd start making demands."

Smug asshole. I'd hate him if he wasn't making me feel so unbelievably fucking good.

Whimpering when he released me, I watched as he descended to the aching center of me. I still wore my skirt, but he unbuttoned it and helped me slither it off.

And then I was on the end of my bed, a man hesitating by my pussy lips, his breath dancing on my cunt, separated only by a thin, dripping-wet lace thong.

If I had any hang-ups about sex, about the way I looked or the way I smelled or my inexperience or the fact that Hudson was a coworker and sort of a stranger, those hang-ups disappeared in the wave of lust currently dominating me.

He toyed with my underwear. I opened my mouth to beg him

again, but before I could, he yanked at the fabric, ripping it right off me.

I gasped, and opened my mouth to protest, but the only thing that came out was a wall-shaking moan.

Because right at that moment, Hudson parted my pussy lips and kissed my cunt deeply. My eyes rolled back in my head. My hips bucked into him. And he pinned my willful body down to the bed so he could worship me fully.

I'd never . . . this was . . . I mean, I had a Womanizer, which was supposed to mimic oral sex. But there was nothing, no toy on planet Earth, that could possibly feel as good as Hudson's mouth as he focused on my clit, sucking it between his teeth and activating every sensitive nerve ending.

We worked in tandem, me rolling against him, begging for more contact and friction, as he happily obliged. My hands flew up to my breasts, and I worked my hard nipples, playing with my body to heighten my pleasure.

But I wanted more. I needed—

"Hudson, could you please . . ." I could barely get the words out between shaky breaths and cries of pleasure.

He withdrew from me. The loss of contact made me weak. "Could I what?"

"Can you please put a finger inside me? Maybe two, actually?"

"Would you rather I use a dildo? I might have been in a horny haze, but I specifically remember you mentioning that I should introduce toys into my sex life. I specifically recall that my future girlfriend will appreciate your tutelage."

A flush crept up my cheeks. I loved my dildos, but . . . "I want to feel *you*."

"Thought you might say that. But I wanted to hear it. It would be my pleasure, Scout. One condition, though. You have to watch me."

My eyes, to this point, had been slammed shut. It seemed so

intimate, to watch him enter me. But I wanted it bad enough, so I propped myself up on my elbows and locked eyes with him as he dragged his fingers along my wet folds. He circled my tight hole for a few turns, teasing me.

But then he plunged two fingers deep inside me, and after he'd captured the sight of me keening and crying out from the delicious pleasure of it all, he buried his face in my cunt once again.

The pleasure was too much. I fell back onto the bed, gripped my nipples in my ready hands, and rode my climax higher and higher, and higher—

"Hudson. Hudson, I'm going to—"

I didn't need to say it. I could feel his triumphant smile forming even as he mouthed my clit.

Then it was all too much. My body tightened and tightened until I fell, shatteringly, over the edge, riding Hudson's face and fingers until I was nothing more than a glistening, exhausted, spent heap of pleasure.

It took a few moments of aftershocks, but eventually I relaxed my internal grip enough for Hudson to withdraw his fingers with ease. He made his way up to the bed, where he lay beside me, still fully dressed.

All at once, the initial wave of want dissipated, I felt silly. I'd been such a mess, begging him and whining. "I'm sorry if that was—"

"Don't you ever say sorry to me. You are exquisite. Now, you want me to get you a glass of water or—"

I narrowed my eyes in confusion. How could he think of water at a time like this? "No, I want you to take my virginity."

"You don't want a break?"

Turning on my side to face him, I lifted my knee, so it lightly brushed his stone-hard erection.

"Hudson, I've been waiting for you for twenty-six years. Don't make me wait another second."

And he didn't. Capturing my face for another kiss, he maneuvered on top of me, pinning me down. My wet pussy spread and ready for him, I tore at his clothes and kissed every bare inch of skin that I could.

Once he was naked, I was confronted with the sight of Hudson's thick cock for the first time. It was perfect. Not too long, but enough that I knew I'd feel full the second he entered me.

I wondered how it would taste, how it would feel down my throat.

Plenty of time for that later, I reminded myself . . . We had the whole night together, after all.

I shifted, dragging the wet line of my entrance along his equally wet cock.

This time, I wouldn't beg out loud. But my body did all the begging he needed. Positioning himself, he looked down at me. "Scout, I—"

Oh no. He had that look in his eye. That sentimental *Let's talk about what's in our hearts* look.

"Do you want to have sex with me?" I asked.

"Yes. Of course. More than *anything*—"

The last line came out a choked cry, because I took the initiative and raised my hips, welcoming him inside me for the first time in one long, hard, punishingly pleasurable thrust.

This time, it was his turn to curse. "Oh fuck. You're so . . . you're so . . ."

He settled there, giving me time to adjust. It was strange, finally having a man inside me. I was no longer a virgin. But that reality was quickly taken over by another wave of lust.

I didn't just want to be a not-virgin. I wanted to be fucked.

"Take me, Hudson," I commanded.

And he did. Gently at first, he rocked in and out of me, giving me his full length in easy strokes. I moved to meet his every gesture, relishing the feeling of being entirely complete.

Dildos were great. I'd never stop using them. We were ride or die. But cock? I didn't know how I'd go back to a silicone-only diet when *this* was on offer.

"More," I said.

Hudson excelled at taking direction. Our passion built together, and we rose in speed and intensity. I gripped at his shoulders, I rocked with him, and before long I felt him rushing toward the edge. I knew he would cum soon, knew I'd been the one to make him so overwhelmed with pleasure.

"Scout. *Scout—*"

"Yes, yes. Please. Please cum inside me."

Our bodies met one final time, and Hudson clung to me as my pussy wrung the orgasm out of him, drip by drip. I held him. Maybe too tight, but I wanted to feel the pleasure leave his body. I wanted to share that moment with him.

When, after a few moments, he exited me, I dashed off to use the bathroom—the last thing I wanted was a UTI—then returned to the warmth of bed. We wrapped up under the covers and looked at each other in the dark silence for a long time. Maybe the moment was too precious to spoil with words. Maybe neither of us knew what to say.

We reeled in the wake of our first time—my first time, his first time with me, and our first time together. But eventually he broke the silence.

"I reject your hypothesis, Scout. My studies have concluded that you are unbelievably, incontrovertibly, scientifically proven to be the sexiest woman I've ever met."

17

Morning Wood-n't You Like Some Coffee?

Some people think that having sex will change you. That one day, a dick will slip inside your vagina, you'll bump pubic bones for 5.4 minutes (the scientific median sex length found in most studies), and poof. You'll suddenly be different! When you walk down the sidewalk, heads will turn in acknowledgment of your newly sexed-up status! The magic of some dude's wand will have transformed you forever!

I never bought into that crap. I was determined that I would be entirely clinical about losing my virginity. No longer being a virgin was just a fact. There. I've been fucked. It's done. I can move on.

That was . . . until I woke the next morning with Hudson's pronounced morning wood lining my ass cheeks, teasing me with what I couldn't have anymore.

It might have been a sweet moment—if, you know, we weren't coworkers who had agreed to a one-night, no-strings-attached hookup. He spooned me, one strong hand on my naked hip. His heart beat against my bare shoulder blade. I might have been distracted by his soft breath on my neck . . . except I was more focused on the erection against my hip bone.

I hadn't seen a lot of dicks IRL, but I knew from my entirely work-related research that his was a good one. One that I wasn't quite ready to have disappear back into his well-fitting pants.

Dammit. The truth was, I *had* changed last night. Just not in the way I anticipated.

All my carefully cultivated, methodical, and clinical thought processes were now infected with the most reactive of human oddities.

Feelings.

Hudson stirred, his hand caressing my side, and I ached for those fingers to move lower. To slip between my folds so I could rock against them and ride all the way to another orgasm. I wanted him to pull me back onto him, gently taking me from behind so I could relish the girth of him again, that fullness that made me deliciously dizzy all night long.

Expectation: Great, now I've had sex.

Reality: Holy fuck, how am I going to not have sex with this man ever again?

A jarring question that only grew more desperate when his fingertips began traveling up my side. It took everything in me not to arch my back against his waiting dick.

"Good morning," he breathed.

And it was. It was the best morning I'd had in a long time.

What a nightmare.

"Good morning," I squeaked. "Did you sleep all right?"

A breathy chuckle. I guess that wasn't what most girls said after a guy's first sleepover.

"You really don't know what you did to me, do you?" he asked.

"I have an idea."

The trail of his fingers up my body was slow—brutally slow—and their destination was clear. My nipples grew hard in anticipation.

"No, you don't." He traced a half moon around the base of my breast. A tease. "You wouldn't ask that question if you knew. You exhausted me. I've never gone to sleep so satisfied. And I've never woken up quite so—"

A thrill of pleasure raced through my body as he brushed my left nipple. My eyelids fluttered closed.

Then I jumped out of the bed like it was on fire.

Problem: I can't have any more sex with Hudson Bailey. It's a distraction.

Proposed Solution: Get the hell out of here. Get *him* the hell out of here before you invite him to stay.

"God, you must be so ready to get going, huh? Don't want to be late to the office." I scrambled around the room in search of clothes. Where had they gone? "You should probably go in first, then text me and let me know when you're in so I can follow. Don't want anyone getting suspicious."

When I couldn't find any damn clothes on the floor, I glanced up at him. He'd sat up against my headboard, legs lazily spread so his proud cock announced its presence beneath the sheet draped around his hips. Hudson fixed me with a look somewhere between amusement and confusion.

It was a sweet look. One that made my heart and not my pussy flutter.

I . . . I liked waking up to him. I liked seeing him in my bed. I liked being the reason he smiled first thing in the morning.

Fuck it. I didn't need clothes right that second. I just needed to get some space.

"I'm going to make coffee," I said too brightly. "Do you want coffee?"

"You don't drink coffee," he reminded me.

But I was gone, escaping into the kitchen. We'd left it a mess last night, having taken snack breaks between sessions.

As some rustling indicated he was hunting for his own clothes, his voice reached me. "Is everything okay?"

How dare he be thoughtful and considerate? I focused on the cabinets, where I had to have *some* coffee, right?

"Never better," I lied. "Just want to be respectful of your time."

"And what if I want to spend that time with you?"

"We have work."

"And after that?"

My chest tightened. "Well. I mean. That wasn't the agreement."

"Ah."

Ah. That was all he said. *Ah.* My mind rushed to fill the gaps of that syllable, to turn it over as if it were a complicated engineering problem that I needed to find the right angle on. Was it an *Ah, you're right, how silly of me*? Was it an *Ah, that's disappointing, I'd give anything to fuck you again, you glorious goddess*? Or maybe an *Ah, that's where my socks went.*

I snapped the cabinet in front of me shut, and the air brushing across my skin made me aware all over again that I was extremely naked.

Emotionally and physically.

"Would you mind grabbing me some clothes? There should be a robe in the top drawer of my dresser."

"No problem. Happy to—*oh*."

What was it with this guy and single syllables? Had my pussy been so good that it robbed him of the ability to speak, or was he just not at his sharpest in the morning?

Then it hit me. *Oh* was not *ah*. *Oh* told me exactly what I'd done wrong.

Shit. Shit, shit, shit. I couldn't even avoid sex right.

I hadn't specified that he should look in the top *left* drawer. A fatal error, because the top *right* drawer was one of three dedicated entirely to my collection of sex toys.

Right then, Hudson was likely looking down at my extensive arsenal of "sexual health aids" like it was the friggin' suitcase in *Pulp Fiction*.

Every inch of me wanted to sink into the floor in embarrassment. Which sounds stupid, considering he knew I used them, and we both worked on them. But it was the difference between wearing a bikini on the beach and getting perved on in your bra and underwear through a window: all about context.

A long, low whistle came from the other room. At least he had the decency to sound impressed.

"You are . . . dedicated to your job."

"I told you. I'm an expert."

The sound of his laughter carried through the apartment. I smiled along, trying to slip back into teasing-colleague mode. I could handle that, right?

Nope. Not when, wearing only a pair of gray briefs stained with pre-cum, he emerged from the bedroom holding a robe in one hand and a powder-blue finger vibrator in the other.

I bit back a groan. This had to be a joke. Of all the ones he could have fished out of the drawer, he picked one of my favorites? Impossible.

"Is this one good for beginners? Maybe you could show me."

He gestured to the vibrator again. It was a small device that had a massaging head attached to a ring, which could be fitted over the finger so the user could easily stroke their clitoris with it. It gave more control than a traditional vibrator and allowed for more rolling movement.

It certainly wasn't the biggest or flashiest toy in the drawer, and I wondered what had made him pick this one. A raised eyebrow from Hudson quickly turned my wondering into imagining—imagining things I could not allow Hudson to do to me with that vibrator. I'd never be able to pry myself off his dick if he did. The orgasms last night were bad (read: mind-blowing) enough. I had to draw the line.

"As much as I'm sure your future girlfriends would *love* that, we agreed. No practical demonstrations."

I snapped my robe out of his hand. Time to get dressed. Back to reality.

"Again, I reiterate. Agreements can change." Easily, he pulled me away from the counter and into him. His erection pressed through his briefs and against my belly. "Ours could change. If you wanted."

And there it was. Out in the open. He still wanted me. All I had to do was say yes.

Enthusiastic consent. What a concept. If only my heart got the memo.

18

Start the Morning with a Bang

How is it that the things we want the most are the things we're most afraid of? Of course I wanted to say yes. The sex last night had not just been amazing; it had shifted the ground beneath my feet. For years, I'd seen myself as a defective piece of machinery. But after we tinkered together for a few hours, I realized I was never broken in the first place. I'd just been forgotten up on the shelf, left to rust.

I didn't want to lose that feeling.

And I especially didn't want to lose the feeling of him rocking his cock against me like he was doing right now.

But . . .

"I told you. I can't let myself get distracted. This was supposed to be a one-and-done. I just wanted to prove to myself that I could do this."

"And you did. Now, what are you going to do with that information? Go back to your old self? Keep coloring inside the lines? Following all these ridiculous rules you've set for yourself?"

He wasn't unkind. Far from it. He was like a coach giving me a pep talk, hoping to inspire me to more. And God, did I want more.

"It doesn't have to be a relationship. It can just be sex," he offered.

"You'd be okay with that?"

"I'll want whatever you're willing to give me."

He sounded so sincere that I almost melted right there.

I'd learned my lesson, though. I wasn't a good judge of character. I didn't know enough about people to be able to tell the difference between a truth and a lie. Case in point: Lloyd Exeter. He'd told me he loved me and respected me and wanted to be with me for more than sex. In hindsight, I could see the faults in our relationship's design. The clandestine meetings. The expectation that I give and never receive. At the time, it looked perfectly engineered all the way.

Sure, Hudson seemed sincere now. But if I looked back in six months, a year, two years? What would I see clearly that I'd missed this time around?

Saying no to him was safer. It was much, much safer.

Sure, Clara had given me the green light to take some risks. But *I* couldn't give *myself* the same unbridled permission.

"I just don't trust myself, Hudson. I've made so many mistakes in the past. I don't want to repeat them."

"You're never going to learn if you don't try."

I dropped my head. He cupped my cheek and lifted it back up.

"Look. Maybe last night really *was* all you needed. That's fine. If that's the case, I'll go right now and we'll never talk about this again. But I just don't want you to throw me away because you're scared. Like I said, it doesn't have to be serious. We can just have fun and enjoy ourselves." When I didn't respond, he added, "You should get whatever you want, Scout. All you have to do is decide what that is."

I wanted to be the person who did that. Wanted to be the type who threw caution to the wind and slipped into a casual FWB situation with the hot guy who liked her. Wanted to believe someone like Hudson could like her without ulterior motives—uncomplicatedly and earnestly.

And him. I wanted him.

"Getting what I want is exactly what I'm afraid of," I confided. "I always screw it up somehow."

"Me too. I told you about my last relationship. It really messed me up. I'm not good at science, but what's that principle? About two negatives equaling a positive? Maybe this will be like that. Our bad luck will cancel each other out."

Even like this, with my heart in disarray and my pussy aching and my world in the balance, he could make me laugh.

"What do you want, Scout? You have to tell me or I can't give it to you."

"Right back at you, Mr. I Don't Care What We Eat for Dinner."

He rolled his eyes as if to say *Okay, you've got me there.* "Well, right now, what I want is you. Can I have you? Will you have me?"

Problem: I don't want to stop being with Hudson.

Proposed Solution: Stay with him.

Test: Say yes.

Result: Who knows?

I hated the scientific uncertainty of it all. But it was decision time. With Clara's voice in my head urging me to take risks and Hudson's encouragement ringing in my ears, I made mine. Reckless and stupid as it was. "Yeah. I want you."

He shrugged. "Then everything else is secondary."

Attacking his lips with my own, I grabbed him by the waist and pulled his body flush against mine. I'd never put my robe on, so I was still completely naked. With only his briefs between us, he could be inside me in a second. I was certainly wet enough, having never really recovered from last night's peak horniness.

But he threaded his hands through my hair, twisting the locks slightly to keep me in place. Like he was doing everything in his power not to let me go. My hands fumbled with his briefs, but he pulled back, keeping me just far enough away that he could dip down and take my left nipple in his mouth.

I moaned. Nipple clamps and stimulators were all very well and good, but—

Oh!

He bit down slightly on my hardened bud, then made up for the tweak of pain with a deep kiss. He repeated the process on my right, removing his hand from my hair long enough to ensure that both nipples got equal attention—one from his mouth, one from his fingers.

I had spent twenty-six years without ever once having a real dick in me, and yet my pussy had never felt so empty.

As if reading my thoughts, he turned me around to face the kitchen island. A strong hand cupped the back of my neck, guiding me down until I was bent over the counter. Hands on the faux marble, framing my head. Feet wide on the floor, so my legs were spread for him. I was exposed, his for the taking.

My breath made fireworks of condensation on the countertop. Every one of my internal systems hummed in anticipation.

Arching my back, I presented my ass, waiting for him to enter me from behind. When he didn't, I offered:

"Aren't you going to . . . ?"

He tutted, then stepped forward, closing much of the gap between us. The head of his length danced against my dripping entrance, teasing me with what I wanted most. "I told you. I can't give you what you want until you ask for it."

My mind flashed for a moment to the folder of diagrams and specs on the BuzzCorp servers, the results of lab studies on stimulation and arousal. He was pushing every button, playing out the science on my extremely willing body. Delay and denial were useful tools in the sex toy department. Now I understood their merit in real-world applications.

His cock slipped against my clit for the briefest of seconds.

My entire body shuddered from the contact. I could almost hear his self-satisfied smirk.

"Please . . ." I swallowed hard, barely able to form a complete thought except: "I need you inside me."

He was more than happy to oblige. I cried out as he filled me with one long, perfect thrust. My hands splayed across the counter; my nipples stung from the sensation of the cold surface underneath them.

Once inside me, he hesitated. No thrusting. No movement. Just the solid all of him stretching my walls, waiting for permission to continue.

Instinctively, as if urging him to come the hell on, my pussy seized around him. But he held firm.

"And?" he prompted.

I swallowed. "Fuck me. And don't stop."

His cock probed once against the back of me, and then he was fucking me like he wanted the memory branded into my skin. Like he wanted to write his sex into my core's memory. Like he never wanted another man to compare. Like no other pussy had ever compared for him.

It was every bit as fulfilling as last night had been. But where that had been the work of a man who believed it was his last time—a man who wanted to savor each sensation—this was the work of a man who wanted me to come back again and again and again.

I met him every time, yearning for more, faster, deeper. When my hand wandered down to my clit, however, he grabbed my wrist and firmly directed my palm back to the counter. From the corner of my eye, I watched him retrieve the finger vibrator.

All this he did without missing a single stroke inside me.

How was it that he was this flawlessly competent at every single thing he did—including me?

"So. Are we also going to revise our agreement on practical

demonstrations? I think they would be very instructive for my sex toy education."

I would give him anything he wanted if he made me cum right now.

"Yes. Yes. I'll show you. I'll teach you—"

Each word was more strangled than the last.

"How do I turn it on?" he whispered against my neck.

"Slip it onto your finger and press it down hard against the counter. Three presses will turn it to its highest setting."

He clicked it only once.

"Tell me what you want," he reiterated.

It was hard to talk when he was pounding me breathless, but at this point, I knew how to get what I wanted. "Please make me cum."

The vibrator stunned my clit. It was on its lowest setting, but still, the relief of its pressure was enough to make me mewl.

"And after that? After you've finished all over me?"

I tried to put thoughts together, to form a plan, as this man used me like my pussy was built for him. Eventually, I managed through moans:

"I want you to keep fucking me. Until you, mm, finish your contract at BuzzCorp, let's, ah, keep doing this. Fuck—please."

"Agreed," he managed, barely able to keep his own tone in check now. Our peaks were fast approaching, we could both feel it.

"But we, nnnh, can't tell anyone."

He grunted. "Fine."

"And," I hissed as the stroking of the vibrator and the pounding of his cock hit a sloppy, unrelenting rhythm my body could no longer hold at bay. I was climbing, my orgasm so close, and I could tell he was close now, too. "You can't—*ah*—you can't fall in love with me or, *nhhhh*, anything like that—"

"How does this feel, Scout? How does the vibrator against your clit feel? Remember, this is for my education—"

He pressed his finger *hard* against my clit. I shook as the vibrations reached their second-highest level.

"It feels like all my muscles are shaking at their highest frequency. Like I have no choice but to tighten around you."

A growl from over my shoulder. He pressed me again. The vibrations reached their apex.

And so did he.

"Fuck, Scout—!"

Hudson roared his climax. The shock waves only accentuated my fast-coming orgasm.

I wanted to return to our deal-making. To make it absolutely clear that I wouldn't repeat old mistakes by mixing the dangerous chemicals of pleasure with business.

But then, at the very same moment, his cock hit in just the right spot and his fingers dragged the vibrator over my clit in a furious, final crescendo.

My words came out as nothing more than a strangled scream. I toppled over the edge, squeezing the last drops of his own orgasm from him until we fell into a toppled heap on the kitchen counter.

For a few moments, we lay there. Breathless. Limbless. And I, for one, was scared shitless. I mean, I'd just agreed to six more weeks of this man. Six more weeks of his jokes and his warm heart and his beautiful cock and his knowledge of exactly what to do with it.

"Miss Porter," he said, turning off the vibrator and kissing my shoulder. "That was one hell of a lesson. And as for your demands, you've got yourself a deal."

Yeah. We *did* have a deal. A deal with the devil, probably.

But hey. At least the road to hell would be paved with good sex.

19

Friends with No Benefits

Last night I'd asked Hudson how you could possibly sit across the table from a stranger, knowing you were about to have sex with them. At the time, I couldn't imagine anything more disconsonant, that partnership of desire and pleasantry.

Turns out I was wrong. There was a weirder feeling.

"So," Leelah said. "What did you get up to last night?"

The *real* worst feeling was having amazing sex and not being able to talk about it. Today, I'd had to face Clara and feign that nothing was different. When I'd first agreed to sex with Hudson, I didn't tell her because it wasn't a big deal. It would be a one-night stand I could mention in passing sometime in the very, very distant future, when he was long gone from BuzzCorp. Now that he would be a more semipermanent fixture in my day-to-day, I didn't want to tell her because . . .

Well . . .

What if I failed?

What if my great attempt to balance personal affairs and work was a total bust, The Fantasy flopped, and I disappointed her?

No, I couldn't handle it.

So I kept my mouth shut and continued to do so with Leelah that afternoon.

As promised, she and I had hit up some trendy sandwich place for lunch so I could get to know her better. Thankfully, she'd spent much of our meal talking about herself: where she grew up (Paris, Texas—home of the Cowboy Boot Jesus, look it up), her hobbies (dance classes, volunteering), her vices (maxing out her Ulta card), her obsessions (rom-coms, hot Formula 1 drivers, and providing free medical intervention to underserved communities). She also took the time to critique my management style, which she described as "hands-on to the extreme."

She spoke quickly and excitedly, like she was afraid if she came up for air, she'd lose her chance to become my friend. I listened as best I could, all while trying not to think about Hudson and how badly I wanted to gush to *someone* about him.

Listen to me. Gush. I never gushed.

After lunch, instead of returning to the office, she dragged me to Pacific Plaza and ordered us drinks from a takeout stand near the entrance. Coffee for her, hot chocolate with whipped cream for me. It was then that she turned the conversation my way.

"Scout? I asked what you got up to."

"Me? Oh, nothing. Had some food. Stayed up too late."

"Doing what?"

I stifled a truthful reply with a long sip of my cocoa. "I was experimenting with some new equipment."

God, this was killing me. How was I not supposed to scream from the rooftops that Hudson had an amazing mouth and hands and that I would let him take me right now on a park bench if he was here?

Right. Because after our morning liaison, we codified several rules of procedure. Simple stuff, mostly. We would have a mutually beneficial sexual relationship, no strings attached. Friends who fucked by night and coworkers by day. We would *never* let our escapades interfere with our jobs or the launch of The Fantasy, and if it ever felt that we were, we would immediately end the association. I would continue to teach him about sex toys, including during our sex sessions. Our safe word was *cosmos*. We would always practice enthusiastic consent. And once Hudson's contract was up in six weeks, the affair would be over, too.

The rules were designed to protect us both. Especially that last one. If we both knew that he was going to leave, then there would be no chance of us developing complicated emotions. Like an element with a short half-life, we would enjoy what we had while we had it, then not mourn it once it was gone.

But our most important rule? Never, ever, under any circumstances, let anyone know what was going on between us. This was for my sake.

After the Lloyd Exeter *thing*, and after my blowup at the bar, I wanted nothing more than to put a reinforced titanium door between my work and sex. In *Jurassic Park* (the book, not the movie . . . the movie didn't have enough science in it), there were these big barriers designed to keep poor, unsuspecting humans from getting trampled by ravenous monsters.

Only in this analogy, my career was the precious tourist, and my apparently insatiably horny vagina was the extinction-level threat.

Leelah clucked her tongue. "Okay. So, you *didn't* hook up with Hudson last night?"

The *Jurassic Park* metaphor was fucked from the start. Those walls never worked on Isla Nublar. Why did I think they would work for my muff monster?

I tripped. "What? No. Why would you even say that?"

"When he walked in today, he had this super dreamy look on his face. Like he was the luckiest guy in the world—or he would be if you'd just look at him. But no matter how hard he tried, you wouldn't even acknowledge his existence. The sexual tension was unbearable."

"It was not!"

It was, but I thought that I was the only one who'd noticed.

"I mean," I corrected, "there wasn't any sexual tension. You're seeing things."

"You're really trying to convince me that *nothing's* going on between you two?"

Damn, she was good. Perceptive. I needed to throw her off.

"I'm the unfuckable nerd who hasn't been able to get a guy in twenty-six years, Leelah, remember? You thought I went from that to raging sex maniac with some office rando overnight?"

This was not the first time I'd described myself as an unfuckable nerd out loud or to myself. But it was the first time the words actually hurt. They used to be a statement of fact. I spent all my time buried in math and gears, so *nerd* was accurate. And no one had ever proven me wrong about the unfuckable thing, so . . . the logic was sound.

But after last night, I knew the truth. Nerd? Yes. Unfuckable? Decidedly not. And I'd wasted years not having the sex I deserved because of that insidious fallacy.

This is why you don't accept a scientific principle without doing the research to back it up.

"Scout, I'm one of the smartest people I've ever met. You're not going to gaslight me into disbelieving obvious evidence."

"And what evidence is that? Just some accidental glances?"

"I'll have you know that I'm extremely perceptive, Scout. I walk into a room, I survey the landscape, and I instantly know what's going on with people. I may only have been at BuzzCorp for a day, but it's obvious what's going on between you two. He wasn't just *looking* at you. It was more than that. It was like . . . relief."

The gates of the park suddenly loomed very close, which meant that our office was only a few blocks farther.

"Relief?" I asked, hating how such an idea made my heart palpitate.

"Yeah. He would focus on work for a little bit, then he would scan the room for you, then when he saw you again, his whole face would relax. Like he was worried you would disappear and was relieved every time he saw that you were still around."

I stepped aside to let a roller skater split between Leelah and me. I was grateful for even the brief distance. She was too close—not just physically, but emotionally, too.

"What guy looks at a woman like that if he's not gagging to get back into her pants? Well, I guess he could be in love with you, but you guys barely even talk, so I'm assuming the sex reason is more realistic."

He could be in love with you. Not likely. I wouldn't let it happen.

"Or," I retorted, "what's most realistic is that you've been watching too many rom-coms since your breakup and now you want to see the world through Hallmark-tinted glasses."

Leelah rolled her eyes. "Well, then I guess I just *imagined* the text he sent you when you got up to get our order at lunch?"

"What text?"

I dug into my pocket for the offending iPhone. Leelah reminded me that earlier, I'd given it to her so she could watch some video of drag queens talking about our products on their podcast, but I tuned her out.

When I put in my passcode, I found the offending text immediately, spelling out my doom in thousands of pixels.

Scout, I can't stop thinking about you—or last night. Hope you're more focused on work than I am today. I'm finding it impossible to code when all I want is to feel you cum around me again. Dinner tonight?

There was another text, too. It had followed five minutes later.

> Shit. Too much? Sorry, new to this friends-with-benefits thing. Be prepared to endure many cringey texts as I navigate this learning curve.

A million thoughts crossed my mind at once. Shock . . . and frustration . . . and a whole lot of relief.

"You *didn't* catch him looking at me! You made all that up to cover up the fact that you saw this text!"

"Yes, but I had a good reason to lie! If I told you I read the texts earlier, you'd've totally been mad at me, stormed off back to work, and not been my friend anymore. I was trying to preserve this very new gal-pals thing we've got going on here!"

The air rushed out of my lungs. "I'm not mad, but you scared the hell out of me! You made me think everyone in the office already knew! I thought I was going to have to call it off with Hudson because we were being too obvious!"

Her face drew up in horror. "Don't do that! Oh my God, you *can't* do that! You two are perfect for each other. I've been here one day, and I already know that."

Not this again. Even after admitting her bullshit, she was still trying to convince me we had more than sex going between us. "*Leelah.*"

"It's true! You're this stone-cold badass steminist loner and he's this cheerful sex helpmate. He's going to break down your walls and you're going to, like, make him fall in love for real for the first time."

I had a choice before me. Tell her the truth or let her walk around thinking we were in the middle of some great love story. I chose the former. Did I want to? No, not really. Every anxiety about mixing up sex and work bubbled to the surface. But I didn't have many options, either. I outlined the entire plot of casual sex and absolute (almost) secrecy. Opening up was not my strong suit, though, so it came out in awkward fits and starts.

When it was over, a strange sense of peace washed over me. I wasn't alone now. I wasn't keeping a secret. This wasn't like back in the day with Lloyd, where the lies piled up around me and I took his request for privacy as sexy gospel.

Now I was having sex with a totally amazing guy. And I just got to . . . tell my friend about it. Trusting someone, which had seemed unconscionable just a few minutes ago, now didn't just feel doable. It felt vital.

When I finished, she tossed her hair smugly. "You've never seen a rom-com, have you, Scout?"

"I don't watch a lot of movies. But when I do, if it doesn't have laser swords or robots in it, I'm usually not interested."

"Fine, then. Just know that I've seen this movie before." She beamed and threw her arm around my shoulder. "I won't spoil the ending for you. But be prepared for a few plot twists."

20

Friends with Whatever-It-Is

I swear that I didn't mean for her to see it. And I'm sorry. But I don't have to keep, you know, talking to her about it—"

We were in my apartment, halfway into a glass of wine, when I realized I couldn't carry on without Hudson knowing the truth. That our little experiment had broken containment and infected the office—or, at least, my friendship-by-fire with Leelah. But now that I'd done it, he looked at me like I was the silliest woman who'd ever lived. "Scout, do you think I'm mad at you?"

He didn't look mad. But that didn't mean he wasn't. People lied all the time. I did, anyway. "Maybe a little?"

"You're the one who wanted to keep us a secret. If you want people to know, then you should tell them. If I had my way about it, I'd probably be taking out an ad in *Popular Science*."

It was the fastest resolution to any relationship conflict I'd ever been involved in. I didn't know how to proceed.

Well. Okay, then. Might as well get on with the real purpose of his visit. I reached for the buttons of my shirt.

"Okay, you ready?"

"For what?"

"For sex," I said, obviously. "What else?"

Hudson shifted on the couch, eyeing me curiously. "Aren't you sore after last night?"

"A little. But studies show that muscular stiffness should generally be worked out, not rested. At least, that's what Clara told me when she tried to trick me back into going to reformer Pilates with her. Let's go in the bedroom—"

"Do you *want* to have sex, Scout? Like right now, in this moment?"

"What about you? Do *you* want to?"

"That wasn't the question."

"It is now. What is this conversational anaphylaxis you experience every time I ask you what you want?"

"I just want to make sure you're comfortable. And happy. I don't want to chase you off."

"You couldn't chase me off. I don't think you could ever chase anybody off."

"Wanna bet?" he grumbled.

I thought about his vague story about his ex-girlfriend. Was that what he meant?

"Care to expand on that, sir?"

"No, thank you."

Silence lingered between us for a beat too long. I gestured to my bedroom door.

"So . . . sex? I mean, it's just that you're here and I thought most guys would jump at the chance to skip foreplay."

"If I were most guys, I don't think you would have decided to sleep with me."

I scoffed, but admittedly . . . it was a turn-on. Did this self-confident nerd bring out the slut in me? "I don't think I'll ever be *not* surprised when you pull that arrogant stuff. It's so unlike you."

"You and I are honest people, Scout. You're a scientist. I'm an engineer. We trade in reality. No bullshit. It's not arrogant to think I'm at least a little special to you. It's just a fact. We wouldn't be here right now if you didn't enjoy my company—even a little bit."

"And you? Am I special to you? Do you enjoy my company?" I asked, once again thinking about how deftly he dodged answering my questions.

"I trust that I can make you happy," he said, after a beat of hesitation. "I *like* making you happy."

It seemed that was all he felt comfortable giving me now. Which was fine, I told myself. We didn't need to add any more depth to this relationship. We were friends with benefits. Nothing more.

"What else do you like about me?" I asked, slowly lowering myself down onto his lap.

A silly question. I braced myself for the obvious attributes everyone always ascribed to me. Hardworking. Smart. Diligent. Disciplined.

But he surprised me. "You're kind."

"I'm *what*?"

"On my first day at BuzzCorp, it was raining, and I didn't have an umbrella. I was standing outside the building, but the security guard wouldn't let me in. You saw me from your window, not yet knowing that I was the guy Clara had hired, and you came down with your umbrella because you'd seen a stranger in the rain who looked like he needed help. You didn't have to do that. But you did. Just like you always leave the everything bagel for Addie on Bagel Wednesdays because you know they're her favorite, even though you love them, too, and just like, when Terrence leaves his sweater at the office on Friday, you send it to the laundry so it's clean when he gets to the office on Monday."

I reeled. I didn't . . . he'd noticed all of that?

"You keep hinting that I'm too accommodating or whatever, but you and I are the same," he said. "But where I want everyone to know what sort of guy I am, you want to hide it. I don't understand."

Oh, the unbearable weight of being perceived. Sex would have been so much easier. I squirmed.

"What? Are you surprised?" he asked.

"I just never thought of myself that way."

"How *do* you think of yourself? You don't really let me see a lot of you. I'd like to know more."

"You already know everything that's worth knowing. The old career, the old flame, the new career, the new fuckbuddy."

As if to prove my point, I settled in deeper on his lap. His cock stirred. Excellent. Only a few more minutes of distraction and we'd be off the *Me* topic and onto the *We* topic.

"So I know your LinkedIn profile, basically. I want to know *you*."

"I don't want to talk about me."

"Too bad." He smirked and rebuttoned my top shirt button. "You're not getting dick until you do."

"There's nothing to know! I'm just . . ." I sighed. It was big of him to demand answers from me when he wouldn't give me any about himself. However, lunch today with Leelah showed me how nice it could be to talk to someone. "I didn't have the normal experiences other people had. I was obsessive about school as a kid, and then I became obsessive about work. My . . . me and Lloyd Exeter, that was the first time I'd ever given myself permission to do something for me. And it almost ruined my life. I know I like sci-fi and bagels and that friendship and dating terrify me. But other than that? I guess maybe I don't even know who I am. There. Is *that* enough?"

Petulantly, I undid my top button again.

Hudson nodded. Batting me away, he started down the buttons, slowly exposing my chest. "You know what I see when I look at you? Someone smart, and sexy, and funny, and you really care about people, even if you're too afraid to let them get close . . . and yes." He pressed a kiss below my ear, tickling the sensitive skin of my neck. “You’ve earned a reward. And I think it’s time for *me* to have another lesson.”

Thank Christ. Now in my bra and skirt, I freed his cock from his briefs and his jeans.

I slipped easily out of my panties, crying out as I sank onto him.

It was my first time being on top. I guess that should have been intimidating. It wasn’t. It felt too right.

Before I could ride him in earnest, though, he held my hips fast, freezing me in place.

“But you should know—I’m going to help you figure out who you are.”

How did one find themself at age twenty-six? He could think that way all he wanted, but I foresaw this dalliance between us as a means to a very specific end. Which I could have gotten if he stopped holding me down and started letting me ride him. “Good luck. Even when it comes to sex, I don’t know who I am. I mean, I read smut and watch porn and have fantasies, but fantasies aren’t wishes. I don’t know if I’d be into half the stuff I daydream about with my vibrator, you know?”

“Well. Why don’t we figure that out together?”

In a sweeping gesture, he lifted me off him, ran to my bedroom, and came back with his laptop and a small utility box I kept on my bedside table. He gave me the latter and opened the former.

“What are we doing?” I asked, hating the emptiness between my legs.

“An experiment. I’m going to look up some kinks online, and we’re going to decide if you’re into them or not.”

“How will we know—”

“I’ll feel it. Your body can’t hide that.”

Another experiment. He knew the way to this girl’s heart. I was tempted to see if *he* wanted the same treatment, but I feared I already knew the answer. He was a black box of a man, hiding himself from me. “Okay.”

Situating himself back on the couch, he propped the laptop onto the tufted fabric arm. A lurid web page in black and pink glared out from the screen, but I was too busy digging through the utility box he'd delivered. Eventually I pulled out a small handheld device. Another one of my favorites.

"And what do we have here, Dr. Porter?"

"It's a suction toy. It feels like I'm having my clit worshipped while I . . ."

An eyebrow quirked. "While I fuck you?"

I settled back into his lap, one leg on either side of him. He shifted upward, filling me to the brim with him. My hand, the one holding the toy, immediately descended to my clit, latching onto the swollen bud.

"Why don't you turn it on," he prompted.

"But don't you want—"

"Do you have any idea how amazing an orgasm is after a woman has ridden you for twenty minutes and cum all over your cock?"

"No, but I take your point."

"Please, Scout. Touch yourself. Please. Teach me how good this feels for you."

The *please* convinced me. I didn't want a hard-core Dom, no matter if those tropes sometimes popped up in the porn I consumed. What I wanted was a partner. Someone who could bend me over a kitchen counter and fuck me one minute, lovingly lay me out like a queen the next, *and* stern-brunch-daddy me into making myself cum after that.

Hudson was all those wrapped up in one very sexy package. I couldn't help but melt for him.

I pressed the first button. The toy's internal mechanism whirred to quiet action, slowly tonguing my clit.

He explored the curves of my bra with his palms. My nipples pressed against the fabric, but he pointedly refused to expose them.

Thighs tightening, I tried to work my way up and down his shaft. But he held me firm, eyes coyly trailing from my face to the screen at his right.

"Now, let's see," he said with professorial detachment. "How do you feel about . . . hair pulling?"

I must have thrust a little deeper or tightened involuntarily around him, because he grinned.

To my surprise, his cock twitched inside me, too.

Oh. Our bodies really *couldn't* hide from each other. I understood the science around involuntary sexual expressions, but to experience it in real time was nothing short of a research revelation.

"We're going to learn a lot about each other today, aren't we, Scout?"

Torture. Trying to keep myself from working my clit hard and fast and in the exact places I needed was absolute torture. But I did my best to follow instructions. My reward wasn't just that delicious feeling of teetering on the brink, but also of his praising moans every time my body reacted to his words.

"What if we role-played? A doctor and his pent-up patient? A professor and his TA desperate for a letter of recommendation?"

Nothing. The sex still felt amazing, but the little *hm* Hudson gave me indicated I must not be into that. He didn't show much sign of interest either.

Thankfully, he took the opportunity to relieve me of my bra.

"How about this. The website says that many women like to hear . . ."

He leaned up, collected one nipple in his mouth, and breathed against my sensitive skin:

"Good girl."

I continued to crave more of him, but while his hands tightened around my waist, I felt no marked change in my state at the sound of those words. Being a good girl wasn't currently my fixation. Being bad with him was.

"Interesting," he murmured against my hard nub.

His worship of my tits continued, and I rode him at his pace, exploring my clit with every motion. I didn't know it was possible to feel this good, this complete. I wanted more, stroking myself upward and upward . . .

"You seemed all too happy to get fucked in your office the other day. Is there an exhibitionist somewhere in you, Scout?"

Yes. I shuddered, clenching almost painfully around his cock. He kept glancing at the screen, hunting for new kinks to explore.

"What if I tied you up?"

Another hit. I cried out, the pleasure coming hot and fast now.

"Or maybe *several* of us could tie you up?"

I couldn't help it. I turned the toy sucking my clit to its next highest function. Randomized for maximum excitement, it teetered between hard and fast, light and soft. Each time I crashed down on Hudson's cock was a new adventure as the mechanical tongues worked their magic.

Then a slight *smack* on my ass sent my eyes flying open in shock . . . and pleasure. I looked down at him, only to find Hudson already staring back at me, wide-eyed.

"I'm sorry—it said—did you not—"

My shoulders shook as I fought to keep my orgasm at bay. Instead of retreating, I curved my ass back into his hand. He then gave the offended cheek a playful squeeze.

"Then you *are* into power dynamics," he murmured. Just like I would have if I were looking at test results in my lab. Maybe role play didn't do it for me, but being his little science experiment definitely did.

He cycled through more of them. At least, I think he did. Maybe blindfolds or being fucked by someone else while he watched or humiliation play or me dominating him? It all became a blur as my mind focused on nothing but the pleasure, on how my wet, swollen clit ached for release and how each thrust of my hips filled me with him all over again, as good as the first time I'd sunk down onto it.

But by the time my orgasm threatened to take hold of me, I was hit with a realization.

He'd done all the talking.

"What about you?" I panted. "What about . . . would you like me to dominate you? Hm? Want me to fuck you with that strap-on we saw the other night?"

A growl tore through his gritted teeth. It wasn't an actual answer, but it was enough to get my mind racing.

Bending him on all fours in bed, lining a strap-on up at his entrance, hearing him moan as I entered him . . .

Too much. I arched my back, bucking into my hand, fighting for that last bit of friction that would throw me over the edge. "Hudson, I'm going to—"

Another glance at the screen.

"What about this one?" Firmly, he grabbed my wrist and removed the toy from my clit. His grin was unfairly hot. "Or delayed gratification?"

"What? No, no, no—" My voice was panting and pathetic. The orgasm slipped out from under me, leaving me hanging in the terrible balance between frustration and pleasure.

I was a sweaty, exhausted mess of a woman with one goal in mind now. Orgasm. But Hudson brushed a stray strand of damp hair from my face, looking up at me as though we were across from each other at a fancy restaurant on a date night.

"You are so beautiful."

Then he rocked his cock into the depths of me. The marriage of his member against my G-spot and the brush of his body against my clit hit exactly the right notes, and suddenly I was flying into a climax, shuddering around his cock and screaming until I was sure my walls would shake.

I rode him all the way through it, drawing every aftershock into my core, relishing the completeness of the sensation.

When I was finally spent, I tipped my forehead against his. The bastard was smug. Absolutely beaming.

"Praise kink." He tapped my nose. The sexiest, smuggest *boop* in human history. "Number thirty-two on the list. I *thought* you might like that one."

Not wanting even a second of separation from him, I allowed him to tip me back onto the couch so he could be on top. We took a moment, though, to catch our collective breaths. "You were very bad, Hudson," I said. He tensed. "I still don't know what you like."

"I want to explore anything that interests you, Scout."

Yet another evasion. My curious mind couldn't give that up. Dating him or getting close to him was not on my agenda—far from it. But now that I'd noticed him dodging my questions, I wanted to know why. I was a scientist, after all. Questioning the unknown was part of my nature.

"But—"

He tried to silence me with a kiss, but I dodged. When he saw I wouldn't give in, he replied: "Listen, the only thing you need to know about me is that we're going to have a *lot* of fun together."

"Maybe I don't need to know more. But I . . . I want to," I said. "I get what it's like, for people not to listen. Not to care. Or to feel like they don't, anyway. As long as you and I are in this together, we both deserve to feel safe enough to explore what we want. You've been here for me. I can be here for you, too, even if this is just a fling."

His Adam's apple bobbed as he swallowed. His lashes brushed the skin beneath his eyes. He let out a small breath. And something, something I'm not sure I could name, shifted between us.

"Just consider it. Offer's on the table if you want it."

I'd barely finished the sentence before he kissed me like I'd never been kissed before.

21

Business Lunch

A few days went by like that. With sex-ploration. Boldly cumming where many men, women, and beyond have cum before. We settled into an easy rhythm, showing off my impressive toy collection as we worked our way through (I'm assuming, having never read it) the first several dozen chapters of the Kama Sutra.

We were emphatically *not* dating. Not dating, you hear me? I was just insatiably horny for him, he for me, and sometimes he fell asleep at my place, holding me in his arms like a sexy, naked security blanket. Nothing more.

I'd done a decent job of maintaining work-life balance. We both stayed focused and disciplined at the office. Deadlines were met. Progress reports completed. Notable improvements to The Fantasy prototype turned in. Every once in a while, intrusive thoughts about wanting to have sex with him in the supply closet imposed on my mind, but like a normal, high-functioning adult, I nudged them aside until after close of business when he could fuck me in the privacy and safety of my own home.

One morning, though, while I was tying my shoes for work,

Hudson kept rearranging my collection of bedside erotica. First alphabetically, then by color.

"Everything okay?" I asked playfully.

"Hm? Me? Yeah. I was just thinking . . . what are you doing tonight?"

"I was planning to stay late at the office and get some work done," I said, without giving it much thought.

A copy of *Good Girl's Guide to Kink* dropped to the floor. Hudson rushed to pick it up.

"Oh yeah. Cool. Cool." He cleared his throat not once but twice. Adjusted his glasses. Put the book back on the table. "Well. You enjoy that. Let me know how it goes. I was thinking about maybe doing some mini golf or whatever. Just a fun thing to do on a random evening. The weather's nice, you know."

I did know. Leelah, who'd become my most constant text companion, had woken me up with gushing messages about the crisp fall air. We were having lunch to celebrate. "Great. Maybe we can link up after I'm done with work?"

"I'd love that."

That was what he said, anyway. His tone, though, lodged in my head like an annoying math problem I couldn't quite figure out.

It still bothered me that afternoon, when Leelah and I found ourselves together at lunch. In the center of the Trio Towers, where the BuzzCorp offices were located, sat a fabulous outdoor oasis, where every day new vendors would come to hawk their wares and entice the office-dwelling ghouls to come out of their cubicles for lunch. I absent-mindedly chowed down on a Korean burrito with one hand while scanning Addie's latest marketing report.

"You know," she said, picking at her salad, "when I said we should hang out more, this is *not* what I had in mind."

"What do you mean?" I asked, mouth full of bulgogi and rice.

"Can't you put the laptop away for, like, a *second*?"

"Why?"

"Because this isn't what friends do. Friends don't work through lunch, Scout. They gossip and laugh and talk shit about their coworkers."

Not that it was worth mentioning, but now that Jared was gone, I liked our colleagues. I flipped a page in the marketing report and frowned. The campaign, which would debut at OFest in New York, was not shaping up how I wanted. "Our deadlines are agnostic on the topic of friendship. No, in fact, they're actively hostile to the concept."

"Scout," Leelah groaned.

"What? We're work-eating outside. This is practically, like, a friendship field trip for me. Now, do you have that performance data we discussed earlier? I want to rerun your numbers after I double-check the tests that Terrence proposed today—"

"No. Close your laptop."

"But—"

"I said *close it*. I thought you were trying new things. Based on what I've heard, working through lunch is not new for you."

Finally deigning to look up at her, I found my friend—still weird to think of anyone as a *friend*—glowering at me with a mixture of frustration and concern.

"I'm trying new things in moderation," I explained. "I am *not* letting this get in the way of The Fantasy. I've got to be responsible here, not go on a 'normal human experiences' bender and wrap my life and career around a tree."

"That's too many metaphors. Stick to STEM, babe. Well, STEM and sex. How *is* that going, by the way?"

Ah, so we'd reached it. The *real* reason she wanted me to take my head out of work and place it firmly back into my bedroom. So she could get that sweet Hudson-and-Scout-Kissing-in-a-Tree gossip.

Heat flooded my face. I returned to my work. "Good."

"Just good?" The wind kicked up, feathering her blowout so it perfectly framed her sneer. "What's wrong with him, then?"

I spit out my water. "Excuse me?"

She snatched the laptop out of my hands and used the hem of her sweater to wipe it down. Clever woman. Now I'd never get it back. "If he's *just* good, and not, like, spectacular and stunning, then he's got to have red flags somewhere. ACAB? More like, yes, ACAB, but also AMAB. All *Men* Are Bastards."

"Bold statement coming from Miss Rom-Com. Weren't he and I supposed to be in love by now?"

"Not yet," she said, sounding it out like I was a small child failing a phonics lesson. "You only *just* broke your 'we're only having sex for one night' rule. This is the *getting to know you*, fun-and-games phase. You can't expect to fall in love with him after just a week."

"I don't expect to *ever* be in love with him," I retorted.

"And why not?"

Because I ruin everything I touch. Because no one has ever shown me before that I'm lovable and I'm inclined to believe them, no matter what Hudson says. Because I was burned on love once; now I'm not even sure I'd know what it looks and feels like.

"About a million reasons. But . . ." My emotional walls tried to slam shut, but I forced myself to talk anyway. This was what friends did. She wasn't going to be giving my laptop back, so I might as well get this off my chest. "He won't tell me anything about himself."

"That's the most ridiculous thing I've ever heard. What man doesn't like to talk about himself nonstop?"

"Okay, I'm glad I'm not overreacting. Like, I asked about his ex-girlfriend, he was super cagey. I asked him what he wanted for dinner, he never gave me an opinion, just agreed with anything I offered. We talked about kinks and interests, he just said he wanted what I want."

Leelah thoughtfully opened a candy bar and gave it a long chew before answering.

"Maybe he's just insecure. Maybe he's afraid if he says the wrong thing, you'll ditch him and never look back."

"I'm no prize. I can't imagine anyone being sorry they missed out on me."

She blinked at me. "Amazing. That minds can defy God to send man to space and defy man to give women the best orgasms of their lives . . . yet you don't have imagination enough to think of yourself as valuable. Some inquisitive mind you've got there, Scout."

Oh God. Was friendship just saying nice things about each other all the time? Abort. Abort.

"It's probably for the best, anyway," I said, dismissing the backhanded compliment. "I don't need to like him any more than I already do."

"Isn't liking him more a good thing?" A retort danced on my tongue. She cut me off. "And I *swear* if you say a single word about The Fantasy and the OFest deadline, I'll smear this nougat and caramel all over your tablet screen."

"He's leaving at the end of his contract. Liking him would be a complication. And long-term, I don't think I could handle a relationship *and* all my work stress. He's just a way to blow off some steam. To get some worldly experience in a safe environment."

"Famous last words," she snarked.

Wrapping up my burrito, I scrubbed at my hands with a nearby napkin as vigorously as if I'd just spilled coolant on them. As if I was trying to rub Hudson's increasingly viscid self from my mind. "Besides, he's got his own stuff going on. He probably wouldn't *want* anything else. This morning, for example, he asked me what I was doing, and when I told him I'd be working late, he said he was planning to take advantage of the weather and go mini-golfing. See? He doesn't need me. Or want me, probably, beyond sex."

For a long moment, Leelah stared at me and said nothing. It was the stare I gave to Clara every time I had to re-explain why I couldn't magically make the C690 axis in our Final Thrust toy work silently when paired with a standard G570 lever: a *Why aren't you getting this?* look.

Now that I knew how it felt to be on the receiving end of such a look, I owed Clara an apology. A big one. "What?"

"He was trying to ask you out," Leelah said.

My first instinct was to shut her down. No one ever asked me out.

But then my scientific brain took over. His nervousness. His casual question about my plans. The anxious book reordering. Our conversation the other night about opening up to each other, my impulsive, curiosity-driven desire for him to tell me about himself.

Ohhhhhhhhhh.

The evidence was conclusive. He was trying to ask me out the only way a people-pleasing, never-wants-to-say-the-wrong-thing person could. By making it seem like an accident. He was trying not to push me too hard, trying to back-door his way into the kind of intimacy I'd hinted at during our talk.

I'd made him feel safe enough to try and take our relationship in a new direction . . . but he was still too nervous of my boundaries to come right out and say it.

"You know, now that I've run the data back, I believe your logic is pretty unimpeachable."

"Great!" She practically cheered. "Now that you know, you can tell him you'd *love* to go mini-golfing."

"I can't" was my sharp, knee-jerk reaction. "I'm working late."

"You're *not* working late, Scout. There's absolutely no reason for you to work late."

While *I* didn't have anything in particular that *I* needed to stay late for, *so* many things had gotten away from me in the last week during my and Hudson's sexual bliss-out. I hadn't kept up on any of the follow-ups and double-checks I did on my team's work . . . Hence my lunchtime review of Addie's marketing schemes. "I've been slacking—"

"You mean you've been working normal business hours, but go on." She dropped her chin into her hands and batted her eyelashes sarcastically. "*Please.* More excuses."

"I need to stay on top of things, that's all," I grumbled after a beat.

"Jesus, Scout! This isn't fucking rocket science. It's not *fucking* science, either! Just text him right now, tell him you're not working late, and ask if he has room on his scorecard for you. Literally and metaphorically."

"I'm drowning in work. Speaking of, when are you going to send me that data we were discussing earlier?"

"I'm not. And you're not working late tonight."

"But I'm looking through the marketing concept Addie is drafting up with the PR team. They're just not getting it right. I wonder if I should start sitting in on the meetings. Maybe I should call a few, just to make sure I'm getting my two cents in. And I would just feel more comfortable if Terrence—"

A small, soft, perfectly manicured hand, with each nail painted like Warhol's soup cans, came to rest on top of mine, weighing it down until it came to rest on top of the notebooks stacked up in my lap.

Until that moment, I hadn't even realized that I'd been gesticulating like a malfunctioning armature robot, frantically cutting through the air with each word, letting my stress carry me away.

"Addie and Marketing are perfectly capable of doing their own jobs, Scout," Leelah said, her voice full of empathy. Care.

"Just like I'm capable of running my own numbers and Terrence is capable of running his own tests. And if you weren't trying to do everyone's job on top of your own, maybe you wouldn't be so freaked out about failing all the time. Maybe you'd have more time for sex and friends and lunch and Hudson."

It was so tempting. I'd already gone this far, after all.

But old habits died hard. And old fears died harder.

What if, one day, after BuzzCorp shuttered and I was the laughingstock of the mechanical engineering world (again), and Lloyd Exeter was dancing on my grave (*again* again), I looked back on this moment and regretted my choice? What if letting myself go on a date with Hudson was the decision that ultimately ruined everything?

"I'm responsible for The Fantasy, Leelah. Everyone's jobs. Everyone's futures. Clara's money. The investors' money. My own reputation. I can't risk it."

She assessed me. All around us, workers laughed and chatted and devoured oversized sandwiches and coffees, enjoying the sunshine tainted by the first throat-clear of fall. But she did not look at anything but me. I was under her microscope.

For years, I'd looked at people like complex machines. Ones that I could figure out and navigate if only I could study them long and hard enough.

Was this what other people felt when I looked at them? Like they were being unraveled?

"Now, I know this is going to sound cheesy," she began, thinking through each word before carefully releasing it like a test balloon between us. "But you are your most important experiment. One that you'll be iterating on forever. You have a handsome, smart, thoughtful, funny—if a little personally reserved, for reasons we have yet to discover—guy who wants to spend time with you. Dating is just data. You find out what you like, what you don't, what makes you happy, *who* makes you happy. That's *data* for the experiment that is your life. Data that could make your time on this rock better. You don't have to go steady with him. You don't have to get emotionally involved. But you should let yourself *try*. At least for the purposes of science."

Her microscope intensified around me. I struggled under its white-hot light.

"Just think about it. You'd never deny yourself the opportunity to learn about anything else. Why deny yourself *this*? Especially when you can let the rest of us pick up the slack. To help you at work so you don't have to worry so much. So you can have a real existence outside of these walls."

I was used to people knowing more than me. About pop culture, about driving cars, about how to interact with other human beings.

I was *not* used to people knowing more about science than me. Or at least seeing science in a more accurate way.

She was right, of course. I did owe it to myself to learn. To indulge my curiosity. After all, I'd never been on a date before—or anything that even *looked* like a date.

It was . . . nice to think of myself as an experiment to cultivate, to nurture, to feed and cherish.

I took such care with my experiments. Why didn't I ever take care of myself?

Besides, Hudson *had* taken my virginity. Why not my date virginity, too?

"And barring that," she said, tossing a piece of gum into her mouth, "I've read plenty of peer-reviewed articles that say work performance significantly improves when one has fresh air and exercise. What's mini golf if not highly concentrated fresh air and exercise, hm? You might actually be *imperiling* your work projects if you don't indulge this one little outing."

She popped her gum. I said nothing. She did me the solid of

changing the subject. With casual offhandedness, Leelah passed along tidbits of office gossip, pitched some ideas for a new twist on a sex machine we were brainstorming, and got in a few sharp digs about her ex-boyfriend for good measure. It was an unconventional lunch for me, but at least I didn't look down at my laptop anymore. At least I spent a good twenty minutes handling something *other* than work.

That pleasant joy ended when, horror of horrors, Hudson showed up to interrupt our little luncheon.

"Hi, Scout. I—" He waved at me, then stopped when he saw that I wasn't alone. For the first time, I got to see the subtle differences in how Hudson treated me versus other people. He was always polite to a fault, but when he saw Leelah, a veneer fell over him. It wasn't fake, per se, but there was a shift. It was the difference between the cozy warmth of a fireplace and the artificial hum of a space heater.

"And Leelah, it's so good to see you. How have you been?"

Leela waggled her eyebrows. "Hello, loverboy."

Hudson tipped his head, but there was no mistaking the beginnings of a blush at the tips of his ears. I swooped in to rescue him, tossing her candy bar wrapper at her.

"Can you be somewhere else, please?" I asked.

She took the dismissal in confident stride. "Sure." Before she left, though, she tossed Hudson a piece of her gum. Spearmint. "Take this. You'll need it. You're welcome, by the way."

He blinked at her. "For what?"

"For whatever is about to happen here and whatever amazing sex you get out of it later. Ciao."

And then, she was gone. With a flounce of her oversized Fleetwood Mac sweater, she disappeared, leaving Hudson and me alone.

"Sorry about her," I said.

"Don't worry about it. I interrupted."

“No, we were wrapping up.”

“Cool.”

Everyone around us carried on their conversations. The food pop-ups slung their final meals. A fountain trickled slowly. All as if to highlight our awkward silence.

But then, at the exact same moment, we said:

“Anyway, I wanted to apologize for this morning—”

“Were you trying to ask me out?”

His eyes widened. He’d been caught.

“I didn’t want to scare you off. I know we talked about getting to know each other better, but I don’t want you to think I’m rushing or pushing you. It’s one thing to be confident in the bedroom, you know, but another thing to ask a girl out, believe it or not, especially when she’s said she isn’t interested in that kind of thing—”

“Yes. I want to go.”

I forced the words out, but as soon as they were, I realized how much I loved saying them. Yes, it was terrifying, thinking that I was, little by little, relaxing my white-knuckle grip on all aspects of my life. But hey . . . it was *one* outing. One night with Hudson that wasn’t one hundred percent focused on sex.

Problem: I’ve never been on a real date before. And Leelah was right. That was a missing data set.

Proposed Solution: Go on a date with Hudson. Simple as that.

Hudson eyed me, surprised by the sudden change of heart. “But what about work?”

“I’m researching better work-life balance. Among other things. Cursory exploration of the studies in this area have informed me that it’s beneficial for my in-office performance.”

His chuckle moved through my entire body, making me glow from the inside out. He liked it when I talked nerdy. “Whatever you say, boss.”

Boss. The way he said it—or maybe the way I heard it—came across like *beautiful* or *lovely* or *woman I can’t wait to kiss again.*

My walls shot up again. This would not be another Lloyd Exeter situation. I would not let myself fall for a guy in the office. I would not give someone else the power to destroy me. Even if Hudson somehow didn't ruin my career like Lloyd had, he was going to leave at the end of his contract. No point in getting attached. Sex was fine. Surface-level enjoyment was perfectly acceptable. Feelings were not.

"But let me reiterate . . . This is one date. We aren't dat*ing*. The rest of our rules and guidelines are still in effect. I just want to make that clear."

A muscle in his jaw twitched, causing his smile to falter for the briefest of moments. After all my study of him, I still didn't know what that slight gesture meant. "Crystal."

22

Sex on the First Date

So how did you come up with the idea for this little outing?" I asked, staring up at the faux UFO looming overhead.

"Easy. I thought to myself, hey, what's the least sexy first date? And thus, mini golf."

Minnie's Golf was a kitschy roadside attraction–inspired mini golf course tucked away in a Dallas suburb. With holes themed to everything from dinosaurs to kaiju battles to alien invasions to giant robot attacks, it was basically built for someone like me.

Only one small problem.

"I've never golfed before. Miniature or otherwise."

"Really?"

"Yeah, believe it or not, my parents didn't exactly consider knocking a ball into the Creature from the Black Lagoon's mouth vital to my education."

"You don't talk about them much. What were they like?"

There was a reason I didn't talk about my parents. Actually, there were countless reasons. So I offered the bare minimum. Lied by omission. "They're great. I wouldn't be where I am today without them."

"That doesn't sound like the whole story. What's going on behind those very nice, very sanitized words, I wonder?"

"They put me through school and spent every spare second they had helping me go over flash cards or rushing me to extra classes or buying me more books," I said, my defensive hackles rising. No one had ever called me out on my bullshit about my family before. "I'm only this person because of them."

"And that person is brilliant. But she's never mini-golfed before."

Despite his breezy tone, the meaning was clear.

They'd given me an education. But they hadn't necessarily given me a life.

I'd always known that. But hearing it reflected to me in Hudson's understated way nearly knocked me on my ass.

Remembering Leelah's experiment suggestion, I filed away this emotional information for later examination. It was more data. That's all.

"Come on, then," I said, smiling. "Show me how it's done."

He led me over to the check-in booth, which, in keeping with the retro theme, was styled like an old drive-in movie ticket stand. The lady behind the counter, with her long silver braids and collection of mood rings on every finger and her name tag with MINNIE written on it, looked exactly like you'd expect an eccentric mini-golf-owning lady to look . . . but she wasn't smiling.

As he booked our game, though, I watched his small talk slowly open Minnie up. By the time she disappeared behind a door to retrieve our clubs and balls, she wasn't just smiling. She was beaming.

Hudson, I realized, was a friendship whisperer. I'd never seen him meet a stranger, never seen him treat anyone with anything less than extreme kindness. It was uncanny, his way of making people feel at home with him.

"You're staring," Hudson said, as we waited for our clubs.

"You're hot," I replied.

"Why thank you. But that's not why you're staring."

No, it wasn't. I was staring because I'd never met anyone like him, and I didn't think I ever would meet anyone like him again.

And the knowledge of him leaving at the end of this contract suddenly felt not like a fail-safe, but like a threat.

Picking another line of inquiry, I followed my curiosity about him to safer discourse. How did a person become a Hudson Bailey?

I had no idea. But for the first time, I wanted more than sex from him. I wanted . . . him. This didn't feel like before, when I wanted to pick him apart and dissect him to better understand him as a subject of scientific fascination. This felt personal. Intimate.

"I just don't really know you. Like, anything about you."

"You know plenty."

"Not really. You are so good at making me feel like it's okay to talk about *myself*, but you never talk about *yourself*."

His gaze shifted.

"What would you like to know?"

"Everything."

He shrugged. "Sounds very personal, Scout. I thought you weren't into the personal stuff."

"I told you. I'm experimenting."

It wasn't an argument or anything, but his resistance to telling me more was clear.

He brightened, though, when Minnie returned to the booth with our pink and green golf clubs and their corresponding, color-coordinated balls.

"I got good news and bad news for you kids," she said. "Good news is, these are brand-new clubs. Bad news is, they've got a slight bend in 'em, so I'm going to have to send them back. I tossed the old ones, so these are the only ones we got. Sorry 'bout that."

We both dismissed the apology. After all, it was only a game. I took green. Hudson took pink.

It was instinctive, as if we both knew that the other was going to pick the non-obvious choice.

After collecting the tools of our temporary trade, we wandered to the practice hole so I could get my bearings. This was a simple one with less theming than its official counterparts. At one end was a clown head with sharp teeth, very *Killer Klowns from Outer Space*. Hudson went first, showing off so I could observe his technique.

"What's with the sudden change of heart?" he asked, lining up his first shot. "You seemed pretty keen on keeping me at arm's length."

"I'm trying to look at myself like a project. Giving myself permission to stretch and learn more about myself."

"Clever."

He bent over to place the ball on the green, then positioned himself with his club. I made no secret of the fact that I was checking out his ass the entire time.

But . . . I also couldn't let his perfect, carved-by-Michelangelo ass distract me from my goal.

Plu-doonk. The ball landed perfectly in the hole. Was that a birdie? An eagle? What was with the confusing names?

Then it was my turn. I prepared to shoot, but Hudson came up behind me, slipping his hands down my arms. He stood close enough that if this were a real golf school and he a real teacher, he definitely would have gotten complaints from the husbands of his desperate-housewife clientele.

Unbidden, my back arched so my ass brushed more firmly against him. My mind temporarily blanked.

This was what we in the scientific research industry called an unexpected setback. His touch was enough to distract me from almost anything.

Not that you could blame me. Our bodies fit perfectly together. To borrow another scientific framing, for two perfectly matched people to find each other on a planet of almost eight billion people was an anomaly, and such an anomaly required extensive study.

With a flex of our bodies, we tapped my neon-green golf club against my ball, sending it sailing . . . straight into the water feature of the next closest hole.

Okay, so maybe couples weren't meant to mini-golf together. We stepped apart, and the sudden post-touch clarity got me.

"You know, you're hiding just as much as I am," I insisted. "Maybe even more. Being nice and pleasant is not a substitute for being *you*. Let me see you. I've been trying to do that. With you and Leelah. Maybe you should try it, too."

"Why? You want to ditch me when my contract is up?"

Every so often, he got this *air* about him. A melancholy that pierced his otherwise sunshiny persona.

"That doesn't mean we can't have fun now."

"And what if you don't like me once you know more about me?" he said quietly.

I promised myself I wouldn't let my heart complicate this fling with Hudson. And I stood by that.

However, I also didn't fail.

Failing would be to let this man think I didn't like him. If he walked away from our relationship—such that it was—truly believing someone couldn't both see him *and* care for him, I wouldn't just *fail*. I would consider myself a *failure*.

"That's it. I'm instituting new mini-golf rules," I said. "Winner of each hole gets a prize."

"I'm listening. What's at stake? Sexual favors?"

"Information. I get lowest score, you have to tell me a fact about you. Of my choosing."

He raised an eyebrow. "And what do *I* win?"

It was nearing six o'clock, which meant the course was switching from family friendly to adults only. A gaggle of kicking and screaming children passed us on their way out, so I whispered my filthy suggestion. His face lit up.

"All right, you're on."

23

Fore-play

By the time we reached the climactic hole (pun absolutely not intended), I'd made nine perfect shots and come in at two par on the other nine.

Hudson, for all the fun he was having, did not fare so well. At the Mars-themed green, with its rotating rover protecting the cup, it took him twelve tries to finally get it in.

He was, it turned out, excellent at getting a hole in one in *my* hole, but not so great at any others.

Which meant that I'd gotten eighteen uninterrupted answers to my most pressing questions, all while he ogled me from behind as I bent over to line up my shots.

He grew up in rural Kentucky. His parents divorced when he was five. Without reliable childcare, they both took him on their dates with potential new partners. He didn't resent that fact, but he did wonder what effect it had on him growing up.

After the fallout over his and his girlfriend's tech security company, he took his buyout, freelancing and working on contract so he'd never be tied to a desk again.

(Briefly, on that point, I wondered if this was part of his *I don't want people looking too closely at me* thing. Did he *really* not want a desk job? Or did he just say that so he could be surface-level agreeable, survive a brief stint at a company, and leave before anyone could meet the man beneath the friendly persona?)

He wanted a dog but couldn't get one with his consulting schedule. His home base was a tiny apartment in rural Colorado, but usually, if he had time between jobs, he traveled instead of going back there.

He loved driving, the mountains, hole-in-the-wall restaurants with questionable health ratings but amazing dishes, and cookies with potato chips in them.

Every month, since he moved too often to properly volunteer anywhere, he spent one Saturday going through GoFundMe and anonymously donating to random projects or fundraisers. He'd sent sixteen different high school marching bands to Disney World that way.

When I asked him what he thought his greatest failure was, or his greatest weakness, I waited for him to feed me bullshit like "I care too much" or "I give other people everything and they barely give me anything in return." You know, one of those weaknesses that's really a humblebrag. Instead, he finally copped to my accusation.

"I never really thought of this as a weakness, but maybe you're right. Maybe I'm too afraid to let people get close. I like to be liked. But I don't want to be examined. Whether or not they mean to, people always judge. I'm afraid of coming up short."

His body language told me that follow-up questions would not be permitted on a mini golf course. However, it still baffled me that a friendship whisperer who could melt the hardest-hearted engineer was afraid of people not liking him.

Out of respect for his boundaries, I didn't push further on that particular point. It didn't feel fair to keep digging at a wound that had clearly not yet become an eschar. Lighter topics followed.

I learned favorite foods (pineapple, bacon, and hot honey pizza), dream job (being a vineyard dog or a bookstore cat), love language ("That's ridiculous pseudo-science peddled by religious weirdos . . . but that being said, words of affirmation"), greatest accomplishment (restarting after leaving his company), the last playlist he listened to (a collection of upbeat one-hit wonders, because he doesn't want anyone to ever be forgotten, not even cheesy 1980s bands), and his most embarrassing moment ("I shit myself on a bus once after being discharged from the hospital. There was this medicine they gave me that wrecked my stomach and I was too poor to get a cab at the time, so I took the bus but it took too long—hey, stop laughing! You asked!")

I'd also learned something I long suspected.

I loved making him laugh.

Just like he was laughing when, at the final hole, he pointed at me and exclaimed, "You're a total mini golf sharp!"

The final hole was a rocket ship, impressive in size, scale, and theme, pulled straight from a 1950s B-movie. Its central door was carved out on one side, so you could see the hole you were shooting for. The inside was painted black with thousands of stick-on glow stars.

"I'm a mathematician," I retorted.

As it turned out, mini golf, a game that literal children played for fun, *was* incredibly easy. It was even easier when one had three advanced degrees in the sciences and math. Mini golf was nothing more than angles, force, momentum, and watching your date bend over in tight pants. Four things at which I excelled.

"Next time, I'm taking you to an arcade and I'm going to absolutely destroy you in *Dragon's Lair*."

"All right, computer nerd. I'll make sure to lose as graciously then as you are right now."

The two of us wandered around the grand decor of this final

green, taking our time before shooting our last shots. Maybe because it looked so cool, this space-age scene tucked away in a random suburb. Or maybe because neither of us wanted the date to end.

"It's not so bad, right?" I asked. "Telling me about yourself. Look, I haven't run away screaming yet. I still like you. Maybe even more now that I heard about that bus story."

The tips of his ears went pink.

"All I'm saying is," I continued, "I think you can trust me. And I think you should. At least enough to let me in and know you better."

"Yeah, well . . . Same."

Called out. I tipped my head in a *touché* gesture.

"All right, then. I'll give you a freebie. What do you want to know about me?"

"What would your dream date be? Assume that you can have anything you want—sky's the limit."

I'd never get over the weirdness of it—that I could handle sex no problem, but the minute he was nice to me, I instantly went lightheaded and dizzy.

"I've never thought about that. I guess it's sort of like my virginity. I never thought about how I would lose it because I never felt like I, you know, would get anything special," I said honestly. Then, as we looked up at the sunset, I felt my head tip sideways onto his shoulder. "But this . . . this is pretty close to what I'd imagine."

"Mini golf?" he asked. I could almost hear the raised eyebrow at that one.

"Sure. A weird sci-fi setting, a new game that I absolutely rule at, and a hot guy staring at my ass all night? If I get sex and bagels in the morning, then I'm pretty sure we hit the exacta on this one."

"Bagels."

"Mm-hmm. Everything with garden veggie cream cheese.

Or blueberry with butter, if I'm feeling dessert-y." Spinning away from him, I stepped across the green to inspect the rocket ship closer, almost tripping over several "moon rock" obstacles on the way. "Listen, I didn't get to go to birthday parties or playdates. For a long time, food was the only fun I got to have. Sometimes, it still is. I have very high standards."

"I'll keep that in mind. Now, about that sex part . . ."

As if summoned by a sex siren, he was on me in an instant. Throwing aside his club, he stood behind me, dragging his hands up my hips. The gesture might have looked innocent and flirty to anyone passing by, but his energy—as well as his cock, which pressed proudly into my backside—radiated want.

"We can't really have sex here," I giggled.

"That *was* what you offered me if I won. It stands to reason that you'd be interested in such a thing."

The giggles continued. *Really.* Imagine it. Us. Having sex. *Here.* It had been a joke! . . . Right?

Hudson turned me around.

"Haven't you noticed how quiet it's gotten around here since I went to get more balls after the Black Lagoon green? I *might* have paid off the owner to let us have the place to ourselves."

I *had* noticed the quiet, but I'd thought it was one of those rom-com-y *it felt like we were the only two people on earth* things, not a real phenomenon.

"You didn't," I breathed.

"Your physiological response," he said, reminding me about our recent kink experiment, "indicated you're excited by sex in public. This felt like good training wheels. Outside, in public, but no risk."

My stomach twisted with a fierce wave of lust. He was right. The slut in me *did* like the prospect of sex in public, but the louder Goody Two-shoes in me screamed that it was a terrible idea. There were too many unknowable factors, too much unmitigated risk.

But if he'd accounted for those factors and risk . . .

"C'mon," Hudson said, taking my hand in his and leading me toward the rocket ship.

Inside, the shoddy construction was well on display. The walls were cardboard-thin, the starry-sky painting on the walls and ceiling was chipping in places, and the conical design meant that every breath echoed. Disney World, this was not.

But the shape also meant that the walls were curved at such a degree that if you were in the deep bend of the wall, you couldn't be seen from the outside. Partly public, partly private.

Hudson had learned one of my kinks, remembered, heard the serious desire beneath my earlier joke offer, and found the perfect place for me to explore that safely.

I cleared my throat to keep the emotion out of it. "I can't believe you did this."

"I think much weirder people have had much weirder sex in here. Minnie was happy just to get paid for it."

Laughing, I fiddled with the cuffs of my sweater. I was going to do this. I was going to have sex with Hudson in a mini-golf rocket ship.

My eyes drifted to his big hand, which was wrapped around his golf club. A thought occurred. A ridiculous premise, really.

It was so dirty. So unexpected.

And yet, I wanted it. I was instantly wet. Not just wet. *Soaking.*

"Can I be vulnerable for a second?" I asked.

"Please do."

"She said she has to return the new golf clubs, right?"

"Mm-hmm."

"How much do you think it would cost to buy this one off her?" I asked, approaching and letting my fingers brush over his. "I don't think anyone else will want to use it once we've done what I have in mind."

A wrinkle appeared between Hudson's eyes. His glasses slipped down his nose slightly. Then he relaxed when he realized my meaning.

I didn't want him to fuck me. Not with his cock, anyway.

"Think of this as part of your sex toy education," I explained. "Anything that *can* be a dildo likely *will* be used as a dildo at some point. It can be instructive to experiment with nontraditional toys. One never knows what one might learn. What do you think? Do you want to try it? And I mean *really* think about that before you answer. Don't just say yes because I want it."

His smile was infectious. I knew whatever was about to come out of his mouth was the truth. "Scout, how could I say no? You know what they say about having sex in a rocket ship, don't you?"

I cringed as the joke came flying at me, too fast to evade. "Don't—"

"It's outta this world."

Eye roll of the century. "Shut up."

"Make me."

So I did.

24

Going Clubbing

Given our relative exposure, taking our clothes off wasn't an option. So as we attacked each other with kisses, our hands traveled straight to the source of each other's pleasure. I grappled with his belt, desperate to free his already ragingly hard cock. He did the same for me, hiking up my dress and exposing my embarrassingly average cotton panties. I didn't have time to be self-conscious, though. All I could think about was him touching me. From the speed with which he ripped those panties down my legs, I could tell he was on the same page.

He roughly spun me around. Hands braced on the wall of stars. Back arched. Tits begging to be touched. With a little nudge against my ankle, he also spread my legs.

My pussy was bare and open. Wetness slathered my thighs. And if anyone happened by, they would see me like this. Desperately at his mercy.

Then I heard the foil crackle of a condom wrapper behind me, freed from his wallet. He slipped the prelubricated condom over the handle of my club, then positioned it at my entrance. The makeshift dildo waited patiently at my wet hole. With its soft grip covered in a condom, it was unthreatening—but exciting.

"Are you ready?" he asked. "Tell me what you want. Let me give you what you want, Scout."

I nodded, biting down hard on my bottom lip. "I want to feel dirty."

Grabbing my breast, he used it for leverage so he could work the club inside me in one hard thrust. I cried out, not out of pain but surprise. He must have heard the difference, because he continued using the club on me, pounding it so hard into my cunt that the sounds of my wetness echoed high above us, reinforcing every rough entry into my tight center.

"You like that, huh? Being pinned up against the wall and used?" he asked, breathing against my back, never once letting up on the pace.

"Yeah."

"Anyone could walk in here, see you getting fucked. Aren't you so filthy? You want to be watched? You want people to see that you're so cock-hungry you'll use anything to get off?"

I bit my lip to stifle my groans. God, he felt so good. I decided to play the game. The good-girl-goes-bad game. "No—"

He began stroking his cock. The pre-cum splashed against my ass.

"I think you do. I think you want someone to see you taking it, moaning for me. Begging for it. Maybe they'd even take their cock out and stroke it to the sight of you. Or put their hands beneath their skirts, playing with themselves as they watched you get fucked. How would you like that, hm? Someone cumming to the sight of your wet cunt dripping all over this toy of ours?"

I could feel his thrusts inside me fall out of rhythm. He was going to cum soon, all while he fucked me with a golf club. I tightened around it, eager to relish every inch of the staff for as long as I could. "I'm not—"

Every instinct told me to touch myself. I even had two miniature vibrators in my purse, begging to be used. Problem was, there was no way to do that without losing my position against the wall. All I could do, then, was buck myself back onto the foreign object inside me. Savor the swell of it inside me, stroking my G-spot with every breach Hudson made. It was torture. It was delicious. It was everything.

"You get one taste of cock and suddenly you're a slut, aren't you? You can't stop cumming even if it means using this thing to force an orgasm out of you."

"Yes. Yes, I am. I'm a slut—"

His orgasm came hot and fast. His scream of pleasure was so loud against the cavernous, curved walls that my ears rang with the force of the echoes.

He moaned my name as his cum lashed my bare skin. My swollen clit twitched with the unfulfilled desire to cum myself.

Somehow, though . . . not cumming made the entire experience hotter. Dirtier. I'd been marked by him—and left with a waiting pussy and pleading cunt as a thank-you.

As he came down from his orgasm, his hand and the club stilled. That wouldn't do. I started throwing my ass back, fucking myself on the thing as he held it firmly in place. Again and again, it struck my G-spot, and when Hudson wrenched his free hand from my breast and directed his energies onto my clit, I knew I was a goner.

My screams filled the rocket ship all around us. My cunt contracted around the golf club deep inside me. And my eyes filled with stars as an orgasm hit me with the strength of a thousand solar flares.

Once I returned to earth, Hudson slipped our makeshift toy out of me and held me close to his chest. But when I eventually peeled away from him, I was still twitchy. Every brush of my legs against each other sent a new twinge of debilitating aftershocks through my body.

Skin flushed, I pulled my panties up from their resting place around my ankles.

"You don't want to clean up?" Hudson asked, gesturing to the cum on my ass. He tucked his own wet cock away without a second thought.

"Sort of hot, isn't it? Walking out of here still sticky from you . . ."

Slick underwear clinging to my skin, I readjusted my clothes. Just because the owner knew we'd been fucking in here didn't mean I had to *look* like we had.

"Did you like that?" he asked.

"You were very sexy. And for your first time using a dildo on someone, you were exceptional."

"Beginner's luck. Hopefully you'll give me plenty of opportunities to practice."

I lifted one side of my mouth in a half-hearted smirk. "Don't worry. I'm still very happy to train you for your future girlfriends."

He captured my chin in his hand. So swift it made me dizzy. "Scout?"

"Hm?"

"I don't want to think about any other women when I'm with you, okay?"

That shouldn't have made me melt. But it did. "Deal."

THE FIRST THING I saw when I opened my eyes the next morning?

A still-steaming cup of hot chocolate, the latest edition of *Popular Science*, and an everything bagel from Bernie's, slathered in veggie cream cheese.

He'd remembered. He'd remembered my perfect date. And after yesterday, when I said I didn't feel like I would ever get my perfect date, that I wasn't a girl to whom things like that happened, he'd served it up to me on a platter.

The bathroom door opened, and Hudson stepped out, resplendent in nothing but a towel and shaggy wet hair.

"Sorry," he said, ducking his head. "I'm an early riser. I didn't wake you up, did I?"

"I usually am, too. Twenty-six years, I wake up at five thirty like clockwork. Then, all of a sudden, I get some dick and it's like I don't even recognize myself. Sleeping in, making friends, going on dates, asking boys to come up to my room for a nightcap . . ."

"You know what they say. To be fucked is to be transformed."

"I thought that was to be *loved* is to be transformed."

"Same-same."

I laughed and drew the covers around me, suddenly shy at the word *love* being thrown around. Stupid slip-up. I wouldn't make it again.

"Thanks for breakfast," I said later, once he'd coaxed me out from beneath the duvet. "You remembered."

"Don't mention it."

As I sat up, the covers slipped away, revealing my chest. Hudson's gaze wandered.

Must have been a real show, considering ten seconds later I chomped into my bagel, spilling garlic flakes down my body.

"You've got a good memory," I said as I chewed.

Slowly, he crossed the room and rifled around for his overnight bag, which he'd oh-so-smoothly brought in last night during our nightcap. "I've got a terrible memory, actually. Deadlines, phone calls I need to make, my library card number. No way I remember any of that. But I learned that about myself years ago, so now I write everything down in my Notes app. My calendar is literally documented to the minute. And when I meet someone, when I like them, I write things down to help me remember."

"Likes everything bagels with garden veggie schmear."

Or like fucking me dirty against a mini golf rocket ship because of one offhand remark made during your little kink experiment.

"Don't forget your dessert breakfast. Blueberry bagel with butter."

He gestured to a brown paper bag on my bedside table, which I hadn't seen before. My pulse fluttered.

"But there are other things, too. If someone tells me their birthday or this movie that I 'have to see' or what baseball team is their favorite, I just jot it down. That way, I keep on top of our friendship." He scrolled down his Notes app, the lighted screen illuminating his handsome face. "Like, Terrence is a level 82 mage in *World of Warcraft*. Addie's mother makes the best chili momo in the world, apparently. Clara's home FC is Tottenham. I just . . . This is a really messed-up world. It's so easy to feel lonely and miserable, like you're totally forgotten by everyone else. I don't want anyone to ever experience that if I can help it. I always want people to feel comfortable. Considered. Cared about."

He trailed off. The weight of his words hung in the air, heavy as storm clouds. I'd never thought of Hudson as a frivolous person by any stretch of the imagination, but this added a new depth to him I hadn't expected.

I *liked* that depth. He wasn't just a happy-go-lucky golden retriever of a guy. He was intentional with his kindness. He recognized that he wasn't perfect, wanted to be better, and found a way to be good to people anyway.

It made me like him even more, which was quickly becoming a recurring theme—and a huge problem. *He's leaving at the end of his contract and you don't have the time, capacity, or experience necessary for a relationship.*

It worried me, too.

He refused to pick dinner on our first date. Refused to even give input. He refused to say whether he'd be into pegging. He never took the lead on anything. He always wanted to do what I wanted to do. He'd dropped a not-insignificant amount of money to rent out a mini golf course so we could fuck on it *and* bought the slightly wonky club we'd used as a sex toy.

All just to make me happy.

Did anyone do the same for him?

And, given what he'd told me about not wanting people to get too close, would he even accept it if they did?

"You said you're afraid that people won't like you if they get to know you, Hudson. But the exact opposite has happened."

He could no longer meet my gaze. I pierced the intimate moment in the only way I knew how: terrible humor.

"So, you want people to feel comfortable. Considered. Cared about. The three C's. Or four. You forgot *cocked*."

A hungry but playful look overtook him. On instinct, I tossed my bagel aside. Prowling up the bed, he moved along my body until I had no choice but to sprawl out beneath him. He brushed my nose with his own. "There's only one person I want to feel cocked right now, and that's you."

"Well," I said, nudging his head down toward my now aching cunt, "why don't you start by being considerate and caring about me first?"

"My pleasure."

No, the pleasure would be all mine. Spreading my legs, he gently kissed my left thigh. Then my right. He took his time. Dragging his nose along my folds. Breathing me in deeply.

I fisted the sheets. I didn't want teasing. I wanted his mouth around my clit and a dildo deep inside me. I wanted to cum. I wanted him to make me cum—

That was when someone knocked on the door.

No, not knocked. *Pounded.*

We both stilled. "Landlord?" Hudson breathed against my folds.

"Definitely not. I own my unit."

I moved against him, wanting more friction, wanting his tongue to part my lips and give my clit the attention it deserved.

Instead, I got more knocking.

Hudson raised his head. I took his hand and placed it on my waiting pussy, trying to entice him back. No dice. "Maybe you should check it out. Could be Girl Scouts."

"Girl Scout cookie season isn't for another three months," I snapped. "Don't be ridiculous."

"I love that you know that."

"It's literally more important to me than Christmas. Ugh, I do *not* feel like answering the door right now. Forget them."

My hand drifted down to the knot of his towel, which was keeping him from being fully exposed to me. He groaned and twisted out of my grip.

"Fine, *I'll* go check it out."

He planted a kiss on my forehead.

"Thanks," I grumbled, not feeling particularly grateful.

Leaving through my half-open frosted French doors, Hudson disappeared. I dropped my head back onto the pillow and let my eyes close. By the ticking of the clock and the padding sound of his footfalls across the poured concrete floors, I could calculate his stride length, how many steps he'd taken, and both how long and how many steps it would take for him to reach the front door. The math played in my head like music from someone else's balcony, sketching out in front of me in soft inclines and reversals of quiet intimacy.

It felt right, having him here. Using my towels. Walking across my floor.

Opening my front door.

"Oh, hello?"

"Who the hell are you?"

The quiet comfort of universal math shattered at the sound of that second voice.

I'd never moved so fast. Before Hudson even had a second to formulate a full, coherent sentence, I was on my feet, in a robe, and tearing out of my room like hell was chasing behind me.

Which, of course, was ridiculous. Hell wasn't behind me. Hell was standing at my front door, looking between the half-naked man and their half-naked daughter with profound disappointment.

"Mom! Dad! What are you doing here?"

25

Meet the Parents . . . of the Girl You're Fucking

A bitter, irrational part of me wanted to scream at Hudson. *This* was why I didn't talk about my parents, like he'd tried to do the day before at the mini golf park. Because they were like uber-Beetlejuices. They didn't need to be invoked three times. If I even *thought* about them for too long, they appeared out of nowhere.

Carol "Carrie" Love Porter was a short, spindly woman who lived in Chico's petites businesswear. She had an unfussy, blunt bob, which was always pinned back with two twin tortoiseshell clips. My father, Bill Porter, was a tall, generically white man with bushy eyebrows and the disposition of a disgruntled bank manager. Until I'd gotten my job at GalacticSolutions, my mother clerked for the local school board, and my father managed a small building and loan. After I'd started working for Lloyd, they both retired early, lived off my salary (hey, they'd gotten me to a half-million-dollar-a-year job by the time I was twenty-four; I owed them), and enjoyed life in quiet and comfort in a Connecticut golf course community. Once I'd been fired, they both went back to work but graciously accepted a portion of my severance and settlement package so they could do so only part time.

I loved them so much. They were my parents. But every time I saw them, I just felt like a failure. And seeing them here, now, rattled me back to square one. Why had I been trying so hard to expand my horizons again? Mom and Dad would *not* approve.

Standing in the entryway, neither of them looked at Hudson. Apparently, he wasn't even worth their attention.

"Scout," Mom said by way of greeting. "Aren't you going to invite us in?"

"Of course! Sorry. Um, please—"

I gestured them inside, tightening my robe. Hudson took the momentary distraction to dash back to my bedroom. I knew it was so he could change, but still, I wanted to hiss *traitor* after his retreating form.

"Glad to see you're keeping this place in good shape," my dad said, picking up Hudson's coat, which we'd left on the couch en route to the bedroom last night.

"I didn't know you were coming," I said. *What, a girl can't leave a few pieces of clothing hanging around without being treated like a slovenly college mess?* "I would have tidied up a little bit."

"Don't apologize on our account," Mom said. "I just can't believe you live like this. All that settlement money and you can't get some help in to clean for you?"

"I'll have a look. I'm sure that I can find someone."

Reemerging from our room in a perfect boyfriend outfit of jeans, a button-up, and a sweater, Hudson came to my side and gave me a little squeeze around the middle. His firm touch brought me back to earth.

"You really should," Mom continued. "It's so bad for your mental health. And dirt and crumbs can build up, you know, which could tank the resale value. Not that you'll be selling, of course. I'm sure you want to keep that little job of yours for as long as humanly possible—"

"Carol," my dad muttered. "You haven't even said hello."

She hugged me. As always, it was bony and angular. Like she'd somehow missed every session in *how to have human contact* class. "Hello, dear."

"Hi, Mom. Hi, Dad."

I hugged him, too. He was marginally better at it, but not much.

It then occurred to me how little physical contact I'd ever had. My parents were emphatically *not* huggers. I didn't have boyfriends or partners or even casual hookups.

Hudson was the only person who'd ever held me.

Dad must have picked up on how quickly I returned to Hudson's side, because he gestured at my general state of undress. "I see you're keeping busy. Research for your work?"

"Uh, yeah," I said, trying to ignore the disdain dripping from Dad's tone when describing sex toys as *my work*. "A little. It's not a big deal, though. It's just—uh, this is . . ."

"Hudson Bailey. Her boyfriend."

Matching his perfect *meet the parents* outfit, Hudson flashed them both a winning smile, took one bold step forward, and extended his hand like it was the most natural thing in the world.

"Boyfriend," my mom repeated, sounding as skeptical as I felt.

He didn't let his demeanor falter, not even for a second. "It's sort of new."

You can say that again.

Neither of them stepped forward to accept his handshake, and I wanted to melt from embarrassment. He inched backward, away from the wall of indifference they jointly projected. "But yeah. It's great to meet you. Scout talks about you both all the time."

My mother turned on me, the wall of indifference crumbling like rubbled fallout all around my head. "You didn't tell us about this, Scout."

"You didn't tell me you were going to be in town. If you'd told me, I would have filled you in," I replied in what I thought was a mild tone. I should have known better.

Dad lashed out. "You're talking to your mother that way?"

"I'm sorry. I'm still a little groggy after, uh—"

"You just woke up?" Mom crowed. "It's nearly eight o'clock."

"I know." *Get control of this situation. You do it with awry experiments and tests all the time. Get control of your variables.* Taking a cue from Hudson, I slapped on a smile, pretending that I was excited to see them. "But what are you two doing in town? I didn't think I would see you until OFest in New York later this year."

Mom and Dad looked each other.

"Well."

"Well."

And then I knew. This was about fucking Lloyd Exeter. God damn him.

"Your father and I saw some chatter online. About you-know-who. We worried."

"That's so sweet of you . . ." I said through my clenched jaw. I didn't believe them. I just needed a way to get my parents out of here. "But I'm *really* doing fine. You didn't have to come all this way—"

"You've always been our first priority. Your mother and I know that this is a real ground shift. You need us."

"We kept it to ourselves because you would have told us to stay home," Mom explained.

There it is.

"You're way too dismissive of our help. If things are a mess," she continued, the implication clearly being that I'd caused another mess that my parents thought me incapable of cleaning up on my own, "then you'll need us."

Which, to be fair, was how I'd always thought of myself. A mistake made up of mistakes. That was why I worked so hard at

BuzzCorp, why I had such a hard time letting go. I didn't *want* to fail. Didn't *want* to feel like I couldn't do anything right except math and science experiments.

But . . . maybe that was changing. Maybe I was proving to myself that I wasn't as broken as I'd always believed.

"That was . . . so thoughtful. Thank you so much for looking out for me. I'm fine, though. I'm working through it. Hudson's been a great help." I looked up at him, surprised at how true the words were. But then, so they didn't think that I was suddenly cured by his magical dick, I added, "And so have my friends at work. Everyone's been so supportive."

Mom cast a cursory glance at Hudson. "Hm. You'll do dinner with us tonight, yes? Mazziano's? The usual time?"

"Yes."

We always had dinner at Mazziano's when they were in town. I hated the place, but I was always outvoted. Or I would have been if they'd let me vote.

What was different, however, was the guest list.

"Both of you," she added firmly.

No. No, no, no. There was no way I was forcing him to endure dinner with my parents. "I can go, for sure, but I don't know if Hudson—"

"I'd love to go," he interjected. Then, with an ease and speed I'd only seen in the best hotel managers, he pulled off a feat I'd never been able to accomplish: He got them the hell out of my house without them getting angry. "Wouldn't miss it for the world. You two take care now. Don't have too much fun sightseeing. I'm sure you both have so much you want to do while you're here. Wouldn't want you to miss a second. Mm-hmm! Good to see you. Can't wait for dinner. Yep, see you then!"

My parents disappeared on the other side of my closed front door. It was a miracle, the silence that followed. No raised voices, no condescending tones, no *are you going to talk to us that way*s.

Just Hudson, blinking across the room at me, the most worn-out I'd ever seen him.

"They're . . ." His eyes turned to calculators, running scenarios about what would hurt me the least. "A lot, aren't they?"

Understatement of the century. But I was more preoccupied with him. He'd gotten my parents off my back. "So are you, *boyfriend*."

"Sorry. I just thought it sounded better than friends with sexual benefits."

Long strides brought him across the room. He tipped his forehead down against mine. I held him tight. "You didn't have to do that," I said. "You didn't have to agree to dinner just because she demanded it. Or because you thought it would make me feel better."

"I know you think I'm just some weak-willed guy who will do whatever a pretty girl says," he teased, dancing around my harsher assessment that he faked it for everyone, not just me. "But that's not true. Sometimes it's about you and wanting to do things for you, specifically."

"Just seems like a lot of work," I muttered. "For a fuckbuddy."

His shoulders shifted, arms tensing around me slightly. "Fuckbuddy or not, just so we're clear, it's not a burden to care about you."

I dug my face into his shoulder. "You'd be the first person *ever* to think so."

26

Eating Out

"So, you saw tech's massive postpandemic layoffs and decided that the best use of your talent was to sell off your company?"

Don't look at me like that. I *tried* to get Hudson to back out of dinner. I told him he'd regret the decision to waste an entire evening with my parents.

He didn't listen.

Which was as touching as it was phenomenally stupid. And though I tried to take his *I want to be there for you* speech at face value, it was also concerning, given his propensity toward sidelining his own emotions and needs for other people.

"To be transparent with you, Mrs. Porter, the sale of my company put me in a position where work isn't necessary for me. It's why I am a contractor. It gives me more control over what I do and what I make."

Mazziano's was an old-school Italian restaurant deep in a downtown Dallas basement. The decor was somewhere between *Goodfellas* and an old-school Pizza Hut, with red-glass chandeliers, plastic-leather booths, and wineglasses that were always still slightly stained by the last user's lipstick. A jukebox in the corner played a rotation of Frank Sinatra's six worst songs on a constant loop, giving the entire place an annoying *It's a Small World*–style soundtrack.

I also *only* came here with my parents, dolled up for their inspection and their judgment, which meant that it could have been the greatest restaurant in the world, with Italian food that even the pope would love. But to me, it would always be cursed.

Even more cursed now, because it wasn't just the site of my humiliation, but Hudson's, too.

"If you don't *need* to, then why do you work at all?" my mom probed.

Hudson just dug in deeper to his chicken parm. "I like working. I like staying busy. I like being helpful."

Mom rolled her eyes. "What a waste. Scout, stop picking at that bread, you know our family carries our bread right in our pooches."

I was Pavlov's dog. I immediately put the bread down.

"I'm just surprised, is all," my father said, after slurping back a glass of the two-hundred-dollar bottle of red wine that he'd ordered and I'd be stuck paying for. "If you could do anything, if money's no object and you get to do whatever work you want, why sex toys?"

The waiter passing by stumbled when he heard that, but he made a valiant recovery. Hudson didn't bat an eyelash. Instead, he subtly picked up a piece of bread from the communal bowl and set it down on my plate.

"It's an interesting vertical. I knew nothing about it when I started. I'm industry agnostic, so when I start a new job, I want to go where I can learn and expand my skills."

"But it's such a ridiculous job, isn't it? We tell people Scout works with computer chips."

It shouldn't have surprised me. Of course they didn't tell people that their precious genius daughter was working in the personal pleasure industry. Still, I pointed out, "I'm not that sort of engineer, Mom."

"We know that, but they don't. This way we don't have to answer humiliating questions about your work."

Humiliating. I was humiliating. Suddenly even the bread didn't look appetizing. "Sure. I get it."

"I don't," Hudson said, shocking me right down to my core. He didn't *ever* disagree with people. At least not so openly. "And I don't think there's anything ridiculous about this job. Do you know how much good Scout's work does for people? Have you ever even bothered to ask her? She gives people autonomy over their own bodies. She helps people foster healthy relationships with their sexualities and with their partners. She's made more people happy than the rest of us at this table combined, probably many times over."

My father snorted. "Son, you don't have to flatter our daughter. We're very realistic about her prospects and her profession. Think about *your* career. Are *you* going to put this little dalliance in the personal pleasure industry on your résumé?"

"What, that I got to work with Dr. Scout Porter, one of the most talented engineers in the country?" He nudged me. "Yeah, you bet that's going on my résumé."

"Darling, don't fuss," Mom tutted in my father's direction. "He's clearly just having sex with her for the professional benefits. Let him lay it on thick if he thinks it will help him."

"Mom."

Not very much of a protest, but it was all I could muster. Not only because I couldn't believe she'd demanded it of Hudson, but because I couldn't believe she thought so little of me.

"It's better you find out now rather than later, Scout," she said flippantly, "and I know *you're* never going to ask the question because you don't want to hear the answer."

"I'm not his boss," I pointed out meekly, as if saying it quietly would stem her anger at being questioned. "I don't have hiring and firing or promoting power over him. Having sex with me wouldn't gain him any advantage."

"But you and Clara are close. He must know that."

"Clara doesn't even know he and I are together," I said. Not explaining why—that I was afraid of failing in front of her. "We're keeping everything low-profile."

"Ah, yes," my mother droned, eyes crinkling at the corners, "because that worked so well at your last job."

Breathe . . . breathe . . . "This isn't like that."

"How can you be so sure? Do you really think a girl like you can handle those decisions, Scout?"

"Why do you think so low of her?" Hudson snapped, in the harshest tone he'd used all night.

This was not friendly, guy-about-town Hudson. Not the perfect boyfriend material. Dad blinked. "Excuse me?"

"You think the only reason I'd sleep with your daughter is to get something out of her. That that's the only reason *anyone* would want to sleep with her."

"That's not what we said," Mom hedged.

"No, but it's what you implied, and I find that incredibly offensive."

"Are you going to let him talk to your parents that way?"

They all turned on me. I felt the gravity of their attention shift, but I picked at my veal piccata instead of answering. After all, Dad's response wasn't a denial. It was an evasion.

They *did* think I was stupid and naïve enough to be used that way. To them, my brain and heart were fundamentally broken. I was book smart but incapable of managing my own stuff. It had been that way since I was a kid, confirmed with the terrible Lloyd Exeter debacle, and reaffirmed every time they so much as spoke to me.

And they were right. I really was incapable of managing anything but engineering projects. That was why I'd held back for so long. Even now, I wasn't able to stand up for myself and my partner.

Failure. It might as well have been tattooed across my forehead.

After a moment of my silence, Hudson sighed. "I'm sorry. I didn't mean to offend you—either of you. But to be totally honest, I don't give a shit what you think or have to say. My loyalties are to Scout, and right now, you're both treating her very badly. I'm not going to listen to it."

Mom chuckled. "If you don't like the way we talk to our daughter, you can leave."

"That's the thing, ma'am. I can't. Because for some crazy reason, Scout listens to you, and I care about her too much to leave her in the company of people who will make her miserable."

Mom and Dad's stares burned holes through my curtain of hair and into my cheeks, turning them fire-red, but I didn't look up.

Eventually, Mom threw her napkin on the table and rose. "Fine, then. We'll go."

They collected their things in silence. But before they went, Hudson stopped them.

"I feel sorry for you both, you know."

My parents stilled. He tipped his wineglass in their direction, toasting their departure.

"You've had Scout for twenty-six years. And not once in those twenty-six years did you ever realize how special she was. Not special because of her intellect or the things she did. Just because of who she *is*. You missed out."

My heart, which had sunk to the floor more and more with each passing second in my parents' presence, suddenly lifted. It wasn't just that Hudson liked me. I think I knew that already. And it wasn't just that he defended me against them—though that didn't hurt.

It was that he recognized what I'd always known but never had the strength to say.

I was a person. I wasn't my grades or my degrees or the job I held. I was a *person* and my parents never got to know her.

Braving a glance up, I saw Mom's lip curl. She pulled her jacket tight around her shoulders. Her gaze slid disgustedly from Hudson's face to mine. "We'll talk about this later, Scout."

And then, they were gone. Leaving us with Frank Sinatra, half a bottle of wine, and the check.

Hudson and I finished our dinners in relative quiet. The air simmered with tension—not from me, but from him. He practically radiated with rage from his interaction with my parents, and I didn't know how to pierce it.

Once outside, we walked to his car, which was parked at the far edge of the near-vacant parking lot. We'd parked under the privacy of a tall, shady tree. It had seemed almost romantic around sunset. Now its fractal-patterned arms cast veiny shadows over Hudson's handsome face. Instead of ducking inside the car, though, he lingered for a moment, debating with himself. Finally, he asked me:

"Do you want to talk about what just happened in there?"

"I'm sorry about them—"

To my surprise, he flinched. "Sorry? Why the hell should you be sorry? They were *horrible* to you."

Ever since meeting Hudson, I'd learned that sometimes tenderness was even more painful than cruelty. No one had ever acknowledged the way my parents treated me, much less got outraged over it on my behalf.

I couldn't look too closely at that. I diverted to safer territory. "I shouldn't have let them talk to you that way."

"We're not talking about me, Scout. We're talking about you. How can you let them treat *you* like that?"

"They're my parents, Hudson," I said, as if it explained anything.

It didn't. I knew it. He knew it. And what was worse, we both realized what I *wasn't* saying.

That I'd agreed with them. I didn't trust myself. And shouldn't. Couldn't.

He fiddled with his glasses. "Look, I'm sorry if I made things uncomfortable for you back there. Really, I am. I hate . . . You know that I hate upsetting people."

"It's okay. I'm just sorry you broke your perfect *people like me* streak."

"Scout. I need you to understand." His gaze was ferocious. His lips curled into a snarl. He took a step forward, pinning me between his body and the car. It was the sexiest he'd ever been. "I will not apologize to them. And I do *not* give a shit if they like me or not."

This was a ground shift between us.

This man was constitutionally incapable of *not* being liked. He did everything in his power to earn people's love and affection. Even at his own peril.

And he'd thrown all of that away just because my parents were hurting me.

I didn't know what to do with that revelation.

So I brushed a lock of hair away from his forehead. "I don't want to talk about them. I want to talk about how hard you're going to fuck me in this car right now."

27

Dangerous Curves

Neither of us was in our right mind. I knew that. The correct thing to do would have been to buckle ourselves into our respective front seats, turn the radio so high we couldn't think, and process our emotions safely and separately before coming back together to discuss what the hell had just happened.

But the noise in my head was unbearable. The sounds of my inadequacy rang in my ears. Every fear I'd had about myself clawed its way out of the box I'd been locking it up in every time Hudson was around.

You can't do anything right. The Fantasy's launch is going to fail and it's all your fault. What made you think that you could have a normal existence—friends and sex—without ruining everything? Do you really think Hudson is in this for you? No, of course not. He's just here to take some girl's virginity and use her as a distraction while he's in town for a few weeks. Why are you letting him get into your emotions just like Lloyd did? How could you be so stupid a second time?

However, unlike most times when they swanned back into my orbit, Mom and Dad's sudden reappearance wasn't the *only* thing mixing me up.

Hudson was there, too. While instinct and history and my mother's harsh stare told me again and again that I was a failure, that there was nothing good about me but my skill with complex algebra and mechanical engineering, there were other parts of me just beginning to surface under Hudson's attentions. Now another voice whispered that my parents were wrong. That I was already proving myself capable of succeeding on my own terms. That I could have Hudson and Leelah and a life outside the office without it leading to catastrophe.

I wanted to listen to that voice. Or, at the very least, I wanted to shut up the first one.

So I threw open the car door.

Problem: Too many thoughts. Too many feelings. Too complicated.

Proposed Solution: Get Hudson to fuck my brains out.

"Hey—"

"Don't talk," I commanded, grabbing him by the arm.

He allowed himself to be pulled along into the back seat, laughing like this was all one big tease.

But it wasn't.

The door closed behind him with a *thunk*. The car's auto lights went out, submerging us in darkness. I yanked him close to me and attacked him with a kiss. This wasn't any of that gentle and safe crap we'd been toying with so far. This was a full-frontal assault, with teeth and fingernails. For a second, he tensed, but just as quickly, he melted again, groaning and answering every gesture of mine with a kiss or claw of his own.

Lying down along the back seat, I relished his hot, burning kisses and his hand running up my thigh. Yes, this was what I wanted.

Reaching into my purse, I grabbed a Circler. Instead of using suction like a Womanizer or vibrations like a Rabbit, this one had a simple handle finished off with what looked like the top of a pawn chess piece. It rotated at various speeds, controlled by simple, discreet buttons on the side of the toy.

My pulse and pussy throbbed at what was to come. I didn't want foreplay. I didn't want lingering glances or teasing. I wanted to be used. Reduced to sex and nothing else so I didn't have to think about the grating machinery of conflict currently threatening to go critical inside me.

"I want you to use this toy on me. And to fuck me," I instructed. "Hard and fast and like you don't give a shit about me. Fuck me until I can't string together a coherent thought. Now, take your cock out."

He froze over me, pulling away slightly. After shoving the toy into his hand, I took the opportunity to yank my dress over my head.

"But I *do* give a shit about you," he said.

My turn to freeze. Sure, he'd said as much before, but this was the first time I believed him. The first time it meant something. All those other instances, I could write off as his thoughtful nature. He liked me, yeah, but he liked *everyone*.

Tonight, however, he'd shown his hand. He liked me for real. More than other people. Enough to be disliked if it meant standing up for me.

And that was terrifying.

"Well. Pretend like you don't."

He watched me with a guarded expression, but his hands went to his fly anyway. His cock was incredibly hard already, straining against his zipper. "Why?"

"Does it matter?"

"Yes. To me, it does."

Really? What guy asked follow-up questions when a hot woman in her bra, underwear, and Keds asked him to bang her senseless?

"Do you want to talk about *your* feelings right now?" I asked.

"Only if you want to talk about yours."

It was another dodge. In any other scenario, I would have pounced on it. I would have told him that he needed to tell me the truth rather than what he thought I wanted to hear.

But he'd given me what I craved—permission to stop talking, thinking, and feeling. So, selfishly, I took it.

"Fuck that. I want you. So shut up and take me."

We went at each other again, our bodies colliding with raw, animalistic energy. He was rough, and I was rough right back, tearing at fabric and teething at skin. I rocked roughly against him, brushing his cock with my already desperate pussy. He answered, yanking my panties aside so he could explore my folds with his fingers, which immediately dripped with my wetness.

"Fuck, Scout," he breathed. "You're so—"

That was dangerously close to a compliment. I didn't want to hear it.

"Are you going to fuck me or not?"

Hudson, not wanting to miss a second of my wet, tightening cunt, positioned himself at my entrance, bringing The Circler down to my clit.

He pushed inside me. I screamed. Okay. So he *could* fuck me hard. And he was good at it.

Only it wasn't enough. Intrusive thoughts were slamming at the doors of my mind, begging to get in and ruin everything. And no matter how feral my own body became, Hudson didn't rise to the challenge, instead keeping a rough but measured pace and focusing The Circler on my clit in an equally frustrating manner.

"More," I choked.

Hudson did exactly the opposite, backing off. "I'll hurt you."

"I want it to hurt."

Where was the smug sex jerk who'd smacked my ass the other day? Sure, that had been mischievous, but still. I wanted more, I wanted deeper, I wanted harder, I wanted to see stars instead of my own failures.

"You never have before," he said cautiously. "Not like this."

"I thought we weren't talking right now. I thought we were fucking."

"But, Scout . . ."

I jerked against him, hoping to inspire a spark of anger or sexual frustration that would send him spiraling alongside me. "*Harder.*"

He stopped entirely. I responded by rocking back onto his cock with a fury, knifing myself onto him as The Circler worked miracles on my clit. Close. I was so close.

But it wasn't what I wanted. I didn't want to feel his soft and giving hands on me while I made myself cum. I wanted him to dominate me. To fill my brain with so much sex and lust that there would be room for nothing else.

"I don't think I want this anymore, Scout," he whispered, palming my hips to stop their movement. "The sex, I mean. *This* sex. And I don't think you do, either."

I eyed him, wild and desperate. My gut agreed. I *didn't* want this sex. I was always horny for him, but right now, I wasn't chasing sex, nor was I trying to connect with him. I was trying to do the very opposite—trying to put sex between us.

After a beat he murmured:

"Cosmos."

Our safe word hit me like a sonic blast. I went rigid. Still. Ashamed. Conflicted.

With a press of a button, The Circler died against my pussy. He withdrew from my body, and that—that sudden emptiness, paired with his unflinching gaze looming over me—knocked free everything I'd been trying to hide from these last few minutes.

My brain's limbic system went into overdrive, irritating my lachrymal glands.

In short, tears welled up along my bottom lids. I was on the verge of crying when Hudson moved off me and situated himself on the far edge of the back seat. I tucked my legs up, mirroring his position at the other end to give him space.

"You told me to be honest about what I want and what I don't. Here it is. I don't want to have sex when it's like this."

"Like what?" I asked, still playing dumb.

"I don't want to be used, Scout. And I don't want to use you."

I swallowed hard. Blinked back the tears. Took a shaky breath. He rushed to speak again.

"Sorry if that's the wrong thing to say. I understand if—"

"No," I said, cutting off his self-conscious overexplanation. "It was exactly the right thing to say. It's the truth. You should always feel safe telling me the truth. Always feel safe to be who you really are."

And here's the crazy thing. I meant that. I meant every word. I wanted to be the person he trusted with himself. In a world of people who he craved to please, I wanted to be the one he never worried about disappointing.

"I'm not going anywhere if you're not," I said, trying to reassure him.

"I'm staying as long as you'll have me, Scout."

My chuckle broke the air between us. "Don't worry. I won't call you on that. You'll be free of me as soon as your contract's up. You'll never have to see my shitty parents again."

"Why *do* you let them treat you like that?"

"Not all of us can charm everyone, Mr. Bailey."

He shook his head. "I wasn't exactly charming tonight. They broke me with the way they talked about you. How can you stand it?"

On any other night, in any other circumstance, with anyone else, I would have given some bullshit answer about them being my parents. Honor thy mother and father and all that.

But Hudson, the people pleaser, had stood up for himself and ended bad sex between us despite how badly I claimed to want it. That meant a lot to me. That he believed in me enough to communicate his needs—which he didn't do with really anyone else.

It told me that he cared about me. And cared about this relationship, whatever it was.

And care had a way of frightening me.

"I don't know," I said. "I guess I'm just used to it."

"I hope you never feel that way with me, Scout. I want to be better for you. To show you that people can be better to you. Do you want that, too?"

It sounded like a proposal that went deeper than sex.

That frightened me even more than the care.

Shit. I was going to have to end this, wasn't I? Before it got too serious to take back?

Well. At least I had a sure-fire way to do that. To make sure Hudson wanted nothing to do with me ever again.

"Will you take me back to my house?" I asked.

"Oh. Um. Yeah."

The way he played with his cuffs told me everything I needed to know—that he thought I was ditching him. I backtracked.

"Sorry. I mean . . . will you come back with me to my house?"

Even in the low light of the dark car, relief etched itself all over his face. The sight pierced me straight through. He'd been so afraid of saying the wrong thing, doing the wrong thing, and losing me.

"Of course. Absolutely."

My heart broke for him a little. Because he wanted to keep me. And in a few minutes, he'd understand why he shouldn't.

Why he couldn't.

28

All the Whore-y Details

"So . . . you have to promise you won't laugh. This is pretty embarrassing for me."

My bedroom had two walk-in closets. One I used for clothes. The other I'd briefly considered making my sex toy depository, but that seemed a little sad back in my virgin days. So, instead, I'd made it into a secret workshop. Soundproof and still, it had just enough room for a desk, a chair, and a little bit of pacing space. I'd taken out the shelving so I could paint one wall with chalk paint.

Whenever I had a hard day at BuzzCorp, whenever I needed to put pleasure away and return to my roots, I went in there to work on my own little fantasy projects.

When we returned home, I brought Hudson there. Too big for the small space, he stood in the center, staring at the dozens of computations written on the chalkboard wall and the sketches of rocket ships and thrusters and engines on the other walls. A scale model of the Hathor, the pipe dream of a rocket I'd been designing in secret since getting fired from GalacticSolutions, dangled above our heads.

"What is all this?" he asked.

Nothing. Just a lifetime of abandoned dreams.

Since I wasn't a character in a melodrama, though, I just shrugged. "I don't really talk about myself either, you know. I get that it can be scary, letting people see deeper than the surface." One of my fingers brushed a drafting-pencil sketch of a fuel injector. "This is what I'm hiding."

He slunk deeper into the closet, his own fingers trailing across my hand-drawn design specs. "These are *amazing*. But why are you showing me this?"

"You asked why I let my parents talk to me that way. Why I believe them. Why I can't *do* the normal things other people do."

"I didn't ever ask that last thing. You've always been normal to me," he replied.

"Here's the thing. My parents are right about me."

"Absolutely not—"

He reached out for me, but I held my hands out in a *no closer* gesture. "Just listen, and then make your judgments, okay? I need you to understand why you can't want me. Why we can't be . . . anything more than we are. Why it's pointless to care about me. I've never . . . I've never told anyone all of this. I need you to listen."

A response was clearly on its way, so I cut him off before he could.

"So . . ." I said, taking a seat on the floor. Might as well be comfortable. "You know how I grew up."

"Prodigy stuff," he said hesitantly. "Right."

"Yeah. And my parents were always there. Once they realized how smart I was, they dedicated themselves to making sure I had the best of everything. They kept my schedules, they drove me everywhere, they bought my school supplies, picked my clothes. Everything."

"They didn't give you any independence."

"No," I agreed, "but that's because I couldn't handle it. Like, once, when I was ten or so, I begged my mom to let me pick my own notebooks and binders for calc. I'd seen this *Shake It Up* binder at Target and begged my mom for it. She said no. I threw a fit about never getting to pick my own stuff. Mom said the other kids would make fun of me, that she was protecting me by being so controlling. But I insisted. *I* would never make fun of anyone for their binders. Why would anyone else do the same to me? Well, wouldn't you know it? The football bros in class saw me in the front row, *Shake It Up* binder and all, and played keep-away with it until the damn thing ripped. Taking weeks of work I'd done on a proof with it."

Hudson sank down to the floor in front of me.

"So you went back to letting them call the shots."

"I was smarter than they were, but not in the ways that mattered. Not smart enough to handle myself. Clearly. Then, I got through college and grad school and everything that followed. I became even more awkward and isolated and didn't understand anything about people. Especially men. I was still finishing up at MIT when I was hired at GalacticSolutions, working in their propulsion department."

Happiest day ever, getting that call from GS, learning that I'd be making half a million dollars a year to head up their fledgling propulsion department.

But I guess I just wasn't allowed to be happy for too long. Because soon, that happiest day curdled into my worst era.

"Now, the thing to know about GalacticSolutions is that they're one of those companies that *isn't* a tech company but *acts* like they're one. They said that it made them agile—"

"Let me guess," Hudson mused. "They said it made them agile, but really, it just meant they gave a college-age whiz kid a ton of responsibility because she didn't know how to say no to overtime, and because she was disposable if she fucked it up."

"And don't forget, if she somehow *did* manage to succeed,

which all signs pointed to, then they'd have an amazing Zuckerberg 2.0 story for the media. Look at this young, female engineer, barely out of school and ready to start the new age of space exploration."

He held his hands aloft, framing me like a photographer. "You would look great in *Forbes*."

I chuckled. The sound was barely audible over the hum of the poorly wired overhead light. "So I get there and I was really fucking good at my job. Every minute up to that point had been spent trying to get there. I belonged. I worked my ass off. I was succeeding in literally every way. But then . . . Lloyd got assigned to oversee my division. And I was a stupid girl who'd never been shown any attention before. Boys did not like nerds with greasy hair and no concept of reality outside of its scientific provability. But Lloyd . . . Lloyd *did* like me. He flirted, he gave me his number, he made moves . . ."

A familiar wave of nausea overtook me. I tried to keep Lloyd locked away in a memory vault because any time I examined the memories too closely, I made myself literally sick thinking of what a stupid girl I'd been.

"Of course you felt flattered. Scout, you're acting like you made the worst mistake in human history. *Everyone* falls for the wrong person at least once."

A sweet way to look at what happened. Also an inaccurate one. I ignored him. "After years of having everything dictated to me by my parents, I thought I could finally handle myself. That I was a grown-up with a grown-up job and could make my own decisions. So Lloyd and I started . . . Back then, I thought we were dating. We did *not* date. We didn't even go on dates. We were hooking up. We didn't have sex," I clarified. "I told him I wasn't ready, and I don't know. Maybe he liked the chase. But it worked out fine anyway, because he loved blowjobs. And hand-jobs, too, but only quickies in the elevator. I think it was a power thing."

"Guess I can check *learn about a billionaire's sexual proclivities* off my bingo card."

"He's not a billionaire yet. Daddy has to die first. And speaking of Daddy, Lloyd didn't want to tell him about us. I thought it was cool. Having a secret like that. But then . . . the rocket blew up."

"Not a euphemism," he said, shaking his head.

"I wish. You sort of know this story, right? About the Ilium? My first big project?" He nodded. Its explosion was one of the biggest stories in the tech world at the time, and we'd talked about it that day in the Cleveland airport. "I told them that we were not ready for the testing phase. *Everyone* told them that. But Lloyd told his father he'd been *personally overseeing* my work and that I was just being modest. These guys . . . there's no one else on earth like them. They just don't have any concept of failure. Like, *Of course it's going to work, even if the experts tell me it won't. Nothing ever goes wrong for me!*"

"But it *did* go wrong."

Sometimes, when I put my head down on the pillow at night, I could still see the fireballs exploding up into the sky. It was a remote-controlled ship, not for human transport or operation, so thankfully no one was hurt. But my work exploding before my eyes . . . I'd never forget it. Or escape it.

"And disastrously. There were so many problems. They hadn't given the departments enough time to coordinate before the test. The internal sequencing was busted, the cabling was interfering with the rudders . . . Avoidable problems, if we'd been given the time and the money. But we weren't. And Lloyd and his father were confident, so they invited almost two thousand people to come and view the rocket live. Two thousand people saw my project go up in smoke."

"Tests sometimes fail," Hudson said. "They should have known that."

"Should have. But Senior and the money guys behind him were furious and humiliated. They decided it was my fault. Lloyd told them it was my fault. They wanted a head on a platter . . . and when a corporate raider got hold of thousands of leaked documents and texts . . ."

"They found out about you and Lloyd."

Oh, did they ever. For weeks I was stuck in sterile boardrooms, listening to teams of lawyers read my most base and salacious fantasies back to me in wry, smug monologues. They always followed up with questions about my fitness for my position, if I knew how much money the disaster with my rocket had cost the company, and whether I'd ever had an inappropriate workplace relationship before.

"Yeah. I was accused of sleeping my way into my position, taking advantage of poor, suggestible Lloyd, and ruining the entire project with my incompetence. And that's what they told everyone in the space exploration vertical. And anyone else who might even potentially hire an engineer like me. Silicon Valley, the medical sector . . . Everyone knew that I was a slut who would fuck their sons and send their projects up in smoke."

The shame pressed down on my neck. I couldn't even keep my eyes open. It was a fundamental law of the universe. Every time I'd ever tried to take control of my own life, I'd fucked it up. Whether it was as frivolous as a binder or my first real relationship, I couldn't do anything right.

That was why I couldn't go deeper with Hudson. That was why we needed barriers and guardrails and rules. So history didn't repeat itself.

"But *you* were the one who was taken advantage of," Hudson said.

"I know. And so did they. That's why they gave me a settlement, had me sign an NDA, and sent me off on my merry way *before* they started spreading rumors of my incompetence."

"That's so wrong."

"Yeah. But I was wrong, too." My voice cracked. "How does someone devote themself to knowledge, only to be the stupidest woman who ever lived?"

"It's not your fault."

"I was a grown woman with a multibillion-dollar project under my control. If I was smart enough to handle that, I should have been smart enough to see through Lloyd. It *was* my fault."

"You said it yourself. Sure, you were an adult with a lot of responsibility, but you were still young, and he *knew* that you had no understanding of the world or people outside of your textbooks. He took advantage of that, manipulated you, and then threw you away when you were no longer convenient. He was in the wrong."

Broken clocks and all of that. I *did* hate Lloyd Exeter, but at the end of the day, I had to own up to my mistakes and pay the price for making them. That price was losing my dreams of space, that price was working at BuzzCorp . . .

"My life is my responsibility, Hudson." The echoes of those words rang with the ghosts of my parents' voices. There was no way Hudson could have heard it, but I did. "And it's one I can't trust myself with. I've never been able to. Work, fine. Yes. I can manage. But anything else? I'm incompetent."

"You haven't ruined anything with me."

"Not yet, maybe," I retorted. Then, when I realized what that *yet* signified, that I would be spending more time with him, I tried to cover my tracks. "Not that it matters anyway; you're leaving soon."

He toyed with his shirtsleeves. "Did you ever apply anywhere else after GalacticSolutions?"

"Why would I when they badmouthed me to everyone? It

would have been a waste of my time. No one would hire me. It's why I didn't want everyone in the office knowing I was a virgin. Once you get labeled, it's hard to shake, and people only see you through that lens forever. With Lloyd, I was this man-eating slut who'd blown him and then blown up his rockets. Unqualified. With the virgin thing, it felt the same. That everyone would see me not as a brilliant engineer but unfit."

He flattened his lips, surveying my workshop. "I know you showed me all these designs because you think it's a reminder of your failure, but I think it's a sign of your potential. Have you ever thought about getting out of sex toys and back into rocket ships?"

My reaction was knee-jerk and defensive. "I like my job."

"I know you do. But I think you might love space exploration more. Maybe you should consider a career change."

"I can't. No one would hire me," I reiterated.

No one except Clara, whom I'd met while crying in the bathroom of a Women in STEM networking seminar. I'd tried to make connections that day, but it felt like every woman in that room was side-eyeing me. Judging me for making their lives harder by being branded yet another office slut sleeping her way to the top. Giving women in the industry a bad name.

"It's possible they would now."

The idea that my scarlet letter had somehow expired over the last two years had never occurred to me. I truly thought I'd be doing my penance walk forever, daydreaming about space exploration while tinkering away with my latest cock ring innovation.

And why not? Why *hadn't* I considered it?

Was it because I didn't want to? Because I didn't want to try and fail to break back into the industry? Because it was safer to stay with Clara than chance a new job hunt?

Was I sabotaging myself?

Of course I was. That was why Hudson was here, after all. I was trying to sabotage our relationship before it could even really begin.

"You could have anything you want, Scout. Anything, and anyone. You're the only person holding you back."

I scoffed, if only to hide how much I wanted him to be right. "No one else agrees with you. Not me, not my parents, not anyone who's gotten Lloyd's side of the story."

"Clara does, I bet. She's the one who hired you after you lost your job at GalacticSolutions, didn't she?"

That barely counted. "Clara would have hired a mop wearing a Nikola Tesla Halloween costume if she thought it would improve her bottom line."

"Now you're just being cruel to yourself."

Yeah. I was.

I deflated a little bit and shrugged.

"I don't know any other way to be."

"You really don't, do you?" I tried to laugh it off. Hudson wasn't having it. "No, I'm serious. I don't think I've ever seen you be anything better than *neutral* to yourself."

"Don't be casting stones."

"I'm not mean to myself," he snapped incredulously.

"Yes, you are, but in a different way. You never show anyone who you are because you're afraid they won't like what they see. Well, I *do* like what I see, and I'm glad I got to meet you. The real you. The one you hide from everyone else."

There was a moment of silent fallout between us. This time, I was the one who'd shown my hand. I didn't just like him as a fuckbuddy. It was quickly growing into something more—something I feared I couldn't control.

"I wish I could be better for that guy," I said, emphasizing each word. He had to understand why I couldn't go any further.

"I wish I knew how not to mess this up. I wish I wasn't afraid of you and what you could do to me. But I am what I am. And what I am is *not right* for a guy like you, Hudson Bailey."

The air between us tightened as realization hit him. "Did you tell me all of this because you thought it would push me away? Were you trying to sabotage whatever it is we have going on here? Do you really believe that you could chase me off?"

Two big, firm hands rose to cup my cheeks. He didn't speak until I lifted my eyes to his.

"Scout. I'm not going anywhere. Bad sex, good sex. Dates, no dates. Terrible parents. Sex toy lessons. Whatever lies ahead, I'm here. If you'll have me. If I'm what you want."

My heart swelled. But I cut it before it could burst. "For the next few weeks, anyway. Which is for the best. If we stayed together any longer, I would just blow it. I'm incapable of doing anything right."

"I don't believe that. I think *this* is right." He stroked my cheekbone with his thumb.

"I don't want you to go," I said. "But I don't want to bring you down with me. I'm a wreck. I ruin everything I touch."

"Do I look ruined to you?" he asked.

No. He didn't. He looked whole.

Like I mended him.

A completed circuit.

After a beat, he spoke again. "Can I tell you something? Be warned: It might make me seem like a bad person."

"Sure."

Moving from his place above me, Hudson sighed and settled on the floor at my feet. He placed his head on my knee, cheek pressing against my bare flesh there. His breath danced tattoos on me; I wanted to keep them forever. "I'm glad you didn't have sex with him. Not because I'm selfish and wanted to be your first or whatever, nothing weird and possessive like that. Just . . . I'm glad your first time was with someone who gave a damn about you. He didn't deserve you anyway. You deserved better. Not just from him. But from everyone."

You deserved better.

No one had ever told me that before. Not even Clara. Even in her most supportive moments, she was pragmatic and unemotional about things, choosing to keep our attentions squarely on what we could do going forward, rather than wallowing in the past.

You deserved better.

But Hudson had said it like it was obvious. Like his heart was broken that no one had told me before. Like I needed to hear it. And maybe I did.

You deserved better.

"Just think about it, okay? You. Me. Us. What you want your tomorrows to look like. I really believe it, Scout. You can have anything you want. Anything. Just ask."

I didn't know if I could believe it.

But God did I want to.

29

More Like Bored-Room, Am I Right, Ladies?

There it was. A nightmare come true. That some great, wonderful, giving, undeniably sexy man would care for me. And I would be unable to accept him because of my track record of ineptitude.

So when we talked about moving forward, I didn't acknowledge my feelings for him. Not the depth of them, anyway. I tried not even to consider that. Instead, I put a different wall between us: time. He was leaving in three weeks. We should make those weeks count without complicating it with anything resembling a real relationship. We would just have fun.

Fun, I could handle. At least, I could *try*. Nights spent together. Some outings here and there. Cuddling and affection and orgasms that I'd remember for the rest of my life. What was the worst that could happen?

A week later, as I sat in a BuzzCorp all-hands meeting, all I could think about was Hudson's cock. I'd been doing that a lot lately, thinking about real dick at home when I should have been paying better attention to the artificial dicks I crafted in the workplace.

See, when I said I worried about my personal life distracting from my professional one, *this* was what I meant. Lusting across a *very* crowded boardroom at a man who'd already made me cum twice before breakfast.

I tried to school my thoughts. Back to the task at hand. We were now only two weeks out from OFest New York, the nationwide sex toy conference where we would launch The Fantasy—and where our fates would be decided.

Clara stood, calling the meeting to order without uttering a single word. She had a way of doing that, of commanding a room based on her presence alone.

"At the outset, I want to congratulate all of you. I put an impossible deadline before this team, and you all have risen to the occasion. I know you're going to brief me on your respective timelines and outstanding projects, but I have monitored your progress through Scout's weekly reports. What I've seen already has impressed me. I know that OFest is going to be a resounding success."

A tiny set of creases developed around the edges of her eyes. Did she *actually* believe that with all her heart, I wondered, or was she just pep-talking us into believing she had confidence so we'd work harder not to let her down?

Weeks ago, I would have assumed the worst. That we were on the brink of disaster and she was manipulating us. Now? I chose to buy in.

Then Leelah perked up, looking at me from across the room and raising her voice so everyone could hear.

"And it's all thanks to Scout."

Not used to being interrupted, Clara balked. Then she quirked her head to the side and beamed. She didn't often beam—it caused wrinkles and Botox was getting expensive these days, apparently—so her praise hit me even harder. "Yes, she has been an exceptional leader, hasn't she? Disciplined, knowledgeable, and dedicated to The Fantasy. We're glad to have you, Scout."

The room broke out in applause. I ducked my head to hide my blush. The last time everyone had focused their attention on me, Lloyd Exeter had been telling Joe Rogan about our brief interlude.

Now, despite my fears and hesitations, I was getting praised. Somehow, I'd managed to make a friend, have amazing sex, delegate work to my colleagues without constantly hovering over their shoulders, *and* win their approval. Clara's, too.

What else could I manage, I wondered. Was Hudson right? Was I capable of more than I'd ever dreamed possible?

"Thanks, everyone," I said, meaning it. "I couldn't have done it without you."

Once the applause died down, Clara took her seat. Back to business.

"Now. Shall we begin?"

The department heads wasted no time. While all of them were beneath me in the org chart, the various groups—software, manufacturing, QA, testing, marketing, and, of course, engineering—each contributed their own updates. The briefs were intensive, but promising—just like I knew they'd be. Everyone understood the importance of this product rollout.

However, once marketing piped up . . .

"We're having some trouble," Thomas, their lead, said with more than a little apprehension. "It's an expensive piece of machinery. Hard to market, especially *because* it's so groundbreaking. People may not understand what it does or how it could work for them since they have no point of reference for a toy like this. I mean, it's not even a toy, really. It's an all-encompassing sexual experience."

"And then there's the male problem," someone mumbled.

The energy in the room shifted. For one thing, The Fantasy was a toy explicitly designed with the vagina-having user in mind, so penis-having people wouldn't be able to use it in any capacity, thus lowering our ability to market it to roughly half of the population. Second, though it was *also* built so partners could program the toy's maneuvers, some men might see it as a replacement. A threat to their sexual dominion over the bedroom.

"Yes, indeed," Clara mused. "I am troubled by Mr. Ose's recent comments—and about the rise in popularity of a brand like Lloyd Exeter's. One more catered to the masculine toy-purchasing populace."

"We shouldn't be catering to cisgender men," Addie snapped. From the side-eyes being exchanged, it was clear she and the marketing team had had this disagreement many times. "This isn't about them. Not everything in the world can be about them."

"I understand that perspective. I also understand that we can't continue to prop up a business—especially one with so much on the line—by only appealing to people with vaginas."

"We should be doing both," Terrence said. He wasn't on the marketing team, nor was he liaising with them like Addie. However, that was what this meeting was for. Brainstorming across departments. "What about testimonials? We can have men talk about what The Fantasy has done for their sex lives. We could even talk about our other products, pushing BuzzCorp as a company for all."

Marketing considered this. I knew from their emails that testimonials had *not* been part of their plan. They'd been more focused on displaying the product and explaining how it worked, rather than selling the vibes (pun not intended). "That's a good idea," Thomas agreed. "What about the hype video that we're going to play before Scout's presentation at OFest? We could have a bunch of talking heads from our focus groups, people of all genders, describing their experiences with sex toys."

Murmurs of agreement from all around the room. Then Hudson raised his hand.

"You don't have to raise your hand," Clara said.

He hesitantly lowered it, then fiddled with his glasses. "I know you all know more about this than me, so take what I'm saying with a grain of salt." I almost rolled my eyes. Hadn't he learned anything these last few weeks? He didn't have to couch every disagreement in caveats. "Wouldn't the testers be skittish about appearing on camera? The fuck reports are one thing. They're private and only used internally. Being on screen in front of hundreds of people, maybe even put on social media for the world to see in a marketing push, while talking about your sexual proclivities is another."

"No, none of them are shy," I said, noting the squirming discomfort taking over Hudson's body. The tense shoulders. The hands twisting around his tablet stylus. "They get what we're doing here and why it's important."

"But he's right," said Thomas. "It *will* be a challenge to get guys to go on camera. We'll need to figure out some way to convince them that it's okay to talk about this stuff."

"Big ask," Hudson said.

"We'll figure it out," was Thomas's reply. But he added, with a wince, "Hopefully."

Clara nodded once, definitively putting her seal of approval on this new direction. "I think it's an idea worth exploring. Stay on top of it."

Mumbles of agreement from all quarters of the room.

"Excellent. If there's nothing left to discuss, let's go once more unto the breach."

Eager for the catered pizza lunch Clara had arranged as a reward, the room cleared quickly. Before I could go, though, my boss took me aside.

"Scout. I mean it. You've exceeded all expectations. I'm proud of you. Tremendously."

Pride welled in my chest, threatening to leave no room for

more important stuff like air. Unable to take the compliment, I brushed it off.

"We'll see how everything shakes out at OFest. I don't want to get too cocky."

"Pun intended?"

"Naturally."

"Very well. How has your experiment in normality gone so far?"

"Great. I'm making friends. Doing things outside of work."

"Seeing anyone?"

Part of me wanted to tell her. After all, she knew everything else about me. Why not this?

Easy. Because Clara was like the mirror-universe version of my parents. Affectionate and thoughtful, encouraging and accepting. Where they shared DNA, though, was in how much influence they had over me.

I wanted this for me. A relationship that I controlled and navigated—no one else. I had no doubt that if Clara knew about my relationship with Hudson, she'd go whole hog and extend his contract or start looking at wedding venues.

And if I did tell her and this ended up being just another signature Scout Porter failure, I'd wind up humiliated.

"It's complicated" was the only reply I could give without explicitly lying.

"Ooh, so mysterious," she crooned. "I look forward to hearing about it once it's *un*complicated."

We both joined our colleagues for pizza, where I made a point of talking non-business with some folks I never bothered getting to know before. Every step, though, I felt Hudson's attention on me. The only reprieve I got was when I finally fled to the bathroom, trying to tamp down the lust gripping me.

That was where Leelah found me, interrupting my peace.

"Girl. How do you expect to keep you and Hudson dating a

secret when you're constantly looking at each other with *fuck me* eyes?"

"First, hi. Second, no we don't. And third, we're not dating."

"I bet that would be news to him." Off my flat look, she continued. "What? You guys are going on dates. He met your parents."

"We've been on *dates*. We're not *dating*. We're just kind of seeing each other. No labels. There's a difference."

"Sure, sure." She rolled her eyes. "I forgot—everything you two do together is just foreplay for your hot-and-heavy sexual adventures."

Finally, an opening to turn this conversation around. "More like *mis*adventures. Have you ever had a guy make you cum with nothing but a car speaker? The other day, we—"

Flush . . .

Oh shit.

There was someone else in the bathroom.

And they'd just heard about me and Hudson.

My stomach washed away with that flush. Every neuron in my body vibrated until I was sure they would pull me apart.

Then the door to stall three opened. Addie stepped out, jaw fully dropped.

"You're having sex with the new guy? Like, that wasn't Jared just pulling stuff out of his ass back at the bar a few weeks ago? You're *actually* having sex with him?"

He'd been working here for a while, so *new guy* seemed like an ungenerous characterization of him. Still . . .

"We weren't having sex then."

"And now?"

"I'm not . . . *not* having sex with him" was my brilliant reply.

For a split second, I worried that Addie was going to take this news badly. As it turned out, I was right, but not for the reasons I suspected.

"You told the new girl before me?"

She was jealous. Addie was *jealous.* It took me back to the drinks night at Josie's; she'd been trying to befriend me then, and I'd shut her out.

"I wasn't going to tell anyone," I said by way of defense. "She guessed."

"I'm extremely perceptive," Leelah said. "Which is how I know that you're *super* stoked to be in on the secret now."

Addie practically vibrated, her eyes lighting up. Apparently, being second to know wasn't so bad when the possibility of friendship was on the table. "Are you kidding me? I'm *dying* for some girl talk. For all everyone talks about this being girlie central, there's an awful lot of testosterone swimming around in the office pool. Is this it? Am I in the inner circle now? Can we please go full girl gang on this bitch? *Sex and the City* vibes?"

I'd forgotten how exuberant Addie could be. Once upon a time, I found that rattling. Now, endearing. She just wanted to belong.

"As much as there is an inner circle, sure," I said with a smirk.

"Fuckin' A. Now, how are we going to celebrate our female empowerment era? Do either of you like weed brownies? I made some today, but we can go to my place and make some more soon. You all could make treats, too. We could have a *bake*-off."

Neither of us had any experience with canna-baking, so we declined the bake-off invite, but as we returned to the office, we fell into an easy rapport.

By the time Hudson and I linked up after work for cocktails at a cute bar far from the office, I was practically glowing. I'd done something right. I'd been *doing* things right and people were noticing. Maybe I wasn't such a failure. Maybe I *could* handle letting go a bit.

Hudson, on the other hand, didn't pass the vibe check. He did his best to chitchat at all the right places, even touching my knee below the bar and whispering about the *further study* he wanted to do in my toy drawer tonight, but it all came out perfunctory, like his mind was elsewhere.

"What's going on in that brain of yours?" I finally asked. "You're like an electron caught in a direct-current circuit."

"Hm?"

"You're sluggish. Your energy's zapped. Are you okay?"

For the last ten minutes, I'd been trying to figure out what *I'd* done to upset him. Usually when people got this way around me, I was the culprit of their emotional sabotage.

"I'm still thinking about our all-hands today," he said, swirling the cherry-pink dregs of his piña colada. "Do you really think that marketing approach is the smartest thing?"

"It does seem like a solid strategy. People don't believe companies. They believe other people. And in the end, I think Terrence was right. Most consumers don't buy a product based on what it can do but how they think it will make them feel."

Hudson wouldn't look at me, so I had to observe him in the patinaed mirror lining the back of the cocktail bar.

"I just can't imagine people who would tell the world about their sexual desires," he muttered.

"Sexual desires aren't shameful," I reminded him. It was my motto while working at BuzzCorp. My guiding star.

"They might not be shameful," he countered. "It's just that people can shame you for them. People are judgmental. Small-minded."

That was true. We saw it everywhere we looked—in legislation trying to ban the sale of sex toys, in apps designed to monitor your partner's or family member's porn consumption, in politicians excluding sexual health materials from freedom-of-speech laws. People could be judgmental and take that prejudice to extremes. I couldn't fault him for thinking something that was patently true.

"Is that why you play your fantasies so close to the chest?" I asked. "You know I'll never judge you, right?"

"I wasn't entirely truthful earlier," he muttered. "When we were talking about my ex-girlfriend. I did . . . I *tried* to communicate some things I was interested in. She laughed at me. Basically called me a freak. I never brought it up again. I hated feeling so . . . so wrong."

"There's nothing wrong about you, Hudson. And anyone who won't accept you like you are isn't worth your time."

Finally, he turned from the mirror. His lips quirked. "You're right. She wasn't the one. But still, those are strong words coming from a girl who only let herself make friends a few weeks ago."

"I'm learning. And what's the point of knowledge if you don't pass it on?" I teased.

I thought he might say more. Might accept my advice and admit that I was right, that it was good and healthy to embrace oneself, no matter the social consequences. But I should have known better. He couldn't do that. Instead, he shifted the subject. "Good point. Now, what sex toy knowledge are you going to pass on to me tonight?"

I mulled it over. Then I put my hand on his knee. My pussy clenched for the wanting of him. "What do you know about cock rings?"

30

Didn't Peg You for an Ass Man

You ever wake up and just *know* that everything is going to whomp? Like, before your eyes even open, you have just, like, this sixth sense activate, alerting every sleeper lizard brain cell to incoming danger? I'd read in academic papers that human intuition could be strong, a leftover, involuntary sensory processing maneuver our brains did from back in the days when cavemen had to sense the presence of lurking saber-toothed tigers.

I guess my ancestors only survived the saber-tooths by sheer dumb luck, though, because I didn't have that. When I encountered a bad day, it was like a blizzard of paper clips or getting broadsided by a clown car full of drunk fish—unexpected and inexplicable.

Of all the disasters that I considered befalling me when I started hooking up with Hudson, the one I *hadn't* considered was the one that was most likely to happen.

Getting my period.

So, the morning after our experiment with cock rings (Hudson wasn't a fan; he didn't feel much difference), I woke up feeling disgusting. Cramps. Tight hips. Headache. The urge to puke my guts out. The occasional intense, shooting pain in my cervix, often so painful it made me double over.

Y'know. Girl stuff.

Despite my IUD, I still got hormonal flare-ups consistent with a menses. I cursed my luck but popped some Advil and brushed it off. Not much I could do about it.

Unfortunately, hormonal fluctuations were the least of my issues. While Clara, Leelah, and Addie were sympathetic to my plight (Clara plying me with organic 99% dark chocolate—gross; Leelah bringing me a heating pad from her desk—better; and Addie keeping everyone away from my office like an attack dog), the same could not be said for my mother, who chose the perfect time to make another surprise appearance.

At least this time it was by phone.

"One of us could have been dead," she said by way of greeting when I finally picked up after her tenth attempt. "And you don't answer your phone?"

"Mom, I'm so sorry," I replied, not sorry but knowing it was what she wanted to hear. "I was in a meeting."

"Yes, yes, so important. The fate of humanity rests on your ability to churn out a new personal massager. Excuse me for the interruption."

"We're on a deadline—"

Her eye roll was almost audible over the phone connection. "Or maybe you're just spending time with that *boy*. Is that it, hm? You can't answer your mother's phone calls because of him?"

"No."

I just didn't *want* to answer my mother's phone calls because of him. Our every interaction now chafed against Hudson's indelible declaration.

You deserved better.

"Oh please. Who do you think you're fooling? You're going to throw everything away on some boy yet again, despite our best efforts to keep you from repeating history."

The air around me turned brittle and unbreathable. Of *course* she would lash out like this when she was angry. I should have expected it.

But I didn't. And it hurt more than I could have imagined, hearing her voice the one fear I'd been running from this entire time.

Why did this always happen? Did she have a sixth sense for my happiness? Every time I felt like I was getting my feet under me, she came in to smash my confidence.

"It's not like that." Heat built up behind my eyes. Tears formed. I tried to blink them away, but that only banished them to my cheeks. "I swear."

"Just don't come crawling back to us when you let him ruin you, like Lloyd did. You know how much we love to say *I told you so.*"

A million protests bubbled to my lips. I swallowed them down. What would be the point? My track record for standing up for myself was abysmal. Mom ended the call, but not before making me promise to still see them for dinner when I went to New York for Manhattan's OFest. Part of me wanted to snap. To ask why she'd even *want* to see such a terrible disappointment of a daughter.

I didn't. I agreed.

By the time I arrived back at my apartment, I was hormonal, the Advil was wearing off, my mom's call had gotten under my skin, and I wanted nothing more than to slide into bed and pretend that the world didn't exist.

But there Hudson was. Bathed in light from the streetlamps, carrying several BuzzCorp-branded shopping totes.

"Oh no," I groaned before I could stop myself.

He started. "Shit, what did I do?"

Rubbing at my face, I collected myself. My problems weren't Hudson's fault. It wasn't fair to take it out on him. "Sorry, I've just had a shit day, and I'm not in the mood for sex. You can go home now."

"Do you want some company?"

Annoyance gripped a knot between my shoulder blades. I punched the building code into the security box. "I just said I don't want to have sex. I don't want to be fucked. I don't want you to go down on me. I don't want to be touched—"

The door clicked open. Hudson grabbed the handle, holding it slightly ajar so it wouldn't relock . . . but also, so I couldn't pass. His eyes searched mine. "We don't *have* to have sex, Scout. You know that, right?"

That took the hot air out of my sails.

Right. We *didn't* have to. We could just hang out together. Fuck what my mom thought. Fuck the fact that he and I should only be no-strings-attached sex buddies.

I was tired and annoyed and all I wanted in that moment was to rest in someone else. In him.

So I invited him in.

Once up in my apartment, he offered me a THC brownie. When we wanted to relax, our ritual was usually a cocktail or glass of wine to start the night. However, he explained that Addie was passing them around the office (seemed like bad business practices, but whatever, I'm not in charge of HR) and wanted to share, so I popped it without a second thought, letting the slightly earthy, totally gooey chocolate settle my frazzled nerves.

As I relaxed into the couch and let the chemicals work their way through my system, Hudson briefed me on his day. I wasn't in the mood to talk; listening to him was enough.

How strange it was to spend time with him removed from the expectations of sex. To think that he wanted to spend time with me—no detours into my pants. And even stranger to think that

I relished his anecdotes about debugging Python code and his various, much worse, workplaces before BuzzCorp.

Half an hour later, the pain from my period was basically nonexistent, a bag of Sun Chips from my kitchen had magically transformed from a family size to a personal one, and, as we faced each other on the love seat, I couldn't stop rubbing my legs against his. It was my turn to talk, and of course, I couldn't very well keep the truth about Addie from him. As painful and embarrassing as it was, he deserved to know that this secret between the two of us had ballooned from three (Leelah) to five (my parents) to six (Addie) now.

"We could just go public, you know."

I tipped the Sun Chips bag and tilted the protruding corner into my mouth to get the last of the crumbs. So attractive. "With what?"

"Whatever this is that we're doing. If we don't have anything to hide . . . we shouldn't be hiding."

I'd become friendly with him (broken rule), I'd masturbated over him (broken rule), had sex with him in the first place (broken rule), had sex with him several times after that (broken rule), and started sort-of dating him (broken rule). There had to be a limit. And going public with this information was it, even if it made me feel a little guilty. Lloyd kept me a secret. Was I doing the same to Hudson?

"But you're leaving soon. What would be the point? Let's just have fun. We don't need to complicate things."

"Sure. Sure, of course you're right," he said. When he winced instead of smiling, though, I chalked it up to my high imagination doing some wishful thinking.

Nothing good would come of this conversation. Searching for some way to distract us both, I scanned the room.

Ah, perfect.

"What's all of that over there?" I asked, detangling our limbs so I could inspect the pile of shopping bags he'd brought.

He practically flew to intercept my path. "Nothing. We can talk about it another time."

"You're blushing," I said with no small amount of glee. He was beautiful when he blushed. "Why are you blushing?"

"You said you don't want to have sex. This is . . . sex stuff."

"What sex stuff?"

Shy. He was being *shy*. I'd seen him evasive and sheepish before. In the office, he could be understated and quiet, friendly and affable. Shy, on the other hand, was new.

"Today, when she was offering me the weed brownies, Addie and I started talking about her work with the marketing team. Which brought me back to our conversation yesterday. About people who can just . . . say what they want. No shame. No fear of what other people will think."

"Yeah?"

"I couldn't ever go in front of a crowd and declare my proclivities or anything. Don't sign me up for the video testimonial crews. But . . ."

My stomach tightened. It had nothing to do with the cramps.

Whatever was in those bags, it had to be good.

And when he handed them over, my suspicions were confirmed.

Not to brag, but the fuck reports from our testers reliably informed us that BuzzCorp had the finest line of pegging products on the market today. Hudson had clearly availed himself of our samples closet, picking out a strap-on harness, butt plugs, extra-strength lubricants, and several dildos of various levels of size, turgidity, and realism.

"When we talked about what kinks you had," he said, the words coming out from between barely moving lips, "what stuff you'd be interested in, we talked about pegging, and it seemed like you were enthusiastic about trying it."

"Oh."

"You encouraged me to ask for what I want. That the people who matter won't judge me. And this is what I want. I'm hoping you won't run away. I hope you care about me the way I am. Kinks and wants and all."

He must have taken the tsunami of lust that overcame me for revulsion, because he imploded with the intensity of a collapsing star.

"*Are* you into it? It's not a big deal if you aren't, and even if you are into it, we definitely don't have to do it tonight, especially when you're not feeling well, but—"

"Yes."

He blinked at my abrupt cutoff.

"Yes?"

My face now ached from smiling so hard. "Yes. Very much yes."

The crazy thing was: It wasn't just the pegging that turned me on. It was that he told me about it. The last time he'd shared his fantasies with someone, his ex-girlfriend, she'd laughed in his face and insulted him. It was enough to make him run from his own sexual desires, to defer to his partner no matter what.

Now he was offering himself to me. Kinks and wants and all.

"So . . . we don't have to do it tonight," he said. "I don't want to pressure you, especially when you're not feeling well. But . . . at some point in the future . . . would you want to?"

I would be a novice, to be sure. I'd only ever seen pegging in porn, read about it in books, and heard plenty of horny details from the fuck reports our product testers provided. Still, my excitement threw over any nerves I might have felt.

I wanted him. Every way I could have him.

"You get my virginity and I get yours. It seems like a fair compromise." Chuckling, I brushed my nose against his. A shudder rippled through his body. Pulling away from him, I collected the bags. "All right, let's go."

His eyes widened. "Tonight? Like, right now?"

"I'm ready if you are."

Ready he must have been, because he practically ran into the bedroom.

31

We Cum in Pieces

One thing porn doesn't tell you about pegging is the amount of work involved. Fancy editing tricks cut out the parts where you have to carefully unwrap all of your materials, lay down a towel on your bed (just in case!), clean your new toys, finagle the twisty straps of the harness, and affix your dildo to it.

The other thing they didn't tell you was how much fun those things could be. How you could joke with your partner while you stood side-by-side at the sink, comparing his dick size to your new dildo like two guys at a urinal. How every accidental brush of your skin would set your body on fire with anticipation. How every casual look was seared with *I'm going to fuck you* implications.

Eventually, Hudson and I found ourselves standing on opposite sides of the bed, staring at each other like two virgins on their wedding night. He, of course, had the dignity of being naked and hard-cocked and unbelievably handsome. I had the unique distinction of wearing a strapped-on dildo, a red lace bra, and nothing else.

I also carried a small remote. Hudson, the brilliant man that he was, had opted for a strap-on harness with a built-in tonguing toy for me. The clit-licker fit snugly against my already swollen nub, ready for action as soon as I pressed go. I held off for now, knowing it wouldn't take me long to reach my peak—not with how turned on I already was.

The air crackled with sexual tension. Still, neither of us moved. The bed loomed between us, beckoning.

"I'm sorry. I've never done this before."

"Me either."

He chuckled and ducked his head. "Right. Obviously. Um—"

Given that we had equal experience, there wasn't any initial indication of who should be in charge here. But Hudson's blushing and stammering, so unlike him, clued me in to what he really wanted—whether he actively knew it or not.

I crawled on the bed and patted the empty space beside me. "Why don't you let me lead?"

"I'd love that. Thank you."

Goose bumps. I always got them when Hudson said *love* lately. I told myself it was just my wonky air-conditioning playing tricks on me.

He situated himself beside me in bed, turned on our sides so we could look at each other. My fingers drifted idly across his body, awakening his hard nipples and his own goose bumps.

"Why do you want this, Hudson?" I asked.

Another chuckle. "I think it'll feel good."

"Yeah, but in what way? Do you want to be used, do you want to be fucked, made love to—"

"I want to be taken care of."

Beyond sex, that one sentence wedged in my heart and refused to let go. Hudson took care of so many people—myself included. He deserved the same treatment. Someone who cared about him, his pleasure, his wants above everything else, even if just for an hour or two.

Perfect. That tiny piece of information unlocked the whole

thing. He may not have known the words, but he wanted what I'd sometimes seen on the internet and in the BuzzCorp fuck reports called "soft domming." Unlike a regular Dom, who usually was characterized by discipline and consequences, a soft Dom was more about praise and care. Not imposing pleasure on you because you're a bad boy who needs to be taught a lesson, but coaxing you into it because you're so good and you need your caring Dom to help you feel good.

Even in my wildest fantasies, I'd never seen myself taking the reins—er, chains and whips—in a BDSM relationship. But whispering sweet nothings in Hudson's ears while he took my cock so well?

My pussy clenched at the mere thought.

"I can do that for you. You just need to relax."

"Relax," he repeated, closing his eyes.

He was coiled up tight. Anticipation or nerves, I couldn't tell. But this was never going to work if he didn't unwind.

"I can't help you if you don't relax," I murmured. "Don't you want to feel good?"

My fingers brushed over his nipples. He shivered. His cock jumped.

"Yeah."

"Then do what I say, and I'm going to make you feel really, *really* good."

"Yes, ma'am."

Ma'am. I liked the sound of that. The toy against my clit practically screamed to be turned on, but I refrained. Hudson needed me more than I needed to cum right now.

"I know first times can be scary. Believe me, I know. But opening up can often be the most rewarding thing we do."

His lips twitched, eyes still closed. "I could tell you the same thing."

"I'm not into anal. But I'll keep that in mind."

We both chuckled, knowing that neither of us was talking about back-door sex anymore. Tipping his chin up, I gave him his first command.

"Come here. Kiss me."

Slowly, our bodies moved together and our lips touched. For the first time, he kissed me like a question. Soft and uncertain. I took his cheek in my hand, deepening it, exploring every inch of his mouth. My chest pressed against his, my nipples pebbled against his smooth skin. My own pussy felt empty without him, which only deepened my desire.

"You're an excellent kisser, you know," I breathed.

"Thank you."

My hands traveled down his chest, toward his cock. It glistened with pre-cum. "We're going to take this nice and slow, okay? Just enjoy the sensations."

Fingertips first. Up and down his shaft. Feather-light, barely touching him. He twitched beneath me, hips bucking, desperate for more contact. When I felt like he might explode from the lack of pressure, I maneuvered down and licked the wet head, tasting the salty brine of him on my tongue.

He touched my scalp, not pushing me toward his cock, but pleading with me to take it.

How could I refuse?

I inched his length between my lips, wetting him until he hit the back of my throat. Then I withdrew, teeth dripping with his pre-cum.

"That's a good boy."

The whimper that escaped his mouth was equal parts arousing and pitiful. I may not have been a *good girl* kind of girl, but he was most certainly a *good boy* kind of boy.

"Don't worry. I'll go back to it. Just one second."

His gaze never left me as I lubed up my fingers. I tried to give him the same *I'm going to make you cum so hard* energy that he'd given me so many times; I knew how painfully it heightened the anticipation.

Once satisfied with my lubrication, I returned to his cock and brought my fingers between his legs. As I took him in my mouth again, I pressed them against his entrance, waiting for the pleasure of the blowjob to hit and relax his muscles.

Soon, he opened for me, parting so I could work my fingers inside him—first to the knuckle, then to the hilt.

He whimpered. Pre-cum slicked the back of my throat. My clit begged for attention.

I remained inside him for a few moments, relishing the tightness around my fingers as I worked my mouth around him. His hips bucked—first deeper into my mouth, then back again for my fingers.

He cried out when I lifted my head long enough to breathe, "You take my fingers so well."

"Thank you. But . . ."

"But what?" I asked innocently. "Tell me what you need. I can't help you if you don't."

If he hadn't already been a panting, sweaty, cum-starved mess, he would have seen the irony in that statement. After all, just a few weeks ago, he'd said that very same thing to me.

From under my hooded eyelashes, I watched him swallow hard. The shyness was still there, but it mingled with desire, a heady combination that went straight to my cunt. "I want you to make love to me."

Love. Even clouded by pre-orgasmic fog, that word hit deep inside me, clanging around uncomfortably.

Making love—what did it even mean? Was it an intention? A level of care? Could you rail someone *and* make love to them? Or was it all soft lighting and gentle, Viagra-commercial smoothness?

I didn't know. But I would find out.

"It would be my pleasure. And you've earned it."

Withdrawing from him—much to his chagrin; he mewled like I often did when he pulled out of me—I cleaned my hands on a nearby towel. Then I shifted him to his side, so we were spooning.

The strap-on dildo fit perfectly between his ass cheeks. Whether he knew it or not, his back arched against it.

"I'm going to take my time with you," I breathed into his ear as I lubed the dildo between us. "There's no rush. I'm going to enjoy stretching you around my cock. Relax."

It was quite the role reversal, positioning my cock at Hudson's entrance. Grabbing his hips and lining him up with me. Hearing his every pant and groan, watching him turn into a puddle of lust and want beneath my hands.

When he took my virginity, was this what he felt like? The power, the trust, the rush of accomplishment when I reacted to his touch with such yearning and want?

I didn't know. All I knew was that when I slid my length inside him for the first time and turned the toy on my clit to its lowest setting, I never wanted to stop.

"Are you all right?" I asked, once I'd bottomed out in him.

"Mm-hmm," he murmured.

Running my fingers through his hair comfortingly, I gave more instructions. A great feat considering that I could barely get the words out. The toy did its best work on my desperate clit. "You can touch yourself if you'd like. But don't cum. The only one making you cum tonight is me, isn't that right?"

He nodded, then gripped his cock firmly. Coherency wasn't his strong suit at the moment. The pleasure was too great.

And I knew the feeling. With every meeting of our hips, the toy on my clit tongued harder, rattling me with a fresh wave of delight. I was getting higher and higher, overwhelmed by the combination of my own oncoming orgasm and his melting pleasure.

Still spooning him from behind, I worked to find a rhythm. He arced against me, matching me thrust for thrust.

Soon, I could tell my climax was just a few breaths away. My body tightened.

"Does that feel good?" I asked.

He nodded.

"Answer me."

"Yes. Yes, it feels so good. You fuck me so good."

And that was all I needed. The toy played long and hard on my clit. I pressed fully into him, deepening our contact and the toy's pressure against me. And I dug my fingers into his flesh, trying to hold on to reality even as my orgasm smashed me through waves of white-hot ecstasy.

I screamed out his name. It was the only thought in my mind. Hudson, Hudson, Hudson . . .

And when it was over, I slowed my erratic thrusts and turned off the toy, once again focusing on him.

"I came so hard inside you, you know that? *You* made me cum like that. Seeing you so ready for me, taking me like this, you'll never understand how sexy it is, Hudson."

He was a mess, stroking his cock and teetering on the brink of what might have been the biggest orgasm of his life. "I've never—"

"I know, baby. I know. Just feel me. My hands on your hips. My cock bottoming out in you, pushing you farther, and farther—"

"Oh *fuck*, Scout. *Fuck*, I'm going to . . . I'm going to . . ."

"Cum for me."

Like the good boy that he was, he obeyed. A roar exploded from the depths of him, and he bounced on my cock, determined to make it last as long as possible. Streams of cum erupted from him, streaming across the bed—evidence of just how hard he'd climaxed.

And then, it was over. We collapsed in a sweaty, spent pile of bones and sex toys and slick and cum. Not the prettiest picture, but I didn't care. To me, it was the entire world.

The air around us settled. The world stopped shaking. Our bodies stilled. It was a strange role reversal, to be the one who took care of him after sex. Who breathed against his neck and stroked his tender skin. Who wrapped my arms around him and cradled him back to earth after shooting him up past the stratosphere. I held him like I'd never held anyone before, like he was precious to me.

And he was. He really was.

32

Safe Word

It wasn't the weed that made me sleep so well that night. It was Hudson. This wasn't the first time we'd fallen asleep tangled up together, but it was different now.

No. *I* was different.

As soon as I woke up the next morning, my body instinctively rolled over in his direction. He was still asleep—I must have really worn him out; he always got up before me—and his hair hung in rough chops across his smooth forehead. The light from my windows poured in, casting him in ultraviolet Technicolor until he glowed.

I matched my breathing to his. I memorized his face. I listened to the reverb of the other night's words in my ears. They thrummed in time with my relaxed heart rate. *You deserved better. You deserved better. You deserved better.* They kept coming back, but today, my heart answered.

I deserve you. I deserve you. I deserve you.

Hudson shifted in his sleep. Our knuckles brushed. The refrain rewrote itself.

I love you.

The thought staggered me. Every instinct told me to run. To

flee this bedroom, change my identity, and run away to start anew somewhere. Texarkana sounded good. I'd probably make a passable diner waitress and look good as a boxed-dye redhead, right?

But no. The coziness of bed was too appealing. The thought of staying in it with Hudson too magnetic.

I was in love with him. With his kindness. His sincerity. His quick laugh and easy nature. His whip-fast wit and earnest treatment of everyone he encountered. His perfect cock. The crease between his brows when he looked at his computer for too long. The brush of his fingertips when they traced down my back. His thoughtfulness. The way he opened up to me. Defended me. Honored me. Cared about and for me.

I loved the Hudson-ness of Hudson. In all the universe, I could not imagine another man like him.

And I could not imagine myself *being* with another man—like him or not.

Terrifying thought.

But then again, there was the possibility that I was imagining things. After all, what scientific proof was there for the concept of love? I could be mistaking a mixture of lust and loneliness for the emotions that everyone else described as love. What a humiliation *that* would be.

Problem: I'm in love. Or, at least I think I am.

Proposed Solution: Find out if love is even real . . . and then find a way to measure whether you're *really* in love with Hudson, or if this is just your overactive mind at work.

As slowly as I could, so as not to disturb him, I took my phone off my bedside table and opened up my DOAJ (Directory of Open Access Journals) app. I turned the brightness down—I would have been more embarrassed by Hudson seeing this than my porn search history—and let my fingers fly across the digital keyboard.

Scientific proof of love.

Steeling myself, I pressed search. The page turned over, populating dozens of peer-reviewed research papers on the subject. Apparently, like hunting for proof of God and ghosts, the questions surrounding soul mates and true love were ripe for study.

And just like those other topics, the results were inconclusive.

In my own research, I relished the idea of questions without answers. It meant that maybe *I* could one day be the person to uncover a new secret of our complex universe. It meant that in a world with millions of ready-made answers, there were still mysteries, still new things to learn. It made our planet a bigger and more exciting place to live.

However, as Hudson slept and I read paper after paper, I suddenly hated the very idea of question marks. Science should be able to tell me *exactly* what I wanted to know at that *exact* moment. What was the point of all these papers and research if they couldn't even tell me that love was real—or how to detect it if it was?

Finally, I settled on a review study that aggregated and analyzed the data of all English-language studies done over the last fifty years. Essentially, the research boiled down to three points.

One: There is no conclusive data proving the existence of love.

Two: However, if there *is* such a thing, its most promising evidence comes from EEG readings of the brain and hormonal studies.

Three: The only difference, it appears, between love and lust in the brain is the release of oxytocin.

Thanks, science. Really great stuff. Super helpful.

New Problem: I need to find out if I'm really in love with Hudson before I make any big decisions. Before I take any risks.

Proposed Solution: Replicate the studies I've read on love to see how my brain reacts to Hudson. It won't be definitive proof that we're in love, but it will be as close as I can get, probably.

Luckily, I happened to know someone with an EEG.

"You're deranged," Leelah said later that day when I told her my plan.

Addie didn't agree. "You're brilliant."

"I'm desperate" was my only reply.

At her former job, Leelah's expertise had been in developing portable versions of the world's most important medical technologies. She wanted to make rescue efforts in the wake of major disasters easier and was determined to help refugees in war zones. One of her most promising projects? A device that looked like a wire-toothed headband, with each tooth dotted with a small sensor. A portable proto-EEG device that, while having nowhere near the complex capabilities of a full machine, could, theoretically, give practitioners a baseline understanding of the patient's mental makeup and neurological responses.

In short, if Leelah just let me borrow it for, like, an hour, I'd be able to put this whole *Am I in love with Hudson or am I just horny and lonely* question to bed.

But Leelah, contrary to her usually rom-com-pilled self, was hesitant. As we put together our bagel breakfasts in the office kitchen, she aggressively slathered hers with undue force.

"Couldn't you just, I don't know, look inside your heart and figure it out?"

I perked up. "*Is* there a way to look inside the heart for that sort of thing? I didn't see any research like that."

"Impossible," she scoffed. "I thought I was working with some of the smartest people in the world, and yet you're all talking nonsense."

Always living for the vibes, Addie prodded: "It's for *science*, Leelah. C'mon. Aren't you even the *least* bit curious?"

"Right!" I concurred. "Dating is just data, after all."

The fastest way to a girl in *this* office? Tease her with science.

And that's how it was that, about an hour after BuzzCorp closed, we were locked away in Kevin, threading what I can only describe as the world's most technologically advanced headband through my unkempt locks. The style was very *nightclub chic in the Blade Runner universe*—discreet enough that I didn't look like I was wearing a medical device, but certainly an eye-catching statement piece.

"What'd you tell Hudson about all this?" Leelah asked, adjusting the nodes so they lay flat against my skull.

"I wanted to maintain the integrity of the experiment," I said. "So I just sort of avoided him all day."

"Bullshit," Addie chimed in. "You're just afraid to face him now that you have all these *feelings*."

Okay, one thing I can say for old, friendless Scout. At least back then, she didn't get read to filth so often.

Leelah made a few last-minute adjustments. "There you go. Now, before I turn this on, we need to have an informed-consent conversation."

"I've already read the research. I know what this thing can do."

"I'm not talking medical safety here. I just . . . if we collect data about what your brain does every time it sees Hudson, then you can't hide from it. It will be irrefutable proof of your care for him. Are you prepared for the consequences of that?"

The atmosphere in the small closet shifted. Oh, so that's why Leelah was so hesitant before. She didn't think I was ready for the truth.

"I don't believe that there is a measurement yet devised by scientists to capture true love," she said, ever the romantic. "Its very essence is unknowing. Leaping into what we don't understand, damn the consequences. But if you're convinced that this will help you make that decision, I'm all for it. So long as you know what you're getting into."

This apparently caught Addie's interest. "Yeah. Say you realize you love him. Or your brain does, anyway. What do you do then?"

That one question lit the fuse on a billion of my neurons, each carrying their own renegade thought or anxiety.

I never got the chance to address any of them, much less Addie's question, because the door to Kevin swung open, revealing Clara, standing in her Goop-beautiful glory, sipping a green smoothie.

"Ah! What are you three chickens doing in here?"

We all froze like we'd been caught looking for our Christmas gifts early.

"We were just—" Leelah squeaked.

"We've reappropriated some of Leelah's old tech," I said, gesturing to the headband. "Testing what stimuli trigger what parts of brain activity in non-sexually-intimate scenarios, so we can capture those same triggers in our toys."

"Right," Addie said, catching on fast. "Like, what parts of our innermost psyches are tickled by a man in a rolled-up button-down shirt? Or at a nightclub, when you're dancing up on some cutie? If we understand the brain's reaction in those scenarios, we can perhaps import the data and attempt to excite those same responses by use of our toys."

Clara's face positively lit up. That was the beauty of being the money and the brains rather than the scientific arm of a hardware start-up. You could be easily distracted by shiny things, no matter how ridiculous the explanation sounded. So what if you didn't get it? You probably just didn't have the technical know-how to understand. Just keep smiling and nodding and let the geniuses get to work.

"That's fantastic. What a fresh approach. We should put these on some of our in-house testers."

Leelah tensed. Due to the legal headaches currently swirling around her dissolved former company after her boyfriend embezzled all their funds, this tech from her previous company *technically* wasn't even supposed to see the light of day. "It's not ready for such a mass trial yet."

Clara quirked her head. "Is this your first time using it, Scout?"

"Yes," I said.

"Then you're the perfect test subject. Who better than a virgin mind to research the effects of sexual stimulation on the brain? And if you're willing, I'm happy to bankroll you all on a little fact-finding mission."

33

Stripping His Way Through Head School

Look, I'm sure they knew what they were talking about when they said *money can't buy happiness*. But Clara's money got us into the city's most exclusive, high-end strip club on one phone call's notice, so . . . it couldn't buy happiness, but it could buy a prime viewing location for Texas's premier, 100% USDA prime ass, tits, and dicks.

"I cannot *believe* you two agreed to this," I mumbled, sinking down deeper into my seat.

Addie furrowed her brow. "She's *Clara Mason*. How the hell do you say no to her?"

"Besides, she thinks this is for science," Leelah pointed out. "If we turned her down, she would've wanted to know why, and neither of us wanted to blow your cover."

The atmosphere in this club was nothing like the movies. Its refined finishes and inset lighting made it look more like the strip club on a spaceship for high-end sex fiends, and the whisper-core horny playlist would probably be as dated and cringey in twenty years as the sax solo in "Careless Whisper" is today.

The dancers moved around a central, W-shaped catwalk, with the VIP tables positioned at each of the five points of it.

Clara had apparently called ahead for us, so obviously we were at the central apex—the I-est of VIPs.

The dancers paid us special attention, each of them giving us the best angles, the sluttiest of teases, the most brazen of removals. But every time one approached, I suddenly found the ice in my old fashioned very, very interesting.

"Scout, you're supposed to look at the dancers, you know," Addie said as a particularly flexible blond lady pranced away at the conclusion of her number.

"She's right. Being here *is* a good thing, really. Not for whatever Clara thought we were doing, but good for the purposes of your experiment, I mean. We already have your baseline reading." Leelah leaned across to me, displaying her phone screen. The application showed a readout of my brain, and with a simple slider on the bottom, she could control whether we looked at past readings or current ones. First, she showed me one from half an hour ago, when we were in the car on the way over and I was blissfully unaware of our destination. "Here at the club, you'll experience lust, which we can then compare to your readings when you see Hudson. If the same parts of your brain light up when you see him, you'll know it's nothing more than an infatuation. If this part here lights up, though, it's clear that it's not just his pants you want to get into."

"It's his heart."

"Yeah, I got that, Addie, thanks."

"Might as well enjoy it," Leelah said, pocketing the phone. "Relax. Have another drink. It's on Clara's card. I, for one, am going to have a good time tonight."

Oh, and enjoy themselves they did.

"Can you believe how hot these people are?" Addie cackled. "It's way better than the dancers at Funky Bananas. These guys even have all their teeth."

The cocktails flowed. Many, *many* cocktails flowed. There

were many whoops and hollers. And as the night wore on, my companions only got rowdier and more ridiculous.

I, on the other hand, had a difficult time with my surroundings.

Between sets, several projectors played semi-pornographic videos erratically spliced together to music against the gossamer curtains. They reminded me of Hudson.

Hell, everything reminded me of Hudson. I considered asking Leelah to let me look at my brain scan, to see what areas lit up on the EEG just by *thinking* about him, but I tried to discipline my thoughts.

I needed to think about random hotties. Not Hudson. It was for science, dammit. How the hell could I be expected to know if I loved him or not without a clean brain scan?

A losing battle. I needed a breather. I rose from my overstuffed silver chair.

"I'm going to run to the restroom."

"Try to find a single fun bone in your body while you're there," teased Leelah, scanning the menu for her next martini selection.

Then, noticing the particularly impressive package on the dancer taking the stage, Addie cackled. "Or you could just borrow his!"

Ignoring them both, I beat out a hasty retreat.

In the privacy of the black-and-gold, low-lit bathroom, I wrangled my breathing.

It felt wrong to be here without Hudson. When he'd texted me about meeting up tonight, I'd told him I had "work stuff" and left it at that. But now, in an evening surrounded by nude people with the express intent of testing my brain's sexual responses, I couldn't help but feel dirty.

I knew that I wasn't. Looking at other people wasn't cheating, and even if it was, Hudson and I were not dating. We'd never promised exclusivity.

But that was the problem with opening your heart to someone

else. You start to carve out bigger and bigger places for them to fit. And when they're not there, even for a few hours, their absence hollows you.

The worst part was, I couldn't even talk to him about it. If I rang him up and tried, I'd have to tell him about my experiment. About my scientific pursuit of the truth regarding our love.

No. Too embarrassing. I'd just have to bear the weight of this academic pursuit myself. I stared myself down in the mirror, put on a fresh coat of lipstick, and steeled myself for what was to come.

I would make myself horny at this strip club. Then I would find Hudson, check my neural activity, figure out if the data suggested I love him, then fuck his brains out and/or declare my feelings.

You know. Normal relationship stuff.

What was *not* normal? Returning to my party on the floor to find Leelah and Addie practically bouncing in their seats. We'd fully reached folie à deux territory with these two, them feeding off each other's boundless energies. The empty shot glasses—ordered, consumed, and abandoned all in the span of my absence—only confirmed that diagnosis.

"Guess what?" Addie spluttered.

"What?"

"We bought you a private dance!"

As it turned out, Leelah was a giggly drunk. Any compunctions she'd had about this experiment of ours dissolved in the bubbles of her champagne, heightening her already bright personality.

"*Clara* bought you a dance," Addie amended through rum hiccups. "We just came up with the idea. Unfortunately, this club has *not* activated your horny brain. The scans aren't giving us *anything*. You need a more targeted approach if we want the EEG to register your sexual arousal."

Scientific principle pretty firmly holds the possibility for infinite parallel realities, each slightly different than this one. In any other version of myself and this moment, I would have run screaming (and possibly crying) from the threat of a stripper thrusting their crotch in my face.

Living in this universe, though, I sat my ass down in the chair and waited for my dance.

I needed to know the truth about what was going on in my brain—the irrefutable, data-confirmed truth. This was the best way I knew how to uncover it.

"What, Scout?" Leelah asked after my pause. "You're going to turn us down?"

"I didn't say that. I'm just preparing."

"We can always cancel it," Addie said. "If you're scared about what your brain scan might show."

"Is that it?" Leelah turned on me. "Did you ask me to read your brain and now you're finally scared of what you might see?"

Fuck that.

"No, I'm not scared."

Except I was. At least when I looked up to see two of the most beautiful people I'd ever seen exit the Platinum Room, the special, cordoned-off space for the private dances. The first was a short, stacked blonde with all-natural, all-perk breasts and the body of an Olympic gymnast. The second was a Celtic king with unruly red curls and a promising package hidden beneath his tight black clothes.

Double trouble. I didn't even *want* to know what Clara's credit card statement would look like after this.

"Is that them?" I asked.

"Mm-hmm," Leelah said. "Clara told us to get only the best for you."

My nerves turned to fire. Which then turned into a raging inferno when I just happened to look up and see someone come through the club's front door.

Hudson Fuckin' Bailey.

My vision tunneled around him.

Of all the strip joints in all the world, he had to walk into mine.

My first thought was: *This is the worst coincidence of all time.* My second thought was: *We're dating and he went to a strip club without me?* My third thought was: *You're not dating, you have no right to be jealous.* And my fourth thought was: *There's no such thing as coincidences. Not when you've got meddling friends around.*

I turned on them both, hissing low. "What the hell did you two do?"

Leelah winced. "I may have called him."

"No way!" Addie nearly spit out her drink. "You too?"

"What?"

Leelah's speech slurred slightly as she bristled. "I thought it would be instructive. That you could compare your two options—sexy strangers and Hudson—and see the results more quickly than running the two tests separately. But . . . I can now see from your expression that it wasn't such a good idea."

"You think?"

Addie was much less apologetic. "And I just thought it would be funny."

"What, exactly, did you tell him?"

"He texted me and asked if I knew where you were. He's been trying to get in touch with you and couldn't. He was worried. So I told him."

Leelah nodded. "Same."

With friends like this . . .

"You *both* are on my shit list."

Shrugging, Addie sipped her cocktail again. "We'll live."

A response boiled to the tip of my tongue. She didn't care, waving and raising her voice over the music. "Hudson! Hudson, we're over here! Pull up a seat! We're getting bottle service."

The contents of my nearly empty drink were now incredibly interesting. I'm not sure I was ashamed that Hudson had found me here, and I wasn't embarrassed, exactly.

What was I talking about? Of course I was embarrassed. I was wearing an electrode headband and taunting myself with other sexy bodies so I could delve into my subconscious electrical impulses to determine if I'd really fallen for him. A normal person would have just known. I, on the other hand, put more stock in data than myself.

How was I going to explain this?

"Sorry to interrupt the party," I heard him say from somewhere over my shoulder.

"Not at all," Leelah said. "We're just getting started."

"I didn't realize this was a girls-night activity. I couldn't get ahold of you, Scout, and, uh, so I asked around and . . . You know what? I'll just head out."

That seemed perfectly reasonable to me.

"No way, dude," Addie said. "Pull up a chair! Tonight's on Clara—and you've earned a little R&R. Isn't that right, Scout?"

He deserves all the R&R in the world, but he doesn't deserve to be stuck here, peer-pressured into watching me get a lap dance from two strangers.

I was about to say as much. But apparently my vote didn't count, because no sooner had Addie gestured to a scantily clad waitress for another chair than my two strippers materialized.

I didn't even want to imagine what my brain scan looked like now.

34

Griptease

Hudson's gaze was inescapable. It was like an evolutionary force. If natural selection ensured that humans could fight, fuck, and feed . . . then my biology was perfectly attuned to know when Hudson wanted the second thing on that list.

This current stare wasn't angry. I'd worried that jealousy would burn through him like a lab fire, but it didn't. It smoldered. It yearned.

It possessed.

The strippers' crotches were right at eye level, though, so I didn't have much mental space to dissect Hudson's attention. She wore a spangly silver number straight out of a Vegas cabaret. He was dressed like a vampire from a bad TV show, with tearaway leathers and a dark button-up shirt complete with sleeves rolled to the elbow.

They should have been ridiculous. Instead, they turned me on.

Maybe because of their perfect bodies. Maybe because of the way Hudson's stare scorched as they touched me—the male dancer's hand on my shoulder, his partner's brushing hair from my face.

"Hey there, beautiful. I'm Stephanie."

I swallowed. What the hell do you say in a situation like this? Were goose bumps normal in this scenario? "Oh, hi."

"I'm Rich," the man purred. "Thought we'd come and give you a show in the Platinum Room. Is that all right?"

My chest tightened. This whole thing with Hudson had been about opening my sexual horizons, and this was a safe place to do that. Besides . . . part of me wanted Hudson to see me like this. The object of someone else's sexual energies. "Mm-hmm."

Rich took me by the hand, guiding me up from the chair. Stephanie slid her arm around my waist, hugging her tight body to my curvier one. Her touch gave me goose bumps. I'd only just started seeing a man; I'd definitely never been touched by a woman.

God, these brain scans are going to light up like a goddamn Christmas tree.

The ladies from work whooped and hollered in approval the whole walk to the Platinum Room. I listened closely for any sign from Hudson, but he didn't join them.

"You know the rules, sugar?" Rich asked as we walked.

"No touching."

"Not unless we touch you first," Stephanie crooned, squeezing my waist. "And you're looking pretty damn tempting, aren't you?"

I almost laughed out loud at that. We'd all changed after work, but my black and white skirt and blouse set was far from little. It didn't even show off my cleavage. Of all the talent in this club, I was probably the *least* tempting.

The compliment was strikingly insincere. Not surprising, considering they were being paid for it. But it only highlighted how sincere Hudson had always been.

I'd never heard him lie. Not once. And certainly never about me. *Beautiful. Smart. Kind. Good. Worthy. Deserving.* He'd said all of that about me. More than that, though, he'd believed it. Even now, when his eyes followed me through the club, his gaze was honest. *I want to fuck you and I wish the hands on you were mine.*

Fuck, and now I was catching feelings in the middle of a personal strip dance.

All right, Scout. Focus. You've got two half-naked bodies ready to bare it all for you—bought and paid for by your boss for the advancement of our scientific understanding regarding sex and neural activity. Maybe this isn't what you planned on for this experiment into the dichotomy between romantic brain and horny brain, but it's what you've got, so the least you can do is give them your full attention.

The Platinum Room *was*, admittedly, very sexy. The plush furnishings, the dark crystal light fixtures, the small, central raised platform. Even the tinted glass walls separating it from the main floor were alluring—they gave the illusion of privacy while, in reality, a guest at the tables could easily see what went on inside.

And by "a guest," I meant Hudson, who had ordered an old fashioned and smoldered at me over the rim of it.

I clenched my thighs together.

Stephanie guided me to the couch. Music, even softer and breathier than the music outside, queued up through unseen speakers.

The show began. These weren't cheesy movie strippers but the real thing. A true double act, they began by kissing each other softly, their hands traveling the planes of one another's bodies. Soon he turned her around, pressing her back to his front, so he could slowly peel off her costume and reveal her body to me.

And it was a *beautiful* body. Porn had not prepared me for how gorgeous a naked woman could be. I swallowed hard as he cupped her breasts, pebbling her nipples beneath his fingers. Then he moved the costume down her body until it puddled beneath her feet, leaving her in nothing but a G-string and matching silver heels.

Then it was his turn. Spinning around, she faced him. First, she ripped away his shirt, turning her head to check that I was still enjoying the show.

I was. In fact, I was enjoying it a little too much. My nipples ached to be touched. My clit needed friction—anything to bring me relief. They were incredibly sexy together, and watching them while Hudson watched me . . . it was almost unbearable.

Slowly lowering herself down his body, Stephanie bent her knees to best show off her perfect ass. Squatting at his feet, she worked his zipper down and—

Oh shit. He wasn't wearing anything underneath. His hard, intimidatingly long cock sprang out.

And then I was alone with two naked strangers, licking my lips involuntarily.

To my surprise, though, they didn't stay up on their dais. Carefully, they stepped down and took their places. Her by my side, kneeling on the couch to face me. Him on the floor, ready to part my legs. They hovered suggestively, their lithe bodies glistening with oil. Her hard nipples dangled; another inch and they would brush my arm. His cock was erect, too. Ready to tease me.

Could they tell how turned on I was?

Could *Hudson*? All the way from across the club?

The EEG readouts must have been going haywire.

Rich's hands lingered above my knees. "Can we touch you?"

"Sure," I panted.

Rich spread my knees sharply, exposing my barely there panties to the cold air. I gasped, but I was quickly distracted by Stephanie, who ran the back of her hand down my cheek.

Stephanie licked her lips. Her face was so close to mine. The overstimulation of two people focused solely on me . . . it was unbelievable. "Can we kiss you?"

Jesus, Clara must have paid more *than a fortune for this dance.*

My gaze flickered to the glass wall, where Hudson stared at me with parted lips. Maybe it was my imagination, but the jealousy rolled off him in waves. His lust settled over my skin like a sheen of sex-dew sweat.

Words lost all their meaning. All I could think to say was "Mm-hmm."

"If you ever want to stop, just say 'platinum,' okay?"

"I will."

Afraid my wandering hands would get me in trouble, I sat on them. It was torture, knowing that I couldn't touch myself. Still, I focused on Stephanie's hot breath on the curve of my neck. Rich's knuckles raised my skirt hem as he dragged his hands up the length of my thighs, straight toward the place where I wanted contact the most.

Then he started to kiss me. Up one thigh, breathing on my pussy, then down the other thigh and back again.

Before I could buck my hips against his face, though, Stephanie threaded one hand through my hair and pulled my lips to hers.

I'd never kissed a woman before. She was all sweetness and plump softness. She ran her tongue along my lips, requesting entrance, and I breathed her into me.

Not to be outdone, Rich abandoned my legs, situating himself between them so he could steal a kiss from me, too. As he plundered my mouth, sharp and intrusive, Stephanie's hands wandered down my chest until they found purchase around my breasts.

I moaned into his mouth. *Fuck.* They felt so good.

They traded me like that, kissing and fondling me. Their naked bodies brushed with mine, driving me crazy. I wanted more contact, more bare flesh . . .

And one more body. I wanted Hudson's. Even in the depths of sensation with *two* other people, I couldn't stop thinking about him.

In a rare break from their onslaught of pleasure, I stole a glance at him through the glass partition separating us. He was hungry. His hand was balled in his lap, and I could tell it was taking great effort not to whip his cock out and make himself cum.

A wave of pride washed over me. Stephanie and Rich's treatment of me was just work to them, but knowing that I was making Hudson seethe with jealous horniness was like winning a golden ticket. Unlikely and transcendently lucky.

My thoughts must have been clear. Stephanie's hand descended toward my center, ready to make my wildest dreams come true and cum in front of Hudson by someone else's touch. And . . .

The music shifted above us. The illusion of sex and lust shattered. All at once, Rich and Stephanie stood up and collected their clothes with a clinical but friendly air.

Ah. It seemed our time was up.

My body hummed with unspent sexual energy.

It was then, with the lights up and the tunes down, that I realized I no longer felt the prickle of Hudson's gaze on my neck. Had he left? Gone to get his own dance? I didn't know. But a mixture of disappointment and relief tugged at me.

Stephanie must have noticed. Perceptive. The consummate professional.

"Show's over, honey. Don't worry, though. I think your boyfriend really enjoyed the view."

"He's not my boyfriend. We're not like that," I said, out of habit more than anything else.

Rich chuckled. "He will be your boyfriend once he's through with you tonight. Anyone can see he wants to tear those panties off with his teeth."

"Yeah. There's only so much a man can take before he bursts. And I think we just pushed him to his limits. Enjoy."

With a friendly face—so different from the sexy pout she'd worn just a few seconds ago—Stephanie helped me back to my feet.

As I exited the Platinum Room, ducking my head to hide my blush from the ecstatic ladies back at my table, I turned on my phone.

Time to call an Uber. Gotta get out of here. My pussy was soaking wet—not really from the dance and the kissing (okay, not *just* from the dance and the kissing) but from the heat of Hudson's jealous stare as I received them.

When my phone powered up, though, I was faced with a single text message on my screen.

It was from Hudson.

Men's bathroom. First door on the left. Five minutes. Bring your purse. Come alone.

35

Dirty Deeds Done Skirt Cheap

I probably shouldn't have gone. I should have gone straight home, taken a cold shower, and only re-engaged with Hudson when I was ready to start my EEG experience fresh. When I could be sure that what I felt for him couldn't be blamed on the desire I felt.

But . . . how could I refuse? The threat of sex with him lingered in every syllable and full stop of that text message, and *God*, did I want him.

This strip club was one of those places that didn't have unified washrooms. Instead, tucked away at the back of the building was a hallway lined with doors, each designated with a painted sex signifier and each its own individual, private room.

I approached the first men's room, checked that the coast was clear, took in a deep breath, and walked in.

The black-painted walls were illuminated only by a single neon sign over the oxidized mirror that read *YOU'RE SO FUCKING SEXY.* It took a moment for my eyes to adjust.

"Was that fun for you?"

I startled at the low rumble of Hudson's voice. He slinked out of the shadows, leaning against one of the dark walls to observe me.

The elevator eyes took me in from my kitten heels to my swollen lips. He assessed my body like it was an enemy combatant he yearned to pillage.

When our eyes met, he tipped his head to one side. He was all calm. All control. Almost flippant in his intensity. I, on the other hand, felt like prey, shivering in his thrall.

"I asked if that was fun for you," he repeated.

"A strip club wouldn't have been my first choice for a girls' night out," I said. "But I didn't hate it."

"Yeah, I imagine you're right. I bet you loved knowing I was there, watching you get toyed with by those two beautiful fucks."

The words were harsh and crass, especially coming out of his usually adoring mouth. But that only turned me on more. He stepped forward, closing our gap until I was pressed against the wall.

"Hudson—"

He lorded over me. "Didn't you? You liked me being jealous."

"Is that what you are? Jealous?"

Taking both hands in just one of his own, he pinned them above my head.

"I haven't stopped thinking about you all day. You're everywhere, Scout. You're in my work, you're in my head, you're in the empty spaces between my fingers. Then I come here because your friends lured me, and I had to watch two strippers turn you on and kiss you and touch you, just like I've wanted to do since you vanished out of our bed this morning. Yeah, I'm *fucking jealous*."

He dipped his head to my neck, nipping down at the soft flesh. My knees threatened to buckle. Especially when his thumb brushed my nipple—a frustrating sensation through my bra. I wanted more.

"I had to work from home this afternoon so I could jerk off to the thought of you. And here you were, getting felt up by strangers. I bet you loved being worshipped while I was in the other room, forced to watch someone else bring you so much pleasure. Am I wrong?"

It took too much focus to keep breathing and standing. I didn't have the capacity for coherent thought anymore, just *fuck me fuck me fuck me.*

Hudson quirked an eyebrow. His hand abandoned my chest and slipped down, down, down, until it toyed with the waistband of my skirt.

He descended further, slipping beneath my underwear until he cupped my mound.

"Why don't we *see* if I'm wrong?" His fingers hesitated for a moment. "Or do you not want that?"

Instead of answering with my words—I couldn't find any—I merely rolled my hips forward. My cunt fit perfectly in his hand. He dipped one finger between my folds and shuddered.

So did I.

"You are so fucking wet," he murmured. Powerful. Triumphant.

I nodded. My agreement came out more like a whimper.

He pulled his fingers away. Then, eyes never leaving mine, he licked them clean. "After last night, when you weren't in bed this morning, I worried that I'd scared you off," he whispered. A note of vulnerability struck a minor chord in the melody of his words, but then vindication brought him back to a major key. "But you still want me, don't you?"

"You already answered your own question."

He chuckled, but it wasn't Hudson's usual chuckle. It was darker, headier. I'd never considered that my romance-skittish departure this morning would scare him, but it made sense. And I would give anything to reassure him again. Including my pussy in this bathroom. He returned his hand between my legs, toying with the idea of splitting me in two with his fingers. "Yeah. I guess I did. But I need you to say it."

"I still want you," I assured him.

He slipped one finger inside me to the knuckle. My clit ached for attention. "That's not good enough. You left me in bed this morning after fucking me all night. I want more from you."

"Please," I said.

His thumb hesitated over my clit. "*Beg.*"

It wouldn't take me long to cum. A few choice words and his focused touch on my center and I would be a goner—right here, shamefully, in a strip club bathroom. That was how much I needed him. That was how much I'd been missing him. "Fuck, Hudson, I need you. I'm sorry—please. Please fuck me. Please make me cum."

Without a word, he ripped his hand from my core, wiped my slick idly on my skirt, marking me with the evidence of my own desire, and started giving orders.

"Take your toy out of your purse."

I blushed. "What?"

"Don't play innocent with me," he replied. He ripped his belt off in a single snapping motion. "I know you too well, you dirty thing. Take your toy out of your purse. Any of them will do."

We talk a lot in today's age about the horrors of being seen. But it was even worse to be seen when the person you were was a fucking slut with multiple sex toys in her purse and a pussy aching to be filled by some man in a bathroom stall.

I had no shame, did I? The cock was too good, and the orgasms too close.

Besides, I liked this new Hudson. The one who wasn't afraid to demand what he wanted from me.

Frantically, I dug through my purse for the first toy I got my hands on. A tiny tube of mascara that, when opened, revealed a brushlike wand capable of delivering small but intense vibrations. When I had it in hand, Hudson could no longer hold that simmering lust back. He snapped my head between his hands, kissing me and tearing at my clothes like a man possessed. Gone went my shirt buttons. Out popped my tits from my bra.

He was all over me, dominating me with his rough hands and even rougher mouth. He seemed to be everywhere at once. My waist, my hard nipples, my sensitive neck, the heights of my thighs.

And when he had trouble accessing my pussy, he gave my skirt the same treatment as my shirt.

He simply tore through it until it could be dispatched carelessly to the floor.

Finally, he wrapped his hands around my ass, picking me up until I had no choice but to wrap my wet-pussyed legs around him, exposing my cunt completely to his whims.

I'd always worried about being too heavy for stuff like this, but Hudson apparently had super-lust strength, because he carried me with ease and set me on the edge of the sink.

Breathy, he tipped his forehead against mine. "I'm going to fuck you now. And you're going to cum around my cock, screaming my name."

"What if someone hears?"

He whipped out his cock. It slid along my wet entrance, mixing our matching pre-cum. "Then they'll know you're mine, that I'm yours, and that you're a dirty fucking slut who needed to be punished with my cock."

And then he was inside me. Fast and hard and, true to his word, completely punishing. Balancing on the edge of the sink, I brought my vibrator to my clit and let it work on me—turning it to the highest setting, higher than I'd ever used it before.

Hudson fucked me like a dirty girl. I felt like one. And soon my orgasm was blossoming as he filled and stretched my cunt.

I gripped at his shoulders, fingernails digging in. I couldn't catch my breath. I couldn't get him deep enough. I couldn't stop seeing stars—

"Hudson! Hudson, I'm yours!"

I came, pulsing around his cock, tightening time and time again, riding the thrusts of his cock until he, too, came in a roaring climax.

He filled me to the brim as he rode out the final aftershocks of our combined orgasm.

When he withdrew from me, he helped me off the sink and set me back on my feet. I immediately felt his slick cum slide from between my swollen pussy lips and down my legs. I reached for a napkin—

"Don't you dare touch that," Hudson said, his voice low and dangerous.

I chuckled. "But I've got to walk out of here."

He didn't join my laughter. "I know."

"What if someone sees?"

"We already talked about this. Then they'll know just what you are. *Mine.*"

My mouth went dry. I *was* his. And I wanted to be. Smelling like him, slick with him . . . I had been marked, and I liked it.

Returning my tits to my bra, I managed to salvage my shirt—at least most of the buttons. My skirt, however, was not going to make it without some serious alterations. Maybe I had a pin in my purse . . .

"You really did a number on my clothes, didn't you?"

Hudson shrugged. "They were in my way. I'll buy you some new stuff. Here. You can have my coat." There it was. That smirk that turned me on *and* comforted me all at the same time. "I'm not done with you."

When I hesitated, he added, "Unless you're done with me, that is?"

Always the gentleman. Always asking for consent in a still-sexy language we both understood.

He requisitioned my skirt and abandoned it in the trash can. Whatever I decided, I'd be walking home with a pussy full of cum and and wearing only dirty underwear and a ripped top.

"I'm not going anywhere, Hudson," I said. "I promised you that, and I meant it."

I slipped into his coat like a familiar hug and snuck out of the club with him right by my side.

Later that night, Leelah texted me the complete data set from our experiment.

Whatever happened after your experience in the
Platinum Room, the EEG went nuts. Wanna
see?

I didn't open it. I didn't need to. I knew the truth.

36

Come Again?

Once we left the club, he took me where we'd never gone before.

His place.

Upon arriving at his short-term corporate housing, I remembered our questions game at mini golf. He told me he didn't like people getting too close. Yet there I was. Being let into a new dimension of his existence. If *getting close* had a synonym, it was walking into Hudson's apartment.

Each time he showed me a new dimension of himself, each time he revealed some hidden element of Hudson Bailey, I felt honored. It was an exclusive club. A limited run. A highly rare element.

This home visit was no different. Except in all the ways that it was.

Because I knew now that I loved him. Empirical data or not, I knew. And this felt like proof that maybe he loved me back. Maybe if I jumped, the long fall into love wouldn't be a lonely one.

The decor was all what I'd expected from a place you could rent by the month. Clean, comfortable, and inoffensive. But everywhere I looked, there were new pieces of Hudson lore waiting to be uncovered. Stacks of secondhand western paperbacks on the bedside table. Graphic tees peeking out from a laundry hamper. Franken Berry cereal on the counter.

I felt both like a stranger in this place and perfectly at home. The entire experience was a microcosmic encapsulation of my relationship with Hudson. Familiar and alien all at once. I wanted to dive through everything, to unpack these fragments of him.

He gestured me to get comfortable on a kitchen barstool while he hunted through the cabinets.

"Are you hungry?"

"Starved," I admitted.

We'd been in such a rush to get to the strip club that we'd not eaten anything before arriving. I eyed the Franken Berry on the counter. Fruity, fun cereals were not in my household growing up; I coveted them, especially on a sloshing-booze stomach. "I'll throw some dinner together," he said, as if answering my unspoken request.

"You can cook?"

"Basic skill."

"You'd be shocked how few people understand basic skills," I mumbled, fully aware that I was one of those people. I could cook a takeout menu and popcorn—and sometimes, depending on the microwave, not even popcorn.

"Ramen?"

Men. I hadn't had much experience with them, but saying "I can cook" when what they meant was "I'm a bachelor who can throw noodles in a pan" seemed typical.

My reaction must have been written all over my face, because he waved not a bag of instant ramen at me, but the fancy box I'd only seen in specialty grocery stores.

"This is the good stuff. You're going to love it. Did you know there's a Japanese word for the slurping you make when you eat ramen? *Zuzutto.*" He mimicked the sound. I smirked.

"Sort of sounds like the noise you make when you go down on me."

"Hmm," he said with a playful tilt of his head. "I don't hear it. I'm just going to have to investigate your hypothesis later."

So, sitting at the bar, I watched him roll the sleeves of his buttoned shirt to the elbows, slip into an apron, and go to work. Not to get romantic about it or anything, but every movement enraptured me. His hands beneath the faucet as he washed them. The precision of his knife cutting through green onions. The tosses of the wok cooking our ground pork. The dexterity of peeling the soft-boiled eggs.

I was so lost in him that I didn't register our silence until he set the steaming bowl in front of me.

After everything that had happened tonight, the quiet domesticity was jarring, but not unpleasant.

We slurped—zuzutto'd—for a while. I, however, felt like I was carrying a ball of electrons in my hand. Now that I had finally copped to loving Hudson, I wanted just the right moment to come out with it.

"You've gotten pretty quiet for a man who just fucked a woman in a strip club bathroom," I said by way of an opener.

"I'm still waiting for you to explain what you were doing there," he said, lips curved.

He doesn't need to know that. "I told you. Girls' night."

"Wearing Leelah's EEG headband?" My entire body tightened. Off my look, he shrugged. "She showed it to me the first week she got here. She's damn proud of that thing."

Damn. I'd been caught.

"We were running an experiment," I conceded.

"Oh? And what experiment necessitated deep brain scans while at a strip club?"

Okay. Not only caught, but trapped. He wasn't going to let me go without an explanation.

"I'm not a person who understands feelings," I said, after a bit. "I have them. A lot of them. But I don't necessarily *get* them. When I run up against something I don't understand, I try to analyze it."

"What feeling were you analyzing at a strip club, then?"

I chose the safest answer. An evasion. "Lust."

He chuckled. "You understand lust."

All I wanted to do was stare at my hands, but I forced myself to catalog every microexpression crossing his face as I explained myself.

"Yes. But I don't understand the . . . other things I'm feeling. The things I'm feeling for *you*. And we thought the EEG—if I compared pure lust to whatever it is I've got going on here, I might be able to get a handle on it."

My attention wasn't rewarded. His face remained completely impassive. "I see. And what did you discover in this little experiment?"

"I didn't check the data."

I didn't need to.

Finally, a flicker. His lips turned down at the corners. "It's a little worrying. That you feel the need to *check the data* on us."

"You're leaving. Our time's almost up," I said, feeling defensive. "This was only temporary, you and me. I wanted to know the facts before I did anything reckless. You know how I am."

The sad set of his mouth did not correct. I panicked.

"How familiar are you with the concept of entropy?"

"I'm a glorified IT guy, Scout," he said with a self-deprecating shrug. "Entropy sounds above my pay grade."

"Well. Entropy is basically how much chaos is in any given system. Evolutionarily speaking, entropy is an enemy. It's dangerous. So our minds learned to compensate for entropy by developing predictive powers. We take all of the inputs and information we're getting, our mind makes snap judgments about what could happen next, and we make decisions that keep us alive, unhurt, and functioning. A predictable existence is a safer one."

I fiddled with my chopsticks.

"I have always—especially after everything that happened with Lloyd at GalacticSolutions—tried to minimize entropy. I thought that maybe the EEG, the data, would help me reduce my entropy in our relationship. It's especially scary now, with The Fantasy launch approaching. I've been getting better at delegating in the office, but in other areas, like with you, I don't know how much uncertainty I can handle right now. This seemed like a solution."

"I see."

"You do?"

My heart swelled. Of course he would understand. Hudson always understood. Now he would take my hands in his and say he didn't need an EEG either—he knew that he loved me, and we should be together, walking bravely and certainly into our future . . .

Only . . . that didn't happen. He reached into his breast pocket and fished around.

The topic shifted on a dime. No more love talk. In fact, the further we got away from that subject, the more he perked up.

"Speaking of uncertain futures, I wanted to pass this along. I was thinking about your rocket problem—"

"I don't have a rocket problem. And all this thinking you did—was this before or after you went home for lunch so you could jerk off to the thought of me?" I teased.

"Ha-ha. Look, the *world* has a rocket problem and that problem is you not making rockets. So, here."

"What is it?"

Having found it in the depths of his breast pocket, he handed over a small card. It was worn from years inside a file folder, meaning he'd had the thing for a long time and only fished it out for me.

"This is the contact info for my friend, Malcolm McEwan, CEO of SkyTech. Brilliant scientist. Always looking to expand his team. I think you two would get along really well. You know, if you ever wanted to go back to aeronautics. No pressure or anything. I don't want to commandeer your choices like everyone else does. I know, I know. Entropy. You don't want to rock the boat now. But if you want to get coffee while you're in New York, maybe after the product launch, I think he'd appreciate the phone call. You have a real gift for design and engineering, Scout. I want you to work on whatever will make you happy. You'd be an asset anywhere you went."

It wasn't a declaration. It wasn't his heart on a silver platter. But it was a considerate gesture that left me with hope.

"Thanks," I said, meaning it. "Is there . . . is there anything else you want to tell me? Anything else we need to get out in the open now that I've totally embarrassed myself with my EEG story? I mean, we're going to go our separate ways after OFest. If there's any time to be honest, it's now."

He searched my face. What he found, I couldn't begin to guess. "We're here. That's all that matters. Who cares about the details?"

I did. I cared about the details. Details were everything to a scientist.

More importantly, now, as a woman falling in love, the details were more than everything. They felt like the *only* thing.

To press him, though, would be to push him away. Or worse, he might just lie to avoid hurting me or rocking the boat. I couldn't have that.

I could bide my time. He just needed to trust me with his heart the way he trusted me with his cock.

I'd wait, I decided. We had until OFest, after all.

Time to change the subject. I'd at least enjoy him while I had him.

Sitting up from my barstool, I crept onto the kitchen counter, crawling along it until I was in front of him, breasts dangling right before his eyes.

"Can I ask you a question, then? I've always wondered . . ."

As he traced the line of my bra, he chuckled, breathy and low. "You can ask me, tell me, *do* anything you want to me right now. I've never been so suggestible."

"How did you know? Like, when you touched my leg in the office that day, how did you know I'd be into it? That was a time when you were afraid to tell me anything else you wanted, but you still told me that you wanted me. You had to have some inkling that I felt the same."

"Bold of you to assume I knew that. Could have just been a shot in the dark."

"C'mon. You were so confident. Was it *that* obvious I was into you?"

"We had adjoining rooms, Scout."

Those words were heavy, like I should have been able to read some deeper meaning from them. But without any context, I was just as in the dark as I was before he said it.

"At the conference we went to right before the Lloyd thing came out," he explained. "We had adjoining rooms. You didn't know, did you? Anyway, the walls were not very thick. The night before we left . . . I heard you."

Oh.

Mortification infected every inch of me. Retreating off the other side of the counter, I put as much space between us as I could. This new information might as well have been an unleashed toxic spore I was trying in vain to escape.

"You heard me masturbating that night?"

His lips quirked ever so slightly. "And screaming out my name when you came. Yeah."

I slammed my eyes shut, as though that would keep the truth out. Hudson had heard me masturbating over him. We were basically strangers and he'd caught me fucking myself to the very thought of him.

Cringe. That was all I could feel. Cringe.

Moving to my side, he tucked a stray strand of hair behind my ear.

"It was very flattering, really. Especially because I'd been fantasizing about you since the day we met. I just can't believe you didn't hear me screaming *your* name about ten minutes later."

In that moment, through the haze of humiliation, I knew that he had to love me. We were made for each other.

37

Post-Orgasmic Bliss

The week and a half before OFest was the happiest time of my life.

I say that fully aware that it wasn't a high bar to clear. I wasn't a particularly happy person to begin with, and my career and personal peaks never lasted long.

Still. For a lonely, sad girl, those precious days meant the world to me. Hudson and I spent every waking moment together. I hung out with Addie and Leelah, even inviting Clara along to join us for coffee a few times. Aside from our current marketing hiccups, the work on The Fantasy couldn't have gone better. Now that I had let go of my white-knuckle grip on the project, the teams felt more confident than ever to press forward with their work. We'd fixed the bugs, the design looked fantastic, ecstatic fuck reports poured in, and Hudson impressed everyone with his newfound, comprehensive sex toy knowledge.

In short, we were ready to knock our OFest presentation out of the park, I was having incredible sex daily, I began to feel like a real adult instead of a cog in a machine, I had friends, and as for love . . . ?

It was so close I could taste it in every single one of Hudson's kisses.

Naturally, this put me on guard for calamity to strike.

"I've got a bad feeling about this," I muttered as I placed my luggage on the X-ray machine at DFW.

We were all heading to the national OFest convention. None of that rinky-dink regional shit that Hudson and I had first visited all those weeks ago. Our equipment and prototypes had been shipped ahead of us, but the team was flying together to JFK for the big event. Usually I attended alone, but given everything that was at stake for the company, Clara decided that all personnel were essential this time. Besides my keynote speech and product rollout, we would need people to staff our booth on the display floor, make sure that the marketing materials were properly organized, keep our prototypes in fine working order, have face time with potential buyers, run the focus groups and testing, finish the hype video for our presentation . . . it was a massive operation.

Before Hudson, before Addie and Leelah, before the events of the last few weeks, their presence would have annoyed me. I would have wanted complete control. Now I looked forward to letting the team flex their muscles to our competition.

In short, the nerves in my stomach had *nothing* to do with OFest and everything to do with, well, something else.

Someone else.

Addie grumbled beside me, still groggy from the four a.m. wake-up call for our flight. "All right, Han Solo-Play. Cool it with the ominous portends."

"I don't know," I said, bouncing on the balls of my feet with pent-up, nervous energy. "I'm just *too* happy. The universe must be waiting to pull the rug out from under me."

Leelah, looking perfect in her head-to-toe matching athleisure, struggled to fit her carry-on through the machine. "You're only worried because you're going to see Lloyd Exeter again. Don't worry. You're going to ace your presentation, show all the haters wrong, and then become a millionaire with your stock options in BuzzCorp. We'll see who's laughing then."

"I don't know. This doesn't feel like a Lloyd Exeter worry."

"What, then?" Addie asked.

Finally free of her bag, Leelah shuffled into the body scanner line behind us. "It's Hudson, isn't it? You know he's leaving soon."

"Jesus, Scout! You haven't told him how you feel yet?"

"I can't," I spluttered.

"Why not?"

"Because he has to make the first move."

Addie tightened the strings of her Eras hoodie. "This isn't the 1600s. We have feminism and dating apps. You don't have to wait for the guy to take the lead."

Believe me, I knew that. It was all I'd been thinking about since my EEG experiment. When he hadn't immediately jumped on the opportunity to tell me how he felt that night over ramen, I posited that I should have confessed my feelings first.

But it wasn't so simple as that. Not with Hudson.

"He is the worst people pleaser I've ever met," I said. "Once, I ordered Thai takeout, and he literally made himself physically ill because he didn't want to disappoint me by saying it was too spicy for him. He told me he signed up for a pyramid scheme, fully knowing it was one, because he didn't want to hurt the essential oil lady. He's *still* technically a Junior Scent Queen in that company, paying money every month because he's too afraid of what canceling will do to her downline."

"And?"

"And if I tell him that I'm in love with him, he'd probably lie and agree just to keep the peace. Just so he wouldn't hurt me. That's who he is."

"Seems like a stretch," Addie groaned as the body scanner line inched forward.

"Have you asked him about love?" Leelah asked.

"I hinted at it once." *I don't understand the other things I'm feeling. The things I'm feeling for you.* "He didn't bite."

"Maybe he's scared."

A TSA agent waved me through. I stepped into the scanner, feeling less transparent there than I did talking with my friends.

Once we regrouped on the other side to collect our bags, I continued:

"I want him. More than anything. And I'm ready to take the leap—whatever that looks like. But until he *tells me* what he wants, I can't risk it. I need to know that he's genuine, not that he's faking it to keep the peace until after OFest."

"If only someone had an EEG machine and we could empirically see if he was telling the truth . . ." Leelah joked.

"We're not hooking Hudson up to your sci-fi headband." I'd already considered it and dismissed it as an option. He'd never agree to it. "Does it really count as a declaration of love if a machine tells me and not him?"

Our bags plodded out onto the conveyor belt—a bright purple number for Leelah, a sensible backpack for me, and a crossbody with barely enough room to fit a book for Addie. As she threw the latter over her shoulder, she asked: "What if he doesn't confess his undying adoration for you in the next few days?"

"He will," I said, my voice a little shaky.

"You think so?"

"That's my hypothesis, anyway. C'mon, ladies. It's New York City! It's the fall. And time is running out. I believe that he does love me back. He just has to find the courage to say it out loud."

Neither of them looked very sure. Rather, they looked about as sure as I felt. But they respectfully bowed out and we went our separate ways—them in search of coffee, me in search of the gate.

"Excuse me, ma'am. I think I need to pull you for a secondary search."

I giggled as Hudson's breath tickled my neck, spinning out of his grasp and righting my suitcase as I went. "Don't! Clara might see."

"What?" he said oh-so-innocently. "We're just two colleagues messing around in the airport."

Joining the throng, we walked past duty-free shops and cheap barbecue joints.

"Well, last time we messed around together at an airport, we ended up fucking each other's brains out just a few days later."

"I'm not waiting a few days this time," he purred. "I intend to have you all over New York City as soon as possible. How much do you think we'd have to pay a cabbie to let us fool around in the back of his car?"

My stomach tightened at that mental image, but . . . "I wish I could. Unfortunately, I'm on a tight schedule today. I need to visit the convention center first. Get some work done."

"Can I go with you? It's a perfectly acceptable place for us to hang out together. Just work, you know."

He winked at me, and I could practically read his thoughts. He wanted to go to the convention center to get some hardware or ideas for our later play. Dirty man.

Not that I could blame him. I wanted that, too.

Soon we rejoined our group. After loading up on breakfast Panda Express and Auntie Anne's pretzels (hey, it's an airport, the concept of "temporally appropriate food" does not exist), we all boarded our flight.

I sat a row behind Hudson, on the opposite side of the plane. From my place, I watched him settle in. Once he was . . .

Mile High Club? I texted.

His shoulders shook with laughter. He typed; then his response pinged through.

We literally did it in the strip club like two weeks ago. Maybe we should pace ourselves with the semi-public sex.

I typed my reply through a pout. Spoilsport.

Don't worry. I'll make sure you get plenty of attention in New York. Share a room with me?

Wouldn't have it any other way.

We took off moments later. And as the hum of the plane's engines sang me to sleep, a saccharine-sweet tang coated my tongue, sharper than the ice-cold Diet Coke served to me by Delta's finest.

There it was. That hope. I was feeling hope, not forcing it this time.

I was going to New York with my friends. My future looked bright. The industry would see me as a force to be reckoned with. And Hudson *would* finally tell me how he felt.

Nothing could go wrong.

I wouldn't let it.

38

Giddy Up-Yours, Pal

Once we landed, the rest of the BuzzCorp crew elected to go to the hotel, explore the city, and rest up for the company dinner Clara had booked for us at "one of the hottest restaurants in Soho."

I, on the other hand, had volunteered to check our team in, confirm that Terrence had transported the last of our equipment to our showcase room and successfully parked the rental truck in the Javits Center parking lot, and begin the process of sorting through our things and preparing for the expo.

The schedule was scrambled eggs, basically. All mixed up in a confusing hodgepodge of networking and interfacing and glad-handing and presenting. But we would make it work. For once, I had complete faith in my team.

Still, having Hudson tag along behind me to gawk at the opening booths and experiences wasn't exactly what I had in mind when I planned this all-day prep extravaganza. If Hudson had been overwhelmed by that pissant convention we'd been to in Cleveland, then I was surprised he didn't pass out the minute he walked through the doors of the Javits Center.

It was too distracting, watching his eyes widen at sex swings and fucking machines and the posters for the "Be Your Own Pornstar" experience—whatever *that* meant.

And speaking of distractions, about halfway through our expo floor walk . . .

Lloyd Exeter appeared from nowhere, chatting with some suits near a display of electro-stim taint massagers.

"Oh Jesus," I muttered. "Here we go."

Obviously I knew that he would be here this weekend. But in a crowd of thousands, I'd hoped to avoid him. Small parts of me even hoped that he might have some sense of shame and go out of his way to avoid me.

Nope!

Not only did he spot me, but he diverted straight toward me.

No sense in running. That would only make the humiliation worse. I stood my ground and waited as he approached, suits peeling off until only he and *Jared Fucking Blotcher* remained.

I tried to swallow my surprise.

"Well, look who we have here," Jared crooned by way of greeting. "The competition."

"Hi, Jared," I said. *Play nice.* "I didn't realize you'd gotten a new job. Congrats."

"Some people in this industry appreciate my insights," he replied, preening. "And my sense of humor. I'm sure it was a shock to you all when I left BuzzCorp, but I had to go where I would be valued."

"Of course."

A flicker of annoyance crossed Lloyd's face. He shooed Jared away. "Leave us."

Chastened, Jared frowned, but I wasn't surprised. Lloyd never knew how to be anything less than the center of attention. I bit the inside of my mouth to keep from smiling at the cosmic justice of it all. Jared got a job with Lloyd's company to get one over on us at BuzzCorp . . . and now he was reaping the consequences of that decision. Newton's Third Law hard at work again.

Once Jared was gone, though, my own smugness melted away. Hudson might have been standing beside me, but I felt totally alone under Lloyd's stare.

"Scout Porter," he said, voice smooth and cold and artificially beautiful as carved butter. "What the hell's a girl like you doing in a place like this?"

"Hi, Lloyd."

"Funny, running into an old friend. Such an *old*, *good* friend."

Fuck.

I'd talked such a big game to Leelah and Addie. Been so confident that Lloyd would *not* get under my skin again.

Reality was different. Seeing him was like getting knocked through space and time.

I was once again the sad, scared girl who'd been called to the CEO's office to have her sexts read aloud in front of the all-male board who would determine her fate.

"Yeah," I said, eyes tracing patterns across the carpeted floor. "Good to see you."

When I added no follow-ups, he turned his attention to Hudson.

"Lloyd Exeter."

"Hudson Bailey."

Neither of them seemed particularly pleased to make the other's acquaintance, but they shook hands anyway.

"Name sounds familiar," Lloyd said. "Do I know you from somewhere?"

"I sincerely hope not."

Not the response Lloyd was looking for, clearly.

"I hear you're doing well for yourself, Scout. That's great news.

I was so worried about you when you left GalacticSolutions. You weren't ready for the big time, but you had potential."

Gee, they really put a lot of work into the carpet patterns of the Javits Center. By the time this conversation was over, I'd have the whole design memorized. "Thanks."

"Loquacious as ever, huh? Hudson, I assure you, she used to be *much* better with her mouth."

Vomit burned the back of my throat. I would not let it make an appearance. *Don't be rude. Just endure the interaction and get out of here unscathed. Do not let Fluorine Scout out of her containment unit. You have got to keep yourself under control—your career is at stake here.*

He clucked his tongue at my nonresponse. "Anyway, I want you to know, I don't hold a grudge."

"About what?"

"About everything that happened back then. I mean, I'm sure you know that *I* don't hold a grudge, considering how well we set you up for success when you left GalacticSolutions, right?"

Finally, the anger broke through. Not enough to say anything, but enough that my stomach roiled with unspent adrenaline.

Hudson, on the other hand, didn't know how to keep his mouth shut.

"How well you set her up? I've never heard such horseshit."

"Some friend you've got here, Scout. Sorry, buddy, we weren't talking to you."

"You didn't do *anything* for her. You ruined—"

Lloyd breezed past Hudson's rage, like it was nothing more than a troublesome fly he'd batted away. "And in return, I hope you don't take me starting this new company of mine personally. It's just business."

Finally, the carpet ceased to hold my interest. The blank cheerfulness in his eyes cut me to my core. He wasn't checking in on me. He was bragging. This was his victory lap.

"Just business, like when you fired her and blamed her for damages that weren't her fault? You're a real piece of work."

Lloyd finally snapped; his calculated persona cracked down the middle. "Hey, buddy, I don't think what I do is any of your concern."

Hudson's gaze was devastating steel. His lips curled up tauntingly. "You're right. You're no concern of mine."

The words dripped with unspoken meaning. It was as close to *I don't give a shit about you because you're fucking beneath me, you insufferable cretin* as anything I'd ever heard Hudson say before.

Lloyd picked up on the subtext. He answered by taking a threatening step forward.

Flipping on survival mode, I forced a cheerful, can-do vibe. "Well! We've got to run. Lots to set up. So much to do. It was good to see you, Lloyd. Give Jared my best."

"Who?"

"Jared? The guy who was just standing with you?"

"Oh, him. I'm not sure how long he'll last, to be frank. I needed his particular . . . insights . . . into the current sex toy industry landscape. Now that I have them, I'm afraid he's outlasting his usefulness. You can have him back, if you want."

What a fucking asshole. I didn't like Jared, but I wouldn't wish working for *or* being fired by Lloyd Exeter on my worst enemy. As far as he was concerned, people were disposable.

Especially once they'd given everything they had to give. Now that Lloyd had Jared's "insights" into BuzzCorp, he was going to be thrown away like a used napkin.

I knew the feeling.

"I can't wait to see your presentation. I'm sure it'll be very . . ." His eyes traveled up and down my body. Undressing me without lifting a finger. "Stimulating."

Without another word, he pivoted and returned to his waiting gaggle of fawning hangers-on. But before he completely left my earshot, I overheard a strand of conversation with his lackeys. Jared included.

"Oh yeah. She still wants me."

If I hadn't forced myself to go numb, I would have cried on the spot.

That was all I would ever be to Lloyd Exeter. A piece of ass to taunt.

Hudson turned on me, fire paling in comparison to the heat of his rage. I distracted myself by starting for Conference Room 58, which was our designated home away from home during the convention. There was so much to do. I didn't have time for this—not for Lloyd's prancing smugness, and not for Hudson's righteous fury.

"What the hell was that?"

"What do you mean?"

"I didn't want to butt in like I did with your parents, but Scout . . . you're *shaking*. Why didn't you stand up to that asshole?"

Was I shaking? I glanced down at my hands.

Shit. Yeah. I was. I'd fought so hard to stay numb that I hadn't even realized.

"We're at work," I reminded him. "I can't get in fights at work, especially not with our competition. I'm a representative of BuzzCorp. Anything I do would reflect badly on the company. I'm better at being myself, but I can't be myself at the expense of our launch. Entropy, remember? No chaos. Not this week, at least."

"Right. Entropy. No chaos. I'll remember that."

His eyes darkened and flickered away from me. Something I'd just said had soured his mood, but I couldn't figure out what.

I searched for an activity to pick up both of us. I found it across the convention floor, where a team was setting up a series of enclosed pods along the north wall of the hall. I recognized them from photographs Clara had shown me a few months ago from a C-suite retreat she'd gone to in Bali.

They were sex pods.

No two ways about it, no cutesy names to obfuscate their true purpose.

Taking after that one show in the UK where people would straight-up have sex in an enclosed box on TV and then come out to tell thousands of strangers back home how the experience went, these sex pods were commonplace at higher-level sexpos like this one. They allowed people to check out their newly acquired merchandise without having to schlep all the way back to the privacy of their hotel rooms.

Perfect.

"You know what? Forget Lloyd. I want to have some fun."

"I like the sound of that."

39

It's My Turn to Use the Sex Box

As a keynote speaker at this year's OFest, I had my choice of goodies from the Sex Pod swag table. Donated by the convention's vendors, they were a prize selection of top-of-the-line, high-quality, cutting-edge products.

Instead, I picked the funniest thing I could find.

A Clone-A-Dick Kit.

As we read through the instructions on the kit, we settled into the sex pod together. It was a hyper-sleek room of about 250 square feet with a design aesthetic that could be described as *space yacht for rich perverts*.

"Why would you want a copy of my penis when you can just have the real thing any time you want?" Hudson asked.

Because unless you tell me you love me and want to try a relationship, you're leaving in a few days, and I want a souvenir to remember you by.

"Because it's hilarious," I said instead. "Also, how sexy would it be if I cucked you with a copy of your own cock?"

He grabbed my ass, dragging me against his hard length, already straining against his jeans. "You're diabolical, you know that?"

"I'm an evil sex toy genius, what can I say?"

Familiar with the features of the sex box, I opened one of the wall panels to reveal a small sink. I set about mixing the solution.

"How does this thing even work?" he asked, gesturing to the box.

"You get hard. You put your dick in this solution. And fifteen minutes later—"

"*Fifteen minutes?* I've got to sustain an erection for fifteen solid minutes?"

I laughed and nudged him back onto a plush chair, curved for maximum spine arching—very sexy. "Yes, and then once it's finished, you fill it with liquid latex, wait a few hours, and *bam*. You've got a clone of your dick. I'm not sure why you're complaining, by the way. You once said I made you hard *all day* at the office."

"*Emotionally* hard. *Sexual-tension*-ly hard. Not *literally* hard. I've gotten very, very good at putting that thing down when you make it crop up in uncomfortable situations."

"Well, then. You'll need some encouragement to keep it up."

"Hm. I have an idea."

The room was filled with sex furniture and paraphernalia. I'd fully expected Hudson to select a device off the wall. Instead, he excused himself from the sex box altogether and, a few minutes later, returned with one of the fifteen prototypes we'd built together.

The Fantasy.

"What are you doing?"

He rolled the testing unit into the small room. It was laid out carefully in its clear-top box, ready for its first user. "It occurred to me that I've never seen The Fantasy in action."

I blanched when I realized his meaning. He wanted to use The Fantasy on me. He wanted to run testing protocols on me while he watched.

That was as hot as it was terrifying. Holy shit.

"No. No way. What if it breaks the unit?"

"It's the spare unit, for emergencies only. Besides, have you ever actually used The Fantasy on yourself? How can you be expected to sing its praises in your presentation when you haven't even tried it?"

It was a stupid argument. But then again, it wasn't really an argument. It was a pretext.

"Hudson, we brought a bunch of those prototypes to the convention for a reason. If the main ones on the floor break, we need to be able to pull another model out to replace it. I don't want to put a used model out on the floor."

"What's the likelihood of all fourteen other models breaking? Besides, all of the body-close elements are replaceable. The core mechanisms are all covered by disposable pads and attachments. Nothing that touches you would ever touch a single convention attendee. It's safe."

"That is true . . ."

While none of our product models would be used on attendees, I'd been extremely careful to make sure that every phallus, insertable, and skin-contacting surface on The Fantasy was replaceable. It was like a speculum at the doctor's office. The core mechanism was reusable while the other elements were not. Our sale models wouldn't include this feature, as they were designed to be used by one person and one person only, but the floor models would. For safety.

And now, apparently, for me to enjoy without guilt or repercussions.

"Anyway," he continued, "I've been working on a surprise for you. If you don't use The Fantasy, you may never get it."

A surprise? Damn him.

"You know I can't resist a mystery."

"Or an experiment. I want to run some more tests with the

software. Last-minute redundancies, you understand," he said, taking out his cell phone.

Reader, this is what it looks like when someone talks themself into a bad decision.

"Fine," I said. "But only because I want a Hudson-dildo of my own."

"I totally forgot about that."

"Get undressed."

"You first. Tonight, we're going to write your first-ever fuck report."

Ages ago, when I'd told him I'd never filled out a fuck report of my own before, preferring to test our toys for my own personal gratification instead of contributing to our company-wide knowledge pool, I never imagined he'd use that against me. But as he adopted a clipped, clinical, professorial air, I couldn't help but do as I was told. I dropped my coat on the floor. I removed my shirt, then unhooked my bra. And that bastard didn't even cast a glance in my direction as he input some protocols into the phone app he'd designed for The Fantasy.

Once I was standing there, fully naked, he gestured to one of the lounging options—an elevated perch that was a cross between a doctor's chair and a sex chaise. I sat up on its plush fabric (your mama's OB-GYN chair this was *not*. The sex box was designed bespoke for maximum comfort and user ease) and hooked my feet into the soft stirrup-like lifts.

So there I was. On my back. Legs spread. Eyes on the ceiling. Body on fire with anticipation.

When I reached up over my head to stretch, a strip of downy fabric slipped around my wrists, binding them together.

"What are you doing?"

"You're testing this toy for the first time. Can't have you squirming," he said, using restraints to fully pin my arms and legs in place. "It could adversely affect the results."

"Are you going to tie up *your* hands?" I asked. "After all, you wouldn't want to do anything to ruin the Clone-A-Dick Kit once you get started with it."

"I'm afraid I need my hands. I'll be controlling The Fantasy, after all."

My mouth watered. I was properly helpless now. I was his to experiment on.

I'd always been the tinkerer. Never the toy to be stretched and tested and brought to the limits. I'd never been a *thing* to be worked upon.

The bindings were warm against my ankles and wrists. I didn't fight them.

"Now, here." Hudson approached the glass-top box holding The Fantasy. "Talk me through how to put this on."

Over these last few weeks, I'd found that I liked talking during sex. The conversation made everything hotter, more intense. And it made me feel closer to Hudson. But having to narrate my own sexual manipulation left my words coming out strained.

"You . . . you have to start by ensuring that the nipples are fully erect and the vagina is sufficiently wet."

Leaving The Fantasy behind, Hudson moved back to me. Both of us knew that, by now, my pussy was likely sopping for him.

That wasn't the point, though. The point was that he wanted to completely unravel me.

He captured my first nipple, tonguing it until it strained painfully erect. Then he gripped the second and repeated the process, driving me crazy with the lack of contact to my pussy.

I'd never felt so sexually vulnerable before, so out of control. The restraints didn't just keep me from hooking my legs around his hips or touching myself; they kept me from even being able to arch and buck the way I usually did when I wanted more.

Once he'd lavished my nipples with attention, he stood back to a more professional distance. Now upright, he probed my pussy, entering me sharply with his fingers—no warning. Just a cold intrusion that made me want to rip his clothes off and let him inspect me *everywhere*.

“Is that sufficiently lubricated enough for you?” he asked, the slick patter of his fingers in my cunt filling the air. “For the purposes of testing the machine, that is.”

“Mm-hmm,” I managed to say. “Now you need to affix the nipple stimulators.”

The Fantasy was simple enough. Two remotely controlled nipple stimulators, a phallus that could vibrate, thrust, and change temperature, and a clitoral stimulator with all the bells and whistles one could ask for—sucking, vibrating, tongueing, fingering, even pinching and light stinging. All connected by a slender body-con design that looked like the stripped-back white outfit from *The Fifth Element*, it was sleek, sexy, and powerful.

If it worked, The Fantasy would one day be the final word in sex toys.

It was designed to be user-friendly. Hudson, by virtue of working with me on this project for weeks now, knew exactly how it was meant to be used.

But we both liked this. This call and response of instruction and touch.

He set the nipple cups around my hard buds. They didn’t spring to life or anything, but even the slight contact aroused me further.

“Lay the central cable down the stomach. It should fit like body tape. That’s it. Now,” I said, eyes closing as he touched me all over, awakening every last one of my senses. “Press the clitoral stimulator into place.”

His long, careful fingers set the rubber cover over my sensitive clit. I shuddered but tried to keep my voice steady.

If there was one thing that I loved more than cumming, it was a good experiment. I didn’t want to burst early and ruin this one.

"And then, set the insertable inside the tester."

"What," he said, lining up the phallus, "no anal stimulation?"

"That's an advanced add-on package. Not out of the testing phase yet. Clara is very big on maximizing secondary purchases."

"I look forward to the Gen2 model, then." Hudson chuckled and slid the toy into my center, filling me up. I let out a little gasp at the incursion. "Are you comfortable?"

How cute. He thought I was in pain. Quite the opposite. A few inches of movement without these restraints holding me back, and I probably could have made myself cum in a matter of seconds. "I'm already at a seven."

"What does that mean?"

"We use sliding scales for different points in the testing process. The testers are supposed to note when certain things increase their proximity to orgasm. Zero means that you're not even touching yourself, no excitement at all. Ten is an orgasm."

"Good to know. I'll expect you to inform me if that changes. I want a good show out of you. It's the only way I'll be able to stay hard for *fifteen minutes* while the mold cures."

His every word was a tease. A tease teasing yet another tease. Not only would he be in control of The Fantasy, but he was going to make me wait the full fifteen minutes of his own delayed gratification before allowing me to cum.

Maybe even longer.

As if to punctuate that point, he peeled off his clothes stitch by painful stitch. The sensors across my body taunted me with their stillness. I wanted to keen against my restraints. And then, when he was finished, he sauntered over until his length dangled just out of kissing range above me.

"You said I need to be *fully* erect to use the kit, right? Well, I may need some help with that."

He didn't. His cock was as hard as I'd ever seen it. But when he brushed it against my cheek, my mouth opened for him without a second thought. I didn't even have time to breathe before he bottomed out in me.

I might have been tied up, but that didn't stop me from worshipping his length with a ferocity I'd never before unleashed. He tasted divine, and I wanted all of him—especially since none of The Fantasy components were on. This was the only sexual stimulation I had at the moment, and I was not about to let a second go to waste.

I worked his cock with my mouth, gagging and stretching myself until I thought he would cum right then and there.

Before he could, though, he retreated from me, firmly pressing my head back against my lounger. "That's enough, I think. Don't want you getting too excited before we've even turned The Fantasy on."

What a bastard. I groaned and gritted my teeth against the yearning.

He made quick work of pulling up his own chair to my side and sliding his cock into the Clone-A-Dick tube. He cringed at the cold, awkward sensation, set an alarm on his phone, then switched over to the control app for The Fantasy.

Fifteen minutes. Ready . . . go.

"Engaging first protocol now," Hudson said. "You should feel a smooth, loving set of sensations."

"I do," I confirmed.

"Tell me what you're experiencing in as much detail as possible. I want to confirm that the software is communicating what I want it to be doing."

"It's, hm, brushing my nipples very lightly. Almost too lightly."

He hummed. "It's drawing you out."

"And it almost feels like it's . . . like it's kissing my clit. Really soft, though. Almost more like it's breathing against me than kissing me."

"No internal stimulation?"

"No, and it's driving me crazy."

"Excellent. Exactly what I wanted."

The Fantasy was made for variety, surprise, and best-ever climaxes. It could do anything, and *most things* all at once. But he'd chosen to start off slow, which was driving me crazy. I was turned on, but not close enough to orgasm yet.

I tested my restraints. No, they weren't going to budge, nor was Hudson going to let me out of them. He leaned back in his chair, holding his concealed cock with one hand and his phone with the other, controlling my every sensation.

"How long does this portion last?" I asked.

"Let's call it a calibration phase. I could make it go on forever," he mused. "Keep you whimpering like that. See how long it takes for you to pass out from need."

"You can't do that—"

My words died in a cry when both of my nipples were bitten—or, at least, The Fantasy made it *feel* like they had been. Hudson's fingers, those culprits, hovered over the control app's keyboard, but he couldn't have looked less guilty, especially not when the kissing returned in quiet, reverent earnest.

"Don't you want complete research?"

"Yes."

"Then be a good little test subject and enjoy my coding handiwork. You wouldn't believe how much time I spent designing this protocol for you. The last few days, whenever you were busy with work and I couldn't convince you to peel away for a quick office fuck . . . I built this so my sexual fantasies had somewhere to go. What level are you on now?"

The biting had taken me up a notch. Then, the thought that he'd been in his dark bedroom, poring over his laptop, stroking his cock with one hand while designing a sex fantasy for me with the other, sent me to a whole new level.

"A seven point five."

"We can do better than that."

And he did. All at once, my body was assaulted by the very device I'd built.

"Shit—"

"That's not particularly descriptive, Scout," he goaded.

Fuck. How was I supposed to get words out when my body was overstimulated in nearly every way? "It's like there are so many mouths on me . . . Two circling each nipple. Kissing down my stomach. And fingers running along my pussy while a mouth works my clit. It's like I'm being touched by a couple of people, not just one."

"I made an on-the-fly adjustment. Wanted you to revisit your strip club experience—but even more intense. Is it more intense, Scout?"

"*Yes,*" I hissed. Then the stimulation stopped. "Hey—"

"You were too close to an eight. I had to pull you back. We've barely even started." Oblivious to the little moan of disappointment I let out, he tapped again on his keyboard. "What's happening now?"

"Nothing."

"Don't hold back. Your feedback is very important. I built this protocol for *you*. It should be exactly what you want."

"What I want is to cum."

"If I can't cum for the next"—he checked his phone's timer—"nine minutes, forty-five seconds, then neither can you. Sorry. I think it's only fair. Now. Tell me. What's happening to that perfect body of yours?"

I swallowed, hard. "The phallus filled me, but it's not doing anything."

Tap, tap, tap. A buzz filled the quiet air of the room. And my cunt. "And now?"

"*Yes.* It's slowly vibrating."

Tap, tap, tap-tap. "And now?"

My hips tried to defy my restraints, but I was pinned too fast. All I could do was lie back and be taken. "It's fucking me. Hudson, I need more—"

"You'll get what I give you." He smirked down at me. "For science."

The phallus had hit a rhythm now. My G-spot pulsed beneath it. He let it go on for torturously long. Time stopped having meaning to me. There was nothing in my world but the pursuit of pleasure and the sight of Hudson squirming, desperate to whip his cock out of its cloning mold and fuck me.

"Where are you now?" he asked eventually.

"Eight."

Tap, tap, tap-tap-tap.

Shit, now my clit was being vibrated *and* sucked. The cock inside me was warming and gaining speed. And my nipples were alternately pinched and kissed. It all blurred in a blissful swirl, until I didn't know where I ended and the oncoming climax began.

When the tapping stopped, the ministrations continued.

"How are you feeling?" he asked.

"Like this was a terrible idea, you bastard—"

He clucked his tongue. Somehow, the condescending lilt of his voice only made him sexier. "That's no way to cum. Remember, I can take this mold off and make myself climax any time I want. You, on the other hand, are tied up and at my mercy."

Everything inside me stopped—The Fantasy instantly powered down.

This time, I screamed. Not a whimper.

"Enjoying yourself?" he taunted. "How *is* The Fantasy, Dr. Porter? Everything you dreamed of?"

His fingers danced over his screen. A few clicks and I would be the most rapturous girl in the world, cumming on a machine I built and that my boyfriend controlled.

"Yes," I said. "Yes, it's perfect."

"So you admit it," he said. "You can build great things. You're not a fuckup. On the contrary, you're amazing."

"I didn't say that—"

The toy lowered its intensity to a quiet purr. I huffed.

"Fine, okay? I can build great things. I'm not a fuckup. I can do anything I put my mind to. I'm amazing. I am amazing—"

Another three-word sentence danced on my tongue. I swallowed it back. Not that it mattered much anyway. Hudson was cat-with-canary grinning now, satisfied by my confession.

"How about a little reward?"

Yesyesyes. My body hummed in anticipation. He tapped a few keys, and all at once, The Fantasy roared to action.

A wall of sensation slammed into me. I was so close. I was going to cum, I was going to cum—

Then, as if a massive power outage struck just my table and nothing else in the building, the entire suit died, leaving me wobbling over the precipice of a world-shaking orgasm.

I screamed from the unfairness of it all. Twisting my head, I glared daggers at the so-called scientist in charge of this so-called experiment. "You fucking bastard—"

All at once, he was aw-shucks Hudson again, eyes widening at his phone screen, which wasn't responding to any of his frantic tippy-taps. "No, that wasn't me."

The adrenaline rushed from my body. Oh, this wasn't part of our little game.

Awesome. Just my luck. Sex-tortured and I didn't even get my promised orgasm in the end.

"Shit, there must be a short somewhere in the wiring," I said. "Get me out of this thing and I'll have a look."

No dice. The timer went off.

Fifteen minutes was up.

Giving up on his phone, Hudson withdrew his cock from the

mold, removed the protective condom separating his cock from the solution, cleaned himself with a nearby intimate wipe, and stalked across the sex pod.

"I don't think that will be necessary," he said. "No offense to your ingenious engineering skills, but I'm going to fuck you better than this machine ever could."

Without bothering with my restraints, Hudson moved between my legs. The insertable no longer useful, he took it out of me and disconnected it from the larger system until he could discard it to the side. The clitoral and nipple stimulators stayed on, despite the loss of power.

But he hesitated.

"Tell me one thing," he insisted.

"Yes?"

"Tell me we're not just having sex to get your mind off Lloyd. Tell me none of this was about him. That we didn't just get off together to spite him or whatever."

I almost laughed at that. Seeing Lloyd had reminded me how happy I was with Hudson. How much I *didn't* want to be the scared girl I'd been back in my GalacticSolutions days anymore.

This wasn't about him. It was about us.

"Hudson, when I'm with you, I don't think about *anything* or *anyone* else. I'm yours."

For as long as you'll have me.

Forever, please.

Tied up, I was powerless to this sex, but he made every touch feel like the loss of control was worth it. Hudson lined himself up and rocked inside me. He found a steady pace, holding me by the ties at my wrists, taking me hard and fast and deep—*so* deep.

Then The Fantasy's short must have unshorted.

"HUDSON!"

I yanked against my cuffs, tugging as power was restored to

The Fantasy. Hudson's cock stroked in and out of me just as the stimulations on my clit and my nipples started once again.

It wasn't going to take me long. I could feel it. I could feel *him* getting closer, too. I could—

My orgasm slammed me into another dimension. My entire body rippled. My vision went white. I couldn't even hear my own screaming.

But I could feel Hudson's cum as it filled me from the back and came dripping past his cock and out of my pussy. *That* brought me back down to earth in the most delicious way.

We fell together in a tangled, spent pile on the examination table. Still strapped to the table, I couldn't do much but catch my breath and relish the weight of him.

"I really need to go meet up with Addie and Leelah," I said once our breathing returned to normal. "They're doing some last-minute prep. Might need my help. And we need to get ready for that dinner with Clara tonight."

"Or, hear me out . . . you could delegate those tasks, skip Clara's dinner, and we could have a real New York City date."

Date.

The word had been tossed around before, usually with me batting it away like an unwelcome fly. But now it relit my already fried nerve endings. God, did I want to say yes.

"We're in the home stretch, Hudson. I really shouldn't."

"I understand. But . . . it's New York. It's the fall. It's beautiful."

"Then you should go out and enjoy it."

He placed his hand on my hip. He might as well have been holding my heart.

"Scout, how could I possibly enjoy it without you?"

That heart, sitting so comfortably in his grip, pulsed with new fire. Could this be it? Were we finally getting to our *Hudson confessing his love for me* era?

Better judgment and sense told me to stand my ground. Stay focused on work. Talk about love off the clock.

Fuck better judgment. Fuck good sense. What had either of them gotten me so far? What about playing it safe, hm? What did that ever get me?

Nothing. Loneliness and isolation and a ball of ghost particles where my heart should have been. A pathetic meetup with Lloyd. Cringe-inducing dinners with my parents. Years of isolation.

Time for a change. Tonight, I would let Fluorine Scout out of her shell. I'd earned it, hadn't I? I'd proven to myself that I wasn't the mistakes of my past, that I had grown. And I would explore New York City with the man I loved, ready for the moment when he finally said those three little words I'd been dying to hear . . .

40

New York, I Love You, But You're Bringing Me Down

"I love pussy."

Yeah, not *those* three little words.

"I love it, but you'd just never see me sitting up there with a camera shoved in my face, proclaiming to the world how much I love it and why."

The next day, we found ourselves at the taping of a focus group. Led by our marketing team, they interviewed some of BuzzCorp's most loyal customers so that their footage could be used in our big marketing hype video before The Fantasy debut talk I would give later this week. Apparently, our male testers felt the same way, because they were steadfastly, to the man, refusing to appear on camera.

Hudson couldn't tear his eyes away from the two-way mirror dividing us from the user panel. He was fascinated by their candor and ease. Totally lost in the moment.

I, on the other hand, couldn't stop thinking about the night before.

We'd gone for a sunset walk, a slice of pizza, and people-watching on the High Line. Without a doubt, the best date ever. Maybe the best *thing* ever. And I know that this is neither a keen, nor original, nor astute observation, but there was a magic about New York City in the fall.

Especially when one was in love.

And I was. I absolutely was.

But was Hudson?

I'd tossed off all my personal and professional obligations the night before in the hopes that Hudson would finally make a move. That he would finally crack under the pressure of his upcoming departure from BuzzCorp and sweep me up into his arms, shouting that he knew I'd wanted to keep things professional, that we always had a deadline to this relationship, that he understood my fears about intimacy, but he didn't care. His heart was on the line, and it was mine for the taking. All I had to do was say yes.

Only . . . none of that happened. The next morning, I was thoroughly sated after a long night of hotel sex, full of breakfast bagels delivered by my oh-so-handsome bed companion, and ready to face a day of BuzzCorp work . . . but I was no closer to Hudson telling me he loved me.

My pre-departure anxiety came rushing back to me. I'd been to New York a few times for conferences like this one, and back in high school and college, I'd attended (and won, thank you very much) more academic contests and quiz bowls than I could count. Back then, I hadn't thought much of the city. Even for someone as studiously disciplined as I was, the constant, inescapable cacophony of bumper-kissing cars and yapping sidewalk strutters and rattling construction drove me to the brink of distraction. An unsettling feeling for someone who'd been able to bury her head in a book and escape the world anywhere else.

In short, in times past, I'd always come to New York with a timer on my heart, counting down until the very blissful second when I got to finally leave.

Now I wanted time to slow. To defy all laws of physics and slow—just to give us a little more time. Surely if we had just a little more time, he'd open up.

Right?

"Scout, what do you think?"

"Hm?"

Yanked from my internal stewing, I returned to the moment at hand. Hudson gestured to the glass in front of us, through which we could see the diverse group of twenty or so testers being candidly interviewed by Addie and several other members of the marketing team. The conversation was lively—laughter and jokes abounded. It wasn't surprising to see the envy in Hudson's eyes, and I felt for him. I really did. He was *terrified* of that sort of openness. Terrified of the rejection that might come with it.

"It's just that they're very brave. I know the men don't want to talk on camera and that's a problem for the marketing team, but still. They're very brave to even talk about it in this setting," he said by way of explanation. "What do you think?"

"I don't think we should be scared of what we want. Ever," I said, hoping the pointed tone might somehow get through to him. "I mean . . . what would *you* say if you weren't afraid of how people would react?"

We both tore our gazes away from the focus group and met somewhere in the middle. His eyes brimmed with promise. Was this the moment? Was he finally going to—

Crash.

The suite door slammed open. Clara stood there, framed by the blue metal, her hair out of place for the first time . . . I want to say *ever*?

"What the hell are you doing here?" she asked, flailing wildly.

I frowned. "Observing the focus group."

A knot tightened in my stomach. Clara was *never* out of sorts.

Never allowed herself to be flapped. If she was like this, then we must be in a DEFCON 1.

"Haven't you checked your phone?"

"No, it died last night and—"

Unwilling to finish that sentence with *I was in Hudson's room and since he has a stupid Android, I didn't have anything to charge it with,* I trailed off.

"I've been looking for you everywhere. Jared is claiming to own a patent on the slip-stick wire coupling we use in The Fantasy's major control systems. He somehow got into our storage yesterday and looked at the final prototypes. No idea how the hell he did that, but he's ready to sic Lloyd's legal dogs on us."

I knew how he did it.

When Hudson and I returned the test unit we'd "borrowed" yesterday, we must not have locked the door behind us. I'd been so wrapped up in my flirtations and my *feelings* and my stupid dream of a New York City rom-com moment that I'd forgotten the most basic thing about a top-secret product rollout.

Double-check all the locks.

"It's not his design, though," Hudson said. "Right?"

"No, of course not. That's not the point. They're just saying this to spike our launch. Which means that if we're going to make all of this go away by then, we're going to need to find a new coupling to use. Which means we need to update the prototypes, adjust the costings, revise the specs we give to investors. It's fractions of a dollar per unit, but we must be up front with them."

My world narrowed around me. I barely had the breath to reply:

"Okay."

Two hands wrapped around my shoulders. Clara steadied me. "Four days. It's going to be rough, but you can handle this. I know you can. I believe in you."

You shouldn't, I thought. *No one should.*

"Tell Addie and Terrence and Leelah to meet me in our HQ. I'll be there in ten."

With a nod, Clara evacuated the room, leaving me to spiral.

My existence abided by Newton's "universal" law of gravity. (Shut up, science nerds—I know about Einstein's theories of relativity, but I'm trying to make a simple point for the normies.)

What goes up, must come down. That is the basic, observable principle. A pendulum abides by that principle, yes. But there's an arc to it. A rising action and a similarly arcing decline. A slow burn of movement. A downward curve that gives one time to prepare for the lowest point.

I was a brick dropped from a twenty-story window. A crushing drop straight to the unforgiving pavement below.

I'd fucked up.

Again.

And in the exact same way as the last time.

I'd trusted myself.

Rookie mistake. Everyone knew that Fluorine Scout couldn't be trusted. Not with men. Not with business. Not with keys, apparently. And certainly not with her own heart or future.

Moving without seeing, I shoved my things into my backpack, saying nothing until Hudson appeared at my side, extending my drafting tablet in uncertain hands.

"What can I do to help?"

"You've done enough, thanks," I said tersely.

He recoiled. "What's that supposed to mean?"

The guilt that flooded me was almost as sharp as the bitterness. "No. I'm sorry. You're right. This wasn't your fault. It was mine. Totally mine. I should have known better."

"Scout. What is going on?"

"What's going on is that I did it again. I did what I wanted, I chased after some guy, and I put *everything* at risk. And for what?

For some sex? For a little bit of fun? For the hope that you might . . ."

"Might what?"

"Nothing. I gotta go."

I shoved my bag over my shoulder and started for the door. He followed.

"I'll help you."

"No, you fucking *won't*. Because this is what I'm good at. My work. It's the only thing I've *ever* been good at. And this is what happens when I let something get in the way of that. I'm not cut out for romance or friendship or anything else, and it's time I remembered that. I'm sorry, Hudson. But I can't do this anymore. I can't be with you anymore."

They were the hardest words I'd ever forced myself to say. They were inevitable, though, weren't they? I'd been living in a fantasy world, buying Hudson's bullshit about me being able to handle myself, about me not being a total failure in everything that isn't STEM. It was time to wake up.

Hudson scoffed.

"I can't believe this."

"Can't believe what?"

Circling me with long strides, he put himself between me and the door, blocking my path. His face contorted with emotion in ways I'd never seen before. Gone was happy-mask Hudson. Gone was vulnerable Hudson. This was someone else. Fluorine Hudson, perhaps. More reminiscent of his takedown of my parents than anything else we'd been through so far. "That you're just going to give up. That you're running away at the first sign of minor trouble. You always do this, Scout. You didn't fight after the GalacticSolutions disaster. You don't stand up to your parents, to Lloyd, to *Jared*, even. You didn't lose your virginity, for God's sake, until you were twenty-six. Entropy, entropy, entropy. It's all bullshit. What you really mean is that you're *scared* and you're letting it hold you back. You're running away from everything real. Including us."

"There is no us," I snapped, thinking of every missed opportunity he'd had to tell me there was one. "You've made that perfectly clear."

"No. *You've* made it perfectly clear. *You* keep reminding me that I'm leaving at the end of my contract. *You* refused to let our relationship get deep. *You* couldn't even decide if you liked me enough to keep seeing me until you hooked yourself up to a goddamn EEG machine. And now *you're* running. All because you hate yourself too much to let yourself live a little."

Until those words, my temperature and my volume had been rising with my rage. But he'd thrown a bucket of liquid nitrogen over me.

You hate yourself.

"No, I . . . No, I don't."

He wouldn't be deterred. "Yes, you do. You hate yourself so much that you sabotage every chance you have to be happy. Relationships, work, your friends. The man who nearly destroyed you showed up and you didn't even have the strength to hold your head up when he talked to you, much less give him a piece of your mind. And when I try to care about you, when I try to get you to see that you're not the worthless nobody you seem to think that you are, you run. I *have* made it clear that I want there to be an *us*, but you don't know how to let someone love you because you can't fathom it being real. You despise yourself, deep down, all the way to the core, and assume that everyone else should, too."

And I'd not realized it until now.

I *did* hate myself.

Maybe because of the way I'd been treated as a child, maybe because of those years of loneliness growing up, maybe because of Lloyd and what happened at GalacticSolutions. I didn't know. But . . . yeah, I hated myself. Deeply. Abidingly. Maybe it was the only thing I'd been able to count on. I wore that self-hatred like a winter coat, clutching it tighter whenever the wind got too sharp, and sweating in it through the summers.

I hated myself. Constantly. Immovably. And yet I hadn't ever been able to face that reality before.

Now I had nowhere else to look. And the truth stared back at me with big, wide, understanding, loving eyes.

And I hated him for it.

"Don't stand there and claim you want to protect me when you're not even man enough to admit you love me."

"What?"

"I went out with you last night, totally abandoning my work responsibilities, because I thought you'd finally say it. That you didn't care about your contract ending or our agreement. That you want to be with me for more than just sex. I was so sure you would . . . but you didn't. And now everything's fucked up because of me and my stupid lack of judgment. Chasing after some guy who doesn't even love me."

I spit out every last word like it was poison. The hurt of the last week and a half, of waiting for a confession that might never come, bubbled to the surface.

Hudson reeled, falling back a few steps.

"Is that what you think?" he asked.

"Yes."

This time, it was his turn to spit the words. "You don't know anything."

That was, I'm sure you've noticed, not a denial. It wasn't a love declaration. And it wasn't what I wanted to hear from him.

"I know how to replace complex couplings," I said. "So, if you don't mind, I'm going to do that."

A sigh. Long and labored. He pinched his nose, rubbing a few soothing circles over it. "If that's what you want."

No. It wasn't what I wanted.

I wanted him to hold me and force me to understand that this wasn't worth throwing us away over. That it was a small mistake. Fixable. That I wasn't a failure. That I *was* lovable. That there was more value to me than my work.

I wanted him to fight for me.

I wanted him to love me.

Since I never got what I wanted, though, I retreated from the room, trying not to think about how the color went out from my world almost as soon as he did.

41

Cutesy Titles Are so Pre-Breakup of Me

Believe it or not, I didn't sleep very well that night.

Shock of the century, I know.

I tinkered on The Fantasy prototypes at the Javits Center until around two a.m., when a janitor alerted me he'd be calling security if I didn't vacate the premises. Then I returned to my hotel room, which I hadn't yet stayed in, as I'd been sleeping in Hudson's. I stared at the ceiling for hours, running over my to-do list for the next day and trying not to think about the way he looked when I walked away this afternoon.

The inability to sleep ran so deep that I didn't even reach for my travel vibrators, which usually knocked me out five minutes after use. I briefly considered using my Hudson dildo, but what was the point? It wouldn't be like my night in the Cleveland hotel, gleefully getting off to the thought of him until I collapsed in ecstatic exhaustion. I would have been left unsatisfied. I wouldn't have been able to cum, and I wouldn't have been able to sleep, and I would have been frustrated by both realities, and the combination of both things would have been enough to make my chest-racking sobs even worse than they already were.

When my alarm went off at six in the morning, I was already

staring at my phone, counting down the seconds until I could crawl out of bed without hating myself even more.

I tried to remind myself that I'd done the right thing. Without Hudson in my life, I was *safe*. I had been foolish to try and change things these last few weeks, and I should not be crying over a man who wouldn't tell me he loved me.

It was all for the best, reverting to my old self.

And if I kept repeating that, maybe one day I would convince myself that it was true.

As soon as I knew the doors would be open, I went back to the Javits Center, where I refused to speak to anyone, kept my distance from Hudson, and tried to get my parents to cancel our family dinner tonight.

To no avail.

Whatever. It's not like I could feel any worse.

We met at a dimly lit French bistro somewhere in the Village. They were already two cocktails deep by the time I arrived. Not that I was late or anything. They probably just wanted drinks on my tab and arrived early to maximize their get.

I tried to play it cool, all while my heart felt like breaking. "Hey, Mom. Dad."

"Scout. How are you?"

"Great, thanks," I lied like I'd never lied before. "Glad you could make the trip down to the city."

I took my seat. The wall of conversation built up around me until I was insulated by it from everything else.

"It was a *nightmare*," Mom said. "Tell her about the train—"

"The train! We really should have just brought the car down."

Her face tightened. "But then we'd've had to park. We talked about this."

"I know we did. But the delay at Williams Bridge . . ."

Their bickering turned to white noise. Not difficult to do, as I'd endured a billion of these arguments before. The white noise, though, turned my thoughts to Hudson. What was he doing tonight, I wondered. Did he miss me?

And what about that love question? Did he not have guts enough to say it? Or did he just . . . not love me? Had I misread the signs and now he was embarrassed for me? What did he mean when he said *You don't know anything*?

The questions hollowed me out. The waiter eventually put me out of my one-track mental spiral. I blankly asked for the first thing I saw on the menu. My parents ordered four appetizers, an extra basket of bread, and the two market price specials.

"So," my dad said over his cocktail once the waiter vanished. "I'm glad to see that you've dumped the dead weight."

Great. Love talk. Perfect timing. "He wasn't dead weight. But no. We're no longer together."

My mom clucked her tongue. Her sympathetic tone grated against my ears. "Ah. Then we were right. It was a mistake from the start, you two. Oh, I do so hate it when we're right."

"It's better that way. Now you won't have any distractions. You can finally put yourself fully into finding a new job. Out of the sex toy industry. Into a career worth your time. One I can tell the guys at golf about—finally."

"We've been over this, dear," Mom countered. "She *can't* get another job."

"Ah, yes. That's right. My apologies."

The bread basket refresher arrived. They both dug in as though they hadn't just brushed me off without a moment's consideration.

Hudson's voice played in my head, louder than their chewing, louder than the din of the restaurant, louder than the music slipping through the tastefully hidden speakers.

I want you to work on whatever will make you happy. You'd be an asset anywhere you went.

He'd told me that the night he'd tried to get me to call his old work buddy, the one who ran one of GalacticSolutions's competitors. The card with his info was still in my purse, tucked between my insurance card and a frequent-buyer card from my favorite bagel place.

You don't know how to let someone love you because you can't fathom it being real. You despise yourself, deep down, all the way to the core, and assume that everyone else should, too.

Oh God.

A black hole of realization swallowed me.

All my parents ever did was belittle my work. They wanted me to leave because they were embarrassed of me. They wanted me to keep my world small so I didn't make any more costly mistakes. They wanted to constantly be in my business, so I never stepped out of line.

That was the treatment I'd gotten used to accepting from people who were supposed to love me.

That wasn't love, though, was it?

No. It couldn't be. Because Hudson was never once embarrassed of me. He took me seriously. He championed me. He listened to me. He trusted me. He encouraged my impulses. He suggested I leave BuzzCorp not because he resented my work there, but because he believed in my potential and my dreams of getting to space. He showed me, time and time again, that I wasn't a failure. And even if I did botch things, I could *always* fix them.

Maybe he couldn't say he loved me. Maybe he *didn't* love me. Maybe we wouldn't be together after all.

But he'd *shown* me what being loved felt like.

I'd changed so much since my last dinner with them. When I thought about the progress I'd made since I shrank from their every word, when I needed Hudson to stand up for me, I knew I could never go back. Hiding in my shell, protecting myself from the world and everyone who *could* love me, was no longer an option. I could not be a lab creature, contained and chained to my work. I could not be the Scout I was six weeks ago. I was a new creation, changed by my brief experiment with love.

"I could get a job," I said, gently pushing back on my parents' discourse. It came out more like a question than a statement, but still. It was a start. "If I wanted to."

"You were blacklisted, honey. Your father's right. No use in setting yourself a goal you can't meet."

"Exactly. As much as I hate to admit it, I think you're better off where you are."

That was two years ago. Surely someone needed an engineer with experience, fresh ideas, and a (mostly) winning track record.

Hudson was right. My talent spoke for itself.

My parents talked around that problem, as though the blacklisting was an afterthought. Like I wasn't even *enough* to get hired no matter what.

"But I'm . . ." I twisted my napkin in my hand, losing myself in the strange designs, distracting myself from the terrifying implications of standing up for myself for the very first time. "I'm really smart. And I'm good at my job. I've created bestselling products. I've made my customers happy. I'm a competent manager. BuzzCorp is lucky to have me. I think, you know, maybe, *any* business would be lucky to have me."

I'd been sabotaging myself, hiding myself, all because I was terrified of trying. Terrified of anything good happening.

My voice was very small. "I just haven't tried."

"Scout, really. Don't be dramatic. You *know* you can't leave BuzzCorp. It's silly to even discuss it. I'm sorry we ever brought it up."

The double act continued, trampling over any intermission I tried to insert. "Besides, all you ever do is castigate us for not appreciating the, I'm sure, world-changing work you're doing at your little sex toy operation. Why now, all of a sudden, are we public enemy number one for not thinking you can do better?"

I didn't blame her for that last little snipe. No wonder she was taken aback. I'd always let them bully me, shove me in little boxes and throw away the key. Bowing and scraping and apologizing for things that weren't my fault, doing their bidding no matter what they asked, picking up the checks and dropping my ego at the door.

Of course they would be surprised when I showed the tiniest hint of a spine.

"You really don't think I could do anything else?" I asked.

I made that small distinction. *Anything else*, not better. Buzz Corp was wonderful. I just wondered . . . was it not for me anymore? And more than that, if I succeeded in selling The Fantasy to the masses, in making the next leap in sex toy innovation, hadn't I achieved my objectives there? What more could I accomplish?

I still had my dreams of space. So much there I still wanted to do. Maybe it was time to try and go back to it.

My mother grew tired of this back-and-forth. "My dear. We gave you everything a girl could ask for. We got you into the best programs, the best schools, took you across the world to further your progress. There's no doubt that you're smart. But businesses—the businesses you left behind—need strong, straightforward, clear-minded people at their helm. Not silly little girls who let their vaginas think for them. Come to think of it, you *are* in the right profession. It's the only one that suits you."

"That's not fair."

She rolled her eyes. "You are moping at this table like a half-drowned kitten because that man had the good sense to dump you. It's more than fair: It's accurate."

"You really don't believe in me," I muttered.

"We're realistic about what, and who, you are," my father conceded bloodlessly. "That's the only way to really love a child."

If someone had asked me two months ago if I had a bad

childhood, I would have emphatically said no. My parents kept a roof over my head, they pushed me to greatness, they were always there, they stayed together, our situation was stable . . . all things I'd associated with a "good childhood."

But now I realized there was more than one way to have a bad childhood. Like, for example, they could withhold all affection from you except when you aced a test or skipped a grade or got an advanced degree . . . leading you to feel like you're only worthwhile to other people if you're perfect. And, since you know you can never be perfect, you isolate yourself until you're completely alone in the world.

Yeah. There was more than one way for your parents to screw you up forever.

And oh boy, had my parents screwed me up.

I analyzed the situation.

Problem: Being around my parents makes me miserable, reinforces all my worst fears about myself, and leaves me feeling unloved and unlovable.

Proposed Solution: Detach from the parental units.

Engage Primary Experiment.

"I need the two of you to listen to me," I said. "And I need you to not interrupt. Can you do that?"

"We're not stupid, Scout." This time, it was Dad's turn to roll his eyes. "Don't talk to us as if we—"

Deep breath. Here goes everything.

"Yes, you gave me an education. Yes, you worked hard so I could fulfill my academic potential. But you also robbed me of a *life*. When was I supposed to make friends between lectures and studying? I don't know how to cook. I can barely make friends. Navigating relationships? Forget it. And after the Lloyd Exeter thing, you made me feel like I was a broken machine that I could never fix. But *you* raised me that way. You made me ignorant about the world. You made me not understand. You put me in a position to be taken advantage of . . . only because I didn't know any better."

They both spluttered, trying to break their *no interrupting* agreement. I raised my voice and powered on until they stopped.

"I hate myself. You *made me* hate myself. And I can't begin to describe how exhausting it's been, sabotaging and holding myself back at every turn because I don't think I deserve anything better. Here's the thing, though. I can change that. I have that power. Starting right now. *Because I don't hate myself enough to sit here and listen to this anymore.*"

I reached for my jacket. Mom and Dad entered panic mode. Their threats bounced off and burned away like pebbles against a rocket booster.

"Scout. Scout, don't you dare get up from this table. After all we've done for you—"

"You're not thinking this through. If you leave now, we may not come back."

I left without any hesitation. Once I was in my taxi uptown, the adrenaline subsided, giving me just enough brain space to evaluate that little experiment.

Experiment complete.

Result: Immediate relief.

Supplemental Notes: I wish I could tell Hudson about this.

42

What's Your Greatest Weakness, You Piece of Shit?

A humble redbrick building on a quiet side street, from the outside, SkyTech looked nothing like I thought an aerospace company should look. It was soft, almost. Warm. And when I approached the glass doors, the inside matched. Yes, there were LED screens mounted on the brick walls, displaying their latest projects. But there were also comfortable furnishings and tables that didn't look ripped out of an Apple store.

It was *so* unlike my time at GalacticSolutions.

Ringing the front bell to be buzzed in took more courage than I'd like to admit. Last night, after leaving my parents, I texted the number Hudson had given me, and Malcolm McEwan responded lightning-fast, working his schedule around my frantic BuzzCorp one so we could meet up during my lunch break.

I wasn't in there to get a job. I was just there to prove to myself that I could try. That I was more than my mistakes, that I was more than my flaws. That all these lies I'd been telling myself—that I wasn't competent enough, that I was a perpetual failure, that I was too emotional to lead, that I was only good enough to make sex toys, that I needed to minimize myself in order to stay safe, that I was unlovable and unimportant—was just bullshit holding me back.

That being me was all that was necessary to live the life I wanted.

Moments later, I found myself in a large office on the top floor, sitting across from Malcolm McEwan, a tall, heavyset gentleman from Alabama. His story was legendary. His great-grandfather, a Black pilot from northern Africa, had married a French expat during the Second World War, moved to the States, tested aircraft for the Navy for twenty years, and was followed by three generations of young men who worked in aerospace in one way or another. His grandfather was a propulsion expert, his father was a Blue Angel, and now Malcolm was a titan of industry. SkyTech was the global leader in sustainable space exploration with a *Star Trek* future in mind—sort of a dream place to work for me, considering I'd never super loved GalacticSolutions's "hypercapitalism hitting hyperspace" ethos.

"Dr. Porter," Malcolm said, shaking my hand. "It's so nice to meet you. I've heard so much about you."

"Oh, I dread to think what you've heard," I joked awkwardly.

So much for my newfound self-confidence, huh?

"Don't worry. When Hudson told me about you, he sent over some of your specs, but I did my own research, too. Made a few calls. And, uh, if you don't mind my saying so, you come very highly recommended by my wife."

The ice between us broke. I laughed.

"Why, thank you. BuzzCorp aims to please."

He had an affable air that calmed my nerves. No wonder he liked Hudson. No wonder Hudson liked him. Good people had a way of finding each other.

"Do you like it over there?" he asked.

"I love it. But I'm not sure the sex toy industry is my forever home."

"And aerospace is?"

"I've missed it," I said, hedging.

He hummed. "I have my sources over at GalacticSolutions. Management gave you a raw deal, didn't they? Your work was flawless."

"Right up until the rocket exploded."

The joke should have been an easy one to concede. Instead, he let it land flat, unwilling to engage. "I know there was more to it than that. Anyone could see that the propulsion systems weren't the problem. It's funny that you and Hudson are close. What happened to you reminds me a little of what happened to him. Damn shame."

It wasn't any of my business, but my ears perked up anyway. "What do you mean?"

"You don't know what went down with his company?"

"No. He didn't really talk about that."

We were too busy boning to talk about it.

"Didn't look him up?"

Felt weird to look up *a guy who knew me biblically.*

"I didn't hire him."

"Well, uh, Hudson was the cofounder of a tech security company with his college buddy, Mike, and his girlfriend, Daisy."

Ah, yes. Daisy. Once, when I'd asked Hudson more questions about his last big relationship, he'd said she was just not the one. I guess now I was just another Daisy. Another *not-the-one*. That hurt me more than I cared to admit.

"The company was great. Top-of-the-line stuff. Made them all a *ton* of money. Daisy and Mike decided that they wanted to sell. But they didn't care about who they sold *to* or what their tech did *after* it was sold. They wanted to auction it off to the most interested party—who was going to use it off-label. Basically turning a "security" product into a data-scraping application, giving people the illusion of safety while selling off their information to the highest bidder, whether that be advertisers or governments who want to monitor their citizens."

I shivered. That was one of the worst things about being an inventor—worrying what your products might do in the wrong hands.

"Hudson was the only one in that little triumvirate with a conscience," Malcolm continued. "He thought that was a gross invasion of privacy. An evil way to manipulate the tech they had created together. He refused to sell. So they elbowed him out. Broke off the friendship. Daisy shacked up with Mike. I think they're engaged. And now . . . Hudson's a free agent."

The impact of Malcolm's story lingered in the silence that followed. It put Hudson into complete perspective.

No wonder he tried so hard to be loved. To never give someone a reason to leave him behind.

Because the two people he'd loved most had ditched him the instant he disagreed with them. He didn't want to get hurt that way ever again.

My guilt over our argument returned full force. No, double force. Triple force. Hurricane force.

"I didn't know that," I muttered.

"Of course you didn't. Do *you* go around talking about the worst thing that ever happened to you?"

I shrugged. "No, most people do that for me. I'm sure rumors of my ruination in this field have preceded me."

"And they're greatly exaggerated, I'm sure."

Over the years, I'd heard variations on that same theme from industry folks. He was the first person I truly believed. "I don't know about that. But . . . thanks for seeing me anyway. It was nice of Hudson to connect us."

"Nice? He is nice, but not *just* nice. He's *good*. Good in a way you don't see a lot anymore. Poor guy just always wanted to do the right thing, you know? Always wanted to make sure he was useful to someone. That he mattered. After all that with Daisy and Mike, I think he got even worse. I offered him a job here, but he likes the whole soldier-of-fortune thing. Mary Poppinsing to anyone who needs him the most. I hope he finds someone to take care of him someday. A man needs his people, you know?"

Like I'd needed him. Like I still needed him.

Clearing my throat, I tried to talk through the lump of emotion there.

"Sorry, we got sidetracked. Were there any business questions you had for me?"

At once, Malcolm schooled his expression. "Right. We're having a little issue with our propulsion systems. Care to take a look?"

I itched to be helpful, but I forced my hands to stay in my lap. "I don't work for free."

"We've already figured it out. I think. I just want to see how you'd tackle the problem."

When I didn't shut him down again, he handed me a tablet, already loaded up to a spec screen. For a few minutes, I read through the doc, crunching numbers in my head. When my head wasn't sufficient anymore, I swiped a pen and pad from his desk, scribbled down a few calculations, and then returned the tablet.

"You need to change your fuel source. Believe me, no one knows horrific, fiery explosions like I do, and if you don't pivot, that's what you've got ahead of you. Here." I slid him my calculations. I'd been doing private research on alternate fuel sources since before my time at GalacticSolutions. I knew even my offhand math would be sound. "Check this out."

I guess I should have been nervous, watching him evaluate my work in such a formal setting. But I knew I was smart. I knew I could do this. I knew engineering better than I knew myself.

My brain had never been the problem. It was my heart that gave me trouble.

Besides, there was a certain emotional high to *knowing* you were right. And I'd been missing that rush at BuzzCorp.

Eventually, Malcolm let out a low, impressed whistle. "That's good. That's real good. Better than what we've got now."

"And cheaper, too, isn't it?"

He smirked. "Well, you don't have to rub it in."

"Sorry, it's been a while since I've gotten to do this. It's going straight to my head."

"This is incredible work. Where *have* you been hiding?"

"Your wife's bedside table drawer, I guess." We both laughed. "Any other questions for me?"

We chatted for a few more minutes. Eventually, though, my lunch break grew short, and we rose to shake hands.

"We'll be in touch. It was nice to meet you, Scout. It's not hard to see why Hudson thinks so highly of you."

They were the sweetest words to ever punch me in the gut, but I took the pain in stride.

Maybe I'd never be able to get Hudson back. That ship had probably sailed. But maybe I could become the sort of woman who didn't need a man to point out her worth.

Maybe I could just be valuable all on my own.

Another successful experiment.

43

What the Fuck Were You Thinking?

We managed it.

Somehow, God help me, we managed it.

Finding new couplings, retrofitting our prototypes and floor models to use them, adjusting our costings, and redrawing all our manufacturing specs . . .

Done.

Now all we needed to do was launch the damn thing.

Over the last few days, I was too swamped to think about much besides work. I hadn't had the time to talk to Hudson, and even if I had, he was always running around doing some errand or another, so I couldn't grab him. By the time the final day of the convention, the final day of Hudson's contract, rolled around, though, I couldn't ignore the dread pooling in my stomach. Not about the presentation. That, I could handle.

But saying goodbye to Hudson? How was I supposed to weather that?

As the last half hour before my rollout speech ticked away, I paced around our HQ in the bowels of the Javits Center, stewing over my presentation. The rest of the team was high above-ground; they were finishing up with the last of the rollout details.

Clara was no doubt glad-handing with the likes of Mr. Ose, while the rest were handing out swag bags and checking that the AV elements of the talk were all ready to go.

I was alone. Until I wasn't.

The sight of Hudson in the doorway robbed me of my breath.

I hadn't been expecting him. Yet there he was. Looking handsome as ever . . . and heartbroken. The circles under his eyes told me I wasn't alone in my postbreakup insomnia spell.

"Hey," he said, weary but warm.

"Oh, hey." I overcompensated for the awkwardness with a false friendliness. "How's the crowd looking up there?"

"Very eager. The marketing department has the crowd in the palm of their hands."

"Are you staying?" I asked before I could stop myself.

"Wouldn't miss it for the world. My contract technically ended EOD yesterday and I do have a flight to catch right after, though, so . . . I think this might be goodbye."

Goodbye. I'd never hated a word before. Words were neutral tools. But that word, wielded against me by Hudson . . . I discovered a new way to despise syllables.

Tell him you love him, you idiot, my brain told me.

He's leaving. He wants to turn the page, I replied. *I have to let him go.*

"Right. Well. Thanks for staying. It'll be good to look out and see you."

"You don't need me. You'll knock 'em dead."

"I hope so."

His reply teemed with confidence. Like it was a foregone conclusion. Like I was foolish for thinking anything different. "How could they not love you?"

You didn't was my first thought.

You didn't love me enough to say it was my second thought.

Okay, maybe you loved me enough to say it, but then you got scared was my third.

And then *I don't really care about being loved by anyone but you.*

"I met with Malcolm, by the way," I added, trying to divert from any love talk. "You were right. We got along well. I think . . . I don't want to jinx it, but I think he's going to offer me a job."

"He'd be crazy not to."

We lapsed into silence. Hudson went for his pullover, which he'd left carelessly tossed over a chair yesterday. Ah, so that was why he was here. Not for me, but for that damn sweatshirt—the same one I'd borrowed during our flight from Cleveland. The one he'd given me after our first kiss.

The memory ached. An old bruise made fresh again by new pressure.

"He told me about what happened with you and your business," I said.

Hudson's cheek jerked. Not quite a smile. I wondered if I would ever see a smile from him again. "Malcolm's got a big mouth. Always has."

"I'm sorry that happened to you. You didn't deserve that. And . . . I'm sorry that it's still eating you up, all these years later. That you don't feel safe to be yourself just because of what some assholes did to you back then." And there it was. Laid out in front of me like a big sign that read *Hello pot, this is kettle* . . . "I guess we're not so different after all, huh? Still letting our pasts get the better of us."

Hudson gave his head a little shake, sending a wave of his signature scent wafting on the AC right in my direction. "Not anymore."

"What do you mean?"

"I decided to take your advice. Just like you took mine. I guess we'll see how it all pans out, hm?" His dimple appeared. I was gripped by the urge to kiss it. "See you around, Scout."

Just like that, he was gone. For a moment, I hesitated, totally torpified. I wanted to run after him, to try and fix this. But it was too late.

I was too late.

He'd all but said he wanted to start over without me. Without the baggage of the past. I guess it was my turn to do the same.

No matter how much it hurt.

I sank into one of our chairs. There was no telling how long I wallowed there, head in my hands. But eventually, Clara materialized, breezing over to me with her usual flair, completely oblivious to my overwrought emotional state.

"So! How ready are you to crush it out there?"

"I'm having sex with Hudson Bailey."

The confession came out like a sob—unprovoked and unstoppable. Not the way I'd planned on telling her, but there was no holding it back now.

"You're *what*?"

When I looked up, she was blurry through my tears.

"I'm having sex with Hudson. I mean, I'm not anymore. But I've *been* having sex with him. When you told me to live a little, I went out, and I did that with him, and we've been having sex basically since the Lloyd Exeter podcast thing. But now we're broken up, and my world is totally upside down, and I don't think I can go another minute without telling you, because I've been hiding it for so long and I still love him more than anything and I needed you to finally know."

Slowly, Clara lifted one hand to her temple and rubbed it in tight circles.

"That was a lot of information to have thrust upon me in thirty seconds. And at eight in the morning, too."

"I'm sorry. It's just been weighing on me."

"Why?"

I blinked. A few of the tears trickled down my cheeks, clearing my vision so I could see her again. Wasn't it obvious? "Because I'm about to go out and do the biggest presentation of my life and if anything goes wrong, I need you to know that it's my fault. I'm distracted. I've wrecked everything. I *always* wreck everything."

Her eyes snapped open, giving me the full force of her emotions. To my surprise, she wasn't angry. She was hurt. "You do *not.* And when you do, you fix it. Just like this week with the couplings. I mean *why didn't you tell me*?"

"I didn't want you to think I was taking my eye off the ball at work."

"Oh no." She snorted. "Your eyes have been very much *on* the ball. Two of them, in fact. Hudson's."

Cringe. "I deserve that."

"You know I wouldn't have minded you being distracted. In fact, I think I even told you a little distraction might be healthy for you. What's really going on here?"

"I didn't want you to see me fail again. I *couldn't* let you see me fail. If I told you about him and we didn't work out or if our time together made me blow it with The Fantasy debut, it would be yet another misfire in front of the one woman I always want to impress."

The clock was ticking toward my presentation. I struggled to get my emotions back in check, to cordon off the horrible disaster area that was my heart so I could continue my work.

But my breaths were shaky. My shoulders shuddered. And when Clara wrapped her arms around me, tight and fierce, I couldn't stop my tears.

She whispered as she held me.

"I couldn't ever have children, you know. It wasn't for lack of trying. But I just couldn't. And I know I can never replace your parents. But I hope you know that I've always thought of you as my daughter. I've loved you and looked after you and there's nothing you could *ever* do that would make me leave you behind, Scout. Nothing you could ever do that would make me love you less. Not a botched job, not a busted product launch, not a failed relationship. *Nothing.* I love you because you are Scout Porter. And Scout Porter is *fucking awesome.*"

The tears were hot and fast. Inescapable. "He told me I hated myself."

"He's right," Clara said, not unkindly. "You do."

"He tried to help me with my parents," I explained. "And he tried to get me to stand up to Lloyd. And he tried to help me find a job in the aerospace sector. And he went and made me fall in love with him, the big dumb idiot."

"A new job?"

Shit. Pulling out of her embrace, I tried to explain. "Right. About that, I'm sorry—"

She brushed one of my tears away. "Don't be. I always knew I would lose you when you saw your own potential. I'm just glad he said it instead of me. You'd've never gone job hunting if I said so."

"I barely went job hunting when *he* said so."

A ghost of a smile haunted her thin lips. "Journey of a thousand steps and all that."

With that, she took my hand and helped me to my feet. Together, we walked to the green room. Once inside, I was set upon by the management staff of the conference, who started hooking me up with a wireless microphone system for my presentation. A makeup woman helped me fix my tear-stained face. Someone else swapped my jacket with a loaner, since this one was wrinkled now. But once they were gone and there was nothing left to do but wait, I sank against the nearest wall and miserably returned to the topic.

"He tried to help me with so many things, Clara. And every

single time, I shot him down. And he was here. He was *right here* just a few minutes ago and I didn't try to fix things. I let him leave. I didn't fight for him."

"Because you don't think you're deserving of love. You don't think you're deserving of *anything*."

There it was again, that casual acknowledgment. "Does everybody know? I feel like I'm the last person to learn this about myself."

"Pretty much. But there are many things you can tell someone and they believe it. *Looks like rain. There's spinach in your teeth. When you get to the light, take a left. This is Tottenham's year.* But how do you tell someone that they'll never be happy until they stop despising themself? You don't. You just love them until they realize that they're worth loving." Her eyes swam with silvery tears. My own mother had never looked so proud of me. And I'd never felt more loved than in that moment. "It took you a long time. But I think you're there. Welcome to the rest of your life, Scout. It's going to be beautiful."

"How?"

"It's like I've always said. You can have anything you want. You just have to believe that it should be yours."

The unspoken question hung in the air. It echoed through my mind in Hudson's voice.

So what do *you want, Scout?*

I knew that answer better than I knew my own name.

I wanted to stop being afraid all the time. I wanted to stop questioning myself. I wanted to stop hating myself. I wanted friends. I wanted a fulfilling career. I wanted a life that was thoroughly and messily and unapologetically my own.

But most of all . . .

"I want him, Clara. I *love* him. I just don't think he loves me back."

Her eyes glistened. "What a fascinating hypothesis. And,

what's even more exciting—you'll get to test that hypothesis very shortly."

"What do you mean—"

It was at that moment that a set of nearby curtains twitched and a stagehand in uniform black clothing and a headset appeared, calling me forward. Here it was. The launch. The moment we'd all been waiting for. Once I stepped out, I would be in front of a crowd of thousands, selling them on the future of sex as we know it.

All while trying to decrypt not one, but two ominous warnings about my romantic prospects.

No pressure.

44

Standing O

We'd gone over the order of operations a dozen times in rehearsals. I would step out. Wave. The crowd would roar. I'd introduce the hype video. The hype video would play. And then I would give the pitch to end all pitches, selling this entire room, from Mr. Ose in the front row to Lloyd Exeter glowering on the sidelines to the sinfluencers in the back, on the fact that The Fantasy was the future of our industry. The future of pleasure. The future of sexual autonomy.

It went according to plan. The reception from the crowd left my ears ringing. My team cheered loudest of all, shooting me encouraging thumbs-ups from the middle of the convention hall, each decked out in a wall of matching black-and-pink BuzzCorp T-shirts.

However, then the auxiliary lights went out, and the hype video began to play.

Only it wasn't the final one that Addie had shown me last night. Not the one I'd given dozens of notes on over the last few days. It was similar, to be sure. The theme of the video was "I want." I want freedom. I want to feel good. I want to chase excitement. I want to explore. I want, I want, I want . . .

It was part Apple commercial, part "Why I Love Chick-fil-A" ad, and part manufactured authenticity, featuring testers and BuzzCorp superfans talking candidly about their sex lives and the ways in which our products have helped them. A group of older married women who had their own "postmenopause book club," only instead of reading the same book every two weeks, they tried the same toy and swapped reviews and stories over chardonnay and pot brownies. The newly disabled woman who rediscovered her sexual power after an accident. The dead-bed queer couple who rekindled their spark. The religious apostate who took control of her own sexuality. A trans man exploring his true body. Divorcées, college kids, pensioners . . .

And Hudson.

Yeah. Hudson Fucking Bailey, staring right down into the barrel of the camera.

I startled at the sight of him. As he spoke, though, the coiled muscles in my body relaxed until I was totally transfixed. Hypnotized by the larger-than-life motions of his lips and the sight of his big hands gesturing across the screen.

"Hi. I'm Hudson Bailey. I actually used to work at BuzzCorp. Don't anymore. But when I came here, I thought it would be just another job, you know? That what I was building was just the same as weather systems or online payment processors. I didn't know anything about sex toys. There's a million reasons for that, but mostly, I think, I was afraid of such intimacy."

Oh my God. He was doing it. He was stopping his ridiculous people-pleasing act on the most public stage of them all.

"It takes guts, you know, to be vulnerable enough with someone to bring them that pleasure and let them bring *you* pleasure, too. What if you say the wrong thing or suggest the wrong toy? What if you're so inexperienced and weird that your partner, the person you care about most in the world, decides to stop calling you?"

Those words lingered in the air. My stomach twisted. I wanted to reach up, grab video Hudson, and hold him until he *knew* that there wasn't anything he could ever do to push me away.

"Anyway, as I got more familiar with sex toys, I realized that I hadn't just been holding myself back in the bedroom, but in so many other ways, because I was afraid. So as I got more confident in the bedroom, I got more confident in general, too. I . . . I fell in love. And I guess doing this little interview is my way of expressing that love. Of finally refusing to let myself be silenced. My time at BuzzCorp taught me we should never be afraid of who we are or what we want. Or *who* we want."

With that, he looked down the center of the camera once again, as if he knew he was talking directly to me, despite this being recorded (I could only guess) a night or two before. His smile was honest and sincere. *My* Hudson smile, not the one he usually reserved for everyone else.

The music behind his confessional swelled. Here it was. The big finish.

"My name is Hudson Bailey. I'm a big fan of The Penetrator. And I want to take my voice back. Because I want the woman I love to know that I'm hers forever."

He loved me.

He loved me. And I'd let him go.

As the video played out its final moments, I realized that Hudson wasn't the only man in the video. There were several of them in this edit, each speaking more enthusiastically than the last about BuzzCorp and our products.

Oh my God.

He'd given them the courage to come forward.

Him going on the record in front of the camera gave the other men in our focus groups the belief that they could do the same.

Hudson had solved our marketing problem.

I scanned the crowd, hoping to find him. The real him, not the projected image.

It was really for the best that I couldn't. I probably would have pulled a silly stunt, run off the stage, jumped into his arms, and kissed him like in one of Leelah's rom-coms.

Instead, with the confidence of a loved woman—a woman not just loved by a man but by her cheering friends in the audience and by, maybe most importantly, herself—I gave the rest of my launch speech.

Reader, I don't like to brag.

In this case, though, I will make an exception.

I fucking crushed it.

By the end, the entire auditorium was eating out of the palm of my hand, and when it was over, a mob of financiers, led by a beaming Mr. Ose, cornered us for handshakes and congratulations.

I was Cinderella, magically transformed in a matter of minutes from forgotten business outcast to the belle of the ball.

A state of affairs that deteriorated like hydrogen-5 when Lloyd Exeter rocked up to congratulate me.

"What a triumph, Scout. You should be proud."

"Thanks."

"Don't thank me. Thank God for making you better at fuck toys than rockets."

Experimenting was the furthest thing from my mind. I was no longer interested, for the moment anyway, in guesswork and trial and error. I wanted unflinching fact. What happened next wasn't an experiment, it was a newly discovered universal constant.

And that universal constant?

Fuck Lloyd Exeter.

"You know what, Lloyd? I'm going to say this because I don't think anyone else is ever going to tell you. You're a guy who doesn't ever hear the truth, so listen up. You're a bad person.

You're lazy. You're entitled. You have a much higher opinion of yourself than you deserve, and at the end of the day, you're going to die alone surrounded by people who only suffer you for the paycheck. And you may not believe me now, but when you're lying on your deathbed, you're going to remember this moment and say . . . *Oh my God, Scout was right.*"

His eyes burned. He worked his jaw. Mr. Rich Boy had insulated himself from face-to-face criticism with cronies and lackeys and yes-men and the Jareds of the world, and he'd just been read in person by the one woman whom he'd used up and thrown away like so much useless space debris.

Scout was right should have been my closing line. I couldn't help it, though. Before I left, I added one final parting shot.

"By the way, you have a weird penis."

Not my best work. Still, despite all I'd said, *that* was probably the only thing that would stick.

Good enough for me.

I stalked off, scanning the crowd for any sign of Hudson. Instead, I found Addie and Leelah. Dodging potential investors and engineers looking to talk shop, I cornered them.

Waving off some nearby chatty dudes looking to talk to anyone in a BuzzCorp T-shirt, Leelah engaged me first. "You were giving total girlboss up there."

"Ugh, Leelah, don't say *giving*. Or *girlboss*. You're such a millennial."

"Shut up—"

Not the time for their bickering. "Guys! Do you know where Hudson is?"

The two shared guilty looks. My stomach dropped. "I think he left."

"*What*?"

"He had a flight to catch!" Leelah said in his defense. As if he needed defending.

The entire OFest audience wanted a piece of me. Clara would, no doubt, be engaged for the next few weeks, talking about fulfilling orders and expanding our product line. I should be there with her.

But I couldn't. "Well, I'm going after him."

"Obviously," Addie said, rolling her eyes. "After us and like three of the marketing people stayed up all night last night to get that footage into the hype video, you'd *better* be running after him! He recorded his part, then showed it to the other focus testers so the guys would go on camera, too. It was amazing. You should have seen it."

"Why didn't you tell me?" I hissed. "And if he was in love with me, why didn't *he* tell me?"

"Besides the fact that you pushed him away at the first sign of trouble?"

I shot Addie a sharp glance. "Before that, I mean."

"We *might* have had a few drinks with him after you two broke up." Off my look, Leelah added: "What? We were *worried* about you!"

Addie took up the baton. "He mentioned entropy?"

"Right. That he wanted to tell you he loved you. And he wanted to ask you to be with him after The Fantasy rollout and his contract ended. But he was going to wait until *after* OFest because you told him that you couldn't handle anything serious right before the launch."

"And then when you said all that shit about him being a coward during the breakup, he decided to try and win you back . . . with this video thing today. He wanted to finally be honest. And boy, was he ever."

This news rattled me. He'd been holding back because of *me*? Because of some stupid offhand comment I'd made about entropy?

Because he was so kind and so good that he was willing to

play friends with benefits until after the convention just because it was what I wanted?

I twisted my hands together. "You mean . . . you mean he's loved me this whole time?"

Addie boxed out a strange man approaching us for conversation. "C'mon, Scout. You're one of the smartest people we know. Figure that one out for yourself."

"Classic rom-com misunderstanding bullshit. Why didn't you just communicate?"

"Not helpful, Leelah! I've got to go."

"You do," she agreed. "But first!"

She threw her arms around me, hugging me like I'd never been hugged before. It was a teenage girl hug, a hug you only saw in movies about finding yourself at cheer camp or whatever. But when Addie joined in, however reluctantly, I couldn't help but soak in the moment.

I had friends. I'd finally opened up and found my people. My life was finally, *finally*, falling into place.

Damn, did it feel good.

"I love you guys," I said, squeezing them both tighter.

Addie was the first to let go. "We love you, too. Now run. We'll hold off this crowd of vipers."

Over her shoulder, it felt like the entirety of OFest was waiting for their moment to pounce and monopolize my time.

"But—"

"We've got this! Trust us."

She didn't have to ask me twice. Because, I realized as I walked away, I *did* trust them. And what a beautiful feeling that was.

They reached into their shoulder bags and produced The Fantasy swag—koozies and T-shirts and scrunchies. The crowds immediately flocked right to them, giving me a chance to sneak out.

On my way, though, I passed Clara, who eyed me with her usual knowing expression.

"Clara . . ." I began, but trailed off when I realized I didn't know what to say. How do you thank someone for saving you? For being there when no one else was? For walking alongside me without judgment as I figured out how to unfuck all my messes?

For being the first person who ever really loved me and saw me?

No words would ever be good enough for that.

Turned out, I didn't need words. Clara had them. Just like she always did.

"I know, darling. I know. And you have my blessing on the new job—wherever it may be and whatever you may want to do next. Not that you ever needed it."

She pressed a kiss on my cheek and wished me her most heartfelt *namaste*. This time, I wished it right back to her. Not because I believed in her brand of spiritualism, but because I knew it would mean the world to her.

When I left, bouncing my way through the crowd as Leelah and Addie cleared it for me, my mentor had tears in her eyes. I blinked back my own. This wasn't goodbye. Just a *see you later, old friend.*

And speaking of seeing old friends later . . . I had a date with Hudson Bailey.

I just had to find him first.

45

Big Finish

The reckless, rom-com-brained part of me wanted to run straight to the airport. The rational part of me knew I needed things like, you know, a phone. And a license.

So once I was free of the convention hall throng, I raced back to our HQ. There was so much to do. I needed to book an earlier flight home. I needed to catch Hudson at his apartment. I had to convince him that I loved him.

Oh God. How would I do that?

Just come out and say it? *Hello, I'm in love with you.*

Nope.

Or a video of my own?

Hard pass. Not photogenic. Also, the marketing team were probably sick of getting bribed to work off the clock.

Maybe a lab report? I could explain in detail how my experiment in sex turned into a successful proof of love.

Only . . . Hudson wasn't an experiment. Our relationship wasn't a proof. I didn't need to analyze or explain what I felt for him or what had transpired between us.

It just *was.* He'd made me fall in love with him, beyond all boundaries of known science and logic. It defied everything I understood about the universe, which somehow made it even more real than if I could put it in a box and study it.

However, I didn't have time to make a decision.

One was made for me.

When I returned to our empty HQ, I found that it wasn't so empty after all. Hudson sat there, drinking a glass of the celebratory champagne we'd stocked there for after The Fantasy's big moment in the spotlight.

Every neuron within me vibrated with an intensity even the Richter scale couldn't measure.

He'd stayed.

"Thought you had a plane to catch," I breathed.

"Turns out I have terrible hand-eye coordination. Couldn't catch a plane to save my soul."

"Very funny."

"Girls like funny guys."

Forget the Richter scale. I wasn't an earthquake right now. *I* wasn't anything on my own. When two black holes merged, their gravitational forces were said to be the most intense thing in the known universe.

We were two black holes.

Destined to merge.

Destined to rattle the entire cosmos with our energy.

"I thought I was going to have, like, a whole flight back to Dallas to figure out my grand gesture. And my speech," I said.

He tipped his champagne glass, amusement toying at the edges of his otherwise placid expression. "Yeah? What were you planning?"

"Pffft. Like, fire-breathers and tap dancers and stuff. Maybe call my friends at NASA for a flyover."

He let out a low whistle. "Sounds expensive."

God, I loved this man. Even in this dramatic and important moment, he still managed to make me smile.

"It would have been. Do you mind if I just . . . talk from the heart instead?"

The champagne found its way to a nearby table. He then leaned forward, elbows on his knees, giving me his entire attention. "I've been waiting for you to say that since the day we met, Scout."

My prepared statements now gone, I dredged up the truth from the bottom of my heart and laid it out bare for him.

"I'm not good at this stuff, but I want to try."

Deep breath, Scout. You can do this.

You're worth fighting for. He's worth fighting for. This love is worth fighting for.

"All my life, I've made a mess of things. Or I thought I did. And I was so hard on myself about it. With my work, if an experiment with one of my projects failed, I knew what to do. I could scrap the whole thing, approach it from a new angle, and refine it until I got the correct outcome. But I didn't know how to do that with myself. My parents taught me that I was only good enough to love when I did everything right, so when I messed up, I just learned how to hide. Because I convinced myself it was better that way. That I was broken and couldn't ever be fixed."

With every word I spoke, they were no longer theoretical. They were real, writing themselves into my very DNA. I knew I would never again go back to the girl I had been.

"But that's not true. I'm not broken. There's nothing unlovable about me. And I can have what I want. I can have it *with you*."

He sucked in a sharp breath. I approached him, closing the gap until I stood right before him, laying myself bare.

Emotionally, that is.

"I'm sorry that I made you think that you couldn't be honest with me about your feelings. Addie and Leelah told me that's why it took so long for you to say it. I was waiting on you to say *I love you,* all the while you were trying to follow my lead and do what I wanted, and then I made everything worse by calling you a coward who can't express himself. I was wrong, Hudson. And I'm sorry. And I'm sorry that I pushed you away. You were never a problem. You were never a distraction. You made me believe, for the first time ever, that *I'm* not a problem, either. You made me . . ."

His eyelashes fluttered. One second there were glistening tears along the rims of his eyes, and the next, they were gone.

"You made me fall in love with you. I'm in love with you, Hudson. Without fear. Without reservation. Without the need to analyze it. I just love you.

"I'm tired of limiting myself. I want to jump in. I want to live, not just muddle through. You inspire me. I stood up to my parents. I stood up to Lloyd. You make me better. Stronger. And I want to love you every single chance I get. To show you that you deserve to be loved just the way you are—the real you. The one who hates spicy food and loves pegging and makes a mean bowl of ramen. And I want to be the woman who loves you that way—every day, for as long as you'll have me."

No response. I couldn't watch his face in the reflection anymore. Trying to read him was impossible. I tripped over myself to fill the silence between us.

"I guess I learned that there's a reason we tangle up love and sex all the time. Because they're both about giving and receiving. We give and receive in the bedroom. Just the same, we have to love, *and* we have to let ourselves be loved back."

He stifled the last words with his lips. Jumping to his feet, he brought his lips down to mine in a brush of a kiss that quickly turned into more. It was a devouring kiss, a kiss that tasted like forever.

I could get used to kisses like that.

When we finally parted, I could barely even open my eyes. I didn't want the moment to end. "That was—"

His grin was as crooked as ever, but somehow even more perfect. It reached not just his eyes but the rest of his body, brightening him in a way I'd been missing these last few days without him. "You just used a sex metaphor to explain why you've finally admitted that you're madly in love with me. What, was I *not* supposed to kiss you?"

Tears were inevitable now. I didn't wipe them away. Sad tears? The worst. Happy tears, though? Is there anything better than the subversion of a sign of misery into such sublime joy?

He took my face between his hands. I leaned into his touch. "I want this, Scout. I've always wanted it. I just needed you to be ready, too."

"I'm ready. I love you."

Another kiss. This time, I put every promise for the future into it. *I'll always love you. I'll always be here. I'll never run again. I'll build a life that I've always wanted—and you'll be there with me, every step of the way.*

When we parted, though, I knew I wasn't going to be able to end this moment with *just* a kiss. So I laced my fingers through his and led him toward a nearby maintenance closet door.

"Where are you taking me?" he asked.

I winked at him. "You're leaving BuzzCorp, aren't you? It's time for your exit interview. Don't worry. I'll be very, very comprehensive."

Problem: It had been several days since I'd last had sex with Hudson.

Proposed Solution: A little closet quickie to seal our new romance. Our real romance. A romance that would last forever.

EPILOGUE

Blast-Off

Two years later, I sat in an office in Huntsville, Alabama, perched on the edge of my desk watching a closed-circuit TV monitor like I'd spontaneously combust if I took my eyes off the screen.

Malcolm offered me a job at SkyTech a few weeks after OFest, and I took it. Got promoted six months in. Now today was our first big test launch.

Hudson came up behind me and pressed a kiss to the crook of my neck.

"It's going to go fine," he breathed against my skin.

"You don't know that."

"Yes, I do. Because you designed it."

When I first met Hudson, I would have been terrified of failing on this scale. But now failure didn't scare me so much. If this rocket blew up, I knew I wasn't going to get kicked out of the industry again. Malcolm would give me the space, resources, and time to diagnose the problem, fix it, and have a successful takeoff next time.

Just like in my relationship with Hudson, I finally had a soft place to land. Somewhere to make mistakes, try again, and grow into someone better.

The relief was nearly indescribable. After a lifetime of flinching and running at the slightest hint of trouble, I now belonged somewhere. I wasn't scared of my own shadow. I was finally free to be the person I'd always been, deep down inside.

On my television screen, our rocket went through its final-stage checks. At this point, there was nothing I could do. The math had been run. Every bolt and weld checked. Every ounce measured and remeasured for maximum lift. So I sat on my hands and tried to corral the butterflies running roughshod through my belly.

"We can go join the rest of the team in Mission Control, if you want," Hudson said. "It's not too late."

"I know. But . . . I think I want the privacy. If it blows, I want to process it before I talk to the team. If it's a success . . . I don't want to cry in front of everybody."

"This is a big deal. Of course you're gonna go through it when everything's said and done. They would understand any emotion you threw at them."

"Trying to get rid of me?" I teased.

"No, trying to distract you before you kick a hole in the carpet."

I glanced down at my leg, which had been absent-mindedly tapping out a drumline chorus on the floor below. "Oops. Sorry."

Removing himself from his sentry point over my shoulder, Hudson sauntered over to the television, cutting into my line of sight for the first time in hours. Now remotely developing an app for an amusement park company (you know the one), he'd taken the day off to support me in the launch—and for his trouble, he'd done everything from holding my hand to drinking my hot chocolate when I was too nervous to finish it to listening to me ramble about The Math™ for an hour and a half.

Leaning against the wall, he drank me in. I flushed under his scrutiny. Even after two years, moving in together, and adopting a mutt named Moogie, he still knew how to make me feel like the most beautiful woman in the galaxy.

"You know what? I think I have a better way to distract you."

"Is that so?"

"Mm-hmm. Come here."

Without further ado, he was on his knees in front of me, gently nudging my thighs apart.

Oh shit.

I giggled and tried to push him away, to no avail. "I really can't—"

He kissed the inside of my leg and raised one challenging eyebrow. "Really can't what?"

My cunt flexed at his intimate touch. A firm *this isn't the time or the place* danced on my lips, but then his hand drifted upward, nudging my skirt up around my waist.

Fingertips taunted the edge of my panties.

"Fine," he said when I came up short in the reply department. "If you really want to know, I think *I* need a distraction. I'm losing my mind. I'm so excited for you, I can hardly think straight."

"Well, if it's for *you*, then . . . how can I refuse?"

A chuckle and his stubble brushed against my sensitive skin. "You can keep your eyes on the screen. Just pretend I'm not even here."

Impossible. I could never think of anything else with Hudson's mouth around my clit.

Still, I indulged him.

He'd read me perfectly. I *did* need a distraction. And now, even if the launch didn't go as planned, at least I would get an amazing orgasm out of it.

We'd made love several times this morning, and from the way

Hudson gripped my hips and yanked me to the very edge of the desk, I could tell that he was not going to go easy on me now. He would not leave any quarter for my mind to wander back to the stress of the launch.

He ripped my panties off. In the reflection on the television screen, I saw him shove them in his pocket for safekeeping. Then, throwing my legs over each of his shoulders, he had me stretched and ready for him—a feast for his taking.

No teasing today. Just hunger.

Capturing my clit between his lips, he kissed me deeply, swirling and sucking just the way I liked. His pace was slow but the pressure unrelenting. The orgasm was an inevitability; I could feel it even now, planting seeds in the pit of my stomach.

Eyes still on the television set, I tried to split my attention between my need for him and my professional obligations.

But then, as he tongued my hard clit, he pressed a finger to my entrance, ready to broach me. My eyes slammed shut.

My cunt dripped for him. He slid one finger easily inside.

Not enough. Not nearly enough.

I bucked my hips, demanding more. He smirked around my clit. A second finger joined the first.

That wasn't enough either. I wanted to cum *hard.* I wanted him to break me apart and put me back together again.

He took the hint. A third entered my cunt.

I exhaled, hard. It was very much a *careful what you wish for* scenario. I was full to the brim of him.

When I was fully stretched out and relaxed around him, he curled in the depths of me, tickling my G-spot with slow, easy strokes.

My eyes fluttered back in my head. God *damn*, was he good at this. My entire body tingled, the warmth of pleasure stimulating every inch of me.

But it wasn't enough. Even as I was riding higher, I needed more.

Sorry, sleeved button-up. I hardly knew ye.

Ripping at the fabric, I tore the shirt away and unhooked my front-clasp bra, exposing my tits to the overly AC-ed room. My nipples pebbled, hard and proud for me, and I moaned as soon as my own hands began to toy with them.

That was when the countdown began, crackling from the CAPCOM speaking over the live launch footage.

"Ten."

Hudson gave my clit the smallest of nibbles. I shuddered.

"Nine."

He picked up his pistoning pace in my pussy. I couldn't help it—I wanted more, so I began thrusting against him.

"Eight."

He tongued my clit, swirling and focusing his attentions on it. *Yes, that's it. Right there.*

"Seven."

Fuck, I was getting close. The muscles in my body tensed in heated anticipation of the climax to come.

"Six."

Removing a hand from one of my nipples, I threaded it through his hair, holding him in place. I was not going to let him get away with teasing me today. My touch only encouraged him to eat me harder and faster. I tightened around his fingers.

"Five."

It was all so much. A wet, sloppy cunt. A perfect mouth to worship it. My nipples tight in my grasp. My pussy full of perfectly pounding fingers, taking me again and again.

"Four."

More, more, more. Right there. Don't stop. Fuck, don't stop . . .

"Three."

I was completely riding his face now, fucking myself against his perfect fingers, dominating his mouth with my pussy. Taking control. Using him and letting him play me all at the same time. My orgasm was so close. The rocket boosters on the screen were fully smoking now, their flames spurting out in mad, violent waves.

I knew the feeling.

"Two."

Full ignition. Inside me and on my television screen.

The rocket's first-stage engines caught, and suddenly, the 450-ton sky-traversing contraption I'd built was flying.

Hudson hit my G-spot one final time. His teeth brushed my clit in just the right way. My nipples tweaked at just the right time.

"Hudson!"

I contracted around his hand, tightening my legs around his neck and holding him in place.

A voice from Mission Control crackled through the speakers. *"We have liftoff."*

We collapsed against each other. His head against my thigh, me curled against him so my head could lie along the curve of his shoulders. Our eyes drifted to the footage. The rocket was gliding off against the clear, blue summer sky, and I was still riding the last aftershocks of Hudson's making.

A perfect launch. A perfect orgasm.

The perfect happy ending.

Acknowledgments

In my opinion, acknowledgments are the hardest part of writing any book. Well, besides the beginning. And the end. The middle's pretty tricky, too. Oh, and don't even get me started on revisions—

Where was I? Oh, yes. The people who made this book possible.

To Maggie Cooper, the apex of agents, and Amanda Maurer, my exceptional editor, I cannot thank you enough for believing in this romance of mine. You took a chance on Scout, who is messy, flawed, and almost unbearably horny. You let me give her life and the love story she deserves. For that, I will forever be in your debt.

To the entire team at Berkley, from my cover artists to the copy editor and freelancers to the marketing team—you all made this book sing. You have my undying gratitude.

To Charlotte and Molly, who had to listen to me talk about this book for way too long, thank you for your friendship, your advice, and your book recs. I'm so lucky to have y'all.

And, finally, to the man who got my virginity. You know who you are, and you know what you did. Thank you, cum again.

Acknowledgments

Alys Murray is a novelist and screenwriter based in New Orleans. She received a BFA from NYU's Tisch School of the Arts and a master's in film studies from King's College London. Alys is the author of the sweetly romantic Full Bloom Farm series, and she's the screenwriter behind five films on Hallmark and Lifetime. A Netflix x Inevitable Foundation Visionary Fellow, Alys is a proud advocate for disabled voices and stories in entertainment.

VISIT ALYS MURRAY ONLINE

AlysMurray.com
AlysMurrayBooks

Ready to find
your next great read?

Let us help.

Visit prh.com/nextread

Penguin
Random
House